Praise for Sophie H. Morgan
and
The Witch is Back

"With a sweet and sexy romance, complicated family dynamics, and a few twists along the way, *The Witch is Back* makes for a fun, enjoyable read to pick up this spooky season!"
—Hazel Beck, author of *Small Town, Big Magic*

"With this tongue-in-cheek paranormal rom-com, Morgan draws readers into a world of magical mayhem…. Watching the endearingly awkward protagonists navigate witchy high society is a joy. This is sure to win Morgan some new fans."
—*Publishers Weekly*

"The high-stakes secrets and reveals lead to satisfying moments that make the plot sweet and magical…. Morgan distinguishes her steamy witch rom-com with impressive twists on romance tropes that will bewitch fans of the genre."
—*Library Journal*

SOPHIE H. MORGAN

ISBN-13: 978-1-335-14664-9

De-Witched

Recycling programs
for this product may
not exist in your area.

For questions and comments about the quality of this book, please contact us at CustomerService@Harlequin.com.

® is a trademark of Harlequin Enterprises ULC.

Harlequin Enterprises ULC
22 Adelaide St. West, 41st Floor
Toronto, Ontario M5H 4E3, Canada
www.Harlequin.com

Printed in U.S.A.

For my spaniel, Molly
And all the good boys and girls like her
who teach us every day what it is to be loved
and what it is to hurtle out of bed at the first sound of retching

"Dogs are not our whole life, but they make our lives whole."
—Roger Caras

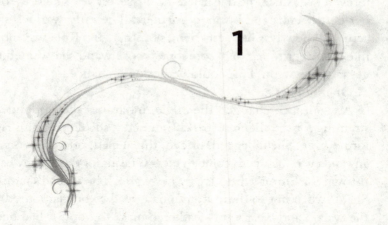

1

*B*alconies were magic, of this Leah Turner was pretty sure. Why else would they appear so often in books and movies? Only a balcony could serve as the setting for a beauty to tell a beast she loved him. Only a balcony could be witness to Richard Gere braving his fear of heights for his pretty woman.

If only those balconies could be this balcony.

Disappointment drowned her as Laurence the warlock crushed his lips to hers, crinkling her ball gown in his grip. He made a passionate sound, deep in his throat. And she…

Felt nothing. No pleasure, no desire, not even a tingle. Unless you counted ones of frustration. They'd been kissing for several minutes, his elegant hands sliding all over, and her stupid libido remained stubbornly stuck in the off position.

She supposed it wasn't fair to have expected his kiss to blow her feathered mask off. But hell, he was a *warlock*. And as a human with limited experience in the magical world, she'd expected something…well, magical. This dude could summon portals, float objects, hell, maybe even start fires. Just…not one in her panties, apparently.

Still, she'd wanted to kiss a warlock for what seemed like

forever, ever since she'd learned the big secret years before from her best friends and business partners. The only warlock she actually knew was her best friend's brother, and Kole was more like a brother to *her* than someone whose wand she wanted to get familiar with. This could be her only chance.

One more try.

As Laurence changed the angle, moaning, she responded, straining for the slightest spark. Damned if she'd taken this risk for nothing. She'd begged, bribed, threatened, offered favors of any and every nature to come to New Orleans for this witchy ball, thrown for Emma's birthday by her warlock boyfriend's family. She'd sworn not to draw attention, agreed to be glamoured to the wazoo and wear a full-feathered mask to boot. It had been weeks before her best friends had caved.

Even their reluctance hadn't dimmed her excitement. After all, Emma and Tia, even Kole, her self-assigned bodyguard for the evening, had good reason to be cautious. Humans were forbidden to know of their kind without permission from their High Family, despite the fact that witches mingled with them all the time. If she were discovered, there'd be consequences.

And if she was thinking about consequences, Leah concluded with a twitch of her brows, Laurence *really* wasn't giving his warlock brethren a good name.

Time to call it. Turns out she'd been wrong; warlocks could be just as disappointing as human men. Every day was a learning day.

She shifted just as his tongue shot to the back of her throat, and her gag reflex kicked in. Her teeth snapped down on the fleshy invader.

Laurence's muffled cry echoed around the intimately lit balcony. He reared back, eyes wide beneath the white mask he'd pushed up on his forehead. "You bith my dunge." Releasing her, he touched it gingerly.

Thousands of retorts sprang to mind, but Leah swallowed

them back. Mostly. "Sorry. I forget that some men can't handle pain."

Wrong thing to say, she judged, as his eyes lit up. He stopped
fingering his tongue and leered at her. "Oh, I can handle it.
Can you, my naughty mystery witch?"

She wondered if it would be considered drawing attention
to herself if she jumped off the balcony.

"Gag me," she muttered.

He made a purring noise. "If you ask nicely." He eased closer
and she matched him backward, the iron railings pressing layers of skirts into her butt. "Your portal or mine?"

She flattened her lips, trembling with the urge to laugh.
Clearing her throat, she gestured to her wrist—which was
naked. "Look at the time. I promised to meet a friend for a
dance."

"So? Send them a mirror message. If they knew you were
with me, they'd let you go." A cocky lift of his chin. "I'm of the
Brochards."

Somewhere in the distance, something jabbered. It was the
only noise for a long moment. "Cool," she decided on. "Even
so…"

"Don't play hard to get now." He leaned in, his smile edged
with that arrogance. His finger stroked down the bare skin between where her sleeve ended and her long white glove began.
"Ten minutes," he reminded her. "That was all it took to get
you out here."

Leah stared him down, flushing under her mask at the
evidence of her determination to bag a warlock. She wasn't
ashamed, exactly; she loved learning, craved new experiences.
But she did wish she'd chosen a different warlock. Now she'd
have to endure Kole's lecture, without even a good kiss to tuck
away in her memories.

Her guard slipped as she sent Laurence a withering look.
"Lesson learned. Excuse me."

"Hey." He wrapped his hand around her arm, not bruising but enough to halt her. "Don't you know who I am?"

"You're a Brochard," she said with admirable patience, barely keeping in a sarcastic "whoopee for you."

"You're a lower born, aren't you?"

"*What?*"

"I can't believe this." He let her go to pace, the tails on his lilac velvet coat flapping. She'd have found the color choice odd if she didn't know from the past six years with Emma and Tia that witches preferred bright colors. "That's the trouble with masquerades," he muttered, more to himself than her. "I should've known the Truenotes would invite all the lower circles. No class."

Okay, Leah understood now why Emma had left this society behind before hooking up with Bastian again. What an asshole.

"They probably wanted some decent people on the guest list, if all Higher sons are like you," she said flatly. She wasn't rude by nature, but bad manners really jammed every button she had. "This is their home. Shouldn't you show them some respect?"

He straightened his tailcoat. "Warlocks respect only their equals." His blue eyes swept over her, clearly cataloging everything as his lip curled. "And you are not mine."

The words slid into her like knives, piercing the quiet insecurity that whispered he was right. That she didn't belong here. She faltered as he brought his face close.

"If you tell anyone about this…"

That piece of ridiculousness snapped her back. "You think I *want* to brag about my kiss with the warlock washing machine?"

"I *beg* your pardon?"

Leah picked up her full skirts, silvery satin that reflected the moon above them. "Get a clue, Brochard. You can't kiss for shit."

She shoved past him, aiming for the glass doors that led back to the masquerade, only to be yanked back when a telekinetic hand seized her elbow.

Two things happened then.

A male voice from the side clipped out: "Unhand the—"

And Leah, considering telekinesis an act of aggression, smashed her fist into Laurence's face.

Something crunched. Blood spurted from Laurence's nose, gushing down his face and onto his pretty clothes. He cupped his nose with a babbling cry—a spell, maybe, or perhaps he was trying to make sense of being punched by a lower born. Imagine if he'd known she was human.

"—lady," the crisp voice finished on a bemused note.

Her eyes flew to the shadows, body tensing in readiness as she supported her throbbing hand. A witness. Was there a fine for punching a Higher son? Would she get sent to witch prison?

Was there such a thing as witch prison?

A question for another time.

Leah stepped away, both from Laurence and from the man hidden by the dark at the side of the balcony. Adrenaline rushed inside her as she wondered if she could make it to the doors.

"I suppose inquiring if you're well is redundant."

It took Leah a moment to realize the question was for her and not the warlock slumped against the balustrade.

Her mind emptied of words. "Um," she said inelegantly.

"You didn't use magic." Curiosity wound through the accented words like ribbons around a maypole. "Why?"

Hoping for an air of mystery, Leah lifted her shoulders.

"You didn't need it," he answered for her. "But did you have to break his nose?"

Leah shrugged again, sidling toward the glass doors.

He matched her step to the right. Now he'd moved, the faint outline of his hair was visible, a dark wave swept back. Light glinted off the sharper features like his chin, nose, a hint of cheekbone. He stood taller than her, not hard since she topped five feet seven in three-inch heels. And, she realized, placing the accent, he was British.

Her heart thudded against her ribs. Fear? Nerves? Delight? All three, maybe.

Her libido cheered.

This was a warlock made for balconies.

"Nothing to say?"

Leah wished she had all the accessories for her nineteenth-century costume. There were only so many times a woman could coquettishly waft a feathered fan. "Maybe I don't want to talk to you."

"I came to your rescue," he pointed out.

"She didn't need rescuing."

Laurence's surly input had the moment shattering. His nose was now intact, though dried blood painted his face.

His lips peeled back from his teeth. "I should give you a taste of your own, *witch*."

"But you won't."

The firm warning from the stranger made Laurence's eyes narrow. "What's it to you, Goodnight?"

"You forced your magic on her."

"So?" he blustered.

"So, it's not done." The warlock called Goodnight cocked his head, light sliding down his face to reveal a perfect pair of lips. He wore his power comfortably as he warned, "Remember yourself, Brochard."

Laurence cast a hateful look at Goodnight, then stomped toward the doors. Leah shifted so they didn't touch, watching as he threw open the glass doors, letting out the ruckus of the party before they closed behind him.

And then it was just the two of them.

"Thank you," she said to break the silence, shifting her weight. "For getting rid of him."

"I suspect you could have done that."

"It might have gotten ugly."

Truth. And, seriously, what the hell had she been thinking, punching a warlock? She really needed to buy a clue and stop being so impulsive before it got her into hot water. Hotter water.

A sudden thought had her head snapping his way. "How long were you standing there?" Had he seen their second-rate make-out session? Embarrassment threatened to curl her toes in her gorgeous shoes.

"I came up the steps as you were scolding him for insulting the Truenotes."

Relief kissed her heated skin. "Manners matter," she told him. Absently, she rubbed a gentle thumb over her sore knuckles. "I should've known it would end badly. It always does."

"It?"

"Me. Men—ah, warlocks. But you have to keep trying. Kiss those frogs."

A beat passed. "Frogs?"

Oh, God. It must be a human idiom. Shoot her now. "I just mean, I have the worst taste."

Clearing her throat, she clasped her hands lightly and wandered toward the view. She settled, choosing to forget that Kole would be furious when he found her. She wasn't ready to leave yet. "So, why were you in the garden?" Behind him she saw the faint shadow of a winding stone staircase leading off below.

He didn't speak.

"Space?" she guessed, throwing him a quick once-over. "You don't strike me as a party person." Not when he stood there, all quiet and solemn in the shadows, posture perfect.

After a beat, he inclined that sharp chin. "Not precisely."

"Me, I love a party." Leah hated silence more than anything.

She'd had too much of that in her teenage years. "Surrounded by the press of people, listening to everyone laugh and talk."

"It's easier to be alone."

The lack of emotion there made her wonder if that was really true. Since she couldn't offer a hug—she doubted that would go down well—she said the first thing that came to mind. A bad habit. "You can be alone with me."

Confusion melded with the accent now. "What does that mean?"

"I'm not sure." A small laugh as her skin grew clammy. Nervous, she was actually nervous. "I guess…it's like this moment doesn't exist. We don't know each other and we don't have to. We can let go of ourselves for a bit. Rest."

Another beat. "Okay."

He didn't get it. She swallowed, turning to the gardens, embracing the press of the night air and the faint sounds that came in from the bayous beyond. She didn't care if the warlock thought she was an idiot, she told herself, gripping the railings. She wasn't trying to impress him.

Then she felt him at her back and knew her words were a lie. She didn't dare move, every nerve turning electric. He didn't touch her, but she felt him everywhere.

"Why do I feel you are never alone? Never someone else." His words brushed by her, along with a hint of scent, nothing she could name. Sexy, like his cultured voice. "Even with a stranger?"

She stared hard at the darkened gardens, trying not to hyperventilate. "I like people. But I can feel alone."

"When?"

The dark pressed around them, cocooning. Intimate. She found herself saying to it, "Sometimes I feel on the outside of things."

"How could anyone keep a witch like you out?"

Because she wasn't a witch. But this was her chance to act like one.

She released the railings and turned, her chest brushing his body. Inhaling at the contact, she looked up. A plain navy mask slicked over his features, hiding what she wanted to see. Except for his eyes. They were an intense green, inhumanly so. As he scanned what her mask didn't cover, they almost gleamed blue.

Her knees turned to Jell-O. "Hi."

Those eyes flickered, puzzled. "Hello."

She pressed her lips together. When his gaze went to them, a rush of tingles swept across her skin. "It's like a secret," she said, surprised her voice came out normal.

"What?"

"Being with a stranger. You can tell them anything. Do anything. And then it's forgotten as you go back to your lives."

He watched her in silence.

She watched him back. Words trembled at her lips and she couldn't keep them in. Didn't want to. "What would you do if you knew there'd be no consequences?"

The wind tousled his hair, but he stood perfectly still. "There are always consequences."

"So, let's pretend."

"I don't play."

"That's a shame." She inched closer.

"I take it you do?"

"Life's there to be lived."

"We're very different."

"Apparently."

"Yet... I find I'm curious."

Her breath lodged in her throat. It took several tries before she could wheeze, "About?"

The wind teased her updo of curls, slid down her skin, had her shivering as she silently begged him to say the words. Complete the fantasy.

And then he did. "What you would do if there were no consequences."

The surge of desire drained any rational thought from her. Like it belonged to someone else, she saw her hand close over his neckcloth, using it to pull him down. Their lips had barely touched, a sizzle of anticipation in her blood, when the glass doors banged open.

"There you are."

Leah jumped away from Goodnight as if he'd burst into flame. Her gaze swung. "Kole," she squeaked. "Hi. Hello. There you are, too. We were just…" She blinked fast. "This is…"

"Lord Goodnight." Kole's voice was as sharp as a blade, his glare even sharper.

Lord? She liked that.

With the doors open, the cozy silence was blasted apart by the thirty-piece orchestra playing to the crowd. When Leah had first seen the opulent ballroom with its gleaming floor, floating chandeliers and white columns around which ruby roses climbed, she'd almost swallowed her tongue. Her family wasn't poor by any means, but even they didn't have ballrooms.

Still, everything else paled next to meeting her warlock. Something Kole seemed to take great exception to as he stiffly walked forward and flung his arm around her shoulders. The gesture wasn't unusual, both of them touchy, affectionate people.

But the last thing Leah wanted was to give her warlock the wrong idea. Unfortunately, when she tried to sidle away, Kole tightened his hold.

She elbowed him in the side and he grunted, stubbornly keeping his arm in place.

Goodnight fell back with the new arrival, eyes darting between Leah and Kole. Then he gave a clipped nod. "Lord Bluewater."

"Didn't realize you had time to socialize, with the business and all."

"Family obligations."

"Naturally," Kole mocked.

Nothing moved an inch on Goodnight's face but Leah felt his annoyance like a whisper across her cheek.

He faced Leah and pressed a hand to his chest, bowed. She noticed the glint of a ring on his pinkie as he straightened. "Thank you for being a stranger with me." His voice was toneless but soft.

Her smile bloomed. "Anytime."

He didn't go through the doors to the party, instead retreating the way he came. Leah stared after him as Kole muttered a curse and dropped his arm. When she went to speak, he held up a hand, casting his other up and around. Something sparked, a faint white light that covered them like a translucent globe. She'd seen it before; soundproofing spell.

His eyebrows were tight when he rounded on her. "What did we say, Leah?"

She ignored him. "Who was that?"

Kole didn't wear a mask so his frustration was easy to read. All signs pointed to pissed. "What did we say? Don't draw attention."

"I wasn't." She chose not to mention Laurence and the punch. "We were just—"

"Yeah, I saw what you and Gabriel Goodnight were *just*." Rich brown eyes that matched his hair raked her with a hot glance. "Don't you have any common sense?"

"Nothing about me is common." She tweaked his nose, smiling when he batted her hand away. "Gabriel Goodnight? You have to be making that up. Sounds like he belongs in a fairy tale."

"Yeah, well, if this was a fairy tale, he'd be a villain."

Her heart dove. "No," she denied. "He was so nice." And he'd come to her rescue.

Kole laughed, then scrubbed his face. "Goddess. I can't leave you unsupervised for one minute. I knew this was a bad idea, especially Sloane coming, too." Sloane was Emma's half-witch sister, who'd been as sheltered from this world as Leah was. When they'd relented about Leah, Sloane had insisted on being her plus-one.

Leah looked past him. "How is she? I don't see you lecturing *her*."

Kole pinched her chin, pulling her attention back. "She's dancing with Bastian. Leah, you could've been found out. You get that, right?"

"But I didn't. It's all good."

"It's not all good when I catch you making out with the Warlock of Contempt."

"We weren't 'making out.'" Barely even a kiss, she thought with some disappointment. "And seriously, you're calling him names now?"

"*Society* calls him that. He's so full of his family and name, of his status. And he's against our people mingling. Thinks witches should stick with witches."

"What?" But that was...

Kole nodded, releasing her chin. "Except when it comes to business, I guess, since his company's mixed up with both witches and humans." He tugged on a loosened blond curl. "See how I rescued you now? How about some gratitude? I have a few ideas on how you could thank me."

She wasn't in the mood for their usual flirty banter, disappointment coating the joy she'd had in the moment.

Kole sighed, reached for her hand—luckily not her injured one, as that would've brought on a whole new lecture. "Let's get back inside. Bastian said he has some big announcement."

She threw one last searching look at the gardens. Kole was wrong, had to be. Not that she'd ever see Gabriel Goodnight again, but she wanted to think of him as the lonely stranger she'd almost kissed on a starlit night. If this was the only piece of this world she could have, that was how she'd choose to remember it.

They'd always have the balcony.

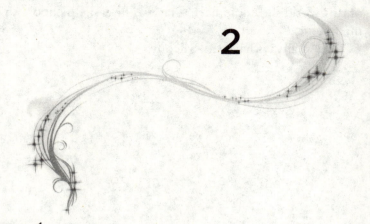

2

*T*oday was the day.

Gabriel stepped out of the portal he'd created, adjusting his sapphire silk tie with a steady hand. Confidence rode his straight shoulders, the lift of his chin, the satisfied air of a warlock about to do what he'd set out to accomplish twelve years ago.

Even though the few human employees scattered around the lobby had signed magical NDAs under the permission of the High Family, he'd still concealed his portal under a glamour and only removed it after snapping the portal shut with a wave of his hand. You never knew if they would have visiting humans from other businesses.

Now visible, he gave a clipped nod to Susan and Eric, who sat at the half-moon marbled reception as his Ferragamo shoes ate up the glossy floor toward the elevator bank. He didn't see if they acknowledged his greeting, too focused on the clench of anticipation in his gut. He could have gone straight to the top floor, but he wanted to appreciate every moment of walking through the New Orleans skyscraper that housed his legacy. Because today was the day.

Today was when the board would finally recognize his years of working his way up through his parents' company and vote him CEO of Goodnight's Remedies.

Along with the wave of satisfaction came the old mingled cloud of sorrow and bitterness. He pushed the up button, seeing not the distorted image of himself in the three-piece silver suit but instead his father, dressed in the same. Although it had been twelve years, sometimes it felt like only days had passed since he and his younger sister, Melly, had got the mirror message about their parents' deaths.

Laura and Alec Goodnight had been helping administer medicines to a village in Colombia when human rebels had blazed through. While his parents had been Higher status, their abilities lay in alchemy. As humans weren't to know of witches, they couldn't portal out; his mother had been trying to help the villagers escape when she was shot in the belly. His father had refused to leave her and had been shot, too. Both gone because of their unwillingness to leave each other—and their determination to be part of the human world.

Gabriel exhaled a slow stream of air as the elevator doors opened, forcing his eyes and attention forward—on the future, not the past. He'd worked his ass off from day one, starting in the mailroom and making his way through each department, learning it, conquering it, expanding it, bit by bit, until he knew how every part of the business interlinked and could function more efficiently.

He'd developed tablets to ease asthma with the skilled lab technicians his mother had once worked with, created marketing campaigns with the silver-tongued suits that worked in advertising. He'd even gone out into the field to harvest ingredients they used in the potions and lotions they bottled and packed up to sell to the masses. He'd earned his place here. He'd done what was expected, what *he* expected from himself. To be the best, to live up to his parents' legacy, even if the company's mission statement slicked salt in open wounds.

To heal, to help, and to engender hope for a brighter future for human- and witchkind together.

His lips flattened as he pushed for the top floor where the board would meet. Gabriel didn't care that the High Family oversaw every initiation of a human into the business—and in general. Inviting humans in, mixing their worlds, was asking for trouble. Asking for someone else to be left an orphan like he and Melly had been.

He closed his eyes, again shoving away any disruptive thoughts. He was an island on a calm ocean and no waves would disrupt his path.

Because today was the day when he would finally step up to meet his destiny. And nothing was going to ruin that.

Except maybe this.

Gabriel wondered if steam was shooting out his ears as he gazed coolly at his uncle and the board across the polished walnut table. Beneath said table, he clasped his hands tightly, wringing until a spike of pain from his family ring allowed him to speak with a measure of calm.

"I think I misheard you." He didn't shift in the leather chair but plenty of the other eleven board members did, uncomfortable with what they thought might become a scene.

They should know better; Gabriel had never made a scene in his life.

His uncle didn't stir under the stare, but then, the man who currently ran the Goodnight empire had helped Gabriel raise Melly—and to some extent, Gabriel himself, even though he'd been eighteen when his parents had died.

August steepled his hands, still looking a distinguished forty despite having one hundred and fifty-two years of hard work behind him. He looked so much like Gabriel's father, like Gabriel, it was almost painful to look at him. They shared the same black hair that had too much body, the same sharp facial structure. Except where Gabriel had inherited his mother's green-blue eyes, August stared sternly at him out of hazel eyes the shade of Melly's.

"I said we can't vote you in yet."

The words hit the same as they had the first time—like shrapnel that tore and twisted its way through Gabriel's internal organs. He'd done all he could and he hadn't measured up.

Noise echoed in his head. "I believe I've proven myself well capable of running this company."

August nodded, as did James, a portly warlock who'd always taken the time to reminisce about Gabriel's parents with him at any event the company had thrown. Across the table, he smiled at him, sympathy obvious.

It made Gabriel's spine stiffer. He didn't need sympathy. He needed his legacy.

"I think I speak for everyone when we say you have more than lived up to the hopes we had," August said, his voice deeper than anyone would expect. It didn't waver. "We're not doubting your ability to run this company."

"Then what is the issue?"

"It's not an issue. It's a clause in your father's will."

That set him back.

August held out a hand and an iPad appeared. Like Gabriel, his primary strength was conjuring, and a small fetch like that was as second nature as breathing. Something Gabriel was finding difficult as he watched August navigate to a page. With a subtle gesture, he projected the section of legal document onto the wall of glass that looked out over the somewhat "newer" section of New Orleans, what the locals referred to as the "American" side.

The lights dimmed and the windows tinted, allowing all of them to read the black type.

Gabriel ran his eyes over it, understanding the words and yet not comprehending how they made sense. "This cannot be right."

August pursed his lips. Another gesture had the document disappearing, the lights to full power and the windows once again reflecting clear blue sky.

"Three months," he confirmed. "Before you assume control, your father wanted you to spend some time living with limited powers amongst humans."

Each word threatened to break him. *Limited powers. Amongst humans.*

"I've never heard this before." Though his tone was even, underneath the table his hands remained tight enough that bone rubbed bone.

Something flickered in his uncle's gaze before he placed the iPad with undue care onto the table. "It was discovered only recently."

"The High Family—" Gabriel began, aware of the straws he was grasping at.

"Have always given this business leeway when dealing with humans," August cut in. "For research, development, testing purposes. You know that."

Yes, he did. They never had trouble finding both witches and invited humans to trial new products, the subjects given the lowdown of the ingredients and the processes before agreement. Their feedback had been instrumental for creating many of their final products which now sat in drugstores across the world. Goodnight's Remedies couldn't function without some degree of mingling. But—

"But," he echoed his thoughts, consciously lowering his tight shoulders. "That is for business. What you're asking...what the contract states is of a more personal nature." And it made something constrict in his chest.

One thought pounded through him. *Don't make me do this.*

August tapped his fingers on the table before rising. "Walk with me. Excuse us for a moment," he told the others and headed for the door, which opened at his approach.

Feeling like a misbehaving schoolboy back at the boarding school all Higher sons had to go to, Gabriel stood with perfect control. He nodded at the discomforted board members, before following his uncle out and into the office across the hall.

It resembled the boardroom, rich with expensive wood and layered with books and artifacts from across the world, articles about the products they'd created, and photographs of family and staff.

Gabriel's eyes lingered on the photo of his family, taken just after Melly was born, back when they'd still lived in England, before he moved to stand by his uncle at the windows.

After a moment, August spoke, keeping his eyes on the figures moving below. "When Laura and Alec founded this company, they did so because they wanted to make a difference in people's lives, behind the scenes, without breaking rules."

"I know, Uncle."

"They started in the back room of their mansion, building it slowly but steadily until it became this." August swept a hand around the opulent office. "A veritable empire that affects so many lives, employs many thousands of people—some human. And they did it because they cared." He turned from the view, hazel eyes direct. "You don't care, Gabriel."

His chin snapped up at the unseen blow. "I have thought of nothing *but* this company since—"

"Not the company." August indicated the people below. "About them."

"I care."

"And that's why you avoid talking to any of our human employees when you can?"

Discomfort crept up Gabriel's poker-straight spine. He folded his arms. "You know why it makes me uncomfortable."

"But not everyone does. There has been talk that you're not suitable to lead this company into its new age. That you would hold us back."

Gabriel's arms drifted to his sides. "Hold you back?"

August clapped both hands onto Gabriel's shoulders, meeting him head-on. "Nobody who knows you doubts your dedication. It's a slap in the face, yes, but we can use this to our advantage. Trust me, I'm angry as hell at Alec for forcing you to do this."

"He knew." Gabriel swallowed, memories clouding him. None good. "He knew I'd fail."

August shook him lightly. "You haven't failed. This is Alec's way of controlling things; my brother was always determined that this company would grow."

And determined, Gabriel thought sickly, that his son never take the reins of the thing he loved the most. Why else force him to live three months with limited powers? He knew it was more likely his son would walk away. The son he knew. The screw-up.

Are you any different now? The thought was a silent jeer hard to ignore.

"If it's too hard for you," August continued, "if you want to step away, I am perfectly happy to keep running the company."

Buzzing began in Gabriel's ears. How had this gone to hell so quickly?

"We can find you a seat on the board or you can pick a department and work there." August squeezed Gabriel's shoulders before dropping away. His face was compassionate. "You don't have to do this."

No, he didn't. His uncle was right; he could walk away. Play into his father's expectations.

Except that wasn't who Gabriel was now. He handled his responsibilities the way his parents had always expected of him.

Except this…it weighed like a crushing curse, bending his body under the pressure.

"What…" He had to stop, start again. "What are the conditions?"

Something flickered in his uncle's eyes before he seated himself on the corner of his desk. "You'd have to stay three months connected with humans. Meaning you have to find a place to live, find a job, get to know your co-workers. Interact. And you'd have to do this with your powers bound."

"Stripped away?"

"Stripped back," August corrected, "and not stripped exactly. We'll limit the level of your magic, but you'll still have access. Though I'm told with a binding spell, the more you use, the more it will hurt." A beat passed. "If you break the binding, use stronger magic, the clause is nullified and you'd give up your controlling share."

Panic burst into a cloud of black dots at the edges of Gabriel's vision. This couldn't be happening.

"I know." August shook his head, gripping the edge of his desk, as if he found this as painful as Gabriel. "I don't know what Alec was thinking. It's not…normal for us to live with only basic magic. And it's not fair to ask you to do this."

No, it wasn't. The walls closed in until his tie threatened to choke him. Magic was what he was, *who* he was.

"Are there any stipulations about the kind of job, the area?" His voice was flat, stripped of emotion. He couldn't afford to give in to it, had to stand alone.

The memory of a teasing witch on a moonlit balcony three weeks ago flirted in his mind, as it so often did. She wouldn't agree, of that he was sure.

"No stipulations other than those stated." August studied him. "I know you, Gabriel. You've worked too hard to give up, but again, I'm fine to continue running the company if you don't want to do this."

Want? No. But he had to.

"However," his uncle continued, clapping a hand on his shoulder again, "choosing to do this will go a long way with the board members eager to explore further growth into the human side of things. After discussion with the High Family, naturally. As CEO, they'd look to you to lead the way. Accomplishing this will help with that."

For a split second, Gabriel thought about breaking something, about screaming. Temptation to refuse played on his tongue, all but purred in his ear. He couldn't do this, he couldn't—

Catching the spiral, he breathed out slowly, willing himself to calm. The tornado slowed, stopped, broke apart as his chest eased. He would deal with this the way he'd dealt with everything. Head-on, one logical step at a time. Alone.

"I need to discuss this with Melly." His sister was fourteen now, still a minor. August had lived with them when he'd first brought them to America, back when it had all first happened, but had moved out of the New Orleans family manor when Gabriel had hit twenty-five. "And ask Mrs. Q if she'll look after her."

August bowed his head. "Of course. And if Mrs. Q feels overworked, Melly can come live with me for the duration. You know I always have room. For you both."

The rush of emotion didn't make it onto Gabriel's face but he nodded. "Thanks, Uncle."

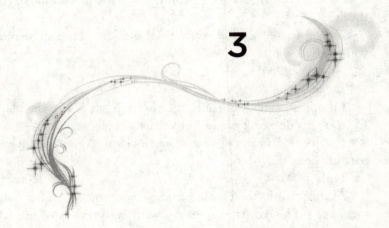

3

*G*abriel took a sip of his wine, a well-aged cabernet, as his little sister doubled over in laughter. It rang around the large room they'd designated as the lounge, sweeping from the Aubusson rug to the twelve-foot ceiling.

"I'm glad you find it so amusing," he commented, tapping a restless hand against his right thigh.

"Oh, come on, Gabriel." She threw herself into the deep cushions of the white couch, curling her legs underneath her. She was dressed casually in jeans and a lavender blouse, the charm bracelet he'd enchanted dangling from her wrist.

"I don't see what's funny." He stared into his drink. "I earned that title."

He felt the slide of a telekinetic touch move through his hair, a sister's comfort. "You'll show them," she said, matter-of-factly, twisting her fall of black hair over one shoulder. "Goodnights always have the final word. Right?"

He put his drink aside on a silver coaster, pushing to stand. He wandered to the mantelpiece, glowering at the fire, which roared to life at a word from him.

His sister didn't let him brood. "What did Uncle August think?"

Gabriel tossed a look over his shoulder. "He suggested I walk away."

"You wouldn't."

"It's tempting."

"Oh, please." She snorted. "You were born to run the place. Even if you don't like, you know, the people part."

He slid a hand into his trouser pocket. "Apparently that's part of the issue."

"Huh?"

"August thinks the clause is there to get me out of my comfort zone." The words were heavy with derision. "So I can take our company into a new era, bring more humans on board."

"You don't agree?"

"I don't see how skipping with humans is going to convince me that they're any less dangerous, no."

Melly clapped her hands together. "*Please* have someone record it if you skip." She beamed at his scowl, but relented. "Okay, so, basically you have to live as a human. It's wild. And it sounds like Dad. At least," her voice got smaller, "from what you've said about him."

"It is." He didn't tell her he thought the clause was actually designed to make him quit. He wanted her to know only the good about their parents since she knew so little. "Mell... I want to know how you feel about me going."

"I'm so jealous. You'll learn loads." She shot him an encouraging smile. "You love learning."

He grunted. "I meant, how you feel about living here alone." He linked his hands behind his back, watching her face. "I already spoke to Mrs. Q and she's happy to stay with you full-time, but if you're uncomfortable at all, I'll speak to the board."

Melly waved that away. "It's three months. And Mrs. Q doesn't need to stay here, I'll be fine on my own."

"No, you won't." He shuddered at the idea of leaving his fourteen-year-old sister, an adept witch, alone for twelve weeks. "And don't even think about visiting."

Her face fell. "Oh, come on."

"No."

She huffed. He knew the subject wasn't dropped; she was just regrouping. "Whatever, I'll be fine. Got my potions to keep me busy." Melly was her mother's daughter and loved messing around with potions, trying to improve them. Something Gabriel encouraged, even if she had blown the roof off her bedroom last year.

Oh, Goddess.

"No potions whilst unsupervised."

She threw up her hands, as dramatic as he was contained. "Am I supposed to sit in the corner?"

"That would be perfect." He almost smiled as he felt the hard *thwack* of a telekinetic forehead flick. "When I return, we'll work on them then."

"You suck at potions."

Affronted, he drew back. "I do not."

"You screw up twice as many potions as I do."

"I disagree."

She began to count them off on her fingers and he hurriedly intervened. "Regardless, it would bring your big brother some peace if you could refrain from blowing yourself up whilst he's away."

She laughed, the Goodnight dimple flashing in her cheek. "Fine. I'll be careful if you're careful. Or maybe I should be getting you to promise the opposite."

He refused to go down that road.

She heaved a breath, drawing her knees up and propping her elbows on them. "So, where are you thinking?"

There was really only one place. "Chicago."

"You're not sticking to New Orleans?"

"No." The last thing he needed was his contemporaries mocking him. "It will be easier somewhere further away."

"Okay, but why Chicago?"

Gabriel grabbed his wine as it slid through the air at his gesture. "Emmaline Bluewater made waves when she and Tia Hightower opened a bar that caters to humans." That idea alone… He'd have wondered how they'd got past the High Family, but the rulers were always more relaxed about business dealings. "I can use my connections to get a temporary position there. Emmaline is recently engaged to Bastian Truenote."

"You know him?"

"Henry does." Henry Pearlmatter was Gabriel's oldest, maybe only, friend. A legacy Higher warlock like Gabriel, he knew every powerful family in the US and Europe.

"I heard he proposed to her last month at the Truenote ball." A down-to-the-bone romantic, Melly sighed, eyes going gooey. "And after everyone was so mean to her."

He hadn't seen the moment that had set witch society ablaze, having been out in the gardens after meeting his mystery witch, wondering who she was and failing to figure it out. All for the best, he supposed, since it appeared she and Kole Bluewater were together.

He drank his wine, washing away the sudden bad taste.

Melly eyed him. "So, you want to work in a bar?"

"Why not?"

"Gabriel." She made a "get real" gesture; one he was often on the receiving end of. "You suck with people."

Gabriel worked his jaw, unable to rebut the point. "I'm sure I'll manage." And at least this job would have a literal boundary between him and the human clientele. Less chance of anything going wrong that way.

Melly wasn't finished. "You'll have to smile, be charming…"

"I'll have to pour drinks and take money. How hard could that be?"

"Ha. Famous last words, brother."

★ ★ ★

Leah charged into Toil and Trouble, letting the bar's double doors swing shut on the sheets of rain pelting the sidewalks— and the people unlucky enough to be on them. Droplets slid down her back as she walked forward, making her squirm as she automatically greeted the customers she knew, smiling at those she didn't.

To the group of men watching an NHL game on the enormous wide-screen hung on the exposed brick wall, she waved, adding some personal insults. The men were regulars, switching sports with the seasons, and she knew with April in sniffing distance, they'd be donning their baseball gear, same as she would. She'd never miss Opening Day. Cubs and proud, y'all.

"It's coming down hard," she announced to her friends when she was close enough.

Tia leaned on the walnut bar that ran the length of the thirty-foot space, where she'd been chatting with their third business partner, Emma, who perched on one of the cushioned barstools. They both smiled in acknowledgment.

To look at them, nobody would connect them as business partners, let alone friends.

Tia Hightower was a witch with capital C confidence, a born leader, no matter that she was currently acting as bartender while they searched for someone to fill the again-empty position. Even though it wasn't a suit, the coral jeans and cream crop tee that set off her brown skin gorgeously did nothing to dim her power. She never had to worry about fitting in as her family made the rules and pretty much did whatever the hell she wanted.

Emma Bluewater, on the other hand, was practical to the bone, though she did take *some* risks, and made worrying about Leah one of her primary tasks. Like Tia, she came from a Higher witch family, but unlike Tia, her family lived on the fringes and witch society had never let her forget it. It was why she could be painfully shy with new people, even when her personality tended toward dry humor.

Leah bet her cautious friend had never imagined running a bar. Toil and Trouble had been Leah's idea, providing Emma with a steady job after she'd abandoned New Orleans for Chicago eight years ago, while also cementing the bonds between all three.

And okay, after they'd spilled the big secret, she'd thought opening a cocktail bar with them might bring a little magic into her own life.

Leah plopped onto a neighboring stool now and used one of the paper napkins out of the nearby dispenser to soak up the worst of the wet. "I lost track of time at the shelter," she said, squeezing her hair into the tissue, "taking photos of the new residents for the website, playing with some of the seniors. Before I knew it, it was cats and dogs outside, too." And the animal shelter where she volunteered was a good twenty, thirty-minute hustle. It hadn't taken two minutes before even her underwear was soaked.

"How's the place doing? Sorry I haven't been by for a while." Emma winced, offering, "Bastian and I took Sloane to Germany for a few days."

"Oh, yeah? She have fun?"

"She and Bastian did something called the Sachertorte challenge."

"How much did she throw up?"

"What happens in Germany stays in Germany."

Leah grinned. "Wise. And don't worry about the shelter. We're fine. I mean, Sonny's moaned about the bills a bit, but I'm sure it's just a rough patch." She waved that away. "Okay, I need you to tell it to me straight." She took a breath. "What's the hair situation?"

Tia and Emma exchanged a look.

"That bad?"

"It's got volume," Emma offered. Tia snorted.

That was Leah's hair cross to bear—when wet, her curls expanded like nobody's business.

Philosophically, she discarded the wet napkin and pledged not to look in any mirrors. "So, where is the old soon-to-be ball and chain?"

Emma lifted the latte that sat on the bar. One hell of a rock in a platinum setting sparkled on her hand. Leah drooled just looking at it. "He's with a friend."

Tia grumbled, dark eyes flashing.

Emma ignored her. "He and Henry are apartment hunting since we want a bigger place than my shoebox."

"You want me to ask my mom? She knows everyone; she might know some nice places."

"Your mom's idea of nice and mine are probably a little different."

Leah made a *pshaw* sound. "Please, we're not that rich. I've seen Bastian's parents' house now, remember? Talk about Daddy Warlock with the Warbucks."

"*Stop.*" At the mention of magic, Emma's eyes grew rabbity.

Leah chucked her under the chin but relented. "Best behavior. Promise."

"Hmm."

They passed the time discussing the future wedding, not that there was much to plan since Emma and Bastian had already gone through the motions the year before. Back then, Emma had looked caged. Now, whenever Bastian's name came up, she got the gooey look. After all the shit they'd gone through, God knew her friend deserved it.

And it gave Leah hope that maybe she'd one day find a good guy of her own, as opposed to her last date, who'd brought his mother and aunt along to vet her.

Seriously. Worst taste in men ever.

"All I'm saying is, who wants a gray bridesmaid dress?" Tia's gorgeous face set in mutinous lines. "Why do you punish me?"

"It's my wedding and it's a very pretty dress."

Tia's lips went sulky. "Fine. But at my wedding, I'm making you wear bright red and you'll like it."

"You picked the bridesmaid dresses?" Grinning, Leah jiggled her wet sneakers on the stool's rung. "What do they look like? Will we be matching?"

Emma's smile faltered as Tia's expression melted into sympathy.

And Leah got a reality check.

Masking the sharp ache of disappointment, Leah reassured her distressed friend that she was totally fine about missing out, provided someone record the ceremony. It was Emma's day and she refused to take any shine from her friend's smile.

Even if it did sometimes feel like she was a kid pressing her hand to the glass window, forever on the outside, forever waiting to be let in.

They'd hit the lull hour, the moment when everyone was one breath from leaving the office, so Leah volunteered to cover restocking. She had the time. Her three dogs were at day care for another hour, a new arrangement since they usually spent their days either with Peggy, who rented a room in Leah's house, or with Leah's mom. But Peggy was on a wild weekend with friends and Leah's mom was traveling with her new husband on their extended honeymoon, so it was the delights of doggy day care for the foreseeable future.

Carrying the last bottles of rosé up from the cellar, Leah walked in from the hall as Tia's voice rose with agitation.

"…can't believe he even asked." Her foot tapped a hard beat on the wooden floor.

"Apparently, he's still bugging Henry and Bastian. I wouldn't put it past him to just show up." Emma bent to stroke her constant companion and witch familiar, Chester, a cute-ugly basset hound mix. "We need to—" She cut off, spotting Leah.

Who glanced between the pair as she placed the box on the bar top. "O-kay," she said. "Color me curious. What're you two talking about?"

Tia's sharp gaze tracked the space, making sure they were alone before she said, "A warlock's been asking for a job at the bar."

Leah swallowed the delighted yip before it made it out. *Get real, Turner.* "You said no."

"Hell, yeah." Tia pointed at her. "You can't lie for shit."

"Can, too."

"Emma."

Emma smiled weakly. "Bastian figured you out in weeks."

"He's shrewd," Leah argued, then waved a hand. "Whatever, you guys already ban witches from this place. I don't expect you to suddenly change your tune." Despite how many times she'd argued she could handle it. Didn't she handle it when the Cubs' second baseman had strolled in for a drink? Did she tear open her shirt and ask him to sign her boob? No. She'd only made him pose for three photos, sign her Cubs cap and joked about giving him a child. He'd taken it well. Not that they'd ever seen him again.

Emma fiddled with one of the paper napkins. "You know it's asking for trouble, having witches in here."

"Yeah, and Gabriel Goodnight would definitely be adding gasoline to the fire."

Leah's heart kicked. "Gabriel Goodnight?"

Memories invaded of a darkened balcony, green eyes, soft lips.

Thank you for being a stranger with me.

Oblivious, Tia ripped the tape off the box of rosé with a curl of her lip. "The Warlock of Contempt himself." When Emma frowned, Tia held up a hand. "You know it's not just me that calls him that."

"Still feels like bullying." Something she'd felt herself from witch society.

Tia began to stack the bottles on the counter. "It's true, though. I've never seen the man smile or laugh or show any-thing *other* than contempt."

"Bastian says Henry likes him."

Tia's face darkened further, as it did whenever her ex was mentioned. "Doesn't that say it all?"

Leah made a time-out gesture. "Guys. Why's he called the Warlock of Contempt?"

"Witch is collective for all, warlock for singular men."

"Not what I meant." She bent to Chester as he trotted her way. She ruffled his long ears, placing a kiss on his nose. "I thought all witch society was stuck up like that."

"Even society demands *some* interaction. They tolerate him because he's a Goodnight, but he makes people uncomfort-able." Tia shrugged, reaching for more bottles. "Luckily he only makes the odd obligatory appearance, too wrapped up in his family's business to socialize."

I don't play. His words.

"If he's such a workaholic," she said to Chester, who threw himself on his back for a belly rub. His leg kicked in the air as she obliged and fought to sound casual. "Why does he want to work *here*?"

Emma winced. "Ah, apparently it has to do with some kind of hoop he has to jump through to inherit his company."

"But you said…"

"It was his parents'." Tia opened the under-counter fridge and began sliding in the bottles. "They died, oh, about eleven, twelve years ago, I think? Left him and his two-year-old sister orphans." Her tone was matter-of-fact but she avoided looking at them, as if she knew they'd see the unwilling sympathy in her eyes. She hated showing too much soft emotion.

Whereas Leah couldn't help it. "That's so sad."

"Well, apparently he needs to spend some time living among humans before claiming the CEO title."

Leah frowned. "That's…weird. You guys are so weird. Why is that even a thing? What kind of company is this?"

"Pharmaceutical, medical and beauty," Emma cut in. "You'd know their products. Goodnight's Remedies?"

"Oh, sure," Leah said, startled. "I see their ads all the time. I even bought the wrinkle cream for my mom. She raves about it." Now she knew why.

Emma sent a look toward the door, checking for anyone coming in. "Right. And on top of that, they also manufacture magical medicines. Like for illnesses, accidents, diseases."

"He wants to help people," Leah murmured, a melty feeling spreading throughout her body.

Tia barked a laugh, closing the fridge and picking up the box to flatten it. "His parents wanted to help people," she corrected. "Both witches and humans. Goodnight wants the company. Goddess knows why. I can't see him caring about…well, anyone."

"You have to admire the tactic," Emma said, her tone diplomatic. "Making him interact with humans when he and all the other Higher family snobs usually keep their distance. It'll prove how serious he is."

Laurence flashed into Leah's mind.

Tia snorted. "Who cares? I just want to know what menial job Gabriel Goodnight is going to be forced to do. I'd pay big money to see that." She grinned as she hugged the now-flat box to her chest, then added, "But not here."

"Not here," Emma confirmed. She clearly caught the expression on Leah's face, turning to her in warning. "Don't get stuck on this, Leah. He doesn't need our help."

"Sounds like he does to me." The idea of seeing Gabriel again toyed with Leah's senses. Not smart, not really, but the temptation dizzied her. All that stood in her way was changing her friends' minds.

Piece of cake.

She corralled her expression, deliberately taking a nonchalant tone. "Didn't you say he wasn't taking no for an answer?"

"So?"

"Well, if you keep refusing, won't that look worse for you? Like you have something to hide?"

Tia eyed her with suspicion. "What's it matter to you?"

"I happen to be a nice person."

"Really? What's that like?"

"Just…come on, guys. You want to stand in the way of someone who's only trying to inherit his *dead parents'* company?" She pressed on the weak chink in Tia's armor, knowing her friend well. Sucker for family, that one. "That's low."

Sure enough, Tia's shoulders slumped.

"It's our place, he'd have to abide by our rules," Leah pointed out. Nudging, nudging. "You could do it so you'd be comfortable. A few shifts here and there."

Emma nibbled at her thumbnail, said nothing.

Progress. Leah backed off. "Just think about it. All I'm saying is, if you don't want people suddenly wondering why you don't let witches come around, it might be best to let one in under your terms."

By the end of the week, after much cajoling on Leah's part and apparently some relentless pushing on Gabriel's, it was settled—Gabriel Goodnight was coming to Toil and Trouble.

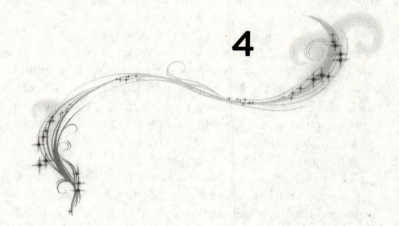

4

Toil and Trouble was every bit as bad as he'd thought it would be.

Gabriel had finagled, twisted arms, pressured and bribed, and yet, as he listened to Tia Hightower list all the ridiculously named drinks on their cocktail menu, he violently wished for a dark corner to hide in.

At least the apartment by Lake Michigan was tolerable, open plan and a decent square footage. He'd left last-minute instructions for Mrs. Q—not that she needed them since she'd kept their houses since he'd been a boy—said a final goodbye to Melly, and portalled to Chicago.

As soon as he'd set foot in his new apartment, the clock had started. When he'd gestured unthinkingly to turn on the lights, a low-grade buzz had vibrated through him. According to James and a few others from the board who'd placed the binding on his powers, he was allotted a certain amount of magic a day. Each use, depending on the complexity of the spell, would increase the feedback from mild irritation to bone-rattling pain. A reminder that he should be learning to live as *they* lived. Gain a new appreciation and empathy for the people the company was trying to help.

The first clue it'd be tougher than even he'd predicted had come when he'd tried to use the toaster. It seemed to need some kind of degree in engineering. No matter the amount of times he pushed the lever, no matter the amount of force he used, the bread wouldn't stay down. Finally he'd just eaten it as is, irritated as the appliance seemed to mock him from its perch on the counter.

It had gone downhill from there.

Tia had met him at the door with a chip on her shoulder similar in size to the bags of ice she'd made him lug upstairs, downstairs and then upstairs again. He needed the job too much to call her out on what was clearly a challenge. Besides, although annoying, he could handle it. And he had a feeling if Tia decided to fully haze him, she'd have him stripped to his underwear and singing along to the karaoke machine in ten seconds.

Karaoke.

Spell him with a sickening curse now.

Three months, he reminded himself as he repeated the drinks back to her scowling face. He only had to make it three months.

Unimpressed with his memory, Tia gave him final directions about the register, carding people who looked below twenty-one—as if he'd know?—and playing nice with others *if he could possibly manage that*, before she set him loose.

He knew she expected him to fail, but he'd prove her wrong if he had to study bartending every night. Goodnights didn't fail.

He tried to remember that he liked learning new things. That was why he'd been so successful at enhancing the different departments at Goodnight's Remedies. Seeing all the parts that make up a whole, how they worked, how they could work even better. This was just one more new thing. One more bleak, miserable thing.

His first customer was a woman in a blue skirt-suit. She looked old enough to drink, but with Tia watching, he dutifully asked her for proof of age.

"You think I'm that young?" The human batted her eyelashes.

"I have to ask," he answered evenly.

She slid her ID over the counter, brushing her fingers along his and keeping hold of the card. "How old do you think I am?"

He paid no attention to her coy tone, focusing instead on sliding the ID away from her. "Forty?"

Offense simmered in eyes gone a dark blue. "I'm thirty-five!"

"If you let go, I'll verify that and get your drink."

She scowled. "You really thought I was forty?"

"You have some lines," he commented, checking the date after she finally relinquished the ID.

That interaction earned him a five-minute lecture on being friendly while keeping his damn mouth shut. When he pointed out he'd just been honest, he thought the vein in Tia's forehead would blow like one of Melly's potions.

Still, he refrained from speaking beyond what was absolutely necessary the next couple of times he'd served. Cocktails were easy enough to follow since they were essentially potions, but the measurements were strange and he had to remake some. Or all.

Tia finally kicked him out at the end of his four-hour shift and he'd never left a building faster without portalling out. He breathed in the crisp air, so different to New Orleans' sultry scent, with a measure of relief. That lasted about a minute as he turned his attention to his next task: grocery shopping.

With Mrs. Q in charge of the domestic tasks at home, he'd never done such a thing and found it strange to be surrounded by humans. Stranger still when a woman with a ponytail and jeans with a hole in the knee threatened him as he reached for the last baguette. Not that he'd been intimidated by her or by the purse she'd wielded like a nunchuck, but he'd surrendered the bread without argument.

But it wasn't just that one woman; the entire atmosphere was discomforting. The knowledge that he wasn't supposed to be there, that he didn't belong, had him hustling through the list Mrs. Q had given him. He was congratulating himself on a job well done when one of the paper bags split just outside the store.

Since he was in public and couldn't use his magic, there was no saving the eggs as they hit the ground like mini grenades, bursting on impact. All over his Ferragamo loafers.

A couple of teenagers loitering nearby on their bikes burst out laughing. Heat crawled up his neck as he tried to scoop the fallen tins and boxes into his remaining bag. And then that split.

He'd finally conjured a folding tote bag inside his pocket. Even that small fetch, something so habitual and easy, piled pressure on the base of his spine. Reminding him that this was his life for the next three months.

One day down, he told himself that night as he lay in his queen-size bed in his empty apartment. His belly grumbled— he'd burned the eggs he'd attempted to fry before settling for a ham sandwich, which, he admitted glumly, would have been better on baguette. He'd work on his cooking tomorrow. After all, tomorrow he'd only have two months, three weeks and six days to go.

Since nobody was around to see, he gave in and pulled the covers over his head.

Leah made it two days. Barely.

She timed it so that Emma would be in the back baking. She'd dressed casually, in worn, comfortable jeans and a sweater close to Gabriel's eye color. Since it was March in Chicago, her trusty peacoat went over the top, along with a thick scarf. She made sure to tuck her curls beneath her Cubs cap. Left to the wind, she'd look like one of those Raggedy Ann dolls, and that wasn't the first impression—well, first daylight impression, anyway—she wanted to make on her warlock.

Nerves jangled as she paused inside the double doors and surveyed the early afternoon crowd. There was barely anyone in, a few friend groups meeting for coffee, Emma's freshly made croissants, and conversation. They didn't do much of an afternoon trade, an area they wanted to work on at some point, but enough to get by.

Gabriel was at the bar.

Hanging back, she drank him in like a parched woman in the dead of summer.

God, he looked good. A little fancy in his three-piece gray suit and white shirt—or would it be two-piece, since he'd shed the jacket and rolled the shirtsleeves up his forearms?

Her eyes lingered there. She'd always been a sucker for a good pair of arms.

Without his mask, he was beautiful, almost too much so. If the devil could take form and tempt her to one night of sin, he would come dressed as Gabriel Goodnight.

The black waves of his hair were styled tidily, the sharp bones of his face contrasting with his soft lips, the faint shadow on his strong jaw. He still wore his tie, tucked into the shirt, under the silk vest. A fantasy made flesh.

His gaze connected with hers.

The impact was like a bolt of lightning, leaving her jittery. She watched for any recognition as she approached, but considering she'd been wearing a mask and had been glamoured when they'd last met, she knew it wasn't realistic.

Green eyes examined her as she came forward. That intense regard—no human man had ever looked at her that way. Her pulse fluttered as she drummed up a smile. "Hi."

She couldn't say his expression was welcoming, but he hadn't been all smiles before either. He'd been... Her gaze dropped to his lips, remembered them barely brushing her own.

"What can I get you?"

She bumped up her smile, wide and warm. "I'm Leah."

He stared at her without reaction.

"Leah. Turner." She gestured around them. "I own part of this place. I guess…" A small awkward laugh left her. "I'm kind of your boss?"

His gaze—God, so green, so breathtaking—flickered. "I don't think so."

What did you say to that?

She shifted her weight. "Well, it's true. Me and Emma and Tia, we all own a third. I just…wanted to come in, say welcome, make sure you're settling in okay."

"I've never heard of you."

Not even a speck of surprise at that revelation. Overprotective: look it up and there would be her friends' defiant faces.

"Really? Huh. Weird." She leaned against the bar, closer to him. "So, your name is Gabriel?"

He stood on the other side, tall, imposing, his mouth a severe line.

She kept the smile, waiting.

Waiting.

Waiting.

Uneasily waiting.

And yet, he did nothing.

She couldn't take it. She broke the silence again. "How are you finding it all?"

Still nothing.

Just as she wondered if she needed to break out her interpretive dance skills, he said, "Why haven't I heard that a…" He caught himself. "…a third person works here?"

"Owns," she corrected, straightening on a small bounce, anxious energy shooting through her from head to toes. "They must have forgotten to mention it."

He absorbed that, face cold even as his eyes flashed.

This could not be the same man from the balcony. Okay, so he hadn't exactly been the life of the party then, but he'd been livelier than this.

There'd been a connection. They'd *kissed*. Well, practically. Her rose-colored glasses slipped down her nose a little.

She gave it another shot, natural optimism butting against the smoke screen he was putting up. "Are you enjoying the job?"

"It's fine," he said flatly.

"I know it can be overwhelming, all the drinks and everything, so if you need any help—"

"I don't need *your* help," he cut in, dismissive as hell and so sharp, Leah felt the prick of the words on her exposed skin.

She tried to keep her cool. "Look, I think we got off on the wrong foot. Once you get to know me—"

"I don't want to get to know you."

Her jaw hit the floor.

"I have to clean." Leaving her gaping, he strode to the other end of the bar, where he picked up a towel and rubbed it over the already-clean surface.

Mortified, she stared at him as anger surged in every inch of her body.

How. Freaking. Rude.

If there was one thing she hated, it was rudeness.

Well...damn it. They'd been right. Kole, Emma, Tia. The Warlock of Contempt in all his glory had just dissed and dismissed her in her own bar. Worse, she'd been weaving this romantic fantasy about how lonely and misunderstood he was because of a few stolen minutes.

And even *worse*, she'd argued for his job here. Like the patsy she was, she'd read into his actions and believed he could be the warlock of her dreams.

Logically, she knew a warlock and a human weren't endgame. But it had been a nice fantasy before he'd dashed any hopes she had on the rocks they served with expensive vodka.

Goddamn it. She finally got it. Warlocks *sucked*.

She watched him, baring her teeth inwardly. He didn't want her help, huh? Well, they'd just see about that. Gabriel Goodnight was going to learn that humans were actually decent people that should be treated with respect and would help out anyone, even a chilly asshole like him.

Leah didn't need to punch his stupidly handsome face when she could kill him with kindness.

Or at least that had been the plan, but the next week proved to her than even a kind heart could hold out only so long against a pretentious dick. And if he wanted a crash course in Humans 101, he was about to learn why you shouldn't piss one off.

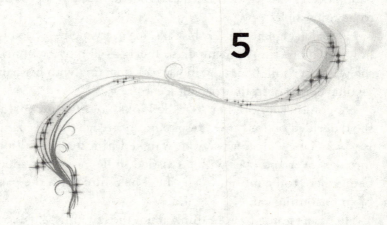

5

It had been a week and Gabriel was ready to wave the white flag. Not just ready; in his mind he'd bought the material, sewn it together and planted it on a pole. Only Goodnight pride stopped him from hoisting it, but he doubted any other Goodnight had ever dealt with anything like this. Not only had he completely failed at being a competent bartender—messing up the drink orders, incorrectly counting change, dropping so many glasses he was pretty sure he'd have nothing left of his salary—but he'd utterly failed at keeping the Goodnight dignity intact.

And all because of one blonde human.

Leah. Even her name made his teeth grind together.

Admittedly, he hadn't handled their first encounter well. Curse him for it, but it wasn't like he was known for his smooth charm, even under normal circumstances. Hearing that Toil and Trouble had a secret human owner was far from normal. Excuse the hell out of him for needing a moment. For needing to ignore her.

Maybe he'd have managed that—if the human in question

hadn't been Leah Turner. Because ignoring Leah was proving to be impossible.

He couldn't ignore the way his ears rang every night—seriously, how could one tiny human talk so much? And move so much; she was never still, bouncing in place or fidgeting with her hair, sending clouds of frothy coconut scent his way.

He couldn't ignore her so-called jokes and the nickname she'd decided on for him—despite his insistence that his name was *not* Gabe—or the way she watched him make multiple mistakes over and over with a satisfied smile, crooning about being there to help him. Yeah, she'd help him. Into the path of an oncoming car.

He wasn't going to even think about the few times he'd forgotten himself and used magic around her, something she'd thankfully missed or they'd all be in deep shit. He was just grateful he could add "unobservant" to her list of flaws—and there were many.

Worst of all, he couldn't ignore that he'd been reduced to trading insults with her, all veiled of course, and each insult that made her eyes narrow proved immensely satisfying.

Like the time she'd suggested a costume day at work and he'd finally got the last word.

"Something fun on today's agenda, Gabe!" she'd sung at him, a mean glint in her eye. "We've decided to have a theme night. How do you feel about *The Wizard of Oz*?"

"My name is Gabriel. And I don't wear costumes."

"Well, with that stick up your ass, I think we've found our scarecrow! Oh, Gabe, it was a joke. Lighten up."

"I don't wear costumes," he'd repeated.

"All right. How about a *Fifty Shades* theme? You already wear suits all the time; you can be Christian Grey. How does that sound?"

"Will I get to gag you?"

Her lips had thinned and every square inch of him had crowed in victory.

Unbelievable. One week in the human world and he'd forgotten everything about being a Goodnight.

And it was all her fault.

A loud whoop by the large mounted TV drew his brooding attention from the glasses he'd been drying to the small crowd watching the sports game. He noted Leah, ridiculous cap concealing all but a few curls, slap hands with a burly human wearing jeans and a beige sweater.

She grinned, mouth moving fast as she gestured to the screen. The group of men around her laughed, all appreciation.

Sure, she might smell nice and, in some eyes, might be considered attractive, but he doubted they'd be so quick with their interest if they worked with her. That one in front most of all needed a wake-up call; he'd already found three excuses to touch her.

Gabriel rammed the next glass into the stack with his mouth a flattened line.

After a few seconds, she winked at burly beige sweater and swiveled to Gabriel. He stuffed his cloth inside the next glass, purposefully watching it twist. He didn't care that she'd prefer to flirt than be at the bar but if she caught him looking, that would be it. She'd get that look in her eye, the gleam of battle. He'd sooner—

"Hey, cutie."

His gaze swung up at the drunken voice. Leah had been caught, clutched by a customer he'd served three neat whiskeys to over the past hour.

Gabriel narrowed in on where the stranger grabbed her. *Can't use magic*, his practical side warned as his fingers curled to telekinetically shove the man away. *Can't risk exposure.*

But as he should've expected, Leah didn't need rescuing.

"Sir, you need to let go." Although an easy smile accompanied the friendly warning, Gabriel noted she'd closed her hand into a fist.

"But I wanna talk to you," the guy slurred, his free hand waving a near-empty glass. "C'mere."

"And wouldn't that be fun?" She nodded in Gabriel's direction, still with that smile. "But you see that brooding tall drink of water at the bar? He's going to scare all the customers away if I don't help him."

When red eyes swung his way, Gabriel stared back without expression.

Leah patted the man's shoulder, easing her elbow out of his hand. "How about we get you some coffee on the house?"

She got him settled, then walked to the bar and around.

Gabriel argued with himself for several long beats before giving in. "Would you have punched him?"

She didn't look up from where she was fixing a strong coffee. "Him? No. Can't own a bar without dealing with frisky drunks." She let the machine do its thing, glancing over her shoulder at him. Her smile was sweet. "Or other annoyances."

His jaw set.

"Now, out of the bar," she mused as the coffee continued to drip. "That's different. I can throw a punch if I need to."

Don't ask, he told himself. "Have you?"

"Punched someone?" The considering expression slid into a wicked smile, an edge to it. "Oh, yeah. And it hurts like a bitch. Another reason for diplomacy. Having said *that*," she added, taking the mug when the machine beeped, "I'd do it again if the situation called for it."

He arched an eyebrow.

She smirked. "Don't worry your pretty head, Gabe. I won't hurt you."

His spine snapped straight. "It's Gabriel."

"Uh-huh." That smirk only grew, lifting his irritation with it. Her sweater slid off one shoulder as she folded her arms.

"Luckily," she continued, "I'm pretty good at talking people into or out of things. And it'd be rude to be punching people all the time."

"Wouldn't want that," he murmured.

"Manners matter," she quipped, heading past him with the coffee. Her elbow grazed his hip but he barely felt it as the words sunk in.

Manners matter.

The memory fluttered, a butterfly caught in webbing. He watched her lips curve as she handed over the drink.

The balcony. The witch who'd punched that pathetic excuse for a Higher son, Laurence Brochard. She'd said it, too.

It was probably a human saying, one of many he'd not heard before. Other witches that spent time with humans used them all the time.

Still, he sent a wary look at Leah, the profile of her lips and chin recalling another's, cast in moonlight. Something twisted before he shoved it away. Ridiculous. Ignoring the prickling sensation prowling down his neck, he concentrated on the female customer smiling at him.

It was incredible, but Gabriel was getting worse with every shift.

Leah winced as he served Scotch to a customer who'd ordered vodka on the rocks, giving them an impassive stare at the subsequent complaint. As if he expected them to simply accept the mistake because of who he was.

Newsflash, she felt like saying at least once every hour. Nobody cared he was a Goodnight, a Higher warlock, or about the fussy designer suits that he clung to. They cared about getting their money's worth.

As the man bristled on the other end of that look, his gestures agitated, she hefted the tray of empties she'd collected with a small sigh and went to play peacemaker for the third time that evening. Her feet ached in her ankle boots and she cursed the decision to wear a heel just so she didn't feel tiny standing next to Gabriel. If she'd known she'd have to run after him putting out fires, she'd have stuck to flats.

It was Sunday evening; the crowd was hopping with office folk craving one last shot of freedom before the daily grind. Tia had been scheduled, but a sudden family thing had summoned her to New Orleans. With Emma out of town with Bastian, Leah had agreed to pull a double with Gabriel. Tia had again lectured her on staying safe, making her promise to stay focused on the work, not the warlock. Honestly, if it wasn't painfully obvious how much Leah and Gabriel rubbed each other the wrong way, Leah wondered if her babysitters would've left her at all. And didn't that make her feel irritated all over again.

Shaking that off, she placed the tray on the bar and cut into the customer's rant. "Gabriel, take these, will you? Hi, sorry to interrupt. Is there a problem?"

It would've been beneath Gabriel to stomp, but she felt his desire to as he silently took the tray away, leaving her to fix his mess. Again. Another man might've said thank you, but he only took up a position as far down the bar as he could get. She'd be lying if she said she wasn't irritated by that. Just as she'd be lying if she said the increase of female traffic to his side of the counter didn't burrow under her skin.

It was the suits, she supposed, keeping an eye strictly for managerial purposes as she served her own customers. The three-piece tailored look swept snugly over his lean, muscular body and only added to his aloof air. Throw in that black hair, those unfairly green eyes, and the rest of what made up a staggering face, and she couldn't blame anyone for drooling. After all, they didn't know his personality sucked.

Don't encourage him, she wanted to shout at the fawning women and men who made eyes at the warlock. He was already arrogant enough for ten men. Not that he ever took any of the unspoken invitations, at least as far as she knew. Maybe Tia was right, maybe he really hated the idea of their worlds colliding.

Or maybe he couldn't get it up. Her smile was on the mean side as she decided she preferred that. Be a dick, lose a dick. Sweet, sweet karma.

When they hit a lull, she deliberately disregarded his no-entry body language and wandered over, nudging a hip on the counter and staring at him.

He ignored her, wiping down the already-clean bar, his favorite job to do when she was nearby.

"So, Goodnight, huh?" She slid her tongue along her teeth as his shoulders visibly stiffened. "As in Goodnight's Remedies?" She wasn't sure why she was playing with fire except that the flame was there and she couldn't stand being ignored. By him. By anyone. "How did you end up working in a bar? Black sheep?" she prompted. "Rebelled against the family's plan? Maybe you wore jeans one day and this is your penance."

"Why would wearing jeans get me sentenced to *this*?"

The way he said it, you'd expect him to be cleaning sewers.

"This," she stressed, "as in the job we generously gave you? You're welcome, by the way." Her grin had bite as he shot a sneer at her. "As for jeans, you never wear them, so I figured there had to be something in the Goodnight charter. Thou Shalt Not Wear Denim."

A muscle flexed in his jaw but he didn't say anything.

He hadn't learned yet that silence didn't work. Leah would only continue to talk at him, and talk and talk until she nudged a reaction out.

"You might not know this," she mused as he dragged the cloth up and down in agitated patterns, "but Turners are Chicago elite, too. Oh, we're more casual than most. Notice, no pearls, no diamonds. I don't even really have a trust fund anymore. Invested in this bar, my place. But my mom is *the* name on the guest list, the donation in the pocket you want. Still, we're not on the Goodnight scale," she allowed, slightly embarrassed she'd felt the need to point out her family's pedigree. Like she cared what he thought. "Your products are in every drugstore across the country. Which again makes me ask, why are you here? Mommy and Daddy catch you getting a little too familiar with a commoner?"

She realized her mistake as soon as he froze in place, audibly sucking in a short breath. Like she'd taken her fist and thumped him solidly in the gut.

"I'm sorry," she said immediately, straightening from her slouch. No matter how irritated she felt, there was no excuse for bringing his parents into it, even if she *had* forgotten they'd died. "Emma and Tia...they told me your parents were..." She swallowed as he continued to stare at her. "I didn't mean to..."

Out of the corner of her eye, she saw the towel he'd been using smoke under his fingers. She took a step to—what? Warn him? She wasn't sure.

But he moved as if it were a dance, stepping back to her one forward. His expression wiped clean as she watched. Without a word, he walked past her to serve a waiting customer down the bar, leaving her alone. The old insecurity slid around her shoulders like an arm from an old friend.

She didn't go after him.

They managed not to cross each other's paths for the next two hours, keeping busy with individual tasks and avoiding even looking at one another. With every minute that passed, Leah felt worse. She wasn't the type to hurt people and though she hadn't meant to poke a sore spot, she had been needling him. And why? Because she couldn't handle the rejection, the obvious distance he wanted to keep between them.

Get real time: she was being a child. It wasn't a realization that went down smooth and she washed out the bad taste with a sip of ice water, battling the urge to exchange the drink for something stronger. Gabriel was in an unfamiliar world in a job he sucked at, away from his friends and family, so he could inherit his parents' company. As much of an ass as he was, she didn't need to be a bigger one.

Casting a veiled look at where he was clearing tables, Leah's chest tightened. She'd have to apologize again. And stop…everything. The teasing, the nickname, the pointed comments and catty smiles. His attention needed to be on the job, not on an internal battle with her.

It was the adult thing to do.

Chugging the rest of the water, Leah cast both her glass and the odd depression at the realization aside. It was still a couple of hours until closing and there were enough tables that needed clearing that one tray wasn't going to do it. Grabbing the other from under the bar, she slipped around the counter.

She kept an eye on Gabriel, as did, she imagined, much of the room. He didn't blend like Emma or Tia, or even Kole. He was simply too commanding to merge with the crowd, even as he picked up half-drunk beers and empty cocktail glasses.

She moved to the table next to his. Bracing herself, she dared to look at his face, pointedly turned away. She cleared her throat. A muscle flexed in his jaw but he refused to acknowledge her. The message was clear: he wasn't going to engage.

"Gabriel," she said, low.

He didn't let her finish. Stiff, he twisted away in a sharp movement. Too sharp.

He slipped, staggered.

And the tray shot out of his hands.

Whether by luck or by magic, the glasses themselves tumbled to the floor, missing the nearest table, a group of chattering women, by inches. The drinks, however, hit the targets dead-on.

Leah winced as they screeched. Chairs scraped back as outrage boiled the air, voices clamoring as everyone zoned in on the culprit. Ruddy color stained Gabriel's cheeks.

And she knew what she had to do. To make it right.

Leah smoothly dropped her tray behind her and inserted herself in between. "I am *so* sorry, ladies. My fault entirely. I walked straight into him." She saw his gaze slide to her, a blink the only indicator of surprise. "Please accept my sincerest apologies," she said, laying it on thick. "All your drinks are on the house, of course, and another round can be on its way."

"This is Dolce," one of the women hissed, pinching the top in question. "Do you know how much it costs?"

Considering she'd been raised in the cradle of wealth before choosing to strike out on her own, Leah could guess down to the cent. But she bowed her head. "I'd be happy to pay for dry cleaning."

"Forget it." The woman grabbed her purse, the rest of them following suit. She brushed her hair out of her face, embarrassment flagged in her cheeks. "Bad service and now this. We won't come here again. Absolute incompetence." As she shoved her chair out of her way, she pierced Leah with a snooty look she'd seen dozens of times before. It was designed to put Leah in her place, remind her that she was at the bottom of the social ladder.

If there weren't people watching, Leah might have responded, but the customer was always right, so all she did was keep up the apologetic expression as the four of them sailed out.

There was a beat. Then, "How 'bout you come spill something on me, Leah?" Tommy, a regular, called out. "I could use a free drink."

Laughter rippled around and Leah sent him a grin before turning to Gabriel.

He was staring at her, eyebrows tugged low. His suit was splattered with pink, remnants of a Cauldron Cosmo if she had to guess.

She nodded toward it. "You should take your shirt off."

Something flared in his eyes. It was gone before she could question it, leaving her throat dry.

Because of that, her voice was a touch hoarse as she clarified, "The stain. We could run it under water before it sets." When he still didn't speak, she avoided that piercing gaze by bending to pick up the broken shards from the dropped glasses. "I have something you could wear. It might be a bit tight, but—" She froze as his hand suddenly touched hers. He removed it instantly but not before the brush of skin to skin had sunk into her bones.

He'd crouched next to her, reeking of alcohol. His hand, the hand that had touched her, fisted in his lap. His eyes bored into her. "Why?"

She didn't pretend not to know what he meant.

"Because," she said, feeling unsteady, "everyone deserves to have someone in their corner." *And I'm sorry*, she wanted to add, but if she did, he'd think she'd done it out of pity. And while she wanted to make up for the line she'd crossed, she didn't pity him. He just seemed so remote, so alone. She knew how that felt.

"I didn't need you to intervene." Although blunt, the words lacked his usual combative air.

She only nodded and continued stacking shards on her tray, saying nothing when he joined her. In fact, neither of them said anything until after shift in the office, where she brought out the oversized hoodie she'd left at the bar a couple of days ago.

Surveying the Cubs sweatshirt, he grimaced. "No."

Leah chose not to be offended by his dismissal of her beloved team. "You don't have any other choices." Unless he wanted to conjure something, but she knew he couldn't explain that away to a human.

She swore she'd aged ten years by the time his pride finally bent to unbuttoning his shirt. Right there, in front of her. Muscled golden skin revealed inch by slow inch. He'd had to pause, look at her before she came to her senses and rushed out, cheeks burning. The sudden spike of desire unnerved her.

But when he appeared in the sweatshirt, logo straining against his chest, and one hundred percent sulking, she flashed him her first smile since their argument.

"You're welcome."

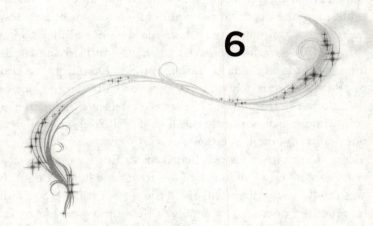

6

*L*eah patted the couch cushion next to her, gently pushing Delilah, her bossy Dachshund, back so lazy Louie could jump up with them. Blinking his one eye, Louie ignored Delilah's snort as he curled up on Leah's bare toes, his squat body barely any weight at all. For a cavalier, he was incredibly laidback and eventually Delilah gave in and snuggled next to him.

Rosie, Leah's eight-year-old sprocker spaniel, watched them from her dog bed by the TV cabinet, tail thumping softly as she saw Leah looking. The cats were off somewhere else in the house, likely sunbathing (Sylvie) or poking into dark corners (Ralph).

Leah smiled and said into her cell, "No, Mom, I'm listening. I'm glad you love Tuscany."

"Oh, it's so romantic, Leah," Joyce Miller née Turner babbled on the other end. "George and I took a stroll through the city at twilight and it was like being in a movie. He even pulled me into a dance on our balcony."

"Hmm." The topic of balconies was still a sore one.

"And the food!"

Leah's eyes drifted around her living room as her mom continued to gush. Her house was a mix of old and new: odd antiques, vintage decoration, bright color and a lot of art. Books sat higgledy-piggledy with fake plants—her ability to keep things alive extended only to animals—and dream catchers hung next to old medical equipment. She liked light, so lamps of all types decorated surfaces except for the large floor one that sat by the front door. The whole effect was colorful chaos and suited her down to the ground. Fortunately, Peggy didn't oppose living like this either.

She'd bought the three-bedroom in Englewood about six years ago, investing a chunk of her trust fund before depositing almost all the rest into Toil and Trouble a year later. She didn't regret either decision, especially as the house gave her enough room to keep her animals. All her babies were rescues from the shelter—Louie for losing an eye, if she had to guess, Rosie because she'd been too excitable, and Delilah who, at three years, was her most recent and had been surrendered because of "difficult behavior" (read: barking and digging, which Leah had got under control after six months of consistent training). Her cats had always lived together and sadly had been given to the shelter when their elderly owner had died.

It had broken her heart; they all did, which was why she was at the animal shelter every second she could spare. Sonny, the owner, had pretty much single-handedly run the place until she'd wandered in ten years ago. He was still in good shape for sixty-seven, but even he couldn't manage the constant upkeep and get new adopters in. She now ran the website, the social media and the volunteer walks, taking peanuts for pay because she'd rather him give to the animals than her. Emma hadn't been wrong; Leah's family was comfortable enough that what remained of her trust helped pay for her admittedly hefty animal bill and the mortgage, and her income from the bar paid for the rest.

"All right, enough about me," her mom wound down after

making Leah envious over gelato. "I want to know what's been happening since last week."

Leah shifted the phone, laying a hand on Louie. "Well, your grandbabies are all healthy."

"I miss them."

"Them, not me?"

"You give me too much lip," her mom teased.

"That's genetics."

A light laugh. "Can't argue with that. Of course I miss you, sweetheart. I miss our movie nights."

"Me, too."

Ever since Leah had been fifteen, after The Divorce, they'd made movie night a tradition. Every month, three movies in a theme—same genre, same year, same actor, etc.—and a bucket of buttered popcorn. This had to be the longest time they'd gone without movie night.

Still, Leah couldn't begrudge her mom. In fact, she marveled at her. From depressed divorcée to hopeful newlywed in thirteen short years. She could honestly say she was happy for her, even with the small worry of what would happen if this marriage turned out like the first. Those years had been rocky to say the least. At least George was a sweetheart, unlike Leah's dad.

"We'll do a marathon when you get back," she told her mom, pushing the discomforting thought away. "Don't worry about it. I know how much you wanted to travel."

"You sure you can't ditch work and come meet up with us someplace?"

The last thing she wanted was to crash her mom's honeymoon. There were certain sights in this world she didn't need to see.

"I've got too much going on here at the moment," she side-stepped, smiling as Rosie sighed loudly from her basket.

"How did the new bartender work out?"

"Um…" She tried to think how to describe Gabriel without

clueing her mom in. "He's…adequate. I'm not sure he'll last."
And if he hadn't been hired under special circumstances, she
doubted he'd have lasted as long as he had.

"That's a shame. You can't seem to keep someone in that
position."

"Maybe we're cursed."

"Well, you did name the bar Toil and Trouble."

Leah chuckled.

"And the shelter?"

Her mood took a nosedive and she began to fidget with the
loose material over her knee. "Sonny mentioned the bills again
yesterday. We need to bring in more people, I think, cover more
of the jobs. It's just finding volunteers to give up the time."

"You'll do it, baby." Her mom's voice was warm, unwav-
ering. "You never met a rock you couldn't bulldoze your way
through."

"Is that your way of calling me hardheaded?"

"If it was?"

"I'd say apple and tree."

They chatted for another ten minutes before hanging up,
leaving Leah in a pensive mood. She tossed down her phone,
making Delilah grumble, and tipped her head back to study
the ceiling. The shelter was a growing worry, the flare of an
ache that worsened with every grimace or frown Sonny wore.

If they only had more hands, she could concentrate on
their website, maybe bring in more donations, facilitate more
adoptions. It wouldn't solve everything, but it might erase the
pinched look from Sonny's face.

He'd joked about retirement yesterday. She couldn't blame
him for finding the idea tempting, but also couldn't bear to
think what would happen to the animals if expenses kept climb-
ing and idea turned into action.

She and the dogs passed the next hour watching a documentary on cold cases to get her mind off it. She was so absorbed

by the detailing of one killer's victims that the thump at her door had her jolting upright, a squeal trapped in her throat.

Delilah scrambled up with one yip, parking her butt at the front door alongside Rosie, always eager for a visitor. Louie had to be dislodged from Leah's feet since nothing short of a nuclear blast would get him to move once he was situated.

Commanding the dogs to sit, then stay, Leah looked out her peephole and saw nobody. Cautious thanks to the documentary, she cracked the door. Her eyes dropped immediately to the package with her name printed neatly on it.

"Uh-oh, is this when we find out we have a stalker?" she said to the dogs, using her foot to usher Delilah back in when she tried to charge out. Leah scooped up the package and closed the door with her hip, the dogs trailing her as she walked back to the couch.

"Someone here?" Peggy called from upstairs. At the sound of her voice, Rosie bounded up the steps, her tail thumping the walls.

"Just a package. I think it might be an ear."

"*What?*"

Peggy charged downstairs, closely followed by Rosie. She skidded to a stop, wrapped only in a terry cloth robe, cheeks flushed from the shower. She had a hot date and was determined to spend the afternoon getting ready.

"An ear?" She spotted the bulky package; it was the size of a cushion. "Oh, yeah. That has 'dismembered body part' all over it."

Leah laughed. "It was outside with only my name on it, so someone dropped it off." She considered the padded envelope. "Not alarming, right?"

"Maybe you have a very cheap admirer."

"Who knows my address."

"Okay, you're creeping me out. Open the thing." Peggy ruffled Rosie's ears, staying well back.

Leah threw caution to the wind, slipping her finger under the lining and tearing it open. She tipped the contents onto the nearby coffee table. A sheet of notepaper fluttered out, followed by a familiar sweatshirt and, to her astonishment, several bills.

"What on earth...?"

"Thank God." Peggy breathed out, pressing a hand to her chest. "No body parts. Unless the ear is wrapped up in the sweater. What's the note say?"

"Ever hear of privacy?"

"I've heard of it."

Leah lifted the paper, scanned the lines. Her mouth parted.

"Well?"

"'I trust this settles the debt between us,'" she read aloud with a faint tinge of disbelief. "'You're welcome. Gabriel.'"

"Gabriel. That's the new brooding bartender you're spending nights with?"

"I'm not spending nights with him. At least, not like that." Leah calculated the bills. "Although this would be close to my going rate."

"Uh-huh. But you'd like it to be like that, right?" Peggy snorted a laugh at Leah's bland stare. "We've lived together too long. I know your lusty eyes. You had them for Anthony Bridgerton and you've got them now."

"Oh, shut up."

Peggy grinned, then studied the envelope's contents. "So, why's he paying you?"

"I lent him my hoodie." Leah flicked through the bills, struggling to understand. "What is this? A weird thank-you? A point made?"

"An excellent move to get in your head." Peggy waggled her eyebrows. "You have to hand it to the guy. At least we know he probably asked Emma or Tia where you lived. No stalker, no severed body parts. It's a good day."

Leah smiled faintly. She didn't know what to think.

"Ask him," Peggy advised, likely reading her face. "Maybe it's, I don't know, for dry cleaning, or maybe he stretched it out and knows you'd need to buy another."

"This would buy four."

"So, maybe he's generous. Another point in his favor. I only pray my date is so giving." Peggy bumped her hip with her own. "I'm going to finish getting ready."

Leah didn't bother looking up as she tapped the bills to her chin.

You're welcome.

Her lips twitched, liquid warmth moving through her even as she fought it. Smart-ass.

Later that week, Emma called a meeting for the owners of Toil and Trouble. As Peggy was out on a third date and had cheekily informed Leah not to wait up, she volunteered her house. She didn't ask why they didn't meet at the bar like they usually did; Gabriel was still a sore topic. With everyone.

His note had become an obsession for her, the subtle teasing pointing to a new step in their—their *situation*. Trying to figure out what that new step was, what she wanted it to be, or wondering what *he* wanted it to be, was a constant loop in her head.

She was sensible enough to recognize the stupidity of that, enough that she'd pulled back on her shifts with him this week. Instead, she'd made an effort to be civil, with him responding in kind. They were like adversaries circling each other, waiting for someone to make the first move. The tension may just kill her.

Emma arrived first. They sat in the kitchen as they made Cauldron Cosmos, Chester and Leah's dogs milling around their feet as they chatted. Leah badly wanted to ask her friend her thoughts on the note, but Joyce Turner hadn't raised a fool, so she focused on the drink Emma handed her instead.

They'd barely cheers'd when Leah heard the front door open and Tia strode in on ice-pick heels.

"You read my mind," she muttered, seizing her glass. "Here's to us, ladies. Strong and independent may we always be." She clinked both glasses before throwing her drink back. Thanks to the falayla root, it had a good kick. Which was why Leah would stick to one—a woman could only perform Instagram Live karaoke so many times and still hold her head up high. Tia nudged Emma with her shoulder, settling next to her. "Even this traitor."

"I'm getting married, not joining a cult."

"Uh-huh. Not that I'm not thrilled to have a legit excuse to hightail it out of the family bosom, but what's with the summons?"

Emma touched her arm. "You okay?"

"You know me." Tia brushed the increasing demands for her time away with a smile. "It'll take more than my nana's will to wear me down."

"Is she the one you went toe-to-toe with about opening the bar?" Leah asked.

"Yeah. And who won?" Tia toasted herself with the empty glass, then gestured between all of them. "Speaking of which, if we're all here, who's babysitting Goodnight?"

"Bastian said he didn't mind helping out."

"Good, we need all the help we can get." Tia selected a nacho from the plate Leah had prepared, piled it high, then caught sight of Ralph, perched on one of the top cabinets and staring. "Your cat's creepy, Leah."

"He just likes to watch."

"Said every woman before being murdered and found in Lake Michigan."

"My cat isn't going to murder me."

"But he thinks about it."

"Wait—do you actually know that, like, with magic, or are you just trying to freak me out?"

Tia's grin was short-lived as she returned to the previous

subject. "Four more bad reviews online. Four. And okay, some social media comments about the grumpy, delicious bartender. But guys, *four*. We're losing business."

Emma bit her lip. "That's why I wanted to talk. It could be a fluke, but we've been less busy the past few nights compared to the same nights last month. I checked the receipts. We've got to do something. Pull him off bartending."

"To do what?" Leah asked, shooing Sylvie away from the nachos she'd made. The cat protested with a miffed yowl. "It's not like he can do our paperwork or bake with you. There's only so much lifting and carrying." Not that she wouldn't mind watching his arms flex in those tailored three-piece suits, or examining how the material stretched over his ass as he bent down.

She gulped some of her cosmo.

"Then he has to go," Tia said flatly. "I hate to be the bitch—"

Leah snorted.

Tia stopped. Considered. "Okay, it's my brand, but still. I relented because of all the bleeding hearts around here. Dead parents, family company, yada yada yada. But if he's actually affecting our business, we can't allow that."

Emma grimaced, but nodded. "That's what I think, too."

"We can't fire him." The words shot from Leah's mouth. When her friends turned raised eyebrows on her, she backtracked hurriedly. Her skin flushed with heat as she toyed with the stem of her glass. "I mean, he's—he's doing it for his family, remember?"

"Here we go," Tia muttered, rubbing her temples.

Leah elbowed her. "I'm serious. He's bad enough at *this* job and we know his situation. He won't last ten minutes anywhere else."

"And this is our problem, why?"

"T."

"Leah, he's a grown warlock. He'll deal. He'll find another job, maybe fifty other jobs the rate he's going," Tia amended, stroking a bare foot she'd removed from one of her heels over Chester's back. "He'll get through the three months. It's not like he needs money."

"I know it sounds harsh, but she's right." Emma lifted her shoulders, let them drop helplessly. "Maybe he'll find a better position. One where he doesn't have to work with people as much."

"Or somewhere so desperate for people they'll hire anyone," Tia suggested.

Desperate. No people. Hire anyone.

"He could work at the shelter."

The silence that followed Leah's suggestion was palpable.

"The shelter?" Emma sampled the words as if they had a funny taste. A groove dug between her brows. "With you?"

"No." Tia lifted her foot—Chester sighed at the loss—and sat up. "Absolutely not."

Leah dealt her a droll look. "Gee, Mom, I wasn't asking permission. We need people at the shelter. This could be perfect."

"If he finds out—"

"Stop. That record is old, play a new one." Leah scrubbed her hands over her face, then deliberately took a breath. "Look, it's not like I want the man there but we're desperate for help and I can stick him in the back with the animals. He might piss off some puppies but besides getting nipped, it won't have severe consequences. And if he accidentally does any magic, again, the animals aren't going to care." She went for a casual shrug, taking a sip of her drink. The magic zinged down her throat, warming her stomach.

"I thought you hated him," Emma said, suspicion carving through the words like a boat through water. "Why would you want him at the place you spend the most time?"

"I don't hate him. It takes too much energy to hate someone, and I don't need that negativity."

Tia rolled her eyes. "Why are we friends?"

"I don't have to like the man to put him to work. It's kind of a win-win because then I won't feel crappy about helping him lose his family's business." She scowled at Tia's mutter. "Yes, I'm a bleeding heart, sue me."

"I don't like it, Leah." Emma's worry was tangible, a whisper along Leah's cheek. Something rattled in the cupboards before Emma got her magic under control. "I was relieved this past week when you stopped working as many shifts together. It's dangerous, especially as you both dislike each other so much. If he finds out you know about witches, he'll report you. He won't think twice."

Leah set down her glass with a clink loud enough that both friends startled. "Okay, I've put up with this for years and mostly I figured you knew what you were on about so played by your rules. And I still will. But guys, I'm not a child and you can't tell me what to do. I'm your business partner. I'm your friend. You don't have to trust him. You have to trust *me*. And trust that when I say I'll be fine, I will be." She kept eye contact with both, hands flat on the counter.

I trust this settles the debt between us.

She was telling the truth; despite the other night, she couldn't say she liked Gabriel. She wasn't going to lie and say part of her didn't find that hint of wry humor intriguing, or that she didn't find him wildly attractive. An irritating fact considering he was an ass ninety percent of the time and potentially hazardous to her health (if her friends were to be believed).

But she couldn't abandon him to her world. It just wasn't in her to be that callous, not even if he was only suffering all this for control of a business.

It might not be smart but she'd chosen her path and she didn't sway from it.

"Fine," Tia eventually snapped, conceding with a bad-tempered glower. "We'll trust you."

"Thank you."

The witch held up a finger. "On one condition." Tia's eyes gleamed like Ralph's as he watched them from on high. "Please let me be the one to fire him."

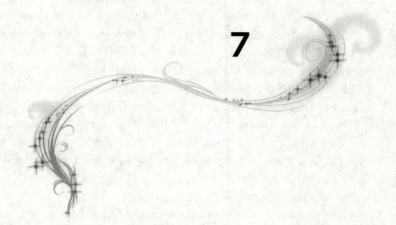

7

*G*abriel's fingers curled at his sides as he strove for outer detachment. Behind him, the sounds of a midweek afternoon at the bar played out: the hum of the TV and its insipid sports game, the murmur of humans discussing the weather or other inanities, the clink of glasses and the occasional laugh.

He felt like it was being directed at him, the laughter, as he stood before an actual firing squad. Fired. He was being *fired*.

His eyes burned as he glanced from Tia to Emmaline to Leah. The latter didn't give anything away, the hint of a tattoo teasing from the slouchy neckline of a too-large sweater. She hadn't mentioned the sweatshirt he'd returned or the money all week, and now let Tia take the lead—which she did with far too much delight, practically cackling as she handed him his last check.

He hated that he'd sought Leah out, unable to help it. Was this her idea? Had the money, the note, prompted this, made her mad at him?

The sensation that uncoiled in his chest was not something he liked.

"I know it's been rough," he said, smoothing his thumb over

his signet ring. *Failure, failure, failure*, his inner voice taunted. "I'll get better. There's never been anything I couldn't master."

"And if our reputation wasn't going down the toilet because of you, that might work." Tia stared coolly back. "We can't afford to keep you on. You're costing us business."

He absorbed the vocal slap without a blink. Inside, mortification squeezed his insides to jelly. His skin grew warm.

"You know I need this job." His voice was quiet, steady.

"You need *a* job," Emmaline corrected, her tone apologetic. She fiddled with her engagement band, color in her cheeks. "Leah has the solution."

He should've seen that coming.

He held his complaints back as she explained about her animal shelter, how they could use a body to fill the gaps. Walk the animals, odd jobs, cleaning, light reception duties if he improved his customer service—this said with the familiar smirk he'd barely seen recently. She'd been civil all week on the few shifts they'd worked together.

He'd been pleased, of course. He didn't want her poking at him, teasing, laughing, playing. And yet he'd been edgier from the lack, every night lying in bed going over the memory of her taking the blame for him. Standing up for him. He couldn't remember the last time someone had.

Of course, none of that mattered now.

Statements of fact, refusals, reasons why he'd be better served in the bar he barely tolerated rose to his lips but he bit them back. He'd been in business long enough to be able to read people. And the three implacable faces staring back at him were united.

If the company wasn't on the line, he would've refused their charity. He detested that he needed their help, but he did. So, he buttoned his lips, gave them a brusque nod and made to leave. His exit was interrupted by—who else—Leah, who piped up that she'd see him bright and early at the shelter before giving him the address.

And now, adding the cherry to this shit sundae, his sister seemed to find this latest twist knee-slappingly hilarious.

He'd begged his parents for a brother…

He tuned out Melly's giggles and thanked Mrs. Q as she patted his shoulder, her ruddy cheeks beaming as she left them to perfectly cooked rosemary lamb and crispy potatoes. He inhaled the scent and felt like weeping at the home-cooked meal. The visit had been just what he needed and since Melly had created the portal for him so he could come home, he'd let her snigger for a solid five minutes without interrupting.

With keen attention he cut a slice of lamb and lifted it to his lips, giving his sister a bored stare. "Are you through?"

Merriment made her eyes sparkle. "I'm sorry, I know this must be hell to you, but now animals? I've never even seen you stroke Uncle August's familiar, let alone any other pet."

Since August's familiar was a hawk, Gabriel felt his reticence was understandable.

Across from Melly at the laden table, August surveyed Gabriel over his wineglass. His eyebrows were drawn, mimicking his pursed mouth.

"And you're sure this is the best job you can find?" he questioned. "There isn't an office somewhere more your style?"

"It's…harder restraining my magic than I thought." Gabriel tried not to stuff food into his face, the enemy toaster still eluding him. "I had a few close calls around the bar. Going into a completely human office would be like throwing myself into the deep end when I've had one swimming lesson."

"Understandable," August murmured, sipping his wine. "Still. An animal shelter? Do you like animals?"

"I don't not like them." He just had limited experience.

"Well, I think it's great." Melly speared a piece of lamb and waved it around. "Think about it, Gabriel. Minimal contact with people. This could turn out for the best."

Exasperation filled him. "Why do you have this idea I am not good with people?"

The silence made him grumble. He chose a crispy potato off his plate to feed his frustration.

"It's nice of them, really."

Gabriel paused mid-chew. "Firing me?"

"Offering you another job is nice," she corrected. A small pot of ketchup appeared at her elbow. Gabriel shuddered as she dunked her seasoned lamb into it. She caught him, grinned, but didn't comment. It was an old battle. "They could've just fired you. They must like you."

He remembered Tia's cool stare, Emmaline's uncomfortable gaze. Leah's sparkling challenge. "Doubtful."

"My offer stands, nephew." August steepled his hands, tipping his chin down. Shadows slicked down his face. "This will be much harder work. More labor-intensive."

Insult turned his head. "Uncle, are you suggesting I can't do this?"

"Of course not. I'm only saying, if *you* don't feel like you can, nobody will blame you if you walk away."

Everyone was determined to think he was useless. But he was Gabriel Goodnight and he'd conquered every challenge that had ever been set before him.

"By the end of these three months," he said, lifting his chin, "not only will I have proven to the board I can deal with humans, but I will have surpassed all expectations." As Melly cheered, he added with bite, "And I'll have learned how to use that damn toaster."

His boastful words seemed far away the following day. Like, Australia.

The mixed scent of disinfectant and something he instinctively took for wet dog swirled up Gabriel's nostrils as he mistakenly inhaled just inside the entrance of Sonny's Shelter. He silently took in the boxy, cheap furniture in what passed for their reception and withheld a grimace. Even worse than he'd pictured.

In amongst the faded furniture and ancient magazines there were touches that made him think someone had tried: thriving plants, framed photos of animals and people—presumably rescues and their rescuers—and many more photos of dogs and cats looking...well, it was ridiculous, but he could swear they looked sad.

He smoothed away a frown as he stepped into the space. His Prada loafers squeaked on the floor.

"Hello?" he said after a moment, strolling to the empty reception desk. A bell sat on top, a sign beside it saying, Ring for Assistance.

He eyed the bell with some distaste, gingerly pushing it with one finger. A cheery sound rang out. Nobody hurried from the corridors that branched off from both sides.

This was not the way to run a successful business, not that he cared. No wonder adoptions were down, as Leah had said, if nobody was there to greet a customer, take them on the journey and make the sale. If he was running things—

He wasn't, he reminded himself. That wasn't why he was here.

A few more seconds passed. Unbelievable. Grumbling, he chose the right-hand corridor at random and headed down it. The rooms he passed had their doors propped open, revealing exam-type equipment and large scales at dog height. The paint was peeling in sections and some of the skirting was chipped.

A dog's deep barks and the peal of feminine laughter pulled his attention onward.

"Hello?" he repeated. "I'm here for..."

He stopped, barely aware that his words had, too.

Leah stood in a large, open room, surrounded by dog toys of every description. She was kneeling, ruffling the fur of a black dog, cooing to him in a low, lilting voice. Her curls were tied back and she wore no makeup. She should look worn, unspectacular. But her blue eyes were bright and her laughter spilled into the room like sunshine.

"Such a good boy," she praised the dog, pressing a kiss to his blocky head. "Such a clever old boy."

Gabriel's eyes tracked down over the navy sweatshirt and jeans she wore, lingering at the rip that showed her knee. Soft. She looked soft.

Which was ridiculous. And had no bearing on the situation.

Annoyed, Gabriel cleared his throat.

He earned the attention of both Leah and the dog.

"Gabe," she said, her surprise obvious. "You came. You're here."

"Gabriel," he corrected, the nickname earning a flash of what he chose to call exasperation. "Did you think I wouldn't show up?"

Her eyes went wide. "Oh, dear."

Before he could even ask, the black dog let out a yip. Muscles bunched as he spun and charged at Gabriel.

Thoughts flared fast and hard. Human. Undercover. No magic.

So, it was with a dawning sense of resignation that he watched thirty to thirty-five kilograms of dog launch at him. Paws hit his chest, a large skull headbutted him hard and gravity kicked in, toppling him like a bowling skittle.

"*Oomph.*" His breath rushed out as he hit, followed by a secondary grunt as the dog delivered a loving lick down the middle of his face. Saliva stuck to his skin and reeked as Gabriel pushed the dog's head back.

"Get down," he demanded, the growl clearly the language the beast spoke; he happily did as ordered. He sat at attention next to Gabriel, panting, pushing against his leg with an adoring look in his soft, brown eyes.

Prone, Gabriel stared sourly back at him. His ass ached, his face felt sticky and his waistcoat had two dirty paw prints marring the silk.

When he looked up, Leah stood over them, hands tucked in her jeans' pockets. She was fighting a grin.

"Clearly, he's learned manners from you," he said as politely as he could, brushing off his waistcoat. He conjured a handkerchief into his pocket, fighting the zip of pain, considering it a necessary evil. He wiped the cloth down his face with a grimace.

"He's much better behaved." A laugh trembled out as she gave in. "You said the magic word. U-P. We think it was a trick his previous owner taught him before she died. That's how Chuck here came to live with us. Nobody else would take him after his owner passed away from cancer. Too old at eight for a lot of people. He's a little needy."

She slapped her thigh and Chuck padded over, leaning heavily against her.

"You should warn people." Gabriel pushed to stand, tucking the handkerchief back in his pocket.

"Where's the fun in that?"

He didn't answer, brushing off his suit trousers. He felt Leah's eyes on him like a physical touch and ignored how his muscles tightened.

"You're wearing a suit."

"Indeed. Your eyesight is impeccable."

"You're wearing a suit at an animal shelter."

"Yes."

"Why?"

"I like suits."

"Then you shouldn't wear them to this job." Leah cocked her head back, and he realized with a jolt how much shorter she was. Her personality more than made up for it.

She sighed. "Don't you own any jeans, Gabe?"

Sardonic, he crossed his arms. "I'm fine as I am."

"Tell me if you still think that by the end of your shift."

"Is this what I'll be doing?" Gabriel glanced around what he assumed to be some kind of playroom. A few cats watched him lazily from their carpeted tower in the corner, whilst a three-legged white-and-ginger dog eyeballed him from a cushion twice its size, a raggedy teddy drooping out its mouth. It looked half a second from charging him as it rumbled a few warning woofs.

"Don't mind Bear." Leah's words pulled his attention back. She kept a hand on Chuck's head as she tipped up her chin to Gabriel. "He's all bark, no bite. Like you."

"I'm not all bark," he responded without thinking.

Those long lashes of hers blinked over ocean blue. He'd surprised her.

Good. Because he sure as hell had surprised himself.

Not all bark? What had he meant by that? Was it a threat? It certainly couldn't have been a playful remark. He didn't *do* playful remarks.

Spooked, he reverted to what he did best. Attack. "It's a bad business that lets its reception desk sit empty."

Her blond eyebrows pinched. "What?"

"When I came in, nobody greeted me. A potential customer would've walked straight back out. Is that how you expect to get these animals rescued or do you want to keep them here so you can play with them yourself?"

He watched with a kind of dizzying relief as anger flooded her eyes and the norm between them clicked back into place.

"Unfortunately, we don't have the staff," she clipped out, folding her arms and mirroring him. "Sonny's the only full-time employee. There are a few of us working part-time, and everyone else is a volunteer, fitting a shift in when they can."

"Which is why you need me."

"Which is why I offered you this job," she countered on a

head toss that sent a tease of coconut his way. He breathed it in as she continued snottily, "Of course, we welcome all advice from men who have to pass a test to succeed in business."

He opened his mouth, closed it with a snap of teeth.

Point to Turner. But the war was just beginning.

Gabriel made it through the day on sheer spite. After Leah had taken him on a whistle-stop tour through the facility, including meeting Sonny, his boss, she'd shoved a mop and bucket in his hands and directed him to the row of empty pens. She'd clearly expected him to balk, so he'd grimly thrown his tie over his shoulder and set to work. It may have taken him the better part of two hours to clean three pens, and he may have had to use a spell to suck up the excess water when he'd been too…enthusiastic, and yes, he may have slipped and fallen on his aching ass again in the small ocean he'd created, thereby ruining his Prada loafers. *But* he counted it a job well done and worth it to see how annoyed Leah was to see he'd finished without protest.

Plus, now he knew how to mop, and he liked knowing things. He'd have to schedule a chat with Goodnight's janitorial staff, see if there were any improvements needed. Something to note down.

He also thought he might have a chat with Sonny about the reception area. Not that Leah would have to know he was helping; he doubted she'd believe it anyway since she clearly thought him useless.

Once he was finished with the mopping, she'd asked him to clear the fenced yard of poop, gather the older beds that would need a wash, and finally, fetch a cat that had refused to climb down from an open vent where the cover had come loose. What Leah had called the Tom Cruise of cats—whatever that meant—had managed to wriggle its way into the vent, which was apparently dangerous and made her voice go up a pitch. He hadn't liked that.

As a result, he'd found himself standing on top of a chair, feeling like an idiot, ordering the cat to come down in his best no-nonsense tone. When that had yielded nothing but a plaintive meow, he'd had to use the cat tower like a ladder, gritting his teeth as he reached inside the vent and grasped the hissing cat. He was now the lucky owner of several stinging scratches across his hand. If he could've used his magic...but he couldn't.

Leah had taken one look and hissed like the cat, commanding him to follow her to the chaotic office, where she'd withdrawn a green first aid box and mercilessly scrubbed the scratches with alcohol wipes. He'd barely withheld a scream.

He'd seen other humans off and on: a man shorter than him with a shock of ginger hair and beard to match had introduced himself as Frankie; another man, with pale blond hair and gray eyes, and built like one sneeze would blow him into the next room, had nodded and said, "Mitch." And he'd seen a young girl around Melly's age, wearing ripped jeans and a top exposing her stomach, talking busily with Leah as they'd sat at the reception desk. When he'd entered the room, her chatter had dried up, but that was nothing new for him. Still, he wondered who she was. A relation of Leah's, perhaps?

Though she looked nothing like the short blue-eyed blonde, except maybe for the clothes and the fact they both wore polish on their nails. Leah changed hers every couple of days, as though she couldn't settle on just one color. It was ridiculous. She was ridiculous.

And if she expected him to fail, he would prove her wrong.

He fell asleep that night, a satisfied curve curling his lips as he pictured her face.

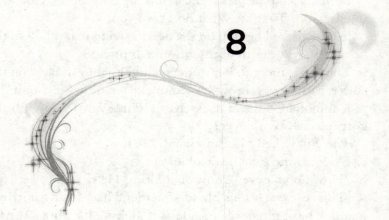

8

*D*espite what Gabriel thought, they did take turns staffing the reception area. With it being her shift, Leah was just finishing up with a burly six-foot-five man and the kitten he'd cooed over—never judge a book—when the door opened for the fourth time that morning. Leah smiled in recognition as Joanne walked in, the coffee shop owner dressed in her work uniform and, best of all, carrying a take-out cup.

"You've been as busy as we were this morning," she declared as she drew near, sable hair bouncing in its practical ponytail.

Leah gave one last wave to her customer. "I doubt that, but it's been busy." Two adoptions and a few people she thought might come back constituted a good morning. It took the worst edge off her worry, enough that her smile was broad. "Is that for me?"

"Figured you'd need the caffeine since you haven't been in." Joanne handed over Leah's usual. They'd met a few years ago when Joanne had first opened across the road and Leah had made a point of stopping in each day to support her. It didn't hurt that Joanne's baking rivalled Emma's and her coffee was superior.

Leah cracked the plastic lid, absorbing the steam. "God, that smells good. Thanks. What do I owe you?"

Joanne parked her hip on the desk, waving that off. "On the house. It gives me an excuse to stretch my legs."

There was more to her smile, enough that Leah blew on the coffee with her eyebrows raised in expectation. "Uh-huh."

Joanne folded like a deck chair. "Fine. What's up with the gorgeous new employee?"

The cup jerked in Leah's hand. "Who?"

Now Joanne gave Leah a look.

"How do you even know about him? He started yesterday."

"I have eyes." The bland statement had Leah snorting. Joanne's head tilted side to side as if looking for him. "What's his story?"

Bare bones, Leah decided. She sipped the coffee, let it dance on her tongue. "His name's Gabriel. He needed a job for the next couple of months and you know we always need help. He's…friends with Emma and Tia."

"The friends you own the bar with, right?" They'd had enough gossipy conversations to get that far. Joanne nibbled her lip. "Single?"

Something in Leah slapped at that, an automatic rejection that surprised her. She hurriedly took another sip of coffee. "Ah, I think so. But he lives in New Orleans so I doubt he's looking to date."

"I could do short-term with someone that looks like him."

"He's kind of abrasive. Not sure he's your type."

Joanne paused, interest dawning in eyes that saw too much. "Am I stepping onto your territory here?"

If she'd have been drinking, it would've been a spit take. "*No.*"

"I won't poach if you've called dibs."

"I haven't—I wouldn't…" When Joanne's smile widened into a knowing grin, Leah took a breath. "It's not like that.

I'm just warning you, his personality doesn't match his looks. If you like that type."

"The tall, dark and take-me-against-a-wall type."

The image that flashed into Leah's brain would need bleach to be erased.

Joanne made a noise in the back of her throat. "I knew it."

"Knew what? You're delusional."

"See, it's the—" She stopped as Leah's phone started to ring. "Saved by the bell. I'd best be getting back anyway."

"Yeah, thanks." Leah moved her coffee to her other hand and picked up her cell. "It's not like that, Jo."

"Uh-huh." Joanne's laugh lingered as she slipped out the door.

"It's not like that," Leah muttered, before pushing answer. "Hey, Tia."

"How're things with Goodnight? You okay?"

Irritation was instant. Leah scowled into space. "Well, I blurted out that I know about magic on his tour, but he took it well."

"Funny."

"Even said he'd give me conjuring lessons."

"Right."

"And then, who knows, maybe he'll spill the secrets of the High Family when we go on our work bonding trip."

"You're a riot."

"No, you are. This checking up on me thing is getting old really fast." Leah swirled her coffee. "Next time you call me, I'm not going to answer."

"Rude. I like it."

Rolling her eyes, Leah turned, intending to sit behind the desk again. "I learn from the—CHRIST." She jerked as she saw Gabriel behind her, coffee a tidal wave out of the cup. She barely registered the burn seeping into her breasts or Tia squawking in her ear. Her words ran on repeat in her head as she blinked fast.

His expression stayed in the same neutral lines, nothing in his eyes betraying shock or surprise. Maybe he'd only just emerged.

He hadn't heard. He couldn't have.

"Tia, I've got to go." Leah didn't bother wasting time explaining as she hung up on her friend. She ignored the persistent ring and set the cup down with her cell. "Gabriel. Hi. Did you need me?"

"That'll stain." His eyes dipped to her breasts where the brown patch soaked her white T-shirt. Beneath the material, her skin pebbled. "You should take it off."

Her smile felt off-center. "Right. Ha. I have that sweatshirt, after all. Thanks, by the way. For returning it." Flustered, she ran a hand down her hair. "Did you need me?"

"Sonny's looking for you. Said I should take over."

He couldn't have heard, she repeated, watching him watch her. He'd have reacted. Shown some emotion. "Right. I'll go do that." She pocketed her phone and picked up the cup. When she got close enough, the intensity of his eyes made her feel cornered. She lingered, doubt nagging. "You okay? With... everything?"

"Fine," he replied evenly.

"Good, that's...good." She had to believe she was in the clear. "You didn't hear... Never mind." Striving for normal, she nodded in the direction of the doors. "Woman who owns the coffee shop across the street has a thing for you."

"Oh?"

"Mm. She was in asking for the gossip. I told her your personality doesn't match your face."

She thought he'd give her a glower and that would be that. Except...

"How does my face look, Leah?"

He didn't say the words with a flirty lilt, didn't lean in and grin, didn't do anything except level his usual gaze on her. And still she felt the impact like a brush of calloused fingers against her skin.

In the end, she conceded the battle, scurrying away with a mumbled excuse and cheeks blazing. He'd definitely not heard. He didn't know. All was well.

Gabriel stayed where he was as Leah walked away, his spine straight, his gaze aloof. He was an island on a calm ocean and no waves would disrupt his peace.

Even a tsunami like this.

Disbelief, shock, horror rocketed through him, crashing against his discipline until his short nails dug into his palms. He continued to breathe, not letting on, not doing anything except managing the emotion as he calmly took a seat.

She. Knew.

Shock sent another ripple through him, even thinking the words.

Their secret, his secret. The secret that had humans dragged before the High Family to be sentenced with who knew what to keep them all protected. It was practically the Golden Rule: unless the High Family specifically granted permission, humans were *not* to know about witches.

Gabriel followed the rules. They made sense to him. He'd lived his life within safe parameters ever since his parents had died and he'd stepped up to raise his sister. He liked the orderly, the lines and neat rows of organization, and the comfortable weight of what he could and couldn't do. What he should do.

And what he should do here was inform the High Family. Emmaline and Tia had clearly not sought permission—if they had, Leah would've confirmed it the second he stepped into the bar. Now the few times he'd lost control of his magic and she'd "missed it" ran through his head. Of course she hadn't missed it. Nobody was that oblivious.

Except him, apparently. And now that he knew, it was safer to follow the rules. To turn her in.

A surge of sickness twisted his belly. It was the shock, he supposed.

She should be turned in.

Rejection at the idea shoved against his skin and he fought to understand why when this was clearly the smart thing, the sensible thing.

Except…if he did that, he'd lose this job. He needed this job to get back to his normal life. It was that simple.

Better to bide his time, he thought, staring at the visitor pad, the lines of precise writing blurred. He could watch her. See how much she knew. Make sure—they were all safe.

Maybe…maybe Leah would be different.

The memory of her eyes staring into his as they'd crouched on the bar floor, glass shards between them. His spine curved to the chair as he released a heavy breath.

He'd pretend he didn't know. For now. At least the pressure was partly off, mistakes he made no longer cause for concern. She'd kept their secret however long.

It was that that had the tightness in his chest easing. He'd play pretend. He was getting good at that.

Like pretending not to notice how the damp coffee-stained T-shirt had clung to her breasts, outlining their shape.

She wore black lace against her skin.

Nope, he hadn't noticed that at all.

Leah wasn't at the shelter the following day. It was a surprise and, Gabriel assured himself, a pleasant one. It was good to have time to process his new knowledge, how he'd react to her and not let her know that he knew. And it was a relief to be left to his own devices. He didn't want her watching him with that skeptical smile. Laughing that deep-in-the-gut sound that absolutely, one hundred percent got on his nerves. Yes, he was pleased she wasn't around.

It was Sonny that greeted him, along with a dog by his side that he introduced as Danny. Goddess knew what the dog was, some kind of mixed breed, but he seemed friendly enough and calm—unlike the bruiser, Chuck, who watched him with near-fanatical devotion whenever Gabriel came within sniffing distance.

"How're you liking it so far?" Sonny led the way to the cat pens where he'd be cleaning out litter trays for the morning. Their footsteps sounded as they walked, accompanied by muffled woofs and whines.

Gabriel held himself tall as he followed the older human, debating how honest to be. He needed the job, after all. "I like a challenge."

Sonny's eyes twinkled as he threw a look over his shoulder. His hair was thinning on top, plenty of white hair threading through the mid-brown shade, but not bad for his age. He pushed the door open on a groaning squeak, gestured for Gabriel to walk through. "Not an animal fan?"

"I don't dislike them."

"Never had pets?" At Gabriel's head shake, Sonny patted Danny on the head. "Damn shame. All kids should have something to love. Didn't your parents ever think to get one?"

"They were busy elsewhere." Setting up the company, running it, putting humans first. He swallowed that down.

"Didn't mean you couldn't have had a pet. It's not just about the love, you see. It teaches responsibility, how to care for someone other than yourself. How to relate to something not like you. And, of course, there's the friend for life factor." Sonny pushed open the next door and the immediate rush of sound from the cats hit them.

"Is that your sales pitch?"

Sonny barked a laugh. "Damn good one, right?"

Gabriel inclined his chin.

"Not a talkative soul." Sonny smiled. "Another good reason for a pet. They don't need you to talk; they just need you to be there."

"I'm just here to work," Gabriel said, polite as he'd been raised to be. He couldn't disrespect elders, even if they spoke a lot of nonsense.

"Apparently so. Give the girl credit, she does come through on her promises."

"I'm sorry?"

Sonny bent, unlatched the door of a gray cat's pen. He reached in and scratched its chin, smile widening as it purred. "Leah. She told me she'd find more volunteers for free. I didn't think she could, everyone feeling the squeeze as they are, but she came through."

It was like the human was speaking a lost language. "Free?"

"Mmm. And I gotta say, thanks." Sonny looked up, nodded at him. "We need all the help we can get and more besides."

Gabriel didn't understand. Leah had promised him a check every week, not that he needed it.

Still, he didn't comment on that, nor the undertone of desperation hinted at in Sonny's words. Discomforted by the gratitude, Gabriel stood silent until Sonny finally left him to it.

So, he thought, as he dumped contents and refilled trays, then cursed as the fresh litter went flying. The shelter was struggling. He couldn't say it wasn't obvious, even if Leah hadn't mentioned it. There were a lot of occupants and not enough staff, and it showed. Unlike an aging society witch who refused to let go of her looks, the shelter couldn't spell itself a facelift. It was sagging at the corners and if it wasn't careful, it would soon deter its customers simply by looking run-down.

Not that it overly mattered to him, but one of the first rules in business was that you projected an image of success, which bred trust. Sonny needed to present the image of a well-run facility, not somewhere desperate for money. Though he had to admit, for Sonny it wouldn't be as easy as finding the right spell to fix the cracks.

He was so lost in thought that he didn't realize Leah's young friend was standing by the door until he was halfway down the line of pens.

He straightened, smoothing a hand down his blue silk tie, then grimacing at the chalky residue left behind. Perhaps Leah was onto something with her advice about jeans. "Hello."

The girl blinked big brown eyes. "Hello."

She was dressed as she had been the last time he'd seen her, ripped jeans and a T-shirt. Her blue nails were bitten down on her left hand, and she lifted her thumb to nibble on the edge.

"I'm Gabriel," he said, discomforted.

"Sloane," she said in a voice just as unsure. She stared at him. And stared.

It appeared neither of them were talkers. Gabriel shifted, trying to come up with a subject to put her at ease. His sister would have fallen into conversation effortlessly, but Gabriel had never been easy with people.

Finally, he said, "You volunteer here?"

She nodded. He noticed she took a deep breath before saying, "I like hanging out here after school."

Now *he* nodded. Slid his gaze to the side and then back. This was like holding a hot cauldron with bare hands. "You must like animals."

"Yeah."

Why was she standing here? He had no interest in talking to a human teenager, but he couldn't flick her off. It seemed too much like kicking a puppy.

"You're doing that wrong, you know." She gestured at the sack of litter he held. Her hair swung forward and she dipped her head, as if she regretted the criticism.

He could choose to be offended, but she wasn't mocking him. "I'll find my way."

"I could show you." She peeked through the curtain of hair. He didn't frown but it was close. "Why?"

"If I show you, you could answer some questions for me."

"About what?"

"New Orleans." She smiled, and something about it struck a familiar chord. Her next words came out in an eager rush. "I've always wanted to go but my sister won't let me."

"Won't let you?"

She shrugged, toed the floor with a sneaker. "Too dangerous still. Maybe someday."

He'd heard that plenty from his own family. "Maybe someday" had been the recurring theme, until it had been replaced with never.

He eyed the sack, the mess he was making and what he'd halfheartedly cleared up. Then the girl who watched him, all hope and shyness. He didn't particularly want company, but again, he couldn't bring himself to shake her off.

"Fine," he agreed, awkward and abrupt. "Show me. And you can keep the cats out of the way as well."

"They're just looking for some love."

"Not from me."

She smiled as though he'd said something funny and pulled out a candy bar. "Want to split this?"

He looked at it dubiously. "What is it?"

Her mouth dropped. "You've never had a Butterfinger?" She tore open the wrapper and painstakingly bent it in half. She offered him the half still in the wrapper. "Try it."

"I'm good."

"Chicken."

He drew himself up. "I am not a child. I do not respond to those kinds of—" He stopped short as she made *bok bok* noises.

Worse than his sister. To shut her up, he shoved the candy in his mouth.

Peanuts exploded on his tongue, the sweet chocolate melting in a soft slide.

He made a noise halfway between a groan and a humming sound.

She grinned and bit into hers, before gesturing at the sack. "So, what you want to do is…"

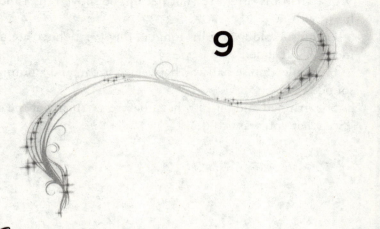

9

*G*abriel watched Chuck watch him as he placed the dog bowl in the kennel. The dog's butt was glued to the floor but his tail swept side to side. Brown eyes melted as Gabriel stepped back.

"Now, wait," Gabriel cautioned, having done this routine before. "Wait. We're not having a repeat of yesterday."

The dog's tail picked up until it was a blur.

"Chuck…" Gabriel hardened his tone. "Don't—"

As if shot from a cannon, Chuck launched forward, his joy too much to bear.

It was, Gabriel thought, trying to be philosophical as he lay under the wriggling Labrador, a work in progress. Like his entire life.

Dealing with things was so much harder without magic. He had to respect humans for that alone. Just because he thought magic should be kept secret didn't mean he couldn't acknowledge they had to be tough to get through daily life. Or deal with the ever-elusive toaster. He'd bought twelve now, all still refusing to work.

"Goodnight!"

Gabriel shut the door on Chuck happily burying his face in his kibble and swiveled to see Mitch and Frankie heading toward him. The two humans had made a point of searching him out to have a conversation whenever they shared the same shift. It was strange.

Mitch was shrugging into a fleece jacket that drowned his skinny frame. "We're heading to T and T, if you want to come."

Mingle with the humans? The idea had something akin to anxiety stabbing into him. "I have plans."

"Hot date?"

Gabriel glanced over at ginger Frankie, uncomfortable with the wiggling eyebrows he saw there. "No."

"Their loss, eh, Goodnight." Frankie clapped him on the shoulder. "C'mon, one drink."

"I really can't."

"You tell me what's so important that one drink would hurt."

He made himself say it. "I don't want to." As their expressions swung to surprise, he shifted, trying to release the unpleasant sensation. It wouldn't do any good to intensify his involvement, he reminded himself, bracing for their inevitable withdrawal. That, at least, he was used to.

Then Frankie smacked Mitch on the chest with the back of his hand, understanding dawning. "I get it. Look, Goodnight, we get you're, you know, shy."

He stared at them.

"No pressure, but we thought we'd shoot the shit, flirt with the pretty bartender."

As Gabriel opened his mouth to refuse them again, Mitch added, "We want you to come. One drink."

Gabriel stopped, twisting in place. He'd said no. He'd meant it.

But... They wanted him to come. Him. Nobody ever wanted Gabriel. They wanted a Goodnight.

He rolled his shoulders against the tide of discomfort, found himself saying, "One, then."

Frankie grinned, clapping him on the shoulder again. "Attaboy. Let's grab the others and we'll head over."

To T and T. Gabriel didn't catch on until he found himself standing outside the establishment that had hired and fired him quicker than some potions took to brew.

And the pretty bartender, he realized as their group of five walked in, was none other than a short blonde whose big blue eyes rounded when they landed on him.

Disbelief? Speculation?

Whatever it was, it made him want to hunch his shoulders like a teenage warlock caught in Jackson Square telling fortunes to drunk tourists.

Mitch offered to grab a booth with Peter and Jasper, the other two volunteers, so it was Frankie and a reluctant Gabriel that went to the bar.

"Rack 'em up, darlin'." Frankie's teeth gleamed out of his beard as he smacked the bar top. "Shots all around."

Gabriel stood quietly. He hadn't seen Leah in a few days and when she laughed, the impact went straight to his head. Not that he showed it.

"This should be good," she commented, with a side-eye at Gabriel. "All right, boys. Pick your poison."

"Tequila. Tequila, lads?" Frankie called back to the others. A cheer rang out.

"Just curious, Gabe," Leah said as she turned to the shelf that was, he noticed with some satisfaction, still organized as he'd set it up one boring Sunday. "Have you ever had a shot?"

"Yes." Years ago.

"Hmm." She poured the tequila into five short glasses and set out a small plate, added five lime wedges, and then a salt-shaker. She lifted her brows when Gabriel stopped Frankie from paying by thrusting out a fifty-dollar note. She accepted it with a finger and thumb, studying him with an interest that made his feet shift. "You don't strike me as a man who gets loose."

"Maybe you don't know as much about me as you think."

"I bet I do."

He scoffed, barely noticing when Frankie grabbed all but one glass and toted them away. "I doubt that."

Challenge gleamed on her face. "I'm a bartender. Some might call us professional readers of human nature."

"I'm different." And she knew it.

"Hmm." The look she shot him under her lashes was poignant with meaning that neither of them would say aloud. "How much do you want to bet?"

"I don't bet."

"Why? Is that a commoner thing, something the glorious Goodnights don't do?"

"You can't goad me."

She smiled. "Want to bet?"

Unwilling amusement moved through him. He stifled it by throwing her a superior look. "I will not argue with you."

"This isn't arguing. This is a conversation. You might not have heard of it but it's where two people talk about something they find interesting."

"And our topic is?"

"You."

Something hot flared down low. He fought the temptation to lean in, sneered instead. "Is this the part where you read me like a cheap psychic?"

"You will meet someone short, blonde and witty," she intoned dramatically, flourishing a hand. She rested her elbows on the bar and his eyes dipped, hunting for a glimpse of tattoo. "I could blow your mind."

His throat tightened. He couldn't help leaning in, inhaling the hint of coconut.

Leah tilted her head, hair tipping over her shoulder. The

background noise was faint to him, a barely-there buzz, his entire focus on her.

"Want me to demonstrate?"

"No," he managed.

She didn't pay any attention, but when did she ever? "You once told me you don't like crowds."

Had he? He didn't remember. "I don't like anyone," he corrected. "I like being alone."

"Nobody likes being alone, Gabe."

"Gabriel."

Her lips twitched.

"It's better this way."

"Better for who?"

He didn't answer.

Looking smug, she pointed out, "You don't like to be in anyone's debt and you don't like being vulnerable. Which is why you sent me money." She was close now, ten inches separating them. "You needed to balance it out."

She was too perceptive for his liking. He rolled his shoulders. "I sent that money for the broken glasses." Lies. And he'd paid for it with pain—the spell to transport the package to the address on her records had taken him out of commission for the rest of the afternoon.

"What I can't figure out is why you're here with Frankie and his boys," she mused.

"Why do you care?"

"Not sure. But then, I do have the worst taste in men."

Gabriel's mouth parted.

Delight lit up her face as she winked and tapped the shot glass with a finger. "And for my final trick, I predict you've never gotten drunk. Because Gabriel Goodnight would never do something so irresponsible. So, I'll take this for my 'bar buddy', for old times' sake."

She took the salt, licked her hand to make it stick. But when she went for the glass, he closed his hand around hers.

Skin to skin. The whisper touch sank into his bones. He dragged his fingers down hers, heart pounding as he slipped the glass free.

Her eyes were pools of deep blue as she watched him tip the tequila back.

The punch of fire shot from his throat down to his stomach, where it curled tight, aching. His breath was short as he upended the glass onto the bar.

Cheeks flushed, Leah silently offered him a lime wedge and he accepted, allowing the tang to mingle with the remnants of tequila. He was dizzy as he stared into her eyes, sucked the lime. The alcohol. It was strong.

"You don't know me." Where he meant to be firm, his voice was deep, soft. A taunt. "But Goodnights always come out on top. We rise to every challenge."

She shouldn't have challenged him.

Last call had come and gone and so had Frankie and the others. Leah had expected Gabriel to last half an hour at most. Be in the company of others? Willingly? And humans to boot? My, what a difference a few days made.

She'd been playing chicken and staying away from the shelter, skittish and half-anxious that witches would portal out of nowhere like a supernatural SWAT team and drag her to their High Family. When that hadn't happened, she'd finally relaxed enough to return—only to learn that Sloane of all people had taken a shine to Gabriel, shadowing him after school and helping him with his jobs. That girl didn't make friends easy, either.

A half witch, half human born from Emma's dad and a human woman who'd died in childbirth, Sloane had grown up with her human aunt, away from witch society. Emma had been agonizing the past year about how to introduce Sloane to the masses without letting the cutthroat attitudes hurt the shy teenager. Still, Leah knew it was only a matter of time until Sloane forced the issue. She was as curious about witch society as Leah was, but at least she stood a chance at being included.

Honestly, that Sloane liked Gabriel and that he in turn allowed her company shocked the hell out of Leah.

But maybe not as much as the fact that he'd shown up tonight, even thrown himself into the drinking games Frankie and the others had played. Tequila after tequila after tequila.

She'd finally suggested a switch to beer when he'd rubbed the lime on his hand instead of the salt.

He hadn't laughed and joked as much as the others had, but he'd been a part of the group. He'd stayed.

Now he sat on a stool, tie crooked, shirtsleeves pushed up to expose those muscled forearms, black hair mussed and eyes closed as he swayed to a Harry Styles song.

She stifled the inappropriate pleasure at the sight of Gabriel rumpled. If it wouldn't be creepy as fuck, she'd take a picture for posterity. Behold the rare items: the four-leaf clover, a big blue moon and Gabriel Goodnight completely trashed.

The doors had been locked ten minutes ago; she'd cashed out the register and had wiped down most of the tables. They had a cleaner that would come in the morning to do a thorough job, but she never stacked the chairs on top of the tables without a cursory wipe.

"Don't fall off there," she cautioned Gabriel as she went around with a dishcloth and a spray bottle.

"Never," he declared. "Goodnights have excellent balance."

"Must be good to be a Goodnight."

He made a noncommittal sound.

She sang along with the chorus as she finished the final few. The last word ended on a squeak as she turned and found her nose buried in Gabriel's chest. Her hand fell to his hip as she caught her balance. She was slow to remove it, heart thudding at the feel of him under her fingertips. She dragged in a breath, tasted spices.

He didn't notice. "You're here alone."

She strangled the ridiculous lust, flustered and irritated to be this affected. "Unless my elementary education fails me, I'm not alone."

"If I weren't here," he said, doggedly following her as she slipped by him to stack another chair, "you'd be alone."

"That's generally how it works."

"But that's not safe."

She twisted to face him, the last chair still suspended in her hands. "Safe?"

His expression was disgruntled. "Anyone could break in here. You could be hurt."

Arrogant, she reminded herself before she completely melted. Disdainful, unfriendly, unhelpful, rude. *Drunk.*

Don't fall for it. She'd been suckered into flirting earlier but that was okay. Flirting was harmless. Feelings were not.

"I can handle myself."

"But you're so fragile."

That quickly, temper grated along her nerve endings. She placed the chair on the table deliberately. How was it he could amuse, arouse and annoy her in the stretch of one minute?

She kept her voice cool. "I bet I could take you."

He didn't laugh—Goodnights apparently didn't—but he did throw her a look that practically patted her on the head.

She spun on him, annoyed. "I think Laurence would—" Her mouth snapped shut. *Shit.*

Anxiety tickled her throat as she backpedaled. "I'm just saying, I'm more dangerous than I look."

He didn't pick up on her slip. Thank God for tequila. "I could tie one hand behind my back and still best you."

"Now, you're just being rude."

"I'm honest."

She decided not to smack him over the head with a chair and finished the rest in silence.

And yet somehow she still found herself escorting her warlock frenemy home. Her decision was made when he'd been unable to work the bar's push door, pulling on the handle like it was a game of tug-of-war, until he'd finally lost his balance and fallen on his ass. She might go to hell, but some things deserved to be laughed at.

"Can you make it upstairs?" she asked now as the Uber waited at the curb near his building. When he'd forgotten the address, she'd had to look it up in their records, unsurprised it was in a ritzy neighborhood that boasted spectacular views of Lake Michigan.

"'Course. I don'need help. I don'need anyone."

In silence, she and the Uber driver watched him stagger up the street.

"I thought you said he lived here," the driver commented.

"He does." Leah dug a finger in her temple as Gabriel continued to walk blithely away from his apartment building.

It took her a minute to catch up with him, to steer him around and to usher him past the well-trained doorman.

"Miss," he said as he held the door for them, unblinking. "Is Mr. Goodnight well?"

"Mr. Goodnight is none of your concern," Gabriel muttered as he weaved through.

Leah ground her teeth and shot an apologetic smile at the doorman. "Mr. Goodnight is about four-tenths tequila right now," she explained, not intervening when Gabriel tripped and planted his face into the wall. Karma in action. "I'm sure he'll be fine in the morning. Thank you."

"No problem, miss. Have a nice evening."

"See, that? *That* was rude," she hissed at Gabriel as she stood with him at the elevator bank.

"Why? I'm none of his business."

"He was being nice."

"Nosy," Gabriel corrected and even tipsy, he managed to look superior. "I'm not going to provide him with gossip."

"News flash, you just did. Nothing people love more than to hate on someone." The ding heralded the arrival of the elevator. She pushed him in. "Manners cost nothing, you know. How you treat people matters."

"Like I care what people think of me." He crossed his arms as he leaned in the corner, green eyes boring into her. Pointed.

She scowled at the dig. "You don't care that you come across as an ass?"

"No."

"Seriously."

"There's only a few people's opinions I care about," he said, mumbling his way through the words.

"And how many of them are still around?"

She hadn't meant his parents, but something dark, raw, flashed across his face until it shut down to ice. She opened her mouth to explain, closed it as he'd closed himself to her.

Sometimes you had to know when to put down the shovel and not dig the hole deeper.

They traveled to his floor in silence.

When the doors opened, she stayed still. Awkward, she gestured into the hall. "You can find your way from here, right?"

"I'm fine." His words were clearer, sharper, stinging in their enunciation.

She bit her lip, shame an oily slide down her spine as his long legs took him away. Before she could think better of it, she darted forward, slamming a hand against the doors to stop them from closing.

"I'm sorry," she called out, softer than a shout, mindful of how late it was.

He stopped but didn't turn around, still stiff.

She swallowed past the uneasiness. "I didn't mean it…that way. But I shouldn't have said it. It was stupid."

When he still didn't speak, she ruefully reflected she shouldn't be surprised. Instead, she let the doors go and stepped back as they slid closed.

Only to jump when they slid open again as if—well. As if by magic.

He stood on the other side. His hair was disheveled, his tie loose, his vest unbuttoned over an untucked shirt, and yet he stood, posture perfect. And though he disguised it well, she recognized someone in pain. Her heart clenched.

Though he'd stopped the elevator, he didn't speak. His expression was guarded, almost like he didn't have the words.

That was okay. Leah always had plenty.

She wet her lips. "You know what I'd love right now? Coffee."

He blinked those stunning green eyes, less glazed than before.

She edged him backward, allowing the elevator to close and return to the lobby without her. "Coffee. Perk me up before I go home."

"It's one in the morning."

"So, you see my need."

"Don't you want to go to bed?"

Unbidden, a shiver brushed against her nerves.

"I do," she rasped and heard the forbidden truth in her voice. "But it's a long journey back to mine. I could use the jolt." She hesitated, realizing she could be misreading him. "Unless *you* want to go to bed."

Flickers of light danced in his eyes as he watched her, then he inclined his chin and led the way to his apartment.

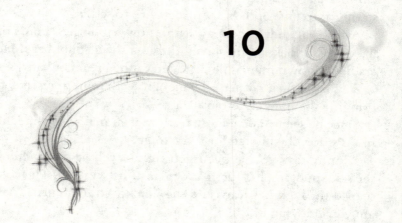

10

Leah wasn't exactly sure how she'd ended up looking out at Gabriel's magnificent view. If she traced a path from the start of the evening to now, it wouldn't have been an obvious one.

She disliked him, right? He was arrogant and rude and completely unapologetic about it.

So why, she asked herself for the umpteenth time as she turned from the city lights to accept a mug of steaming coffee, had she pushed her way into his apartment?

The apartment was nice, big—hardly shocking—open plan. A short hallway led to the kitchen-slash-living room, where a corner sofa done in soft gray dominated the right side. A muted rug in cream and gray lay across the dark hardwood floor and a glass coffee table sat atop it, only a perfectly straight remote on top of that. The wide-screen TV it belonged to was hung on the eggshell-painted wall. She couldn't imagine Gabriel watching TV, couldn't imagine him relaxing at all.

Beyond, a deck of some kind with an iron railing could be seen out of floor-to-ceiling windows. Beyond that was the familiar placid darkness of Lake Michigan, which she'd been staring at to give both of them a chance to settle.

At least he didn't seem as drunk now, either her words or his own warlock nature slicing through the alcohol haze. He cradled his own mug as he retreated to the breakfast bar.

Staying in their corners, she thought with some amusement, bringing the mug up to blow on it.

Since he seemed on edge, a territorial animal with someone in his space, she hunted for a safe topic.

"Sonny says you've been getting on well at the shelter," she said, nudging her hips back against the window. The cold seeped through her jeans and she quickly straightened. "Ah, are you enjoying it?"

"It's a job."

Three words.

Even she couldn't do much with three words.

At least until he added, "I like to learn new things."

Unsure how to respond, she took a gulp of coffee. And spat it back in the mug.

"It's hot," he told her, like you would a five-year-old.

As her mouth burned, she slid him a withering look.

He pressed his lips together and looked down, almost—almost—smiling. She hoped she was there when he finally did.

"You like learning new things?" she managed once she'd assured herself her tongue hadn't boiled off. A swift once-over had her stating, "You should tell that to your face."

"My face is not a billboard of emotion."

"Slap *that* on a bumper sticker." Leah bit down on her amusement. "But you're saying you actually like learning to mop and take care of animals?"

"Knowledge is power."

Now she laughed. "Well, that's on brand."

"On brand?"

Human term. "I just meant," she said aloud, "of course you

have an ulterior motive to learning. Don't you ever just do anything for fun?"

"I enjoy documentaries," he ventured after a moment's thought.

"And here I didn't think we had anything in common, Gabe."

He ignored that. "You like documentaries?"

"Pretty much every type," she confirmed, tucking hair behind her ear and cautiously sipping her coffee. "I'm a bit of a curious nerd. I'll try anything once." She felt the color rise to her cheeks in a wave of heat. "Ah, I meant, like true crime, history, industry."

"You surprise me."

"You surprise *me*. I figured you for alphabetizing your belongings for fun or practicing your sneer in the mirror."

"The sneer comes naturally."

It startled a laugh out of her. "Well, it's good you're enjoying it. We need you."

"You do."

"More honesty?"

He tipped his mug back without speaking.

She smoothed her thumb over the hot ceramic. "Sonny used to have a better handle on things." Her easy humor faded as the worry pinched. "But life happens," she continued. "He got older, more animals needed homes. Expenses go up, bills flood in. People need paid work, so they go elsewhere."

"You haven't."

"I wouldn't. They need me. I run the website, the social media." She shot him a somewhat teasing look. "Almost as important as having someone on reception these days."

He arched an eyebrow but didn't comment. "Do people donate?"

"It only goes so far. We rescued a dog a few weeks back that'd obviously been used for baiting. In fights," she elaborated at his blank look. "He had to go into surgery to save his leg. He's recovering, but that bill alone was thousands." She tapped her fingernails, a jaunty lemon color, on the mug, jittery with excess energy. "He looks so stressed these days. Sometimes I worry—" She caught herself. "Well, anyway, you being around is helpful."

The ring he always wore on his left hand glinted in the low lights as he swilled his drink. "Even taking into account my salary?"

An internal siren blared. "You needed the job and we can afford some part-time employees." Or she could, out of what remained of her trust. As far as Sonny knew, Gabriel was volunteering. She refused to take money out of the shelter when she was the one who'd insisted on Gabriel working there.

His gaze picked her apart. "We can or you can?"

She opened her mouth.

"Don't lie to me."

Deciding she really needed to sit, she avoided that stare and crossed to the couch. So tidy. She resisted the urge to poke the remote control out of alignment.

"Leah."

"What?" She hunched her shoulders. "It's no big deal."

"Why are you paying me a salary?"

"The shelter can't afford to and you needed the job."

His jaw flexed. "You will cease paying it."

She scoffed. "Brilliant plan. And what are you going to live on?"

"I have plenty of money."

She bet he did. Apparently, along with magical powers, witches made a killing at managing their finances, and being the heir of Goodnight's Remedies had to have benefits beyond unlimited access to their wrinkle-free face cream.

She sipped more coffee. "I can afford it." Just.

"Your ripped jeans say otherwise."

"Those are a fashion statement."

"And your sweaters that don't fit?"

She lowered the mug. "I'm feeling a lot of judgment right now from a man who probably sleeps in a tie and cuff links."

He ignored her. "And your cap."

"You say *one* word about the Cubs…"

"You can't possibly afford me."

"Maybe not for the whole night, but is there an hourly rate we could discuss?" She sniggered at his confused expression. "Never mind. Leave it, Gabriel."

"No."

"This is about your whole owing-people issues, isn't it?"

"Keep your money," he gritted out. "Or put it toward the shelter. But I don't want to be in your debt."

She'd so called that one.

Deciding to be nice and not crow, she held up a hand in surrender. "All right, jeez. Hell, you must really enjoy working there to work for free." She slid him a provocative smile. "It's the charming co-workers, isn't it?"

"I find myself dazzled every day."

Her smile stretched into an honest grin. It probably wasn't his intention, but any time a dry retort came from his mouth, she counted it a victory. One more button undone on his serious straitjacket.

"You must like the guys, at least," she pointed out. "You hung out with them voluntarily."

His instant discomfort was obvious. "I was…persuaded," he muttered, lifting his mug.

"And you stayed."

He drank deep before putting the cup on the counter. He kept his eyes on it, then elegantly raised a shoulder. "It was interesting. I've not had much occasion to 'hang out.'" Instantly, his expression tightened and he looked down his nose at her. "Goodnights have far more important things we must do."

"Of course," she murmured, that crack in his façade splitting her own chest. She couldn't stand being alone, hence her "mutt"-ley crew. She wondered if he felt the same deep down, despite what he said.

Flirtation, not feelings, she reminded herself.

She set down her mug on the glass table. "And Sloane? I hear she's become your shadow."

When he approached, her heart rate picked up, practically humming as he leaned down, low enough for her to see a shadow of facial hair along his jawline. Her breath caught as he reached out. When he produced a coaster to slide under her mug, she had to laugh at herself.

He hesitated, then sank down on the other end of the couch. His back was a straight line while hers curved into the cushions. "I find her interesting."

The man couldn't say he liked anything. Why did she find *that* interesting?

"She reminds me of someone," he finished, throwing her nervous system into overdrive.

She forced herself to stay relaxed. "Someone I know?" *Please don't say Emma.*

"No."

Her spine relaxed. Thank God.

When he didn't elaborate, she suppressed a sigh. "Gee, Gabe, you're such a chatterbox."

"So I've been told."

She snickered. "C'mon." She dared to cross the invisible border and poked his leg with her foot. He jerked like she'd electrocuted him.

He recovered quickly. "Why do you want to know?"

"Because when they were handing out patience, curiosity was having a two-for-one sale and I've always been a sucker for a bargain."

"You are strange."

"Like you're a model of normal?"

Green met blue, his searching. His face was shadowed, all angles. "I've never had anyone talk to me like you."

She wiggled her eyebrows. "You're welcome."

The Warlock of Contempt glanced away, but not before she saw the smallest curve shape his lips.

She'd made him smile.

This must be what miracle workers felt.

"My sister."

Her train had jumped tracks and with effort she tried to get back onto his. "What?"

"Sloane." He traced his ring. "She reminds me of my sister."

Right. Tia had mentioned a sister. "How old is she?"

"Fourteen."

"Tough age."

"For some. Melly has always been strong-willed."

"As all Goodnights are."

A dry flick of a look. "Indeed."

"She's back in New Orleans?" He nodded. "You didn't bring her here. I…" She picked her way delicately through the mine-field. "With your parents… Do you take care of her?"

"Yes."

She wanted to ask how old he'd been when his parents had died, but it felt too much like prying open the fist he held around his pain. "You must miss her."

"What makes you say that?"

"Your voice. You love her, even when she annoys you."

He faced the window, all haughty male. "I have a great tolerance for annoying females."

Leah laughed at that.

He watched the darkness as she watched him. "We haven't been apart this long before," he admitted softly. "I do miss her, yes."

"She could come visit."

"No." Now his voice was sharp. "It's dangerous."

"The city?"

His lip curled. "The people."

Leah's heart hitched. He'd been so easy tonight, with her, with the guys, that she'd forgotten he had a hang-up about humans. Still, she plunged ahead, a general paving the way for her troops to win the war.

"Depends how you look at it." She didn't flinch as he cut his gaze to hers, the green sharp enough to make her bleed. "I like to think that people are basically good."

Everything about him tightened, a cork ready to blow and shatter the bottle as it flew. "My parents died because they went out of their way to help people," he bit out, voice sharp, hard. "It's because of…'people' that Melly grew up only knowing them through my memories."

She should go. That was the sensible thing to do.

And yet, her feet stubbornly stayed planted. It didn't take a magnifying glass to glimpse his pain. It was a wound that didn't bleed but wept into his insides, poisoning everything it touched. She shouldn't care, shouldn't want to launch herself at him and hug the ache away. Likely she'd get thrown across the room if she even tried. So, she did the only thing she could think of. Share something of herself.

"You're right." She pulled her bottom lip into her mouth, worrying it. Took a deep breath. "People can be selfish. Weak. My dad." Her skin prickled and she shrugged her shoulders irritably. "He was…well, he was my hero when I was a kid. My best friend. Until he decided he wanted a new family." She sensed Gabriel looking at her but preferred to focus her gaze past his shoulder, on his fabulous kitchen and its twelve toasters. That earned a double take. *Twelve?* And he called *her* strange. "My mom fell apart," she said, picking up the thread. "Wouldn't eat, wouldn't dress, wouldn't come out of her room. She's the happiest, brightest woman, and with one selfish decision, he cut her into nothing."

Old pain blossomed, a bruise that never healed, sore under the surface. He was poker-faced when she dared to look at him. She found it comforting, preferring that to any kind of sympathy.

"So, I get the whole distrust vibe you've got going," she finished, ready to drop the subject back into the do-not-disturb box. She'd made her point. "But you shouldn't let a couple bad apples ruin the cobbler. Most of us are okay."

He didn't speak but she felt his gaze probing, as if he could see beneath the layers. It propelled her upward with a need to hide. "Anyway, it's late. I should get going. Thanks for the drink."

When he didn't move, didn't speak, she grabbed her purse from where she'd set it by the couch. *Home free*, she thought. Except when she sidled past him, his long fingers wrapped around her wrist. His hand was cool. Strong.

She hoped he didn't feel the skip in her pulse. "What?"

He released her, an odd hitch of something causing a line between his brows. "You didn't finish your coffee."

Uh, yeah, she had. Except when she glanced back, the mug was half-full.

Her pulse skipped again before rocketing up. She swung her gaze back to him, assessing, wondering what he was playing at. Was this another of his mistakes? Or... Her skin pebbled. Did he...?

"Sit," he ordered, not commenting on her sudden stiffness. He patted the couch in a move as awkward as it was unnatural. "Finish it. Talk to me about...the Cubs."

She blinked, suspicion temporarily diverted. "You want me to talk to you about baseball?"

"Yes."

The warlock was just odd and with the ghost of her dad lingering, she stepped toward the exit. "I should really—"

"You shouldn't go until you've taught me about baseball."

What *was* this? Gabriel never wanted to talk. He hated company, or that was his party line. So why would he—?

Realization struck. A sleek dart of sensation fired in her chest as she swallowed. "I'm okay, Gabriel. I mean, I'm not upset."

"I know."

"It was a long time ago. I don't need a distraction."

"Who said you did?"

Either she'd read him wrong or Gabriel Goodnight was far sweeter than he let on. And that…that was more dangerous to her than knowing about witches.

She should go.

Instead, she sank back into her seat. "Okay." Her dogs would be fine with Peggy, and Ubers would always be running. Her throat was dry as she cleared it and that damn ache only grew. "Baseball 101. You sure you know what you're getting yourself into?"

He waved an imperious hand. "Of course."

Good. Because she didn't.

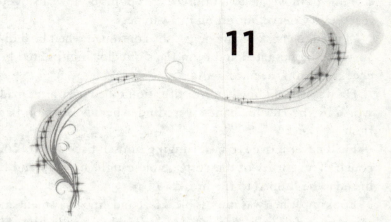

11

*H*e woke tangled in her.

At first Gabriel thought it a dream, a forbidden one he'd not even admitted to himself. His hands on her skin, soft under his fingertips. He skimmed those fingers up her spine, under the clothing that hid her body.

She stirred. Her legs were entwined with his, hips tucked against him. She was short but Goddess, she fitted. She shouldn't, in so many ways, but she fitted.

A truth was easier to acknowledge in a dream and he shifted, trying to ease the ache in his body. He hunted for her scent, dipping his head until his nose found her throat. He breathed her in. Hungered.

"Gabriel."

Like he'd been hexed, Gabriel's body turned to ice. His arms tensed around Leah as he lifted his head, opening his eyes to reality.

Sleepy blue eyes met his as she yawned. Her hair was a blond nest of curls and her cheeks were flushed. "Guess we fell asleep," she said, voice thick. "What time is it?"

Time to move, he told himself. Except his body was slow to react, every nerve humming in awareness.

"I need to check on my dogs," she continued when he didn't answer. She hesitated and twin flags of color highlighted her cheeks. "I, um, need to get up."

He was still holding her. Mortification rolled over him, made worse by the fact his hands were under her sweater, on bare flesh.

He'd never moved so fast, flinging himself backward off the couch. The corner of the coffee table caught his shin and he hissed as he limped to the breakfast bar.

Looking at her was impossible. Heat and embarrassment and something painfully close to desire throbbed inside him. He heard her move, a bag rustle, the dull sound of fingers hitting a cell phone screen.

"Peggy's already dropped them off at day care," she announced, as if he'd been waiting on the news or knew who Peggy was. "Which means I can go straight to the shelter. I keep some clothes there and it'd be easier than traveling across town. After coffee, of course. Who can function in the morning without coffee?" There was a slight edge to her voice as she peppered him with words.

Gabriel wanted her to take them back, wanted her to leave. To leave him alone, let him rebuild. He felt exposed. Weak. He had been weak.

It had been her apology that did it. And then, then it had been the unguarded moment when he'd seen past the sunny façade and glimpsed pain. He should have let her leave, wallow in that pain at home. But he'd spent too many nights alone with his own, and he'd reacted.

He'd listened to her talk about baseball, about her beloved Cubs, about how this year would be the year. He'd listened and learned and absorbed and he'd fallen asleep to the sound of the documentary she'd suggested they put on about the beautiful game.

And woken up with guilt a third bedfellow.

He'd always sworn that humans were dangerous, and here he was "hanging out" with them, talking with them. Wanting them.

Some part of him shook his head, knowing that wasn't why he was pushing her away, but he was skilled at ignoring the things he didn't want to face. So, Gabriel reverted to what he knew.

"This is becoming a bad habit," he said briskly. He affected his society mask as he turned, linking his tight hands behind his back.

She ran her fingers through her hair, combing it as best she could. "Coffee?"

"Insisting on acting like we're friends."

The words hit like a curse. He saw it, how she absorbed them, flinching as the meaning penetrated. "You asked me to stay."

"You wanted coffee and I was raised too well to turn someone out of the house."

Her mouth dropped, ocean blue turning stormy. "Not *then*. When I was going to leave, you wanted me to stay."

"If that's how you want to remember it."

"Don't be a dick."

"I'm going to change if you want to let yourself out." He didn't stop to watch her, but strode down the hall to his bedroom, firmly clicking the door behind him. He sank down, resting his forehead on it. Behind him, a lamp juddered, tipping off the bedside table. The magic squeezed his spine, but worse was that he'd not meant to do it.

"Get hold of yourself," he muttered. He deliberately turned his back on the door to get dressed.

★ ★ ★

Leah didn't waste time leaving his highness' apartment, though she did move several things out of alignment before she went. Petty, yes. Satisfying, *hell* yes.

What a dick. She fumed as she rode the elevator down and Google mapped a coffee shop. Joanne's was too far away and she wasn't in the mood to hear someone wax on about how gorgeous Gabriel was. On the outside, maybe, but inside was a whole 'nother story—one with a dark and twisted ending.

Man, he was lucky she wasn't a witch because she'd have telekinetically kicked him in the nuts for that performance.

"Insisting on acting like we're friends," she mocked, stomping in the direction of the closest L train station. "Like I have nothing better to do than pant after his warlock self. My coffee mug didn't refill itself."

She couldn't believe she'd fallen for his BS *again*. What was that saying? Fool me once, shame on you. Fool me twice, shame I'm such a goddamned idiot.

Under the anger, hurt roiled but she didn't want to focus on that, on the fact that she'd thought they were…bonding or some crap. That there may be more under the Higher warlock guise.

She nurtured her righteous anger throughout her journey and when she stepped off the train, walking the few blocks to the shelter, her resolution was firm. Whatever it was that attracted her to him, it was stopping right now. Even a dog learned its lesson after being kicked too many times. The next time she saw him, she would—

—stop in her tracks as he slid out of a cab that idled in front of the shelter.

Her lip curled, anger riding a fiery line down her body. Of course, he was too good for public transportation. And even if he'd told her he was headed to the shelter, too, she'd wanted coffee first. So she wouldn't have said yes, even if he'd been courteous and goddamned asked. It wasn't like they were friends, after all.

She hated how good he looked in a cashmere overcoat open over yet another stunning three-piece suit. He should look ridiculous, doing shelter work dressed like that, but he never did. Ass.

The cab drove off and their gazes met.

Play it cool, she reminded herself. She lifted the coffee as she crossed the street and took a bolstering sip. "Fancy meeting you here."

The wind blew a lock of black hair across his forehead. It was the only thing about him that moved.

Her jaw gritted and she flicked her eyes away, annoyed. And her stomach dropped, along with the cardboard coffee cup she was holding. The lid popped off and coffee gushed out as she rushed forward, heedless of Gabriel's demand. All of her attention was on the broken glass that littered the sidewalk and the spray paint that shouted obscenities to the public as they passed.

Then Gabriel's hand gripped her elbow, pulled her around.

She wrenched away. "Sonny," she threw at him and fled, hearing his curse and the sound of his Italian loafers pounding after her.

She didn't care as she burst into the torn-up reception, as she took a sharp left toward where the overnight workers slept. It had been Sonny's night. That was the thought that played through her mind on repeat. He was old. He could've been...

Rushing through the door to the room, she scanned it in seconds. Not here. Didn't mean anything, she told herself, her knees weak. Didn't mean—

"Leah."

At his voice, she spun and made a sound in relief, just as Gabriel reached them. Sonny was coming out of the cat enclosures, phone to his ear.

"Calling the cops?" she asked, hearing the quiver in her

voice. Her hands shook, so she smoothed them down her thighs. "When did it happen?"

"I left for one goddamned hour." Sonny's gaze flicked from her to Gabriel. "The animals are all right, thank Christ, but the windows...the walls..."

"We'll clean it up. We'll get it fixed. It's fixable."

"More bills," he murmured, despair heavy in the words before his attention snapped back to the call. "Yes, I'm still here."

He wandered away, talking rapidly. Leah watched him go, helpless.

"Goddamn it," she said under her breath. "*Goddamn it.*" She aimed a kick at the wall, breath exploding out when her foot connected. More bills. More worry. More likely he'd want to wash his hands of the place. If she hadn't plowed so much of her money into the bar, into her house...but he wouldn't accept it anyway, even if she had enough to buy in.

Gabriel was a silent presence at her side. She didn't know what she expected him to do. What normal people did, she supposed. Comfort her, offer words of reassurance, empty though they might be.

What she didn't expect him to do was to walk away.

She deliberately didn't watch him go. Why was she even mildly surprised?

Ignoring the fist in her throat, she went to grab a change of clothes and face the mountain of tasks ahead of her.

Gabriel was standing on the sidewalk, surveying the damage, as Sonny walked out to join him. They stood, side by side and in silence, for a long moment.

"Son of a bitch," were Sonny's first words. Lines dug deep grooves around his mouth, in his forehead, around eyes that spoke of annoyed anxiety. "This is just what we needed."

Gabriel kept his gaze on the broken glass. "I can fix it."

"You know a carpenter, a handyman?"

"Something like that." Give him a moment alone with no prying eyes, it would be nothing to him. It *was* nothing to him.

"That's something, I guess." Sonny rubbed the back of his neck, then his face. "Jesus. I did not need this."

The bite of wind nipped his cheeks as Gabriel slid his eyes toward the older human. "She was worried. About you."

"Leah?" Sonny shrugged, stuffing his hands in his fleece's pockets. "I'm fine."

"She ran into the building." The way his heart had squeezed, the air tight in his lungs. He hadn't cared for it. "It could've been dangerous."

"Leah thinks with her heart. And I'm fine. They took their opportunity, some cash from the office. Some drugs we keep on-site. Expensive ones." Sonny pursed his lips. "Joanne from across the street is checking her CCTV, and Raj from next to her, but I doubt it'll catch anything across the way." He sighed. "I knew I should've upgraded the security."

"Why didn't you?"

"It was that or let a dog keep his leg." Sonny ruefully smiled. "I think with my heart, too."

"It's foolish." Gabriel returned his attention to the sad building. "Being practical is how you run a successful business." It was how he'd increased efficiency in their product development by ten percent, looking at a problem as though it were a puzzle to be solved.

"Maybe. Maybe that's why we're in this situation."

"Situation?"

Sonny dipped his head. "It doesn't matter. We're okay, the animals aren't hurt. The other stuff… I'm sure we'll push through. Like Leah says. That girl always thinks of something."

Gabriel studied the way the paint had stained the brick. "Would you sell?"

"Retire, you mean?" Sonny dragged in a breath, knuckled

his chest as though something hurt. "Time was, I'd have said I'd drop dead in this place."

"And now?"

Sonny didn't answer.

Gabriel thought of Leah. "You could sell it to her."

"I'd give it to her," Sonny corrected. "She's been here since she was fifteen. She's as much a part of this place as anyone. But it's a white elephant. It'll bleed her dry and then take more. I'd never pass over that burden."

Gabriel's business mind told him Sonny was right. Running a charitable organization like this required more money than any one person could supply. It took multiple deep pockets. "You need investors."

"We need a lot of things. Right now, we need to walk the dogs, feed the cats and get this mess cleaned up. Fortunately some of the guys from the music store next door, the bookshop across the street, they're volunteering hands. God knows we need 'em." Sonny clapped a hand on Gabriel's arm and then walked through the carpet of glass, battered sneakers crunching as he went.

Gabriel brooded. The human was right about one thing. Words were useless; action counted. And so, he bent for the broom he'd brought out with him. He surveyed the millions of tiny shards with a sigh. If he had full use of his magic, he could literally evaporate them all in the space of one second.

But he didn't. So, he dutifully bent and began sweeping. It was, he'd discovered, one of the only tasks he didn't suck at.

It took him the better part of an hour. He'd shed his coat, his tie, rolled up his sleeves and was rubbing the ache in the small of his back when Leah stepped out.

She stopped short. "Oh. I thought you'd gone."

He steadied the broom with one hand. "Why?"

"Because you left."

"The glass needed sweeping."

Her eyebrows lifted. "*You* swept up the glass?"

"It needed doing. I'm going to start on the paint."

She held up the bucket she was carrying. "Great minds." But she didn't come closer, feet shifting with edgy energy. "If you want to get inside, I can do this."

He didn't move. "It's cold. I can do it."

"I'm not fragile."

She was tense, body half angled away, but it was her eyes that tugged at him. Shielded. Not friendly, not seething. Nothing.

He'd finally pushed her away.

A sharp ache spasmed in his chest.

"Seriously," she said, still polite. "You've done your share. I can do this alone."

He should do what she said.

But he couldn't. "About this morning."

She blanched. "We don't have to…"

"No. We do." His skin was hot and he welcomed the breeze that kissed his exposed skin. And couldn't think of what to say.

At least thirty seconds passed before she shifted the bucket to her other hand. "Okay. Let's just—"

"I'm sorry." The words snapped out. Not exactly apologetic.

Her cautious face turned to him.

"I'm not…good with…people." Understatement. "I don't want you to be…" A pause as he searched for the words. "At odds with me."

Thoughts rolled through her eyes like a summer storm. She set the bucket down. "Look. Thanks for apologizing. I get it's not something you do and I appreciate it. But we keep hokey-pokeying and I'm tired of being in, out, in, out." As he struggled to understand what she meant, she tugged a curl in obvious frustration. "What I mean is you want to be left alone, and I think it's time I do what you want."

She was really conceding. No more sassy smiles. No more calling him Gabe or teasing him for being serious. No more blue eyes watching him or words intended to aggravate. No more human distraction.

This was what he'd wanted.

Panic, dark and thick, grabbed him by the throat. "No."

"No?"

"No," he said more firmly. He pushed away the voice screaming this was a mistake. "No more in and out." Too late, he realized that was probably not the best way to put it. He stared her down as her lips quivered.

She firmed them. "No more in and out, huh?"

He nodded. "I propose we be friends."

"We can't be friends, Gabriel."

"Why?"

"You just said so this morning."

"No, I didn't."

"Yes, you did."

"I said you were acting like we're friends."

If how fast she blinked was an indication of an impending eruption, he was about to have Mount Vesuvius on his hands.

He hurried on. "I told you. I'm not good at…this. But I want to be. Friends. Or friendly acquaintances, at least."

The pressure inside his chest relaxed as her lips curved.

"That sounds like Gabriel Goodnight," she said dryly. She pressed those same lips together and then sighed. In defeat. "And what do friendly acquaintances do?"

He gestured. "Clean the wall together?"

She rolled her eyes but bent to pick up the bucket. He crossed, taking it from her. Their fingers touched and his heart beat a little faster.

"Lead the way, friend."

Her light words relaxed the last of his tension and he stepped back.

"Gabe?"

He swung his gaze to her, narrowed at the nickname. He'd never let on how his heart gave a small jump at its return.

She held eye contact. "One more time and I'm done."

"Understood."

Yes, he understood. He understood that, even though it'd be smarter to let her back away, to distance himself, she'd become too essential for him to give up entirely.

He let her talk the first half hour as they scrubbed at the wall with sponges, then brushes, applying muscle to the paint that refused to lift. He didn't mind letting her voice wash over him, finding the rhythm unusually soothing.

They'd managed to get half the lettering down to a faint pink line when he said, "I spoke to Sonny."

She blew a curl out of her face as she bent to wet her brush. She'd bundled her hair into a rough, straggly ponytail. He couldn't say why he found it appealing. "Hmm?"

He told himself to stop looking at her butt as she bent over. "You need money."

"I told you that."

"You identified the problem," he allowed. "The next step is how to reach your objective. You make a plan."

"You sure you're not a robot?" She shook off the excess liquid and straightened. "Do you have a plan, or did you just want to rub my lack of one in my face?"

"Would I do that?"

She sent him an arch look.

"You need visibility," he said, returning to the point. "You need sympathy and awareness. At the bottom of it all, this is a charity, albeit for animals. What do charities do when they need more money?"

"You want me to go door-to door?"

"Host a gala," he corrected. "Invite the local businesses, ones that are good fits with the brand, the companies that could use the tax break and are looking to mask themselves as do-gooders. When we do a new product launch, we invite all the tastemakers, the press, even rivals to make as much noise as possible." That, at least, he'd been good at, organizing details and deploying his assistants to speak and cajole on his behalf. "You need to make some noise, draw people in."

She thoughtfully scrubbed the wall, back and forth. "A gala? Isn't that *too* upscale for what we are?"

"You want deep pockets; you need to go to their level. It would need to be a ticketed affair, a dinner paid per plate or an auction—but that would be harder as you would need to secure lots. A dinner, talks, maybe an appearance from some of the more well-behaved residents." He spared her a pointed lift of his eyebrow. "*Not* Chuck."

"You love him, really."

"Hmm." He played his hand over his brush, the bristles sharp against his skin. "What do you think?"

"I think it's a little out of my depth."

"You told me your family is part of Chicago's social scene." Surprise blinked through her eyes. "I did?"

It had been when she'd been needling him, dropping her own crumbs, little realizing he'd collected them to form his own impression. He didn't say that. "I would've thought, grow-ing up in a family that donate to charities and attend functions, you'd be planning events like this in your sleep."

"Maybe…if I hadn't been busy taking care of my mom. After that…" She shrugged. "Do you know none of her so-called society friends visited her or helped at all? A lot of them sneered at us behind her back. Oh, but when she got healthy again and was donating the Turner money, oh, then, it was all smiles and laughs and air-kisses." Her disgust was palpable. "I wasn't about to go into that world of fakes that rejected us. So, I looked for a job, real people. I only took my trust fund be-cause my mom said she'd wire money into my account every day if I didn't." She added on a grin, "But I got rid of it quick enough by investing in my own property and then proposing the bar to Emma and Tia."

He was unwillingly fascinated. "You could have drifted on the money." Most of the society witches he knew did just that, men and women.

"I prefer to work," she said simply. "Like you, Gabe."

The parallel took him aback, more because of how true it was. "I suppose."

"I bet most society women in New Orleans aren't like me," she prompted with a grin, inviting him to comment.

But he couldn't. Because nobody was like her. And to say that aloud felt like admitting too much.

"The worlds sound very similar," was all he said. Human or witch, society stayed society, apparently. Maybe they had more in common than he thought. How unsettling.

As if reading the edge on his face, Leah let the subject float away, returning to their original topic. "Anyway, that's why I'd be out of my depth. I've attended charity things, but organizing one sounds like juggling knives. Spending that money and having everything hinge on it? I could stab myself in the foot."

"I'll help." The words were so out of character that both she and he blinked in unison.

"*You* want to help *me* organize a charity gala?" Disbelief soaked through the words. "Why?"

He masked his uneasiness. "Goodnights happen to be excellent at organizing functions."

"Naturally." A smile played over her lips as she switched brush for sponge, only to fiddle with it. "You'd really help?"

He could assess, implement, better. That was what he did, what he'd done for years as he'd worked his way up through the departments at Goodnight's Remedies. If he were to apply logic to this, it made sense to demonstrate to the board how he'd gone above and beyond while he was here. It really benefited him in the end.

"I'll have to." He kept his tone matter-of-fact, someone superior granting a favor. "You clearly don't know what you're doing."

Her eyes narrowed. That was the only warning he got before the sponge she'd been toying with smacked him in the stomach. Water soaked through his waistcoat, then his shirt, as the weapon plopped to the ground.

His mouth parted in disbelief.

Teeth flashed, unrepentant. "Whoops."

She retrieved her brush, spun to the wall.

He didn't plan it. He didn't think. He simply levitated the sponge, dunked it and lobbed it at her back. Only she unexpectedly turned at the last minute. The wet sponge slopped against her chest, her squeal instant and shocked.

He absorbed the feedback as he watched the wet material cling to her skin. A hint of bra showed through the white tee. Black again. His head went fuzzy. Her breasts weren't big but they'd fit his hands.

"You—I—what the…" she spluttered.

"Your sponge," he said through the gravel in his throat. "You're welcome."

12

It wasn't easy corralling three dogs, two of which hated leashes with a passion, but Leah was a veteran. Rosie and Delilah stared at her as they waited outside Gabriel's apartment, Rosie's eyes soft pools of distressed brown, and Delilah's expressing a cold seething lick of betrayal. Louie merely sat at her feet, easygoing as always and pleased to be somewhere new.

They were all here and ready to plan a gala.

She and Gabriel had decided it was best kept a secret for now. Better to present the idea fully formed to Sonny, less likely then he'd protest it was too much trouble or too big a risk.

As if she didn't have a stake in the place, too. When she'd been young and burned out from caring for her mom, the animals had saved her. When she'd needed to feel accepted, like she was a part of something, it had been there. It was her place in a way nowhere else was, even the bar. She wasn't about to lose it without a fight.

She was lying low with her friends, as well. Not *not* telling them but steering clear. If they knew she was spending time with Gabriel outside of her regular shelter shifts, they'd play cockblockers.

Figure of speech, of course. She and Gabriel were only "friendly acquaintances."

Why was she smiling? He wasn't charming.

Case in point, when she'd suggested her place to start planning, Gabriel had overridden her, stating it'd be too small and his apartment much more suitable. This guy...

Still, she'd got the last laugh when she'd opted not to clarify her "place" was a house and instead insisted on bringing her dogs along. All of them.

The door opened on that note and the warlock himself made an appearance. And not in a suit.

She gaped. "You're in *jeans*."

Sardonic, he focused on her dogs. "Three."

"Very good. You get a gold star."

"You didn't say there were three."

"Didn't I?"

He eyed Rosie as she strained at the leash, desperate to show her adoration for the stranger. "Are they trained?"

"To do what?" Her grin was unrepentant as those fiercely green eyes slid her way. "They won't cause you any more hassle than I do."

"Hmm." Still, he stepped back, held the door for her as she and the others traipsed in.

Once he'd shut it behind them, she bent to unclip the leashes.

Rosie immediately hurtled to Gabriel, stopping at his feet and panting up at him, whining in despair when he didn't immediately coo over her.

"She wants you to pet her," Leah supplied.

"She can want all she likes." Gabriel sidestepped, flummoxed when Rosie matched him. He changed direction and she matched him again. "You're not going to win," he told her.

"Don't you know females always do?" Leah placed the leashes and her purse on one of the decorative tables Gabriel had in the short hall. Once her hands were free, she threaded fingers through her curls. She was pretty sure she looked like she'd been pulled into a hedge, tossed around, then thrust back out. Windy city and all.

After an amusing thirty seconds, Gabriel finally placed one precise pat on Rosie's head. The sprocker all but melted to the ground, flipping to her back and exposing her stomach.

Leah sniggered at the nonplussed expression on Gabriel's face.

Meanwhile, Delilah had had enough of investigating the living room furniture and circled back. She sniffed his feet—bare, Leah noticed with a small jolt—and then huffed as she made a beeline for the kitchen.

"Delilah isn't much for men," she explained, following her dog, making sure she wasn't getting into anything she shouldn't.

When she looked back, she caught Gabriel's hand rubbing the spaniel's tummy. Busted.

He pretended innocence as he rose, cheeks a little pink. "Drink?"

"Sure." She covertly checked him out as he walked by. "I can't believe you're not wearing a suit." And looking damn good out of one, too.

"I'm at home."

"I thought I'd be sipping hot chocolate in hell before you relaxed."

"I'm not so uptight."

She snorted. "Please. If I cranked you one more notch, you'd go off like an alarm clock."

"I don't know what that means."

"It means, you're uptight. But you do you," she added with a bright, quick smile. "As a friendly acquaintance, I think it's endearing." And so were the jeans that hugged his muscular ass. God, she'd thought him annoyingly hot in his vest and shirt-sleeves, but seeing this together man unbuttoned?

Undeniable lust shivered over her skin and she stepped back

in reaction. Louie yelped and she bent, immediately fussing. "Sorry, Lou."

She took a moment, breathing out the lust, breathing in a reality check. So, he was hot. And he'd apologized. And helped clean the shelter. So, what? It wasn't like anything more could happen.

Or would happen. He'd never really given her any indication he thought of her that way. And wasn't that a kick in the ass?

"Introductions," she chirped, puncturing the disappointment before it could inflate. "The sprocker acting like she's been struck by cupid's arrow is Rosie. The dachshund who's getting in your garbage by the sounds of it—" she winced at the clattering sound "—is Delilah. And this," she stroked a hand over Louie's soft ears, "is Louie."

"The calm one."

"Always. He was found wandering on the streets with a bad eye infection. We don't really know what his background is, but he's a sweetheart."

"You rescued him."

"He bonded with me pretty immediately and I couldn't bear to leave him. He's never been trouble; all he wants is love. They all do."

"You rescued all three?"

She nodded. "I have two cats as well."

"You didn't think to bring them?"

She recognized the dry thread of humor, matched it. "Next time."

He watched the small cavalier snuggle into her leg. "You like caring for things."

"I've had lots of practice."

His eyes met hers. Something rippled between them, catching in her chest.

A crash sounded from behind the breakfast bar and she reacted on instinct, bursting upward and hurtling across the kitchen. "Delilah," she reprimanded. "No!"

Having followed her around the counter, Gabriel stared at the recycling littering the floor. "I see why she was surrendered."

"Ha. Ha." Leah shooed the little dog and bent to clean up. Gabriel stooped to help.

"I thought we'd have dinner first," he said, offhandedly.

The can she'd picked up slipped free, bounced and rolled away. She went after it, praying for some sense. *Not a date, Leah.* "Cool. I could eat."

He righted the recycling bin. "I thought we'd order in."

"You don't like to cook?" She glanced at the twelve toasters. "Kinda seems like you have a thing for toast, at least."

"Those are defective."

A detail caught her eye. Huh. "You know you have to plug them in."

He stopped what he was doing. "Excuse me?"

She gestured. "The toasters."

Seconds passed before he answered, a hint of chagrin entering his voice. "Of course I know."

Leah tossed the last can into the bin and hid her amusement. "How can you not know about how toasters work?"

Did witches and warlocks use magic for all their cooking? It seemed a bit lazy.

He paused, tipping his head to the side, a sudden intense look making her go still. He was looking at her like...she should know why. Which, of course, she did—but did he?

The question of the week.

She gave them both an out, far from ready to broach the subject. "Poor little rich boy?"

His slight huff of humor eased the tension. "Something like that." He held out his hand to help her up.

She met his gaze as she gripped it. Stupid to feel breathless, stupid that his skin sliding over hers made her think dark, sweaty thoughts.

His jaw flexed as he exerted pressure, bringing her up to him. Her throat felt thick. She stood, still holding his hand.

It held for three seconds. Five.

"*I couldn't take it any longer.*"

Their hands jerked apart at the interruption, both lurching back, Gabriel into the breakfast bar, Leah slamming into the cupboards. Her cheeks were steaming as she tore her gaze from Gabriel to the source of the interruption.

The woman stood on the other side of the counter. Older by about twenty years or so, if Leah had to guess, dressed in a long paisley dress, her hair was dark blond, tucked up in an intricately braided bun. Crystals swung at her ears as she waved a hand.

"I don't care if you're not supposed to use magic, they said nothing about me—oh!" She stilled as she spotted Leah. Brown eyes studied her and Gabriel, how close they were. "Am I... interrupting?"

Leah didn't dare breathe. What was she supposed to do, now that magic had been mentioned? What would a regular human do? Gabriel didn't look alarmed—but when did he ever? The earth could be imploding and he'd only glower at the inconvenience.

More evidence into the *he knows* column. She should probably worry about that more than she was.

"Mrs. Q." The strong affection in his voice had Leah's lips parting in surprise. "I told you I was fine."

The woman didn't move her attention from Leah.

She took that as her cue, awkwardly lifting a hand in a semi-wave. "Hi. I'm Leah."

"*Oh.*" The sound was knowing, as was the look the older woman slid to Gabriel.

Leah would do many depraved things to know what he'd said

about her behind closed doors. She choked down the desperate curiosity, just barely. "Gonna make introductions, Gabe?"

"*Gabe?*"

Gabriel ignored the woman's choked question, though he did link his fingers at the base of his spine. "Leah, Kate Quinlan."

Obviously amused, she focused on Leah. "You can call me Mrs. Q, dear. Everyone does. I'm Gabriel's housekeeper." Her accent was British, like his, warm and pleasant to the ear.

"I didn't realize you'd hired someone."

"Not here. In New Orleans. I—" She paused, selected her next words with care. "I...took a flight to bring Gabriel some casseroles. Do some general housekeeping."

Leah ran her tongue over her teeth before tucking it in her cheek. "That's very dedicated of you."

"Oh, well, I've been his housekeeper since he was a little boy running naked on the grounds of the manor."

Gabriel put a hand to his forehead, muttering under his breath.

Leah grinned. Her smile only spread when Mrs. Q clocked her dogs and swooped in, kissing them all and fussing like an old friend.

Leah went with impulse. "How about you join us for dinner? I'd love to hear more about how this one came to be *the* Gabriel Goodnight."

"I have so many stories!"

"Don't you have to catch your flight back?" Gabriel said between gritted teeth.

Mrs. Q waved that away and clucked into the kitchen. "Not at all. I'll get dinner on if you open some wine." She opened the fridge, which was fully stocked. "And you can tell me all about yourself, Leah."

"Mrs. Q..."

"Don't sass me, boy. Now, you find a decent bottle of wine— and no pranks. Used to be a terrible prankster."

"When I was thirteen," he grumbled, on his way to the cabinets to, presumably, find a bottle of wine.

Absolutely fascinated, Leah leaned her hips against the cupboards. "Gabriel played pranks?"

"For most of his young life. He loved to play with people."

"And you told me you didn't play."

Gabriel sent her a look. "When did I say that?"

"When—" they'd been on the balcony.

He lifted his eyebrows. Patient as ever. Like a cat with a mouse.

Careful. "I can't remember."

Liar, his eyes seemed to mock.

She bit down on a shiver, swinging to his housekeeper like a life raft. "So. Tell me *all* about the early Goodnight years."

Gabriel's sigh punctuated Mrs. Q's wink.

They had the most amazing pork chops Leah had ever tasted. Bursting with questions about whether Mrs. Q used witchery in her cooking, Leah added them to her ever-evolving list to ask Emma and Tia. Maybe this time they'd open up and answer.

Mrs. Q was a font of information otherwise, keeping them entertained with stories from Gabriel's childhood in England. He'd apparently gotten into one scrape after another, right up until a definite point neither overtly mentioned, but which Leah knew had to be when his parents had died. Before and after. There'd been a line drawn.

She couldn't help but feel for him, for the boy of eighteen who'd suddenly lost everything, including his childhood. How had they died? She had a feeling that detail was significant, but it wasn't like she could blurt out the question. She'd prodded that sore area without thinking too many times.

Part of her also noted that while Mrs. Q featured in the stories, his parents always seemed to have been away on some trip. Great humanitarians etc., but hadn't they spent any time with their son? Maybe that was selective storytelling—and it was none of her business. But still...

Anyway, she was happy to keep the conversation light, enjoying the dynamic between housekeeper and employee, which ran more like aunt to nephew. It was a new side to Gabriel, one that unfortunately was devastatingly attractive to her.

When the housekeeper "left for her flight," she pulled Leah into a hug. "You don't be a stranger," she announced, squeezing the breath out of Leah's body. "Gabriel, when you're next in New Orleans, you bring this one and I'll give her a cooking lesson in our kitchen."

Leah glowed under the unsaid compliment, the inclusion in that invitation. At least until Gabriel flatly stated, "She won't be coming to New Orleans. We're only working together."

Well. The happy drained from Leah as effectively as if he'd stabbed her with a needle. So much for friendly acquaintances.

She kept up the front until Mrs. Q left. The minute the door closed behind the older woman, though, Gabriel pounced. "You're annoyed. With me."

She tried to play it off. "I'm always annoyed with you, Gabe."

A muscle moved in his jaw as he stopped in front of her. "I told you, I'm not good at this. People. If you don't tell me what I did, I can't be sure I won't do it again."

"Why would that bother you?"

"We're...friends." The way he struggled with the word both amused and frustrated her.

Okay. Fine. She busied herself by getting her wine from the counter, nudging Rosie away from the plates. "You didn't say that to Mrs. Q."

Inside, the old insecurities shivered to life. *Not good enough to be invited in.*

It was childish to still feel like this, she knew, especially as she also knew the line she walked was a dangerous one. Witch and human, never the twain shall meet. She shouldn't feel pushed out because he'd reinforced that. But she did.

"It's not you." Out of the corner of her eye, she saw him smooth a hand down the center of his chest, where his tie usually was. "Mrs. Q is a matchmaker. If I'd claimed a friendship with you, she'd have been searching for a wedding gift before the end of the week."

Leah shrugged. "It's no big deal."

"I don't have many…friends." His accent hit the last word hard, locks of black hair slipping across his forehead as he shook it in annoyance. "She'd have taken that as a sign."

The silence was short but tense, all but pounding in her ears. "Which it's not," she confirmed. His gaze returned to weigh heavy on her face.

Rosie bounced in, spinning in a circle and plopping her butt on the floor at Gabriel's feet. Despite his apparent disinterest, her dogs seemed to have fallen under his spell in a finger snap. A recurring theme.

She gave in. "I've got some chews in my purse. Let me get them and we can get down to business."

13

Part of Leah had questioned how much the entitled warlock could know about organizing a charity dinner, but as an hour spun away under the finer details of planning, she had to readjust her expectations.

She should've known better; Gabriel was all about organization. He insisted they make a plan, a list of things they had to do now—approaching sponsors, vendors, venues—before moving on to how much money she wanted to raise and when by. She could see him as CEO of his company now, at the helm, moving the chess pieces as he willed.

Any simmering attraction was quickly buried under the need to make this work. They'd decided on a black-tie charity dinner where guests would pay $500 a plate. Leah knew that was on the lower end of the scale, but it still made her stomach cramp. What if they couldn't convince sponsors to buy in or guests to buy a plate?

Gabriel steamrollered over her hesitancy, clearly comfortable in this environment. It was yet another new side, the business mogul, and one that suited him.

"You're good at this," she commented when he was flicking through potential venues on a laptop, checking availability for the next month or so. She'd doubted they could pull this off, especially so soon, but he'd brushed her off with his usual imperious Goodnight explanations. Who was she to question a Goodnight?

She'd curled up on the other side of Louie, who'd finished his chew a while ago and now snored contentedly. The other two were sprawled on the floor in front of the lit fireplace.

She rested her arm along the back of the couch. "Which makes me ask why you're having to pass a test to get your company. It's clearly more 'you' than mopping pens or slinging drinks."

He shifted to her. "Tia and Emmaline didn't tell you?" Something lurked behind the question.

She considered her words, selected them carefully. "They told me something about needing to prove yourself?"

The fire snapped in the fireplace. He stared at her, long and hard enough that the ground beneath her started to crumble.

Then he glanced down at Louie. "Yes. Proving to the board that I can do the impossible."

Leah knew what he meant. Be around humans. But all she said was, "Manual labor."

"Something like that."

She tapped her hand against the back of the couch. Her fingernails were a bright orange today and out of place against the gray material. "It's very admirable you'd go through so much for your family."

His face was always so serious. He'd mirrored her, one strong arm braced on the line of the couch. Their fingers didn't touch, but if she moved, they could.

"It was my father's request," he said in a low voice.

"I… But I thought your dad was…"

"He is. But his last wishes were in his will, and if I want to be his successor, these are the conditions."

"So, you had no choice over it?"

His jaw tensed. Abruptly he pushed up, striding over to the window. He stood there, framed by the darkness. He looked, she reflected with a clutch in her heart, very alone.

"This company," he said, his voice a mere wisp of sound, "was their entire life's work. They dedicated themselves to it, died for it. A choice?" He continued to gaze into the night. "No, there was no choice."

Gabriel said nothing else, but Leah heard everything in the silence.

She wet her lips, debating. When she gave in and went to him, she didn't look anywhere but out at the night. "They'd be proud of you."

He let out a sound, something between a sigh and a laugh. "This from the woman who constantly berates me."

"That's different. You need to be brought down a peg or two."

"Or five?"

"Or six. But that doesn't mean they wouldn't be proud of your choice to leave everything you know, your…way of life," she said, treading carefully. "Just to fulfill their last wish."

Now those eyes she found so breathtaking found hers. "You don't ascribe to the opinion I'm only after power? I know Tia will have said it. Many will."

"Maybe." Humor surfaced. "But…no. I don't think that."

"Why?"

She gave a light shrug. "Call it a gut feeling."

"Feelings can be wrong."

Newsflash. The feelings flowing through her were all kinds of wrong. Still, she didn't move away. "C'mon, you clearly hate it here. Away from everyone—away from your sister. You told me you miss her. Power-hungry people don't care about that."

"That's naïve." A fine thread of hesitation spun out. "But… she is a large part of the reason I'm here."

What would that be like, she wondered, tracing his face. To be one of the few people Gabriel Goodnight cared for? "Do you talk while you're here?"

"Often."

"You're close." She heard the wistful note in her own voice.

"Yes. It's just us two." He twisted toward her, mirroring again. "You don't have a sibling?"

She shook her head, then paused. "Well, my dad has another daughter and son by his second marriage, but we don't really hang out."

"Why?"

"They're not...we're not family. It's awkward. I don't really see my dad much, not enough to claim them as brother and sister. He calls every few months, we endure conversation until the next time." She passed a hand through her curls, discomfort rolling through her. "It's just me and my mom. And now her new husband."

He was fully focused on her and she wasn't sure she enjoyed it. "She's recently wed?"

"Sort of. They're on an extended honeymoon, so they've been traveling for a while."

"You don't like him."

"What? No." She rejected that with a wave of her hand. "I mean, yes. He's great for her. They're a good match."

"And now you're alone."

"I have my babies," she countered, not liking the hitch the words put into her voice. "I have Tia and Emma. My housemate, Peggy. And my mom will come back at some point. We've always been close."

"You said your father left her."

She didn't like this topic. "How about some coffee?" When she went to walk away, he caught her hand.

"I'm sorry." Sincerity rang in the words. "I didn't mean to upset you."

"You didn't. Yes, he left her, us." She didn't move her gaze away from their hands. Such a simple, strong support. "It was hard, but we got over it. We had each other."

"You looked after her when it first happened. You mentioned it," he explained at her surprised glance.

"Yes."

"How old?"

"Fifteen."

He was quiet, the only sound the soft snores of the dogs and the crackle of the fire.

His silence prompted her to speak. "I didn't mind stepping up. She needed me and I like being useful, always have. I don't hold it against her."

"How long?"

Too long. In her mind, Leah's mind picked over the memories of pleading with her mom to open the door, to get out of bed, to be with her. Shut out in more ways than one. "A while."

When he looked at her like that, it felt like he could see the reasons why, what prompted her to crave people, their voices, their smiles, their friendship.

Always feeling like she was on the other side of that door, pleading to get in.

She swallowed. "In a way, she led me to the shelter. Having that place, my place, to go when everything felt…too much? It would've been a lot harder without it."

More silence wove between them, a tapestry of unsaid things and fast beats of her heart as he didn't let go of her hand and she didn't let go of his. It was too much, the taunt of a future she couldn't have.

"Listen to me, playing the violin for you." She saw his confusion at the idiom, motored past it. "Families are complicated. You'd know that, right? Doesn't mean we have to focus on the bad stuff."

His thoughts were hidden behind his usual veil. "You confuse me."

"I know."

The green of his eyes was startling in the low light, hypnotizing as he stepped closer. Close enough she had to tip her head back to keep eye contact and suddenly that became the most important thing. That and the slow swish of his thumb against her hand.

"I'll help you save your place, Leah." His voice, the lovely low, liquid tone, did things to her. Goose bumps spread up her arm from that rasp of his thumb.

"I knew you liked Chuck," she teased through the wild drumming of her pulse.

His gaze skimmed her face, settled for a brief, heart-stopping, moment on her lips. "I don't like anyone."

"Goodnights have more important things to do?"

"Exactly."

"It's better to be lonely?"

"It's better to be alone," he murmured.

She gazed up at him, barely thinking it through as she let the words go. "You can be alone with me."

He didn't answer; she wasn't sure she expected him to. In the silence, her skin exploded with heat, her knees all but melting under the force as he tightened his hand on hers. And tugged.

Helpless, she went where he commanded, so close now that their feet brushed. He was taller than her, the disparity in their heights causing a raw darkness to twist in her belly. The memory of waking up tangled with him that morning was a beat in her veins. How his hands had been on her bare skin. How he'd pressed his face into the sensitive skin of her throat.

For the first time in her life, words abandoned her, her bottomless energy all directed into quelling the desire that pulsed like a living thing inside her. Her legs clamped together where it beat the hardest.

Sparks danced in her blood, in her vision.

Actual sparks, she realized, with a jolt. Magical sparks.

Gabriel had conjured magic.

She immediately dropped her gaze, pretending not to have seen the floating specks of magic. Firework sparks.

But he'd seen. And knew she had, too.

He dropped her hand, his chest laboring with the same breath she dragged into her lungs. They both stared at each other as the sparks gradually vanished.

She'd only seen sparks a couple times, only when Kole or Tia had been mad about something. This hadn't been anger, but it had been something.

Something she wasn't supposed to have witnessed.

They both stepped away as if they'd choreographed the movement.

"I, ah, should get going." Her voice was a rasp, lust playing with it. "Thanks for your help."

He nodded but said nothing as it took her a good five minutes to gather her dogs up. He had, however, ordered her a town car, she realized when she got downstairs and the driver called her name. She didn't know what to read into that, if she should.

She settled back into the buttery leather and rubbed her face with her hands as the car pulled smoothly away.

They'd crossed a line tonight. And tomorrow they'd have to face the consequences.

After the upheaval of the last few weeks, it felt good to be in the New Orleans office at Goodnight's Remedies. Familiar, and a solid reminder of why he was putting himself through it all. He'd intended to check in with August anyway, but after the night before, Gabriel had needed to get out of Chicago. Find his normal. Which was *not* hanging out with human men at bars or teasing human women, throwing himself into their problems to make the shadow of worry clear from their eyes. Or almost tasting them.

He muttered a curse and August turned from the coffee bar set up in the corner of his office with a quizzical look. "Did you say something?" He proffered the sweet, black coffee he knew Gabriel preferred.

"Nothing important."

His uncle relaxed on the edge of his desk, as ruthlessly organized as Gabriel's own. August had opted for espresso and he sipped it, his magic automatically making it drinking temperature.

Considering his own magic was not fully under his control, Gabriel settled in to wait for the steaming liquid in his mug to cool.

"You look tired," August observed. "Is that why you asked me to conjure the portal? You're not doing well?"

"I am, actually." Which surprised him as much as it clearly did August. "I'm not saying I've developed a burning passion for the work, but I'm learning."

"Is working with humans still causing you uneasiness?"

Not in the way his uncle meant.

Holy hell, he'd almost given in to temptation and kissed Leah last night. If he was honest, if those telltale green lights hadn't sparked into existence, he'd have been swallowed whole by the gut-wrenching desire. Willingly.

Goddess. He wanted to portal to the Sahara, bury his head in the desert sands and scream. Where to begin?

For one, if Leah was a witch and truly understood what those sparks meant, he'd have been mortified. Magical manifestation was something that happened in your teenage years, at least as far as passion went. Anger was allowed, even became a display, like a cobra flaring its hood. But softer emotions like desire?

He blamed the magical binding. His control wasn't at its peak.

The second, more pressing concern was that he now knew who had been with him on that balcony all those weeks ago.

You can be alone with me.

The phrase had slid into place like a missing puzzle piece. Bits and pieces of conversation had all added up to give him the full picture, and it made him sick with dread. Not because she'd been his mystery witch, but because she'd been on that balcony at all. Bad enough to know about witches. By infiltrating their society as she had, she could've courted far worse punishment if she'd been discovered.

Punishment.

His stomach hurt, dark emotions squeezing his chest tight enough to crush his ribs. Every time he thought of it, he couldn't catch a breath. What had Emmaline and Tia been thinking, allowing her to go? Putting herself in danger for—what? The thrill? The impulse to track Leah down, demand answers, to shake some common sense into her, was overwhelming.

He couldn't deal. So, for now, he wrestled it into a box, hid it away. He was good at that.

"I've found it…easier than I thought," Gabriel answered his uncle, mystified that the words were true. "I've even decided to expand my interests and help plan a charity gala for the shelter. We have access to an array of business contacts all over the country that might help, and it's good for the company to put our stamp of approval on a charitable event." All true, but not why he'd offered to help.

August smiled. "Well. That's fine, son. I'm pleased." He cleared his throat. "It's what your father would've wanted."

Gabriel jerked his chin in a nod.

"Perhaps he knew better than all of us." August stood, rounded his desk to sit in his leather chair. It creaked as he leaned back, steepled his hands. His espresso hovered in mid-air. "Maybe immersing yourself fully was the only way to move forward."

Guilt sat sickly sweet in Gabriel's throat. As if he could forget for even a second that his parents had died because they were determined to bring magic, in some small way, to human lives.

Except…he couldn't paint with his bitter brush as easily as he once had.

Before, he'd have said that humans brought nothing but pain. While humans might selfishly benefit from magic, they couldn't give anything back, and their ignorance could only invite danger.

But now…his time in Chicago had tweaked his perspective. He'd never said witches were good, humans were bad. Goddess knew and *he* knew that witches in society could be cutthroat for a slight as simple as ignoring an invitation. And humans could also be selfish and weak. He'd always thought those weaknesses could only implode, like volatile ingredients in a potion. Now he'd begun to consider what each could bring to the other.

Leah didn't have magic, but she demonstrated strength and intelligence, even correcting some of his ideas for the gala, improving on them. Before, he'd been too swayed by childish fear to really look at the impact their human employees were having on each aspect of the company, but he'd stayed up late all this week reading reports he'd had sent over. The results were good. That slight change of perspective humans could offer was often the key to everything.

He wasn't saying he was over his parents' deaths, he didn't know if he ever would be. But holding onto the grudge was like trying to hold wet soap in his hands.

His mind flashed to another memory, a soapy sponge, white T-shirt material. Black lace.

"Gabriel?"

He blinked as his uncle's concern pulled him back to the sunlit office. "It's still an adjustment," he said, sipping the black coffee and wincing at the burn. "But I'm abiding by the board and my father's wishes and throwing myself into it."

"About that." If bad news had a face, it would have been August's. His espresso floated back down to the desk. "I'm afraid not everyone on the board believes you *are* giving your all."

Gabriel stopped moving. "I live in an apartment and spend my days cleaning out animal pens. How exactly am I not giving my all?"

"Some members question if you're still relying on magic too much."

He deliberately placed his coffee on the desk. "Wasn't that the point of the binding, the feedback loop? So I didn't use too much magic?"

"You don't need to convince me, nephew. I know you're doing your best."

And his best still wasn't good enough.

Gabriel slid his mask on before any of the stinging pain leaked through. "What do they propose? That I be stripped of magic completely?" As the words left him, dread curled tight in his belly, poisoning everything it touched.

"No." August sounded appalled at the idea, and Gabriel's taut muscles eased. "No. But they want to assign a...what you'd call a minder, of sorts, to drop in, check up on you."

He shot up in his seat. "*No*."

The vehemence stunned both of them.

August blinked. "No?"

Gabriel didn't want a minder watching him, judging, seeing too much. Seeing...everything. Seeing *Leah*. "I don't see why I should be subjected to such a humiliation."

"As I said, they want reassurance." August shook his head in disgust as he spread his hands on the desk. "I argued, my boy, argued until I turned blue, but the majority wouldn't be moved. It'll only be a few sporadic visits." He rolled his eyes upward and muttered something unflattering about the naysayers.

Gabriel gave in. "Who?"

"Will," August said, naming his longtime PA. "I've ordered him to be as unobtrusive as possible."

Even with that assurance, the humiliation bubbled and burned. "What next, Uncle?" Gabriel's voice was bitter. "Will they all come on a field trip to watch me make a fool of myself?"

"Think of it as one more stepping stone. One more hurdle."

Unbelievable. He'd come to New Orleans searching for relief and it'd twisted around and bitten him. One more hurdle. He felt like he was already running a steeplechase.

But what could he say?

Gabriel gritted his teeth. "Very well."

14

*L*eah slid Emma a look as they packed folders for potential sponsors. Her friend had returned from Brazil that morning, hopping a portal as she and Bastian often did. The Brazilian sun had given Emma's skin a glow, or maybe that was just what being in love did. Or all the sex.

Don't think about sex, she told herself in a tone that would've had her dogs quaking. As it was, they'd disappeared to the backyard to take advantage of the April sun. Emma had placed a protective barrier around Leah's property when she'd moved in, so she didn't worry anyone would get in or they'd get out.

Instead, she scratched Sylvie as the cat purred and lay across her lap. Ralph, as usual, kept to the shadows. Even now, she spied two amber eyes gleaming behind the TV cabinet.

It had been a few days since That Night and Leah couldn't think about it without going crazy with questions about what it meant—or how Gabriel Goodnight might kiss. A mystery it seemed she was doomed never to solve.

In any case, she'd devoted herself to the gala as the ultimate distraction. Faced with facts and figures—and even better, Leah's stubbornness—Sonny had had no choice but to say yes to their gala idea. She'd sensed the worry behind his smile, that they'd be worse off after spending their limited funds on this rather than repairs, but he'd agreed to try.

The next steps were simple: arrange meetings with prospective sponsors, go armed with a folder that included ballpark numbers and budgets, as well as basic information about the shelter and some of the residents' profiles. The animals were the real linchpin; the strings Leah wanted to tug weren't just purse ones. And she wasn't above using her family name to sweeten the deal, even if crawling back to her mother's old crowd stung her pride.

But she couldn't concentrate on stuffing packets when the truth of That Night was trembling on the tip of her tongue. She'd never kept a secret from her friends until Gabriel, but she knew they'd react poorly if she brought it up. The tug-of-war was killing her.

"I have to tell you something," she blurted out ten minutes later. But when Emma looked at her in question, her lily-livered ass bailed. "Um… I love your ring."

Emma glanced at the engagement band. "I know."

"It's shiny."

"Yep."

"Emma?"

"Hmm?"

"That wasn't it."

"I figured."

Leah blew out a breath. "I just…wanted to tell you that…" Shit. She faltered again. "Gabriel's involved in this. The campaign. It was his idea." There. Getting closer.

"He came up with the gala?" Emma's tone fell between wary and intrigued.

"I guess he felt bad for us. Sonny. And you know he can't resist showing how superior he is." Leah winced at the unfairness of the statement, adding, "Though I think he actually does want to help."

"Gabriel Goodnight wants to help you."

Leah shrugged. "Me. The shelter. Everyone."

"Uh-huh." The papers slid away from Leah with a wave of Emma's hand. "Leah."

"Yes?"

"Gabriel Goodnight doesn't *do* helping others."

"How would you know? You haven't socialized with him for eight years."

Emma's mouth opened, closed. "I know his reputation. *And* what I saw of him when he worked at the bar."

Leah waved that away. "He can be an ass," she agreed, meaning it. "But he's also sweet. Kind of. In his own way."

"Holy mother." Emma gawked at her. "You *like* him."

Leah shifted, edgy. "It's hard to define. He's not definable. We're not definable."

"You're a 'we'?" Emma looked pained, like she'd been told she'd have to deal with her bitch of a mother for an hour. "Is this because he's a warlock? Because, honestly, Leah, they're not worth the hassle."

"Says the woman engaged to one."

"After a *lot* of hassle. And I'm sister to many. I know of what I speak."

Leah grinned fondly. "How is my favorite brother?" She hadn't seen Kole in weeks.

"He'd faint if I told you you were crushing on Gabriel Goodnight," Emma emphasized. "And then he'd storm through a portal so he could tell you to your face all of the things that could go wrong with you crushing on Gabriel Goodnight."

"Why do you keep saying his whole name?"

"Because he's *Gabriel Goodnight*."

Unwillingly amused, Leah patted her hand. "Okay. And no, it's not because he's a warlock." She couldn't deny the curiosity, the years of pent-up fantasy. But he could be such a dick. She felt sure that would offset any novelty.

And…Gabriel was more than just "a warlock." Maybe it was his limited powers, but she didn't see that when she looked at him. For the first time, she didn't care that he might be able to answer all her questions about the witch world, and then some. All she thought about was *him*. The man, not the magic.

"You're not telling me something." Emma's eyes narrowed as she peered at her. "Something's happened."

If there'd been a brown bag around, Leah might have hyperventilated. *Shit.* Her friend was way too observant. "What would have happened?" Her voice went up an octave.

"I don't know." Emma's brows knit, confused. "He's always dated legacies. I've never seen him stoop to a commoner before."

"Gee, thanks." Leah rolled the word around. "Legacies?"

"Strong magical families, like Bastian and Tia. Each parent sacrifices a small part of their magic to fuel their child. They're coveted." Emma flicked that off as if she hadn't just confirmed Gabriel had been considered an object all his life. No wonder he didn't trust anybody.

"That doesn't matter right now," her friend continued, scowling. "You've got secret eyes. Something's happened and you're going to tell me what."

Leah grazed her bottom lip with her teeth, debating. "Okay," she said, taking a breath to ease the chokehold nerves had on her throat. "Something *almost* happened."

Emma's face froze.

"Almost." Leah reached out, poked Emma's knee. "Stop overreacting."

It took five seconds for her friend to rearrange her face into something that resembled neutral. "Okay. Tell me. I'm here to listen."

Amusement bullied in, helped pave the way. Still, she had

to take another breath. At least she was getting a lot of oxygen. "A few nights ago," Leah began, "I was at his apartment to talk about all this." She gestured at the folders. "We started talking about other stuff, and we were standing by the window, close, and maybe it was the fireplace or the low light or just how green his eyes are—seriously, how unfairly gorgeous are his eyes? But whatever, we were close and we—"

"You *kissed*?" Emma shrieked, sounding like her teenage sister.

Her shriek brought forth the hounds, claws skittering over the kitchen floor.

Leah shook her head vigorously as the dogs bolted in. "No. But…" *He knows I know about magic*, she finished internally. He had to know, he'd seen that she'd seen. And nothing. No witches, no punishment, no High Family. He'd kept it to himself.

Why?

For her? Or because it was practical, because he needed to finish his time at the shelter without disruption?

She couldn't ask her friend that, though. Emma would lose her shit.

So, she ended with another truth. "I think I wanted to."

"Okay." Emma ignored Louie as he clambered onto her knee, Rosie's nose as she pressed against her. "Okay. Okay. Okay," she repeated one final time. "So, you and Gabriel Goodnight almost kissed." She did fine until the end, when the words emerged as a squeak. Then gave up. "You want to kiss *Gabriel Goodnight*?"

"It can't be *that* unbelievable."

"I don't think you realize. He's never approved of bringing humans into our world. He blames them for his parents' deaths."

Something dark flared in the pit of Leah's stomach, a taste surging up her throat. "What?"

Emma laid a hand on Louie's soft fur. "I don't know all the details, but there was some kind of tragedy overseas. His parents were always gone, trialing new medicines and the like. I think I saw them twice my whole childhood."

That's what Leah had picked up from Mrs. Q. She asked the question she hadn't been able to ask with Gabriel sitting next to her. "Did Gabriel and his sister travel with them?"

"No. They used to leave Gabriel with their housekeeper in England, and then when Amelia, his sister, came along, his uncle stepped in to help Gabriel look after her. He'd have been around seventeen, eighteen, I think?" She shook her head, dismissing that.

Leah didn't want to dismiss it. They hadn't taken him with them. He'd been left alone. Always alone.

"Anyway, something happened when they were traveling, and they died. Some kind of raid, or attack? And because they couldn't use magic in front of humans, they got killed. I remember everyone in society was in shock for weeks. Witches aren't immortal, but we're damn well long-lived. That his parents died so young freaked out a lot of people."

"So, humans killed his parents?" Leah struggled with dismay.

"Yes. And he's always held it as a barrier against integrating with humans. Irrational, but that's Gabriel Goodnight."

She didn't know what to say, what to think. Yeah, it was irrational, but emotions were. She wanted to talk to him, to understand. To see if he still felt that way.

Emma was staring at her expectantly, as if Leah would suddenly acknowledge how weird it all was and make the cross sign against him.

Leah let her shoulder lift and fall, helpless. "He's got me, Emma."

"Even though there can't be any future?"

A direct hit. And still, despite that... "Yeah."

"Tia's going to kill us both." Emma's voice was mournful. "I thought you hated him."

"There's a thin line between attraction and hate and apparently that line is a dog leash. He told me he was going to help save my place, Em. He stood there, all dark and unsmiling and told me he was going to help save *my place*."

Emma sighed. "I'm surprised you didn't just throw yourself at him."

Truthfully, so was Leah.

Gabriel stared at the dog.

Chuck stared back.

"I'm not throwing that thing," he informed the Labrador. The grotty chewed-up tennis ball had been spat at his feet after Chuck had ignored all Gabriel's attempts at recall and dug up the ball instead.

Chuck's tail swept across the yard, back and forth through the dirt.

Gabriel firmed his jaw and his resolve. "I'd probably get a human disease from touching it."

Brown eyes peered at him, full of love.

"It's not playtime. We're here to work." Not that any training seemed to be getting through Chuck's unbelievably thick brain. "Now I want you to sit here, *sit*, and I'm going over there." So saying, Gabriel walked a short distance away. When he turned around, Chuck stopped obediently at his feet and spat the ball out again.

Gabriel pinched the bridge of his nose. Why was it his lot in this city to be surrounded by willful individuals, animal or human?

"You'll find I'm more stubborn than you," he told the dog. "I've had to be." If he was any less stubborn, he wouldn't be on tenterhooks, waiting for his uncle's PA to make a surprise appearance. He'd have thrown in the towel.

Chuck edged forward, plopped his butt on the floor. He pushed his big head under Gabriel's palm. Gabriel stroked the soft fur absently, mind turning to the more immediate problem.

In a word: Leah.

A few days had passed and neither of them had brought up the almost-kiss—that, or the display of magic he knew she'd seen. Now they both knew she knew. That truth was a heavy weight between them whenever they were in the same room. So, like any mature male, he'd made a point to avoid her as much as he could.

What was there to say?

Better that they play pretend, he thought with a grimace. That Leah wasn't a grenade with the pin half-pulled.

Even that wasn't enough to stop the *what ifs* from plaguing him.

What if he hadn't manifested magic?

What if he'd kissed her?

"She's trouble," he said, the words snatched by the breeze.

Chuck snuffled his leg, leaving a trail of slobber on the jeans he'd finally broken down and worn.

He didn't have the heart to chastise the dog. Instead, he conjured a large biscuit, barely registering the feedback as it shocked his blood, and spent a painstaking five minutes convincing Chuck to lie down.

When the dog finally rolled to his back with his legs crooked in the air, the victory Gabriel felt was unmatched. He tossed the biscuit high in the air and watched with amusement as Chuck gained his paws and leaped, teeth snapping.

"We'll get there," Gabriel told him, ridiculously proud, and slapped his thigh. "Come, Chuck. Heel."

He walked into the shelter with the dog glued to his hip. Then Chuck bolted, his body slamming Gabriel's legs so hard he had to slap a hand against the wall for balance.

He winced at the sound of Chuck's enthusiastic barks as he found the cat pens. A multitude of hisses and indignant meows ripped the air and while Gabriel wouldn't say he hurried to catch up, he definitely moved at an accelerated pace.

He conjured a leash with another wince on the run—uh, fast walk—and faced off with Chuck in the cat enclosures. The Labrador shouldn't look giddy but he did, eyes bright with excitement, his whole body wriggling. When he saw Gabriel, he woofed with delight.

"Not playtime," Gabriel said firmly. Desperately. "Come."

He did not. By the time Gabriel had him pinned into a corner, he was sweating.

"It's not done to show so much excitement," he said to Chuck, unable to stop his hand from stroking a reassuring hand down the dog's body as Chuck's head drooped. "Dignity, Chuck."

"I'm not sure he knows that word."

Gabriel froze for only a second before he turned to face his human. Not his, he corrected instantly, as his gaze wandered over Leah's face, the sloped nose, the stubborn chin, the smiling blue eyes. Her curly hair was hidden beneath her beloved cap today. She wore ripped jeans and a pink sweater that was thin and impractical in this weather. He imagined if he said that, she'd roll her eyes.

"He'll learn," he replied.

"When are you going to accept that you can't control everything?"

"Why should I?"

One side of her lips curled. And he found himself wanting to smile back.

He didn't.

"Well—" he said, the awareness tingling across his skin forcing him to retreat.

She interrupted. "Can we talk?"

Instant dread coiled up like a snake. He took one step in retreat before remembering he was a Goodnight. "Talk?"

She nodded.

He began to sweat again. "Uh…"

"Please?"

Gabriel would like to meet the person who could deny Leah when she begged. He conceded with a nod.

She wet her lips, seeming nervous. "Okay, cool. About the other night."

"Yes?" he croaked, alarm and anticipation firing in his veins. Chuck leaned against his legs, nudging his big head in encouragement.

"Leah," Sloane called from the next room. "Mary from the bookshop's here. She said she's giving in to your not-so-subtle hints and wants to have a look at Frenchie."

Considering it was Leah who'd wanted to talk, Gabriel expected her to be irritated by the distraction. Instead, she shrugged as if to say *what can you do*, before dashing off.

Reprieve? he wondered. But now the subject had been raised, it wasn't going away.

Better to get ahead of it, he decided uneasily, take the familiar by the tail. The bull by the horns, he amended, using the human expression. So, he'd talk to her on his terms.

And be damn careful of what was said.

It was late by the time Gabriel could finally approach Leah again. He did one last walk-through, saving Chuck's kennel for last so he could sneak him one final biscuit, before he returned to reception, where Leah was briefing the night volunteers.

As he walked in, all eyes turned to him.

Gabriel nodded hello but his focus was Leah. "Come. I'll accompany you home."

"What?"

"We'll talk on the way." He'd decided that would be best. They'd be limited in how much they could say, and their conversation could only last for the duration of the journey.

"Um…okay." She peered at him, unusually flustered. Her

hand smoothed her sweater. "Are you sure you want to travel across town?"

He merely held out the coat he'd retrieved.

With a small shrug, she slipped her arms into the dark green coat. His hands lingered for a moment on her shoulders as he drew in her scent. Not noticing, Leah waved to the volunteers and then walked with him into the night. "I usually get the L."

His nose wrinkled. "I don't think so."

She tipped her chin up, a spark of laughter he'd sorely missed lighting her expression. "Don't you get tired of being snobby?"

"When one has a natural talent, it should always be employed."

"Uh-huh. C'mon, Gabe. This'll be a good experience for you."

"Leah, I'm not riding in a tin can of strangers. Leah. Leah." With a mutter, he hurried after her. Night had fallen and although the streets were relatively bustling, he didn't trust anyone not to assault her.

Her idea of thanking him for the assistance was making him stand upright in a train car, merrily insisting he hold the pole so he wouldn't go flying and, when he resisted, laughing her head off when he kept smashing into the side. More than his ego was bruised as they exited into a neighborhood nicer than he'd expected.

Small houses lined the street, with yards, rather than the towering apartment blocks he was used to. There were leafy trees, unfurling with the beginnings of green leaves, grass and iron curlicued gates. Someone in their front yard waved to Leah and she waved back without slowing down.

He knew she wanted to talk about the other night, dissect, explore, but as he paced his steps to hers, he shied away from the topic. "You walk alone this way every day?"

"Sometimes." She buried her hands in her pockets. "Sometimes I Uber. Depends on if I'm in the mood to stretch my legs."

"How safe is the neighborhood?"

She flicked a grin at him. "Safe enough. I know how to take care of myself."

He grunted, Laurence's face flashing to mind. Still... "You don't own a car?"

"Had one for a while, but it's pointless when I travel into the center so much." Her sneakers padded over the sidewalk and she let out a breath that curled white into the air. "God, how can it be this cold still?"

Gabriel didn't think; he warmed the air around her with a flick of his fingers and then bit down on the lick of pain. Fuck.

She noticed his grunt, stopped. "Gabriel?"

He motioned her on, setting his teeth against the small ripples that continued to ebb in his system. "It's fine."

"What is it?"

"Nothing."

"You know I'm as stubborn as you, right?"

"I believe that's why we rode in the tin can of death."

Her smile didn't fully light her eyes. "You'd tell me if you were really in pain."

It was a statement, but he answered her anyway. "Likely not."

"Of course." Now her smile was rueful. "Goodnights don't show weakness?"

"Best way to be."

She made a noncommittal noise and indicated to cross the road. "One day you'll open up to someone."

"Have you?" He watched for traffic as she walked ahead.

"No. But then, like I've said, I have the worst taste in men."

Before he could comment, she gestured to a two-story red-brick house with white trim around the windows and a white arch over the door. "This is me."

"You live here?" He couldn't keep the surprise from his voice.

"You thought I'd live in a small apartment with three dogs and two cats?"

He conceded the point. "You said this was one of your investments."

"Yep. Thanks to this and the bar, I'm moderately comfortable, but I'm not in the land of, oh, say, wearing a designer suit to an animal shelter." She paused on the sidewalk and glanced at him. "Bigger than yours, huh?"

His look was dry. "The apartment, yes. The family manor, no."

"Now, now, don't brag about size. Real men don't do that." She stretched up to pat his cheek.

It wasn't a conscious move but he caught her hand on its descent, loosely clasping it. Soft, she was always so soft, where he felt hardened like weathered stone. His breathing was rough as he studied her hand in his before he let them part ways.

She recovered first. "It's, ah, convenient." As if nothing had happened, except a blush scored her cheeks. "Ogden Park is a short walk away, Halstead station about fifteen minutes, and the dogs have a yard. It's peaceful. I love the city and the noise and the rush, but I like having something calm to come back to." She laughed a little. "Well, until I go through the door and the babies realize I'm home. And there's Peggy."

"You live with her," he remembered.

She nodded. "I couldn't live alone. I'd go stir-crazy, and it's helpful for the dogs when I stay out unexpectedly." She walked up the three steps to the small porch. Turned. "So."

He followed like a charmed object. "So."

Her hands drifted together, rubbing fingertips. "We said we'd talk."

He nodded.

The night pressed in as she clearly fumbled for words. "I don't know what to say," she finally admitted in a low voice. "I… it…what happened, I…" She took a breath. "Do you regret it?"

He could cut this off right now, at the knees, no mercy. He opened his mouth to do just that. It wasn't like he couldn't be brutally honest; it was part of his reputation.

But what emerged was a low, "No."

Something moved in her expression. "Me neither."

Everything in him kept still, breathless, not knowing what to do as electricity crackled between them. He knew what the practical thing, the logical thing to do was.

But that wasn't what he wanted.

He stepped forward.

She startled at the movement, and her back bumped the door. Her hands braced at her sides, flat. Unsteady breaths made her breasts rise and fall. Still she didn't speak. Didn't tell him no.

He laid his hands deliberately on the door, either side of her head. He couldn't touch her. His control dangled on a precarious thread. If he even grazed her, it would snap. And they would both fall into the dark.

"Gabriel?" The whisper had him closing his eyes, relishing the sound of his name on her lips. Her scent was stronger this close and he didn't think, just lowered his head to the crook of her neck to inhale.

A short sound burst from her, but she didn't reach for him, as if she knew not to.

"You drive me mad," he murmured against her skin. The need for her was a drumbeat in his soul. "I see you, hear you, *feel* you all day, all night, in my dreams. You've bewitched me."

"I-ironic."

As she couldn't see him, he let his mouth curve into a dark smile. "You should be the very last woman I want." He lifted his head, inches from hers. Every nerve was on fire. "And yet, you're the only woman I've ever craved." He closed his eyes again, tried to reach for control. He shouldn't be doing this. "You make it hard to resist."

Her words were quiet but deafening. "Then don't."

And he was done.

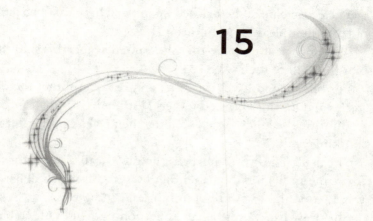

15

*G*abriel's fingers dug into the door at Leah's back as his mouth moved over hers. When he'd let himself imagine kissing her, it was a slow seduction, a display of skill that leisurely built desire in shimmering waves.

In reality, he fell on her like a man half-starved.

Their mouths clashed, hungered. His body pulsed with need as Leah's lips parted and her tongue swept to his, gliding against him again, and again, until a desperate groan rumbled in his throat. He crowded her, stopping just before their bodies touched.

Hold back, he told himself, even as he dove for another taste, as addicted as a magic siphon. He may as well have been leeching power; his skin felt tight, fit to burst at the sensations carving through him.

Wood from the door dug under his fingernails as magic sought to escape, adding a slice of pain to the pleasure. Even that didn't stop him.

Her moan as he changed the angle of the kiss shot to his head, to his cock. He wanted to move against her, into her, trap her with his weight and taste her everywhere. Dizzy, he trembled against the barrage of need.

It was Leah who stopped, who gentled the storm. Her eyes were electric blue as she reached up, nipped his chin. The graze of teeth shot pleasure to his groin.

"Do you want to come in?" she panted against his skin, the words a spell of their own.

For one second, two, three, he was ready to forget the obstacles and just lose himself in her. With her.

But three seconds passed to four, then five. And he started thinking again.

"I can't." The words hurt his throat. "I can't." And for the first time in his life, he hated that he was a warlock. That he was a Goodnight with responsibilities. But he was.

She drew back, eyes big and questioning. And vulnerable.

He couldn't stand it.

"If I were not Gabriel Goodnight," he rasped, wishing he could tunnel a hand through her curls, knowing he was too close to the edge. "I would touch you. Taste you. *Take* you. Until we were both ruined for anyone else."

Her mouth, still damp from his kisses, parted. Her cheeks flushed.

He took in a shuddering breath. "But I am. And so, I cannot."

"Why?" The question was soft. Stupid.

"You *know* why."

The unsaid truth sat between them.

Leah got the stubborn pinch between her eyes. "Okay. Yes. I know why."

Internal alarms flicked on, blaring red, sirens wailing.

"I know that you're a—"

He acted quickly, dropping his head and pressing a firm kiss to her mouth to stop the words, to keep them from the air, the wind. Fear, and yes, it was fear, plucked at his heart. Someone could be listening. Could take her away.

She was not allowed to be hurt.

She kissed him back, a sumptuous meeting of mouths. He allowed himself one last taste, then another, mustering all his control so he could pull away. This time, he leaned his forehead against hers, closed his eyes. "Don't," he murmured. "Some words cannot be taken back."

They were quiet for a long moment, and then he gradually stepped away, until he no longer had the scent of coconut in his lungs.

She remained against the door, lips damp, eyes dark. Temptation in its purest form, an angel lured to sin.

Physically aching, he swallowed hard and dipped a shallow bow, reverting to his upbringing while his mind whirled. "Good night, Leah."

She said nothing and he forced himself to turn, to walk away. *For the best.* It was a mantra in his head, even as he tasted her on his lips. *For the best.*

"Gabe?"

His heart stopped along with his feet. He angled his head back.

She smiled at him, her bright, happy smile that did weird things to his chest. "If you weren't Gabriel Goodnight, I'd never have kissed you."

His mouth was dry. "Everyone always wants a Goodnight."

She shook her head. "But if you weren't *Gabe*, I wouldn't want to kiss you again."

Pleasure snaked through him. "You could do better," he said, softer than the night air.

"I know." Another beaming smile. "You're welcome."

She spun and opened her front door, disappearing through it before he'd processed her words.

And so, she missed the low laugh he couldn't stop, didn't see how he grinned foolishly up at the sky before turning on his heel and heading back home.

★ ★ ★

"Um, who was *that*?"

At the sound of Peggy's voice, Leah froze in the act of peeking out the window. She hunched her shoulders and let the curtain fall back into place. "Nobody."

"Uh-huh. Well, you sure were getting friendly with nobody on the porch."

Leah sheepishly smiled as she looked at her roommate, who was chilling on the couch with Sylvie and Louie. Rosie and Delilah had already found their way to Leah, Rosie parking her butt on Leah's foot and Delilah sniffing her pant leg in suspicion, as if knowing exactly what her mistress had been getting up to outside.

"Okay," Leah allowed, bending to stroke Rosie's soft head and Delilah's wriggling body. "*That* was Gabriel. Goodnight."

"So much for disliking him." Amusement coated the words.

"I don't. Dislike him." Leah headed for the big stuffed armchair and plopped down, accepting Rosie's weight as the sprocker sprawled against her legs. "He can be annoying, but—"

"—so can you?"

"For example." Leah slumped, pressing jumpy fingers to her lap before giving in and tracing her lips. Her heart was still humming, practically a vibration at this point. "It probably wasn't a good idea." But she couldn't regret it.

Peggy snorted. "Screw that and tell me about the kiss."

"How did you even know we were there?"

"You must have pushed the doorbell when you leaned back against the door. I checked the camera and saw enough."

Laughter bubbled up. "Sorry."

"I'm just glad I checked first instead of just answering it."

"Oh, God." Leah covered her face with her hands as her shoulders shook. She breathed out, dropped her hands, still grinning. "Yeah, that would've been awkward."

Sylvie stretched in Peggy's lap, needling her nails into her thin sleep pants. Her roommate winced and shifted the cat. "C'mon, you haven't had a decent date in ages. Spill. What made you take the plunge?"

She hadn't, Leah thought, still processing that it had been *Gabriel* who'd made the first move, *Gabriel* who'd backed her into that door and bracketed her body, never lifting his hands to touch her. As if he teetered on an edge.

It went down as the hottest kiss of her life.

But all she said was, "Let's just say they don't give out names like 'Goodnight' for nothing."

"Tongue?"

"Pegs."

"You get what vicariously means, right?"

"I get that if you're that hard up, it means you need to go out on the hunt."

"You going to come with, or are you and Goodnight now a thing?"

The balloon popped, reality leaking in. Leah's smile faded. "I don't think so. He stopped."

"And I thank him for it, since old Mrs. Malloy across the street would've given us an earful about public lewdness."

Leah winced. She'd forgotten her nosy neighbor. "Oh, God. Well, tomorrow's problem." She waved it away. "No, I mean, he didn't want to come in."

Peggy held up a hand, prompting Sylvie to butt her head against it. "He said no to sex?"

"I didn't *say* sex, but it was implied, and yeah, he said he couldn't."

"He couldn't?" Peggy's expression took on a pained slant. "You mean…medically?"

"*No,*" Leah choked. Delilah huffed at the lack of attention and trotted over to Peggy. "Can confirm, no problems in that area."

"Damn shame if he had. So, is he looking to just be friends?"

"Maybe?" Although she had to choose her words, Leah admitted it was nice being able to talk about Gabriel and know Peggy wasn't going to go shrieking into the night. Leah having feelings for the Warlock of Contempt? The horror. "He's…only here temporarily. Proving something to his family's company."

"Sounds Shakespearean. Where is this company?"

"New Orleans."

"Okay, makes a little more sense. Folks go wild down there, I think it's the heat and the mysticism. Voodoo and witches." She rolled her eyes and Leah tried not to give anything away. "So, you're thinking he doesn't want to get attached?"

Leah imagined what Gabriel would say to that, amused even as part of her flinched. "Goodnights don't get attached."

"Sounds pompous."

"Oh, he is. And rude, blunt, dictatorial, stubborn…"

"Sounds hot."

"You don't know the half of it." But she sighed, slumping, picking at her jeans. "He pretends not to care, but I think he might care too much. And he hates that because…well, he'd rather be alone than have to care or be cared about. Or at least I think that's what it is." It echoed within her, a self-truth she didn't want to acknowledge. Because deep down she knew *she* kept people *close* until they threatened to make her care too much. And— "I—I like him," she admitted, disturbed. "More than I should."

"Why?"

"He makes me feel…not in control. Like life won't be the same when he's gone."

"He might not go."

He would. No amount of charm and vivaciousness in the world could keep him. "He will," she confirmed, hollow. "Maybe it's better to know."

"All right." Peggy clapped her hands, sat forward, eyes direct. "Say he will. What happens if you both acknowledge that but indulge in a little fun first?"

The idea taunted her, a slide of silk across exposed skin. The side of her that hated to be vulnerable shied away, but the other part, the part that craved Gabriel—*Gabe*—couldn't stand the idea of not seeing this through. A few weeks of passion before saying goodbye. An affair with guidelines built in.

She shouldn't even be entertaining the idea. Everyone would lose their shit. But then, it was nobody's business but theirs. Her risk to take. On every level.

Could she be brave enough, was the question.

"Ugh." Leah pulled on her own hair, frustrated with herself. "We got any ice cream left?"

"Whose house do you think this is?"

"Right."

Before Leah hefted herself up, Peggy asked, "How was the kiss?"

"Hormones go kaboom."

"That's what I thought."

The next couple of weeks were busy and Gabriel was grateful for it. Offering more hours to the shelter to cover Leah's need for extra time to arrange the gala, he managed it so they rarely spent more than an hour together—and always with company.

Not that the kiss was forgotten. He woke from dreams of soft skin, hot friction, hard and aching, and nothing he did could dredge her from his system. She was in there, in his blood, his need for her increasing despite spending less time with her.

Through the shelter grapevine, he'd heard that arrangements for the dinner had progressed well. She and Emmaline had hooked sponsors, had sent out invites to Chicago's best and brightest, and had secured an exquisite ballroom for their just shy of five hundred guests. He'd also been doing the rounds, dropping the Goodnight name when needed and using his limited magic to speed up the booking process. In this, he'd accepted the cost gladly. The shelter needed the money and he was only there for a short time; it needed to happen soon. And soon it was—next week.

In lieu of Leah's company, he'd been tugged along for a few "men's nights out" with Mitch and Frankie. He surprised himself by enjoying the time. He liked learning about Mitch's extensive knowledge of Native American history, Frankie's obsession with every Motown hit and the stories behind the label. He liked *them*, and he looked forward to their "hang outs" more and more.

And of course, there was Chuck and his stubborn refusal to be trained to keep Gabriel busy. He'd somewhat mastered sit, though four times out of ten, he'd roll onto his back instead. Gabriel couldn't figure out why that charmed him.

Now he stood and watched Chuck nose about the yard and lift his leg. He'd called Chuck's name thirty seconds ago, and while the Labrador was on his way over, he'd taken the scenic route.

"Gabriel."

The unexpected voice had dread sinking claws into his heart. Society mask on, Gabriel took a discreet, steadying breath before angling his head toward his uncle's PA. "Will."

Short in stature, studious by nature, Will was a bespectacled brunet, always in a suit tailored to his skinny frame. He'd begun working with August a decade ago, fresh from school, and had unswerving loyalty to both him and the company. Gabriel had never minded him. Now he itched under the skin at Will's mere presence.

At least Leah wasn't at the shelter.

"Good to see you." Will cast him an easy smile. "It hasn't been the same without you around."

Gabriel noticed Will hadn't said he was missed. "Is everything well at the company?"

"Very much so. All special projects are proceeding as your uncle wishes and Marketing are already pulling plans together for the hundredth anniversary of Goodnight's founding for next year."

A stab of pain caught Gabriel unaware. He murmured something noncommittal and turned his attention to the dog.

Chuck's head had come up, a predator scenting new prey. With a joyful bark, he rushed toward the newcomer.

Will froze him in place with one hastily thrown-up hand. "Holy Goddess!"

Gabriel resisted the small laugh that tried to escape. He nudged Will over, breaking the holding spell. "Chuck," he ordered. "*No.*"

Chuck's legs pinwheeled as he tried to change direction toward his original target and rammed straight into Gabriel. It took several seconds to sort out limbs and paws, another few to convince Chuck not to try again.

Will was watching them both, wide-eyed, when Chuck finally sat with a small whine. "You speak dog now?"

"More like I'm teaching him to speak human." Gabriel set a calming hand on the vibrating dog, soothed.

"Are you…taking him to be your familiar?"

"No." He didn't feel the instant connection that witches and familiars felt on sight. Not that he needed the big dumb dog tearing up the family manor, shredding the four-hundred-year-old couch, knocking over lamps that had been there his whole life.

"So, you just spend time with him?" Will's voice was curious, startled.

Gabriel withdrew his hand, feeling too seen. "Part of the job."

Will, still eyeing Chuck as though he were a grizzly bear, nodded. "And how are you finding interacting with humans?"

Gabriel curled his toes in his shoes and wished for the armor of his three-piece suit. "Fine."

"Your uncle indicated you've been enjoying their company more."

There was no accusation in the tone, but Gabriel stood straighter. "As expected, I have made an effort to socialize with humans, yes."

"And how is that?"

"Fine."

Will finally slid him a look. "Many *fines.*"

"This is an aggravating situation for me."

"Being around humans."

"Being watched," Gabriel corrected. "Judged. I have stuck to the terms of the contract and dislike these added amendments."

"I understand." Will's hair moved faintly in the breeze and he shuddered, waving a hand and creating a warm cloud of air around them.

Gabriel envied the amount of magic Will had used in the last five minutes. He appreciated magic more now, had learned to cope without relying on it, but Goddess, he missed it.

"It's an intrusion," Will continued, not missing a beat, "but I'll barely be here. I'll be as discreet as possible. Only a few questions."

Gabriel's pulse skipped. "Questions?"

"To prove you've been making an effort. I find it ridiculous but..." Will shrugged. "Don't worry, I'm not canvassing everyone. A select few only. Emmaline Bluewater, Tia Hightower. The third from the bar." A notepad poofed into Will's hand and he flipped a page, reading off it. "Leah Turner."

The only outward show of Gabriel's dismay was the tremble in the hands he linked behind him. "There is no need to talk to Leah."

"I think her the most important. A human witness to prove you've gone above and beyond." Will cocked his head. "Curious that a human who knows nothing of our world should own a third of the bar." He obviously didn't consider that anyone would have told Leah; not surprising for someone who adhered so strictly to rules and order in his own life.

Chuck responded to the tension riding Gabriel by pawing at his leg. He received an absent stroke as Gabriel weighed every word. "Family money. She likes her projects."

"Hmm." Will seemed to lose interest, asking a few more questions about Gabriel's experiences the last few weeks.

When they were done, he considered Gabriel. "The board should applaud you for these efforts. Existing with only scraps of magic, forced to work in a job you're overqualified for, wearing a mask. Knowing the people around you couldn't handle the real you or our world. I bet you can't wait to leave them all behind."

The words hit hard, unexpectedly so. Gabriel managed to murmur something noncommittal, unsure why the truth should so surprise him. Will was right, after all. As much as he liked Mitch, Frankie, Leah, none of them could exist in his real world. They didn't know the real him. And in the end, he would say goodbye. Return to being alone. Just as he liked it.

As Will cheerfully said he'd be in touch and left, Gabriel lowered himself to the ground and sat there in the yard for a moment longer, Chuck's head resting loyally on his knee.

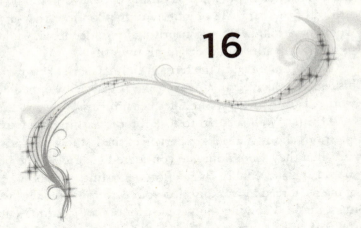

16

When Mitch came jogging up to him an hour later, brows tight, Gabriel felt his heart sink.

And he cursed when he followed Mitch out the side of the building where nonsensical phrases and symbols were spray-painted in garish yellow. Considering the paint was well set, it had to have happened the night before, even if they'd only just noticed now.

"Is this normal?" he demanded, waving a hand at the graffiti.

Mitch hunched his shoulders against the cold. "Not so long as I've volunteered. We've had the odd thing, but this is like we're being targeted."

Gabriel crossed his arms in disgust. "I didn't install a camera here when we put in the new security system. That will be rectified."

In the meantime, they shoved up their sleeves and got to scraping the paint off as best they could. They were soon joined by Frankie and the three of them carried an easy conversation as they worked, easier than most Gabriel had ever been part of. In fact, Melly had been delighted when he'd mentioned his "friends," (her words), and had again clamored to visit so she could meet them. He'd stuck with his refusal, still leery about having her around so many humans where she couldn't defend herself with magic. A dreamscape potion wasn't created in a day.

Once the wall was as clear as they could get it and their shifts long over, Mitch raised the idea of a drink. Considering the only thing Gabriel had waiting for him was a microwaved casserole and the second part of a documentary he knew Leah would enjoy, he'd agreed. If she was there, he could recommend it, they could talk. Safe, easy.

He'd missed her, damn it.

She wasn't at Toil and Trouble when they arrived, but Bastian Truenote was.

Gabriel tried not to let it stiffen him up as he left Frankie and Mitch in a booth and approached the bar. It wasn't so much that he disliked Bastian, more that he was a solid reminder of everything Gabriel was not.

Bastian was tall, golden and handsome in the way of the old movie stars. His grin was charming, his eyes a twinkling navy, his manner easy, and, as had become apparent when they'd worked together, he was as suited for the role of amiable bartender as Gabriel wasn't. He was also a far superior Higher son from what Gabriel had observed. His parents doted on him, their pride open and unashamed. In a word: perfect.

And it was hard to like perfect when he was achingly aware of every flaw he possessed.

"Truenote," he greeted, his accent making the word clipped. "I didn't realize you were in town."

Bastian served his customer, cast Gabriel a casual grin as they walked off. "We came in this morning. Emma needed to help Leah with some gala stuff, and they recruited me to tend bar since Tia got called to New Orleans by her family again." He looked beyond Gabriel. "You here alone?"

"No. I came with…friends." Will's words floated through his head but he pushed them aside. He would focus only on today.

Bastian choked. "*Human* friends?"

Gabriel made no comment, deliberately not rising to the bait.

A dimple flashed. "Well, who'da thunk it? Gabriel Goodnight sliding right into the human world."

"They'd like two beers. Three," Gabriel decided in the next breath, gesturing to one of the taps. "That'll do."

"Gabriel!"

Recognition pulled Gabriel's attention from Bastian to the owner of the familiar voice. Nonplussed, he stared into green eyes paler than his own, set against a shock of platinum hair. "Henry? What are you doing here?"

The tall man Gabriel considered his only real friend offered a hand, clasping Gabriel's briefly. Dressed in jeans and a gray fisherman's sweater, he lifted his eyebrows. "I'd be better if I wasn't in enemy territory."

"Ah." Nobody could forget the intense few years where Henry Pearlmatter and Tia Hightower had been a blazing item. Everyone had expected they'd marry, but instead, their relationship had fallen apart in as passionate a display as it had begun.

Bastian snorted from across the bar. "You have to be in the same room at some point. You're both invited to the wedding."

Gabriel's invitation must have been lost in the cosmos. He was too used to being excluded to take offense.

"How are you finding being here?" Henry perched on a stool, hooking his shoe around the bottom rung. He more than most knew of Gabriel's family history. "Tell you the truth, I half expected you to message me by mirror and request an extraction."

"I came close." Gabriel passed across a bill to Bastian as the latter plonked three pints on the bar. "It's better, now."

"Catch me up."

So, he did, after quickly dropping the drinks with Mitch and Frankie, who waved off his awkward apology for choosing his old friend over them. Henry's family was as old magic as Gabriel's, and just as respected. While Henry played proper in public, Gabriel had always enjoyed the hidden jovial side of the warlock. Goddess knew what Henry saw in Gabriel to hold up their friendship, but whatever it was, he'd always been grateful for it.

Bastian had joined them, settling into the conversation as they swapped stories about working at the bar. Gabriel had relaxed enough not to take offense at Bastian's taunts, had even made several of his own and enjoyed the friendly nature of it all. At least until the conversation circled around to Leah.

"So," Bastian said, drawing out the word, expression narrowing. "You and Leah. Something going on there?"

Caught off guard, Gabriel felt his left eye twitch.

Henry swore. They'd been friends too long for him not to pick up on it. "You're messing with a human?"

"No." The lie seared his insides and he shifted to ease the discomfort. "We're...friends."

"Friends." Henry swiped up his beer and swigged. "How did that happen?"

Gabriel shrugged, uncomfortable. "You'd have to meet her."

"Irresistible, is she?"

Yes. "More like an unstoppable force."

"That's true." Bastian held up an acknowledging finger at a customer. "Leah's kind of the human equivalent of a battering ram. She gets through in the end."

As Bastian ambled off to fill the order, Gabriel watched speculation fill Henry's eyes. And he frowned. "Don't look at me like that."

"You like this woman."

"She's tolerable."

"You *really* like her."

Gabriel pokered up. "I said no such thing."

"You didn't have to. She must be something to get you to see beyond your fears."

"It's not just her." Gabriel unbent enough to smile faintly. "Though she plays a big part. Being here…spending time with humans, it's harder to hold onto the past. I've enjoyed it, learned from them. That has value." He stared at his signet ring, all that it represented. "My parents hoped to take the company forward, expand. At least now I think I might be able to live up to their expectations and carry it through."

Henry said nothing, but set a hand on Gabriel's shoulder briefly. He didn't dwell, didn't point out that most family was held together by love, not cold obligation.

Instead, he lifted his beer again with a quick grin. "So, you're dating this human?"

"You know that's impossible."

"Interesting." Henry drank, set it down. "You didn't say you didn't want to. Have you kissed her?"

Bastian returned at the tail end, cocked his head.

Loathing the attention, Gabriel refused to say anything. Not that it mattered.

"Shit," Bastian said unhappily. "Emma's going to freak." His expression shifted to something Gabriel couldn't read. "Not sure what Kole will say."

The muscles in his back stiffened. "Are they…involved?"

"No." Bastian drew it out, making it sound more like a question. "Though I've always wondered—" He stopped short, gaze going over Gabriel's shoulder. His lips formed a silent whistle. "Well, hell, what did you do, Goodnight?"

Gabriel frowned.

Bastian's smile was more a smirk as he nodded behind him. "Cute blonde, pint-sized, pissed off, and headed your way." As Gabriel swiveled, Bastian added, "Start praying now."

Leah wasted no time as she approached the dark warlock. She ignored the hubbub of the evening crowd, the pumping music, even Bastian's casual greeting as she screeched to a halt, planting her feet and her hands on her hips. She gave Gabriel her best glower.

He didn't react. "Leah."

She threw up an accusing finger. "Don't even. How dare you hide that the shelter was vandalized again? Is that your call to make? Newsflash: this isn't the 1900s, Gabriel. I don't need some interfering, autocratic *man* deciding what I should and shouldn't know. You had no right."

Gabriel didn't stand from his stool, which put them at an even height for once. His startling green eyes surveyed her with careful neutrality.

It infuriated her. How he was calm and contained while she was a bag of hormones and lust. Even now, as pissed as she was, all she wanted to do was grab hold of the black sweater he was wearing and have his glorious mouth locked on hers again. Addiction ran through her bloodstream, hyping the irritation that he'd been hiding things from her.

She'd called in to run through some details with Sonny for the gala, only to be told they'd been vandalized again. But Gabriel had taken care of it, she'd been assured. Read: don't worry her pretty little head.

"I am not one of your minions," she said, poking her finger into his chest. Meeting a wall of muscle. "I am not beneath you. It's not your place to choose whether to tell me something."

He waited. "Are you done?"

Her lips thinned.

"Because I wasn't keeping it from you."

"Bull," she spat.

"Don't accuse me of lying." His eyes shone greener, if that was possible.

"You know I'd want to know. It's *my* place, Gabriel."

"And I wanted to take care of it first. For you."

It made her falter.

"I was planning on telling you tomorrow, when we're both

scheduled to be in. I didn't want it to play on your mind all night when nothing could be done. I won't apologize for that."

God help her. How was a woman meant to deal with Gabriel Goodnight? She stared at him, confused, touched. His actions were sweet and misguided and irritating because he was right. It would have been on her mind all night.

Even so, someone needed to yank Gabriel into the twenty-first century. Good thing she was woman enough to take up the challenge.

She released a breath and stepped forward, teasingly close to touching his knees. "Okay, I appreciate the thought. But you can't make those decisions for me, not if you respect me at all. I had a right to know as soon as it happened, even if you thought it was going to worry me." She quirked an eyebrow. "Do you respect me?"

"Of course."

"Then, respect me enough to tell me bad news."

Mulishly, he stared her down. Finally, he gave a clipped nod. And she could breathe again.

Easing her grip on the righteous anger, she patted his cheek. The barest hint of stubble grazed her palm. "It was very sweet of you, though."

"I am not sweet," he informed her loftily. Cranky.

Adorable. She smiled now, a bright beam. "Goodnights aren't sweet?"

"Sweet doesn't get things done."

Her smile stretched into a grin. "Of course. This yours?" Before he could answer, she lifted his beer, took a swig. Then caught sight of the man on the neighboring stool gaping at her. Mortified, she looked at the beer. "Shit. Is this yours?"

The handsome man with platinum hair grinned. "No, sorry," he said, his voice deeper than she'd expected. "I've just never seen Gabriel admit he was wrong."

Gabriel gave him a bland look.

"You know Gabriel?" It hit her then what that meant. *Warlock.* She disguised the instant of excitement, forcing her expression to stay casual. "You're from New Orleans?"

The stranger lifted his hand in a half greeting. "Henry."

Her eyes widened, mind turning on a dime to race in a different direction. "*Henry?*"

He grimaced. "You must know Tia."

"You ever going to say hello to me?"

Leah swiveled at the mock-affronted question. She grinned, boosting herself up and giving Bastian a smacking kiss on the cheek. "Who could forget about you, handsome?" She winked at him. "How about a beer on the house?"

"Since you own the house, why not?"

Leah shifted back to Henry as Bastian went to fetch her a beer. "So, *you're* Tia's ex?" And he was here, in her bar. Should she throw him out? She studied his arms, the muscled form, reconsidered. Should she get Bastian to throw him out?

"To save you from asking the question that's all over your face," Henry stated wryly, tapping a hand on the counter, revealing some edginess. "I'm only here because Bastian asked me to swing by so he could hit me up for a favor. Trust me, Tia and I know to keep a state between us."

God, she had so many questions. Like, a ballpark full. But, since it felt disloyal to gossip behind her friend's back, Leah focused elsewhere. All innocence, she commented, "A long way from New Orleans for a favor."

She jumped when Gabriel's hand settled at the small of her back. She glanced his way, caught the warning flash. She grinned at him.

Henry merely flashed his own smile. "Private jet. And it gave me a chance to catch up with old friends."

"So, you knew Gabe when he was a boy?"

"Sure, me and *Gabe* go way back."

"Was he always such a killjoy?" She poked his ribs, squeaked when his hand on her back slid down, tapped her ass. A rush of inappropriate lust had her frowning at him.

His lips barely curved. That only made it worse.

"Not always," Henry answered. He leaned an elbow on the bar, the picture of a man settling in for a conversation. "When we were young, he had a real nose for a prank. His parents hated that. Their son shouldn't dishonor the family name, do good and all that. Even if he only went after the bullies."

"Henry."

He ignored Gabriel and regaled a fascinated Leah with more stories that Mrs. Q hadn't known about. She laughed so hard at one point, beer shot out of her nose.

She didn't want to like Henry, out of loyalty to Tia, but it was hard not to get sucked into the charming warlock's orbit. Even so, she occasionally caught the edge of something before he smoothed it over with a grin. As much a mask as Gabriel's, she thought, as they called for a second beer. It seemed nobody survived in Higher society without one. Fake, all of it. Just like…

She swallowed, suddenly edgy. Well, just like the entitled world she'd walked away from. Hadn't thought twice about leaving it all behind, had never been happier than when she could stop second-guessing everybody's smile and words.

Gabriel's society might be magical but it was the same. And this was the world she'd always wanted to join?

As she picked up the beer Bastian brought, she nudged that disquieting thought out of sight to focus on the now. Gabriel didn't have many friends, or not that she'd picked up on. It was important to her that she made a good impression. She tucked the reason away with the other thought, neatly out of sight.

With a cleansing sip of her beer, she angled toward Gabriel's friend and changed the subject. "So, Henry…you're rich, huh?"

Henry's laugh lured a few female stares from the nearby table. "Reasonably."

"You're a good person?"

"Depends who you ask."

Intriguing, but she didn't ask questions. Instead, she batted her eyelashes. "Ever thought about investing in an animal shelter?"

When she saw Gabriel smile behind his beer, everything fell into place.

17

Tonight was the night.

Leah pressed a jittery hand to her belly as she stood in front of the mirror in her bedroom, wrapped in her dressing gown. Delilah and Louie lay on her bed, with Rosie creeping closer to the open closet so she could curl up with the shoes. Sylvie had wound herself up on the chaise longue at the end of Leah's bed, and Ralph was...well, who knew?

She ignored all of them as she stared at herself. Because tonight was the night.

Of the charity gala.

And for her to seduce Gabriel Goodnight.

"Breathe," she told herself as her lungs squeezed. "Just breathe."

Pressure mounted her shoulders, squatted there as she rolled them. More so about the gala than the seduction, though both presented their own challenges. But she was as prepared as she could be, more prepared than she'd even expected, thanks to the planner her mom had hired to help stage the event.

If only she could be there to see it.

Leah swallowed the pang of longing. Her mom and George

were headed to Spain and sounded so excited about it, she hadn't
had the heart to ask them to come to Chicago for one night,
especially since they'd already given a generous donation.

She'd be fine. No, *they'd* be spectacular. Leah—and Gabriel.

Because after days of back and forth, of questioning what was
right, what was wrong, heart or head, she'd made her decision.

She would be brave. Knowing Gabriel would eventually leave
her would help keep her walls, shaky as they were, blocking
any deeper emotions. Sex with friendship was fine. Sex with
feelings was not.

Okay, there might be *some* feelings. But she'd like to meet the
person who wouldn't fall just a little for Gabriel Goodnight. It
didn't change her mind. She had to see this through, be with
him in every way she could. While she had him.

She dressed for seduction: black lace, garter, stockings. And
an utter dream of a dress. A spill of baby pink, the floor-length
gown was halter neck and dipped in a perfect curve to the small
of her back, with shimmering pink-and-silver beading that
caught the light and gleamed.

She left her curls down, arranged over one shoulder, jamming
in enough pins to ensure it, and went heavier on her makeup.
Finally, she stepped into silver strappy heels that would give
her enough height to comfortably tangle with a tall warlock.

Here's hoping.

The doorbell went and Rosie and Delilah took off, Delilah yipping as they charged down to greet who Peggy let in.

Gabriel must have come to escort her. He'd made it obvious he didn't like her walking these perfectly safe streets alone.
Such a father hen.

Her pulse scrambled as Peggy called up. "Leah, there's an
attractive man here for you."

The beading pressed into her fingers as she held her jump-
ing belly. This was it.

She turned off her bedroom light and headed for the stairs,

slowing to a dramatic walk—she didn't want to trip over her heels and make a swan dive—and descended to greet her escort.

The man's hair was dark, but not black, and while he *was* unfairly handsome, this man didn't have intense green eyes, a sharp face and a mouth slow to smile.

Her own mouth dropped in surprise as she stopped halfway down. "Kole. What are you doing here?"

Emma's brother grinned charmingly, outfitted in a tuxedo that had Peggy panting by the window. As she caught her eyes, Peggy pressed a hand over her forehead and pretended to faint.

Unaware of her roommate's antics, Kole held out a hand to help her the rest of the way. "I'm here for you."

Leah accepted his escort, holding up her gown so she didn't tread on the delicate fabric. Confused, she glanced from where her dogs were sniffing his tux to his face. "But you're supposed to be out somewhere doing secret spy things."

He snorted. "I'm *not* a spy."

"Sure." She winked dramatically. "You're not a spy. I get it."

"Give me strength." He lifted their joined hands and made her twirl. "And the tongue back in my head. I'm an old man, Leah. Have some compassion."

"Is it your heart or your knees?"

"You have one already, could have me on the other in that dress."

She crowed a laugh and smacked his chest with her clutch. "Seriously, what are you doing here?"

"Em called, said you'd need some backup." His face stayed casual.

Annoyance scraped down her skin. "She's called in the big guns because of Gabriel, hasn't she?"

"Please, enough flattery." Kole posed, biceps pumped so his muscles were outlined in the tailored jacket. Peggy moaned. "More medium. Bigger applies elsewhere on my body."

"I don't need a brother."

"I thought I was the spy who loved you."

"Try Dr. No. Because that's my answer: *No* to a chaperone." She shook her head in disbelief. "I'm twenty-eight, for Christ's sake. I don't need a babysitter."

"Maybe I'll just…leave you guys alone for a minute." Peggy smiled awkwardly as she backed toward the kitchen.

As soon as she was out of sight, Kole lost the grin. "What were you thinking? Playing around with Goodnight? You know he could recognize you from the balcony."

God, that was so long ago; she'd almost forgotten. He'd become so much more than the beautiful masked stranger fulfilling a fantasy. Now he was…Gabriel.

"If he hasn't by now, he won't," she said, evading the question. "And it's my life, Kole. I don't need another helicopter friend."

He dared her disapproval and cupped her cheek with his calloused hand. "We care about you. We don't want anything to happen."

"I've heard it. I understand. But I've been choosing my own path and lovers for a long time now."

His hand fell away. "Lovers? Are you sleeping with him?"

"Not that it's any of your business, but no. Not yet."

A muscle popped in his jaw. "It's a bad idea, Leah. He's a warlock. You can't have a future with him."

"I'm not writing his name on my binder." Uncomfortable, she shrugged her shoulders, the echo of his words prodding at something raw inside. "I like him."

"The Warlock of Contempt?" he sneered.

Dangerous emotion washed up her. "Don't call him that."

"Unbelievable." He paced away, then back, a show of frustration. "He's not good for you. It won't end well."

"How do you know?"

"Because he's a warlock," Kole repeated. "And you're a human. There are too many obstacles between you."

He was right. She'd already acknowledged that to herself, but it still hurt.

She took his hand, squeezed it, aiming for a light tone. "I'm not looking for forever. You know me, it never lasts. Worst taste in men, right?" She waggled her eyebrows.

His smile was reluctant, rueful. He squeezed back. "You're setting a whole new record this time."

"I hope I'm not interrupting."

Leah's eyes shot to the doorway. In her chest, her heart kicked hard.

Gabriel stood as stiff as his voice, every muscle in his lean body locked and outfitted in a tuxedo that rippled over him like black water. His hair was styled back, ebony silk against the fine bones of his face.

The intensity there made her breathless. "Gabriel. Hi."

When he didn't respond, she followed his gaze to her and Kole's joined hands.

She dropped Kole's instantly. "Uh, you know Kole Bluewater, right? He's come to support the event."

Gabriel didn't soften. "Bluewater."

"Goodnight." Kole's voice was cold as he eased closer to her. She wrestled the unladylike urge to kick him as Gabriel noted the movement.

This wasn't going as she'd planned. For one thing, Gabriel was supposed to be all eyes for her, not her unwelcome chaperone.

Best-laid plans, she sighed internally, and ignored both the idiots as she went to tell Peggy she and her *two* escorts were leaving.

The evening was a smash. The dinner was incredible, the champagne flowed. Leah's speech to thank everyone for coming and supporting the shelter had gone over very well, especially when Chuck and a few others were brought out. Chuck had behaved himself beautifully, giving everyone the big eyes, which had resulted in four—count 'em, *four*—people coming up to Leah and asking about him.

She'd laughed, twinkled, charmed, did everything but tap-dance to keep everyone smiling and open to donating. She'd checked in with Mitch and Frankie, who were in charge of the table set up with materials about the shelter, and they'd confirmed several checks had been slipped in their cashbox. Sonny, ill at ease in an ill-fitting suit, just looked relieved. Leah was sure he would celebrate now he was on his way back with the animals to the shelter. Not one for parties, that man.

With the gala a success, Leah finally throttled back on her hostessing enough to take a sip of champagne. Her feet hurt but she refused to take the shoes off just yet, not when she hadn't had a chance to implement her seduction plan.

God. If the gala was a smash, the seduction was a crash. After Gabriel had seen her and Kole holding hands, he'd withdrawn into his mask and had barely spoken. Not on the very, very long Uber ride into the city—three was definitely a crowd in the back seat of a car—and not to her all evening. Some seduction if she couldn't even pin him down long enough to proposition him.

She kept one eye out for him as she circled the room, shaking hands and directing servers to fill their trays. Impatience twinned with irritation as he continued to be elusive. When she saw her friends, irritation pushed to the fore.

She made a beeline, planting herself in their way. "You got some 'splainin' to do," she accused.

Dressed in a teal sheath that bared her shoulders, pearls gifted from Bastian at her neck and ears, Emma screwed up her face. "Huh?"

Leah pointed to where Kole leaned against the wall, flirting with a pretty server.

Emma's cheeks flushed bright red. "He wanted to come."

"Didn't get an invite, did he?"

"You'd have wanted him here before."

"I do want him here if I don't have to suffer big brother censure."

Tia arched her eyebrows, stunning as always in an ivory mermaid gown shot through with gold overlay. "I'm not sure that's him being a big brother."

"Whatever." Leah struggled not to show her annoyance, aware there was a photographer working the room. "You said you'd trust me. So, do it. I like Gabriel. Deal."

"How, though?" Tia wrinkled her nose. "He's so…cold."

"Not *all* the time."

Two pairs of eyes locked on her.

"Yeah, we kissed." Leah dared them to say anything, folding her arms. Then unfolded them and posed for the photographer as she came up, calling out for a smile. Likewise, her friends moved into position.

All three faced off again when she moved away.

"I supported you," Leah said to Emma, voice tense enough to hum. "When Bastian came back, I supported your decision to make the best of things. I trusted you. Trust me."

There was nothing but the tinkle of the piped-in music, the murmuring of the crowd. Emma reluctantly nodded. "She's right."

"Emma, don't be soft."

"She's right, T," Emma reiterated. She looked away, at her fiancé dancing with an elderly lady dripping with diamonds and laughing her ass off. A soft smile touched her face. "We have to trust her."

"I don't trust him."

"*Tia.*"

Tia held Leah's unrelenting glare for ten seconds before huffing. "Fine. Fine, make a mistake. But *don't* tell him the truth."

Leah made an as-if noise, pretty sure a guilty blush colored her skin.

Tia ran a hand down her necklace to toy with the pendant. "And if he so much as hurts a hair on your head, I *will* use the hex bag that's tucked under the counter at work."

"You already made one up?"

"No." Her eyes gleamed. "I made six."

"You're a scary woman," Leah told her, but had to laugh. She touched each of their arms. "Are we okay?"

"Always," Emma said instantly.

"It'd take a lot more than one warlock to get in the way of us." Tia grabbed her hand, squeezed it, much as Kole had. "You know I love you. It's just…you've never really liked someone before. I hate that it's him."

Instant denial rose. "That's not true."

"Name me one man you've liked longer than a month."

"Well…there was…okay, not him. Paul was…well, he isn't the best example." Leah trailed off, irritated when she couldn't name anyone. That hidden truth mocked her. "I have bad taste," she argued, flushing hot.

Tia snorted. "You're telling me." Leah made a face at her and she smirked back. "I'm just saying, be careful. This isn't the guy to finally commit to—because he can't commit back, and I'd honestly have *you* commit*ted* before it went that far. He'd never choose you over the rules. That warlock is too black-and-white."

Leah wanted to argue, but now wasn't the time to get into it. Besides, "I'm not in love with him or anything. God, Kole was acting the same way. I just…" She tried to find the words to explain why she needed to pursue this, couldn't.

"I honestly don't get it." Tia looked across at Gabriel, who'd emerged from whatever rock he'd been under. "He's too up-tight to be a good lover."

"Shhh," Emma hushed, seeing a woman turn to them in

surprise. She smiled weakly, then swatted Tia. "Would you keep it down?"

"C'mon, tell me you don't agree."

"Don't get me involved." Though she couldn't resist adding, "But if you ask me, he's got a real Tarzan, Jane vibe."

Tia gagged as Leah's smile widened. "I'll find out, report back."

"Please." Tia held up her hands, gestured. "Don't."

It was another twenty minutes before she worked around to where Gabriel was standing alone. Warmed from her friends' wary acceptance—because that's what that had been—Leah was all set to barrel through any objections he had. She was done thinking.

Goodnight, you're mine.

Pleasure bloomed at the sight of him. Not a hair out of place, he looked as suited to this finery as any of the elite here. She knew what they saw: someone cold, someone formal, someone unapproachable.

She saw Gabe.

He looked up, neutral at her approach.

She didn't bother with small talk. "Dance with me?"

Something electric leaped between them as he slid his hand into hers, turned toward the dance floor. Something slow played now, moody, as they joined the other couples.

Bastian had stolen Emma, tucking her into his body and whispering in her ear, making her blush. Tia had struck up a conversation with a good-looking guy at one of the tables but would be portalling off soon to check on the bar, which they'd left in the care of a recent hire.

Leah forgot them both as Gabriel placed a hand on the small of her back, bared by her dress. Skin to skin. The intimate touch ignited a liquid warmth low in her belly as he moved them to the music.

"It's going well, don't you think?" Her eyes traced the dark soon-to-be-stubble on his chin, the angle of his jaw. She wanted to nip there. "Even Chuck behaved."

"Except for the one woman," he agreed.

"I'm sure she'll be able to get wine out of that dress."

"Is that why you threw more on her?"

"Look, I heard white wine helps get red wine stains out."

"Fire also works but I wouldn't recommend it."

She'd have laughed, but it wasn't Gabe speaking to her. He was using his social voice. He was hiding from her.

She wouldn't allow it. "Thanks. For all of this."

"I did nothing."

"Sure." She snorted, enjoying the swish of her skirts as his legs glided against hers. "Except come up with the idea, help plan it, implement it."

"I was bored."

"I think you like me," she teased.

His eyes locked on hers, blazing jewel green for one instant. "Apparently I'm not the only one."

She imagined her eyebrows practically disappeared into her hair. "*Kole?* He's a friend."

"Mmm."

She lifted the hand that rested on his shoulder to poke him in the ribs. He jumped, startled. "Don't do that. I'm serious."

"It's not the first time he's come between us."

Her breath hitched as he referenced the balcony. He knew. How? When?

It wasn't the place to ask, but later…after.

"No," she agreed softly, acknowledging that truth. "He's overprotective. Like a brother."

"Trust me, he is not acting like a brother."

She was hearing that a lot tonight. "Please. I've known him for years. We've only ever been friends."

His jaw flexed. "It's not my business."

"You're being an idiot again," she informed him, delighting in how his mouth turned down in annoyance. "Of course, it's your business. If you want it to be."

He didn't look at her. "I don't know what you mean."

Okay, now she was annoyed. "You know exactly what I mean, you're just not admitting it. Where's the blunt guy who always tells the truth, huh?"

"The truth?"

"Yeah."

"You want me to tell you the truth?"

"*Yes.*"

"You want me to tell you that I wanted to rip his hand off you?" His grip tightened on her waist. "You want me to admit that I hate feeling that way? More, that I despise every man that sees you in that fantasy of a dress, knowing each one is imagining you removing it for them?"

Her heart was in her throat, and it was beating so hard, she couldn't breathe.

His mouth brushed her temple as he brought her even closer, so his words sank into her skin. "I can't think of anything but you, Leah. How I could make you feel just as crazed. Lips. Teeth." He grazed his along her skin and she almost moaned, melting against him. "Body." He dipped his head, whispered into her ear. "I am Gabriel Goodnight. I do not indulge in scandalous behavior. I do not cause scenes. But you tempt me to it, Leah." His breath was hot and made lust pulse everywhere. "Oh, you tempt me."

She had no idea what to say, if there were even words *to* say.

Her head tilted back, watched as his gaze settled on her mouth, lifting to her eyes. Her lips felt swollen, her body aching. Empty.

"Yes," she rasped. "Tell me all of that."

He stared at her, a small smile slowly commanding his face. He shook his head. "You're trouble."

"You're the one asking for it." Leah wet her lips. "But you don't have to."

He blinked in incomprehension, still somehow moving their bodies to the beat.

She grabbed her courage with sweaty hands and went all in. "Ask," she clarified. "Tonight, I'm yours for the taking."

She watched his eyes darken, felt his hold on her change. To her delight, his eyes glittered, as though magic manifested in them.

He might have surrendered then. She really thought he might have gone against all that was Gabriel Goodnight and swept her into a kiss of legend in front of everyone—if they hadn't been interrupted.

"Gabriel."

His hands dropped away fast enough to give her friction burn. "Uncle," he greeted above the music, striding over to welcome the man who'd spoken. A man with a face that resembled Gabriel's—or what Gabriel's face might look like in twenty years. Or longer. Witches were slower to age, according to Tia. Which meant Gabriel would still be gorgeous while Leah was buying up boxes of Goodnight's wrinkle cream.

That thought effectively killed her desire, as much as watching Gabriel walk away from her did.

Well. Fine. That was fine. She didn't need to be introduced to his uncle. She'd just…give him some space.

However, she'd only taken a couple of steps when she saw Gabriel leading the man back to her.

"Leah." Gabriel nodded at the older man next to him. "This is my uncle."

"Um," she said awkwardly, hiding her shock at the introduction. "Hi. Leah Turner." She belatedly held out her hand.

The warlock eyed it before accepting. "August Goodnight." It wasn't welcome that sparked in those eyes, but wariness. Maybe even a hint of dislike.

Perfect. Just what she needed. Cockblocking relatives.

I just want to have sex with him, she wanted to throw her head back and scream. *Throw me a bone here.*

Instead, she chatted politely as August asked her about Chicago, the gala, the shelter, how it came to be. How lucky she was Gabriel had come along at the right time, had done all of this for her. Without her even lifting a finger, imagine, he'd fallen right in her lap. Etc.

After ten minutes of this, she was one dig away from seeing how a warlock went mano a mano with a Cubs fan.

When the conversation lagged, she saw her opportunity. "I'll let you catch up while I go check something out with the planner," she lied, mustering a social smile. "Nice to meet you, Mr. Goodnight."

"I'm sure."

She ground her teeth, sliding a look to Gabriel. "Find me later?"

He nodded and she made her escape.

"Goodnights," she muttered, as she pushed through the doors to the blessedly quiet hall beyond the ballroom. "All of them, a lot of work."

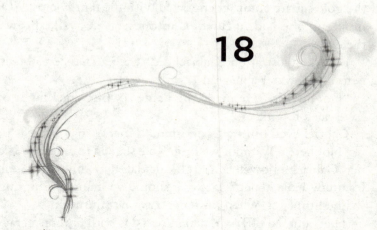

18

To say his uncle's appearance had been unexpected was understating it.

"After Will's report, I had to come see for myself," he insisted when Gabriel rounded on him the moment Leah hurried off. "There was some question about whether the humans are taking advantage of you. I know you must've used magic to get this done in so short a time."

"They're not taking advantage of me." Gabriel could barely concentrate as he answered his uncle. All he heard were the same words, teasing, tempting.

I'm yours for the taking.

A lush hint of desire shuddered through him.

Fortunately, August was far from aware of his distraction, and looked less than convinced. "I just think—" His mirror chimed in his pocket.

He discreetly checked it. "Hong Kong are wanting to pass through the new contracts." He glanced up, around. "Any ideas on finding a space without prying eyes?"

"I've not been here before."

"No matter. I'll cast a glamour barrier." August flipped open the gold square compact engraved with the family crest. "One moment," he said in fluent Cantonese as he walked toward the exit.

Battling frustration, Gabriel didn't get a chance to breathe before Bluewater appeared.

"Goodnight." He made the name a whip, cracking it out. "We need to talk."

Gabriel eyed him with derision. "Fine."

"Not here." Without waiting, Kole stalked to a deserted corner. Gabriel followed at a stroll calculated to annoy. He *wanted* to annoy Kole, a petty fact that should've shamed him, might shame him later, when his temper wasn't simmering.

They squared off, two men in tuxedos with tension a crackle in the air around them.

Kole didn't waste time. "You need to back off from Leah."

Gabriel kept his face expressionless. "I wasn't aware you spoke for her."

"I watch out for her. I want what's *best* for her. And you're not it."

That dug in deep, splintering off to Gabriel's nerves. "I'm a Goodnight," he returned. "A legacy."

"I wouldn't care if you were from the High Family itself." Kole gritted his teeth. "*You* aren't right for her."

"And you know me?"

"I know you're a cold son of a bitch. I know you care more about your family crest than its members."

"Fascinating how you read me like a book, considering I can't think of one instance we've spent time together." Gabriel lifted his eyebrows ever so slightly, too used to society drawing their own conclusions to care. "And you're one to talk about caring for family when you left Emmaline alone for so many years with your mother."

His dart was well aimed. Kole's eyes flashed. "Listen, you arrogant dick. This isn't about me."

"Isn't it?" Gabriel stepped closer, body locked so he wouldn't betray the emotion humming through him. "Because it looks to me like you're having a tantrum about my spending time with your toy."

"*She isn't a toy.*"

"Exactly," Gabriel shot back, angry on Leah's behalf. "She's a woman who makes her own decisions. But you're treating her like a toy. She isn't yours to put down and pick up when you come back. She isn't yours, period."

"And you think she could be yours?" A laugh carved out of Kole's mouth, jagged, threatening to slice Gabriel. "It might've escaped you in this game you're playing, but there are higher stakes here than just breaking her heart." Magic sparked and sizzled around Kole before he pulled it back with visible effort. "If she finds out about witches, she could be seriously hurt."

Gabriel's jaw grated from clenching so hard. "I would *never* hurt Leah."

"You hurt her by being near her. If you really cared, and that's stretching it, you wouldn't endanger her by getting involved."

He had no answer for that, not that he needed one as Kole stormed off with one final warning.

Left alone, Gabriel slumped, mind whirling. It was true. Getting involved with Leah was dangerous, reckless and decidedly un-sensible. And yet...

She wanted him. He wanted her. All the rest was just noise.

She'd asked him to respect her—he did, enough to trust she could make her own decisions, just as he'd told Bluewater. They could do this.

If he could be bold enough to grab happiness for just a little while.

The night stretched on. Every time Leah tried to get close to Gabriel to finish their conversation, something whirled them away from each other. Even the absolute stunned joy of her mom appearing with George, beckoned there on Gabriel's decree apparently, hadn't blocked the raging impatience that hummed under her skin. So, she'd played hostess and danced with her mom, posed for photos and pretended that every second wasn't a century.

Two hours after she'd appeared, Leah's mom hugged her by the idling town car. Her grip was firm, loving, and she smelled of soft roses and expensive perfume. Leah drew it in as something in her settled. "Thank you for coming," she mumbled into her neck.

Joyce Miller née Turner drew away, sparkling in an elegant silver gown and matching chandelier earrings. Her blond hair had been tamed into a classic updo that framed her regal, still-beautiful face. The eyes might have a few lines, but they shone the same blue as Leah's as she surveyed her daughter.

George was already in the waiting car, having said his goodbyes. They were headed straight to O'Hare, back to their honeymoon, but Leah couldn't bring herself to feel too sad. They'd shown up for her. That meant more than anything.

"We wouldn't have been anywhere else. I'm sorry we have to leave tonight." Disappointment shadowed her mother's face. "But we've arranged a wine tasting and a day out in—"

Leah shook her head, interrupting. "Mom, it's fine. I'm just glad you could make it."

"Me, too." Joyce squeezed their joined hands before her gaze slid past Leah. From the appreciative gleam, Leah could guess who she was looking at.

"Your Gabriel," she began, confirming Leah's assumption.

"He's not my Gabriel."

"He would be if you were smart about it."

Leah couldn't help but laugh, even as her heart ached. "He's going back to New Orleans next month."

"There are planes," her mother argued. "People move."

If only distance was the obstacle. "It's not like that between us."

"Well, what is it?"

"I..." The secret fell like weight across her shoulders.

He's a warlock, she wanted to say. *I'm a human. It's never going to work out.*

"It's just not that simple," she settled for.

"It should be. Consider this my motherly advice for the decade: seduce him."

Leah choked. "*Mom.*"

Joyce's grin could only be described as devilish. "Honey, that man is an éclair waiting to be gobbled up." She tugged on Leah's hands. "He called me, a woman he's never met, so I could be here for you. And it was more of a demand than a suggestion."

Leah's lips curved.

"He cares. That's hard to find." Joyce hesitated over her next words. "I know you've always been a little distrustful of men because of, well, your dad, how he left. How I...fell apart. You don't like to let people in in case they hurt you. Leave."

"Mom." Pained, uncomfortable, Leah rolled her shoulders as if she could shrug off the topic. "Don't. It's fine. I'm fine."

Joyce looked like she wanted to say more, but sighed and leaned in to kiss Leah's cheek. "Just promise me you'll think about it." As Leah laughed again, she added, "You deserve happiness, baby."

The words stayed with Leah as she waved them off and saw Gabriel waiting for her with Emma and Bastian. Their eyes locked, and a shiver trailed one finger down her spine.

Happiness, she thought again, exhaling a steadying breath. She was going to go get her some.

"You guys didn't have to stick around," she said as she approached, holding up her skirt and hopping over a puddle. It had rained and the night air was full of the scent of it. "You should've left when Tia did."

Emma smiled at her, tucked under the protection of Bastian's draped arm. She wore his tuxedo jacket and huddled into it as she said, "We just wanted to say how great it all was. Really."

"Loved the little hot dogs," Bastian put in. He flashed her a grin. "Next time my mom throws an event, I'm putting them on the menu. Little wieners for all the big ones."

Leah laughed before registering someone was missing. She glanced around. "Where's Kole?"

Awkwardness infused the air like spice.

"He decided to call it an early night," Emma said after a moment, flushing.

Leah wanted to feel annoyance at the statement but all that came was regret. Despite the fact that she went long stretches without seeing him, she counted Kole as a friend. She didn't want them to be at odds.

Still. It was her life and it was her decision.

He was her decision.

"And you?" She faced Gabriel, who stood slightly apart from her friends. Always apart.

He inclined his head. Unlike Bastian, who'd undone his bow tie, he was as buttoned-up as ever. "I will escort you home."

The hint of care wrapped up in a haughty statement was so like him. "Are you worried about my safety?"

He lifted his chin as if the thought was preposterous. "No. It's good manners, since I escorted you here."

"Uh-huh." She poked him in the rock-hard belly. "I'm onto you, Gabe. You're such a worrywart."

"Goodnights are not worrywarts."

"They might not be, but you are." She grinned at his irritated expression, knowing she was right.

Bastian spoke up. "We can get you home if it's out of Goodnight's way."

Leah didn't take her eyes off Gabriel's face. "That's okay."

"You sure?"

The question seemed double-edged.

Emma reached over and slipped her hand in Bastian's, tugged. "She's sure." She cast Leah a bolstering smile and then, to Leah's surprise, said to Gabriel, "We're trusting you with her."

He gave a clipped nod.

"*Okay.* On that embarrassing note…" Leah nudged Gabriel to walk. "Bye, guys."

They left her friends and the hotel behind, matching strides despite the height difference. Now they were alone, he relaxed his concrete posture, his face sliding into contemplation. "Are you pleased?"

Leah didn't question with what; she was pleased with it all. "It went well. And I loved having my mom there." She brushed her hand against his, the dark pleasure flirting inside her reflected in his eyes. He didn't pull away.

He didn't acknowledge her silent thanks, either, but she didn't expect him to. He hated to be praised. She got the impression he hadn't been on the receiving end much in his life.

Headlights slid over his face, golden, then not. "What?"

Another shiver, this one from cold, tickled her body. She lifted her arms to fold them around herself, chafed the trailing goose bumps. "Nothing. It's just nice, finally being alone with you."

He looked down at her, moving his gaze to where she rubbed her arms. The air warmed around her the next second, a small twist marring his lips as he turned his head away on an intake of breath.

"Are you okay?" she asked, concern overshadowing the jump of excitement at the display of magic. The display of magic *in front of her.*

He nodded, the movement stiff. As if it hadn't happened, he gestured to the street where traffic kept the city active. "Shall we get a car?"

There were tough nuts and there was Gabriel.

Leah stepped closer, slipping her hand into his. With a glow of triumph, she felt the tremor go through him. "I don't want to go home yet."

He didn't turn in to her but he didn't let go of her hand, either. Even this late, Saturday night in Chicago had its own music, its own rhythm. Leah could barely hear it over her own breath as she waited for him to say something.

When he did, the words were low, filled with gravel. "It wouldn't be a good idea."

A car slid past, spraying puddle water near them, but neither paid it any attention.

"I think you're wrong," she challenged, fear of rejection clamoring in her chest.

"Must you always argue?"

"When you're always wrong, yeah."

He finally looked at her. His eyes were brilliant, lightning captured inside green glass. "I'm not wrong now."

"A matter of opinion." Her heart thrummed, so fast there was barely any space between the beats. *Please.* She took a shaky breath and went with her best offer. "Once."

"Excuse me?"

God, she could barely breathe. She moved in so the warmth around her encompassed him. Tipping back her head, she carefully set one hand on his chest. It rose unsteadily under her fingers.

"Once," she repeated, ignoring the few people that passed them. They were ghosts to her. "You. Me. One night."

Something sparked under her hand, like his skin had put out a small charge.

She pressed her advantage. "Forget everyone else, your side, my side. What I am, who you are." A muscle flexed in his jaw and she curled her fingers into his shirt. "The politics, the truth, the lies. Forget everything but you. And me. And one night."

"Leah…" His voice was a rumble of darkness. Of warning.

She didn't heed it. "I know you're all about responsibility. Doing what you think is right. But what if we played pretend? What if, for one night, you were just Gabe. And I was just Leah?"

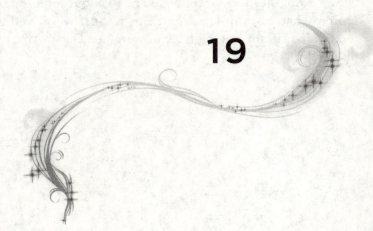

19

*H*e'd portalled them to his apartment. And she'd missed it. Leah's whole focus had been Gabriel as he'd made the decision in the space of two thudding heartbeats. His kiss was consuming, hands grasping her hips as he brought her up on her toes. Big hands. Strong, surprisingly capable hands.

When he'd walked her backward, she'd gone willingly, barely registering the strange juddering around her until her back hit the wall and it wasn't cold concrete.

When she opened her eyes, his expression was drawn, hints of pain within. Then she saw the last flickers of a portal closing behind him and realization hit her like a slap on the ass.

He didn't say anything, only watched her carefully.

Questions crowded her throat. What did it mean that he'd used such obvious magic? Should she comment on it? Was it possible he'd show her more? Could she ask questions about what kind of magic he had? Did this mean he trusted her?

That last question answered itself. He'd portalled her, a human. He trusted her. Gabriel Goodnight *trusted* her.

She untangled the hand in his hair, traced his forehead. "It hurts you, doesn't it?" The lines eased as she ran her fingers across them. He didn't confirm but she knew she was right.

All those times he'd helped her out with magic, looked after her.

And she knew she didn't need to ask anything else. Not now. All she needed was for him to kiss her again.

She threaded her hands through his hair, relishing the feel of the strands slipping through her fingers, and tugged.

She didn't need to ask twice. He bent to capture her mouth in another deep, drugging kiss. His hands skimmed up her sides, making her shiver.

"Bed," she mumbled, dragging her mouth free. "I want to feel you."

His eyes, already hot, went molten.

But he shook his head. "No."

"*No?*"

A hint of humor played around his face. "Not yet," he amended.

"What are you—"

"You talk too much."

"So, give me something to do with my mouth."

A muscle ticked in his jaw and his hands tightened on her hips. "You will not rush me."

"We only have one night," she reminded him. "Let's get to the good stuff."

He took her hand, turned her palm upward and brushed his lips over the pulse point in her wrist before gently biting down. Lust surged into her belly.

"Leah," he murmured. "You *are* the good stuff."

Romance flickered inside her. It made her feel weak. "You're too good at saying the right thing."

One eyebrow tilted. "I've never been accused of that before."

She had to laugh. She smoothed her free hand over his jaw,

his cheek so she cupped it. "Maybe you don't show this side of you enough."

"This side?"

"Gabe."

He looked at her. "I'll never be just Gabe."

She knew what he was saying. "One night," she confirmed, pushing aside the sneaking want that craved more. "If you ever get on with it."

"You're impossible." With an intensity to his face, he pushed her so her spine hit the wall. Abruptly, her arms were above her head, locked together. And he wasn't touching her.

When her startled eyes flew to his, he only said, "Okay?"

Was he kidding? "More." It was breathless, a moan, and she squirmed in place. Reality intruded long enough for her to add, "But doesn't this hurt you?"

"It's worth it," he said, in a voice made for dark deeds done in dark rooms. His eyes roved over her. "This dress has tormented me all night. But not as much as this has."

He stepped in, nudged the pink fabric to the side and exposed her tattoo. An ampersand, smaller than her thumbprint and just below her left collarbone.

His finger traced the design. Everywhere he touched, fire spread. "What does it mean?"

She swallowed against the lust choking her throat. "It's a reminder that there's always a next. That nothing ever really ends, and to stay open to people, possibilities." Like him.

But this would end. She accepted it, didn't want to linger. Instead, she tilted back her head and gave him a sly smile. "It's not my only one."

His finger paused. "Where?"

"You'll have to find it yourself."

"Hmm." He put his mouth to her ampersand, nipped. She jumped.

"You ever consider getting inked?"

She didn't realize it was a dual-edged question until he frowned. She knew in the witch community, the main reason for tattoos was an engagement, for what they called "the Divining." Different traits would show up on their wrists in the weeks following the engagement, showing what each individual would bring to the marriage. Apparently, the majority of witch marriages were magically motivated, purely political.

Was there a political marriage in Gabriel's future? A wife who would ignore him until they had to show a united front to society? Who wouldn't tease him, make him play, make him talk? One who had strong magical bloodlines perfect for his legacy genes?

He hesitated. And she found she didn't want to hear his answer.

So, she didn't let him. "I think you'd look sexy." She wiggled her eyebrows. "All proper on the outside, a little edgy underneath."

"Sexy?"

He sounded like he'd never heard the word before.

"I could show you." She strained forward from where she was chained. Why did she find it so hot he was restraining her with magic?

"Later. I have plans. A list."

"A *list*?"

"I've wanted to touch you for weeks, Leah." His lips curved, small but edged with sin. "I'm a man who thinks everything through. I've thought this through a lot."

"What did you think about?"

"How you'd say my name." He moved closer, pushing his body against hers so she was trapped between him and the wall. His lips hovered over hers, teasing. "How you'd taste."

Her breathing was ragged. "Then kiss me."

Holding her gaze, he shook his head in a deliberate negative. "Not here."

And then he sank to the floor.

It took her a wild second to understand, and in that time, his hands were under her dress, smoothing up her legs. Lust tugged viciously at her insides.

"Gabe," she said unsteadily. "My dress."

"Very nice," he agreed in his polite tone. "I apologize."

"For wha—"

Fabric ripped. Between one second and the next, her dress had acquired a rough slit that hiked to her upper thigh.

Shock obliterated her words.

He didn't even notice, tracing the tops of her stockings, where they hooked to her garter belt. "This...is also nice." His voice was graveled. "Did you wear it for me?"

"Yes," she managed.

"Thank you."

"You're welcome."

Wicked humor danced in his eyes as he slid a look up at her. A fierce wave of desire pounded through her at the sight of Gabriel at her feet, tuxedo-clad, hair rumpled, with laughter in his gorgeous eyes. She bit her lip and squeezed her legs together.

He noticed. "That won't do."

He eased the ripped fabric aside, eased her legs apart with strong fingers. Those fingers left her thighs, trailed upward, over her panties. Her head fell back as he cupped her.

He made a noise, a dark one, as he nudged the panties aside and traced a finger against her, into her. A sound ripped free. Her hands spasmed where they were locked, as he began a slow rhythm, sinking deep, withdrawing, moving, curling.

Her eyes had closed, her fingers clenched on open air as she rode that finger, then the next, without shame, seeking more, always more. Teeth sank into her bottom lip. Hers, she was pretty sure, but who cared when all her attention was on him, his hands, his fingers, his thumb as it circled her clit, pressing hard with every thrust.

"Come for me," he demanded in that haughty accent she loved before he pushed a third finger into her.

A broken noise fell from her mouth as she obeyed, as she flung herself into the dark void of pleasure. When she opened her eyes, he was still on his knees and he had his fingers in his mouth. He kept eye contact as he tasted her.

"Gabriel," she breathed, pushing against the hold on her wrists. "I need to touch you."

"You taste like sunshine." He pushed to his feet, releasing her wrists. She sagged and he caught her, immediately capturing her mouth with his.

It was darker, deeper, and she was helpless to resist, didn't want to. She clutched his shoulders, roamed over them, using his lapels to hold him tighter to her. She'd just come, but it had only whetted her appetite, a starter before the main course— and she'd been starving for him for what felt like forever.

She wrestled with his jacket until she finally tore her mouth from his on an annoyed sound. "Are you welded into this thing?"

"A well-tailored jacket is a necessity," he told her, and she smiled despite herself.

"Not now it's not." She pulled on it, pleased when he helped her, even more so when he stood in front of her in his shirt and pants. She attacked his bow tie next, ripping it free, then started on his buttons. She pushed open the shirt like she was unveiling a spectacular view. And what a view.

She bent her head and pressed a kiss to one pec, trailing kisses to the other. Her hands pulled the shirt free and threw it blindly.

When she went to undo his zipper, his hand closed over hers. "Wait."

Frustrated, she blew a loosened curl out of her face. "Why?"

"Because. It's my turn."

He spun her around, her back to his front, surprising her into a super sexy squawk. It melted into a breathy catch as he pressed a kiss to her shoulder. "How does this come off?" His hand slid down her hip, inching the material up. "Or shall I solve the issue the same way as last time?"

She really liked this dress. But she wasn't an idiot. "Rip it."

He must have used magic because the words had barely cleared her mouth before there was a loud tearing sound and from top to bottom, the fabric of her dress was in two halves. It dropped to the ground, puddling there, leaving her in her silver heels and underwear.

His hands skimmed her body as though committing it to memory. When she tried to turn, he held her in place.

"I dreamt of you." The words whispered into her throat. "Like this. Here. With me."

She arched against him. "With you," she agreed, hissing as one of his hands covered her breast. "Only with you. Gabe."

He molded her, squeezing gently, skimming a thumb over the tight nipple, making delicate sensations shoot between her thighs. She went up on tiptoe as he rolled the bud between his fingers.

"I'm going to lick you here."

She swallowed.

"Then here." His hand moved to her other breast, flicking the nipple so more lightning struck. "Everywhere. I want you to cry out my name."

She'd had enough. Without warning, she reached behind her and palmed him, shaping, squeezing.

His grip tightened as he sucked a breath in through his teeth. "*Leah.*"

"I never thought I'd say this," she said, voice raw. "But the time for talking is over."

And suddenly it was.

She wasn't sure if she'd spun or if he'd turned her, but they were face-to-face. He pushed her so she backed up, suddenly dropping onto the couch. That lovely, long, soft couch.

As she reclined, his eyes roamed her, hot, intense. His hands dropped to his pants, unzipping. The sound reverberated through her, clenching in all sorts of places. He pushed both his pants and boxer briefs down his long legs, stepped out of them.

She was unable to take her eyes off the length of him. She shifted, even that friction amping up her frustration as she ached, desperate for him to be inside her.

A condom packet appeared in his hand. He tossed it onto the coffee table, barely pausing before he braced a hand against her chest and nudged her to lie flat. She registered he'd lost his socks and shoes at some point, before her attention diverted back as he came down over her.

Now, she thought, trembling ridiculously. Her hands stroked over his arms, sculpting the muscles that bunched under her fingers.

But he wasn't done with her, and with every teasing touch, deft stroke, nibble, kiss, lick, he drove her slowly into a fever where even the cool brush of air against her sensitized skin had her quivering. Nothing escaped his attention: her breasts, her stomach, her hips, her thighs, between them. He was a master of control, patiently guiding her to the edge before pulling her back, again and again and again until she reared up and bit his bicep in revenge.

As though his control had slipped, green sparks burst around them, dozens of tiny iridescent lights. One hit her skin and buzzed, a hot vibration that arrowed to her thighs, making her hiss.

His mouth descended, first on hers, stoking the fire that raged, before sliding down her throat, across her collarbones to the tattoo. He'd found her other one, a small arrow in a bow on her left hip, meant to be a positive reminder that when life holds you back, it's about to propel you forward. She felt like that arrow, poised to fly, tense and waiting.

When his knuckles brushed her damp center, she cried out his name.

It was like he'd been waiting for it. Suddenly the condom packet was in his hand and he tore it open. He sheathed himself, fisting tightly as he looked at her spread out beneath him. He'd left her garter belt and stockings, but the panties had been lost some time ago.

"Now," she said, pleaded.

He let go, braced his arms on either side of her. She felt the nudge of him, hard to her soft, and spasmed.

"Now." As he said it, he drove forward.

She lost her breath. Her hands flew up, clutched at his arms. Her nails dug in as he sank in all the way.

Their eyes met. Passion tightened his features, hair disheveled from sweat. Gabriel undone.

She contracted around him and he sucked in a breath.

Holding her gaze, he gradually pulled back before sinking in again. Sweat slicked along her skin as she tried to breathe, pleasure shaking her in its teeth.

She met his next thrust, canting up her hips so he nudged that place inside that made fireworks dance in her core. His hand held her hips up as he reared back and plunged again. Harder, but not faster.

Her breathing was jagged, matching his, but on and on his slow, deliberate thrusts continued. The couch creaked as he rocked his hips, as she wrapped her legs around his waist. He bent, kissed her hard as they climbed, those sparks glittering around them, some landing and sending shock waves across her flesh.

Desperate for more, crazed, she sank her nails into his ass, tried to grind her hips against his, but he resisted on a low groan. He nipped her lip in reprimand.

Her inner muscles squeezed, one step from free fall.

He cursed as he felt it, and finally, finally, his hips pistoned, faster, harder. He let her drop to the couch, followed her. Now he wasn't holding her hips up, he used his free hand to stroke her.

"Leah," he demanded, raw. She wasn't sure what he was demanding but knew he could have whatever he wanted in that moment.

She arched, gasping as he rolled his hips, squeezed, and she shot off the edge, unseeing, unfeeling as she cried out.

He snarled. His hips were almost punishing for the next few strokes but she welcomed it, gloried in it. When he pressed his face into her throat, groaned her name as he shuddered in pleasure, it felt like victory.

Little aftershocks made her tremor as she wrapped her arms around him. His chest moved unevenly against hers. Sweat slicked them both.

She felt used, drained, energized. She felt everything, nothing. As her heart regained a somewhat normal rhythm, she let out a deep, smug sigh. "You're welcome."

And then squeaked as he nudged her ticklish spot.

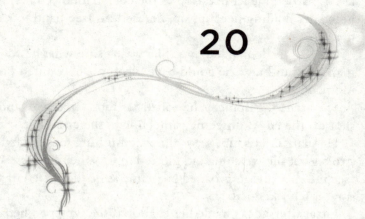

20

Gabriel had reached for her more than once. He'd meant it when he'd said he had a list and if they only had one night, he meant to tick off every item.

He'd tasted her properly, her hands in his hair, her hips rising to his mouth as he drove her to ecstasy. Several times. He could well become addicted to her taste, to the small, sharp pain of his hair being tugged, the sight of her head thrown back, the sound of her voice calling his name.

He'd taken her on the couch, resisting the temptation to have her in his bed. It was bad enough he'd be surrounded by the memories out in the living space; he'd never be able to sleep for the remaining weeks if he had her in his sheets. He'd marked every inch of her skin, unable to help the dark swell of satisfaction every time she cried out *his* name. She would remember him. He would never forget her.

He hadn't meant to sleep. He'd had her draped across his lap, skimming a thumb along her thigh, over the tattoo on her hip, listening as she told him about a dance class she wanted to try. She'd made him smile and he'd closed his eyes for a moment, listening to her voice.

Now sunlight was pouring in through his windows. And the night was done.

Regret clamped a fist around his heart but he didn't show it as he brewed coffee in the kitchen. He'd have conjured her favorite drink from the café across from the shelter, but his use of magic the night before had taken him close to the edge, and he felt drained this morning. All-around lackluster.

She emerged from his bathroom, dressed in one of his shirts and a pair of suit trousers she'd rolled up what had to be ten times. She should've looked ridiculous, but with her curls flying everywhere, her cheeks flushed and some fairly embarrassing marks on her neck, she'd never looked more beautiful.

He cleared his throat, set the mug down on the breakfast bar. "I didn't know if you liked to eat in the morning." If so, he wasn't sure what he could make for her. He still hadn't managed to master the perfect toast.

"I'm easy." She gave him a smile as she came over, picked up the mug. "Is this—"

"Milk, one sugar."

"Thanks." She sipped, gagged. "And hot."

"Coffee generally is."

"You got me there." She blew, took one more careful sip. Then studied him across the curling steam. "So. Last night."

He kept his face impassive. "Yes."

Her fingers, the same ones that had trailed his body so many times, curled around her cup. "I had fun."

"It was enjoyable."

Her grin flashed. "Orgasms generally are."

"And you had your share."

A pink flush spread across her cheeks. "Well, you wouldn't let me take my turn to help you keep up."

"I didn't need it." And he didn't regret it, either.

She gave him a doubting look and tapped her fingers on the mug. "So, did we cross everything off your list?"

"For the most part." It would be enough, it had to be. One night. They'd agreed.

She moved her hair behind her ear, looked down at herself. Rueful, she said, "You don't mind me borrowing this, right? I can't exactly leave in my dress."

Now he felt like his cheeks were flushing. "I apologize for that."

"Don't. I liked it." She flicked a look at him and away, an element of shyness in the way she couldn't hold eye contact.

He bore down on a surge of emotion, ruthlessly squashing it. "Good. And no, I don't mind."

She nodded, drank some coffee. "You don't regret…?"

"No." That, he was decisive about. "And you?"

"Never." When she looked at him in that way, he could see himself clearing the counter, taking her in his arms again.

The silence crackled, much like the embarrassing manifestation of magic he'd displayed last night. Premature sparkage. How mortifying.

When the chirp of the compact mirror on the counter sounded, both of them jolted.

He threw a look at it. "I forgot to call Melly last night."

"Right." She put the mug down on the bar. "I'll get going."

"Would you like me to—?"

"I'm fine. You don't need to take care of me." She gestured. "Talk to your sister. I'll see you at the shelter."

He made no moves toward the mirror. Instead, he watched as she gathered up her shoes and purse. "Leah. We're…good, yes?"

She glanced his way, seemed to read something in his face. Heading over, she crooked a finger from the other side of the breakfast bar. Obliging, although wary, he bent down. She gave his cheek a kiss. He breathed her in as she leaned away. "We're good. One night. Still friends."

He searched her face, couldn't see any hint she was lying. A part of him was relieved. He couldn't stand the idea of her being annoyed with him. The other part was tangled in all kinds of emotions too slippery to get a handle on. So, he nodded, and watched the door close behind her with a conclusive click. The apartment seemed to dim.

Rubbing an ache in his chest, he picked up the compact, flipped it open. As he'd thought, his sister's face filled the screen. "Melly."

"Is everything okay? You didn't call me."

"Apologies. The gala ran late."

"I figured. Did it go well? Was Leah pleased?"

He kept his face bland, hoped his perceptive sister, who had been asking about Leah every day, wouldn't catch on. "I believe she was very pleased with the evening."

Leah hadn't been awkward or clinging or even sad, he thought hours later, sitting at the reception desk for his shift. Chuck lay at his feet, lulled into complacency with the biggest chew Gabriel had been able to hunt down at the local pet store. Along with a new tug toy and a tiny, stuffed Labrador that looked too much like Chuck to pass up. And then, because guilt had stirred about the other animals, he'd also ordered several toys and chews to be delivered to the shelter later this afternoon. It wasn't everything, but small actions counted. He believed that. He knew Leah did, too.

Mercy. Enough, man.

With the current lull in walk-ins, being on reception wasn't the best job when you didn't want to wallow in your thoughts. He deliberately turned his attention away from Leah for the fourth time in ten minutes, searching for a distraction. He'd even make small talk with visitors at this point.

He eyed the sagging couch. The place needed new furniture, he thought again. He'd been sidelined by the vandalism and learning the trade and…other things, but it remained as true now as it had been weeks ago. The family manor had many rooms with furniture he and Melly never bothered with. They could certainly spare a couch. Maybe a few other pieces, to make the reception look more welcoming and less desperate. Especially since they'd had a flurry of phone calls after the gala had been mentioned in the society pages and across social media, at least according to Leah. She'd been so happy, beaming all morning, not at all affected by the end to their agreed-upon one night.

Damn it.

He smoothed his thumb over his signet ring, wondering what his parents would have thought of his affair with a human. They likely would've been pleased, keen as they'd been to bring their worlds together, to the detriment of any family life.

And although he'd let that bitterness shape his life in ways he wasn't proud of, he thought he understood now what had drawn them out of society and toward humans. Though they may be whispers to a witch's shout, humans held their own brand of magic. Potent and real as any other Gabriel had experienced.

Chuck's tail beat the floor in welcome as the outside door suddenly opened, lurching to his feet. Gabriel snapped a hand out, catching his collar with a murmured command. Chuck looked balefully up at him and lay back down, sighed.

It wasn't bright-eyed potential adopters. Instead, two uni-formed police came in. One was a woman, tan and tall, polished and pressed. The other was a man who matched her in height, brunet, and so white he gleamed like a pearl. He tucked his thumbs into his belt and swaggered up to the reception desk.

Gabriel stood. He had a feeling this wasn't a social call.

The male officer stopped, lifting his chin. "We'd like to see the owner."

"He isn't here." They'd gotten a call about an abandoned dog on the other side of town and Sonny had headed right over. Gabriel almost said they could talk to him, but hesitated. As much as he'd like to take care of this for her, Leah was the next in charge, and she'd want to handle it. "If you take a seat, I'll find the next best thing."

They remained standing.

He found Leah in the cat sanctuary, stroking an amber tabby. He'd seen her throughout the day and each time was another nick to his self-control. He cleared his throat. "You're needed in reception. Two police officers are asking for the owner, and Sonny's out."

She pursed her lips as she gently deposited the cat back in its pen and shut the door. "Did they say what they wanted?"

"I came to get you before asking. I respect you." He didn't know why he added it, but it made her grin.

"Duly noted." She set off in front of him, hips swaying as she strode forward. She'd been magnificent in the pink evening gown, but faded denim definitely had its own appeal.

When they walked into reception, both cops turned to her. "You the manager?"

"Essentially." She crossed her arms. "Is this about the tagging? Have you found who was doing it?"

"Afraid not, ma'am." The woman stepped up next to her partner. "Officer Parks," she continued, motioning to herself. "Officer Franklin. We're here on reports of dangerous dogs being let loose around the neighborhood from this establishment."

Leah stared blankly. "Dangerous dogs?"

"Aggressive. Prone to bite."

Now she bristled. "Who told you that piece of garbage?"

"Anonymous tip."

"That's crap." Leah jammed her hands on her hips. "I'm telling you, we don't have any vicious dogs. And if we did, we'd never let them loose. Our insurance wouldn't allow it."

"Well, then, I guess we'll just take you at your word."

Gabriel closed a hand into a fist at his side, wound tight at the sarcasm. "Don't speak to her like that."

Officer Franklin puffed up his chest. "We have a duty to investigate threats."

"Investigate away." Leah flung her hand wide, angry energy unbottled. "But I'm telling you, that report is trash."

They insisted on touring the facility, but even after half an hour and turning up nothing, insisted on coming back to speak to Sonny and their neighbors. They'd been aggressive, patronizing and downright rude from the moment they'd arrived, grating along Gabriel's nerves. For the first time, he understood what Leah meant about basic manners.

"Give Mr. Bradford this card and tell him to call us as soon as he can." Officer Franklin thrust a card at Leah.

She blew out a breath in obvious frustration. "You've just seen we've got no vicious dogs. That tip was obviously a prank. I don't understand why—"

"Ma'am." Officer Parks huffed out a breath. "We've heard enough from you. Just tell Mr. Bradford."

Gabriel's eyes narrowed. As they turned on their heel and walked toward the exit, he debated, reasoned, considered—and lost the battle. With a small cough, he rubbed his chin and sent magic spiraling toward the door.

As Officer Franklin reached for it, it blew inward without warning. Staggering back to avoid being hit, he smacked into his partner with a curse. They went down in a tangle of limbs and in the resulting confusion, somehow the two found themselves handcuffed together. They stared down in bemusement.

"Clive, you idiot," Parks snapped, hauling them upward. "Get the key."

He patted his pocket down with his free hand, then again. And again. His eyes flew up. "It's not in there."

"For the love of…" She yanked at the cuffs, cursing when he crashed into her. They both knocked into the door and through it as it swung open unexpectedly. It closed behind their cries of alarm.

When Gabriel turned to Leah, her eyes were lit with laughter. "How strange for them to get locked together," she commented evenly.

"Indeed."

"And then to fall through the door like that."

"Bad luck. Or perhaps karma."

"Hmm." She tucked her hands in her front pockets. "You know, you don't have to protect me. I can take care of myself."

"I don't like anyone disrespecting you."

She shook her head, a laugh bubbling out. "I'd never have believed it." Her lips were still curved as she angled her head back. "A man of hidden talents."

The amusement quickly drained as she looked pensively at the doors. "It's like someone's out to get us." She slumped, closing her eyes briefly. "I'll have to tell Sonny. Perfect. One more thing. He'll be sure to— No," she decided, slicing the air with her hands. "No, I'm not going to worry because there's nothing to worry about. If they want to waste their time, then have at it. And we've had more adoption interest and bigger donations than we've had in months. Thanks to you and me. Go us."

There was no thought. No plan.

One minute he was watching her babble, finishing with that nervous smile.

The next, he had her up against his body, tasting that smile with his mouth. Her body jolted against his, then her hands were in his hair and she was kissing him back. She thrummed with energy, the wildly beautiful energy he'd noticed from the first. He craved it.

When they broke apart, she was panting. His chest moved unevenly as she braced her hands against him.

"Gabriel," she said, pressing her lips together as if to taste him. He felt it in his gut. "I thought we said…"

"I know." He framed her face. "You make me weak."

"That doesn't sound good." She wrapped her fingers around his wrists, but she didn't tug him away.

"It's not."

"I'm sorry."

"No, you're not."

"No, I'm not," she agreed and grinned.

He loved her smiles.

If you really cared about her, you wouldn't endanger her by getting involved. Kole's words. Guilt shot into him but not strong enough to fight her pull. He'd told Kole she was a woman who made her own decisions. He couldn't treat her as less.

"I can't do it."

Her thumbs gently stroked his pulse points. "Can't do what?"

"I can't have just one night."

She grew very still.

He moved his hands into her wild curls. "I can't stay away. It's stupid. Dangerous. I don't want anything to happen to you."

"Gabe." That one word stopped him. "What are you saying?"

"It's selfish. But I'm asking for one month. My last month. Be with me. And then I'll let you go."

Leah gazed up at him, a million thoughts flickering behind the blue. Chuck had given up on them and had wandered off to find his chew, and the padding of the dog's feet echoed inside Gabriel's deathly quiet mind as he waited.

Finally, she squeezed his wrists. "Yes."

Leah didn't let the small fear of what her friends would say keep her from barreling through the bar's doors.

"Break out the Cauldron Cosmos," she announced, bouncing up to the bar and ignoring the few stares she received at her entrance. Her grin felt so wide, it could fall off her face.

Emma took one look and turned to Bastian, who worked beside her. "Girl time."

He tucked her hair behind her ear. "I could be a girl."

"No, you really couldn't."

He grazed her cheek, grinned. "I'll take that as a compliment."

Leah shooed him. "Leave. Where's Tia?"

"New Orleans."

"Well, poof her here."

"You really have a handle on the magic thing," Bastian said dryly. "We're not genies. We can't poof people."

That distracted her. "Genies exist?"

"Oh, yeah." Bastian picked up a vodka bottle, handed it to her. "Rub this three times and see what happens."

"Rub this." She made a rude gesture at him and he laughed.

"Why don't you go find Tia?" Emma set three chilled glasses on the counter, despite the afternoon trade.

Bastian turned her face to his, kissed her thoroughly. A blush stained Emma's cheeks when he drew away. "Miss me."

"Eh," she said noncommittally and he grinned, kissed her again. Then, with a nod to Leah, strode out the back to portal to New Orleans.

Leah hopped onto a stool, waved at a couple of regulars. "When did Stan dye his hair?"

"About a week ago? Says it's lucky for baseball."

"I'm all for it, then." Leah turned back around. "I feel like I haven't been here in ages."

"Yeah, well, you've been spending more time at the shelter lately."

"Do you know how many adoptions we had today? Six. *Six.* That's more than we had in the last two weeks." She wriggled her shoulders.

"That's amazing." Emma's grin widened. "Congratulations."

"Thanks. I mean, I know we're not out of the woods yet, and Sonny's still being weird and making noises about getting away for a bit."

"You think he'll really retire?" Emma's brows drew together as she selected a shaker.

"I don't know. But anyway, it's a start and that's not why I'm here." Leah shook it off, determined to hang onto her happy feeling.

"Uh-huh. Can I guess from the fat cat expression someone got the cream last night?"

Leah let a beat pass. "That was weird."

"Yeah, I regretted it the minute it was out." Emma added ingredients to the shaker. "You want to wait for Tia?"

"I don't mind bragging more than once."

Emma's eyebrows lifted. "That good?"

"You know how there's sex and then there's forget-your-own-name sex?"

Emma gave her a look.

"Right, your whole I-felt-engaged-so-stayed-true-to-Bastian thing." Leah waved that off. "Trust me, not all guys get the job done, or they get the job done but it's only so-so."

"And Gabriel Goodnight got the job done?"

"Gabriel Goodnight crossed every *t* and dotted every *i*. The man believes in thorough attention to detail. God bless him for it." Leah brushed her nails against her chest, studied them. Then ruined it by dancing in her seat like a child. She sighed, plonking an elbow on the bar and resting her chin on it. "You think it's the warlock factor?"

"Leah."

"Nobody's listening."

Emma shot her a pained glance and topped the shaker, lifted it. The ingredients rattled as she began to shake. "Well, again, you're asking the wrong person. Tia would be best."

"Best for what?" Dressed in a red power suit with sharp stilettos that clicked across the wooden floor, Tia emerged from the back, Chester at her heels. She carried a rosebud, which she handed to Emma. "From Bastian. He says not to forget your date tonight."

Emma's engagement ring winked as she took the flower, smiling dreamily as her magic unfurled the rose petals.

Tia's eye roll said everything. She unbuttoned her jacket, displaying a white silk camisole, and leaned a hip on the counter, oblivious to the stares she was getting from their male patrons. "So, Bastian said it was girl time. Did it not go well?" She reached over, patted Leah's upper arm. "Disappointment, was he? I knew it. He's too stiff to be good in bed." She made a gesture. "And not in the hot way."

"Wrong." Emma set the rose down, poured out the drinks, slid one over to Tia. "Apparently Gabriel Goodnight should be called Gabriel Wildnight."

Leah wiggled her eyebrows as she picked up her glass.

Tia's jaw dropped. "Get out. That broomstick?"

Witch slang, Leah presumed. She debated what to tell them, settled for a tantalizing detail. "He ripped my dress in two."

No two people had ever looked as dumbfounded as her friends in that moment. Leah could've said she'd discovered she could do magic for all their shock.

Tia recovered first. "Well." She picked up her glass, shot it back. "I hate to say it, but good for Goodnight."

"One ripped dress and you approve?" Emma demanded. "Bastian had to work for it."

Tia shrugged, twirling her empty glass. "I don't approve, but it's got a shelf life—unlike your situation with Bastian had. At least this will all be over in a month."

The reminder threatened to pop her happiness balloon but Leah breezed determinedly past it. "So, you're happy for me?"

"You're human and sleeping with a warlock who could find out you know his secret at any time." Tia gave her a get-real look. "I'm not happy, but if I learned anything from Emma, you're all going to make mistakes and I just have to be here to pick up the pieces."

"Such a saint," Emma put in.

"I know, right?"

"Ah, about that," Leah interrupted before she lost her nerve. She sipped her cocktail, let the alcohol warm her belly. Give her the courage to get out the words. "He maybe, kinda, already sorta…knows."

"Knows what?"

"That I know." She tried a smile. "About magic."

Both of her friends stared at her.

One beat.

Two beats.

Thr—

"*What?*" Tia screeched.

Everyone in the bar quietened. A stray cough sounded in the unnatural silence.

Emma cleared her throat. "Um," she said, lifting her voice and a hand. "Sorry about that. Everything's fine."

Conversation resumed slowly but Tia didn't give them a moment's look as she bunched hands in her hair, tugged, eyes a little wild. "You *told* him?"

"No." Leah's toes curled under the stool's rung. "He figured it out. A while ago now."

"He's known for *weeks* and you didn't tell us?"

"I didn't know he knew for a while." Leah lifted a shoulder, toyed with her drink. She couldn't settle. "But after he kissed me, it was obvious."

"You didn't tell me that," Emma interjected, arms folded. Leah couldn't see him, but below the counter, Chester whined in appreciation of Emma's distress. As her familiar, he'd be able to feel it—or that's what Leah had been told.

"Un-freaking-believable." Tia wiped a hand down her face,

did some audible breathing. "A Higher son knows and you keep it to yourself."

"Okay, I know I probably should've warned you, but he isn't going to tell anyone. He cares about me." The glow returned.

"I hope you're right." Emma bit the edge of her thumbnail. "Kole is going to lose his shit."

"We can't tell Kole. He already doesn't like him." Which reminded her. "Do you know what they were talking about last night?" She'd spotted Kole and Gabriel cornered together and from their body language, they weren't discussing their favorite Bridgerton brother.

"Kole was warning him off."

Leah covered her face, mortified. "Jesus. You guys take overprotectiveness to a new level. He had no right." She peeked through her fingers. "What did Gabriel say?"

"This feels like high school," Tia complained. "Can we get back to the whole Gabriel knows thing? What are we going to do?"

"Nothing. Because that's what he'll do." Leah dropped her hands and stared Tia down. The wood pressed reassuringly into her as she braced for her next words. "He's going to finish his last month here and then he's going back to New Orleans."

"You're sure?" Emma asked.

"Like Tia said, I'm human, he's a warlock. A legacy warlock who'll need a society wife and let's face it, that isn't me. I walked away from that life once already." She forced herself to act like it was no big deal, like it wasn't crushing the part of her that still wished for more.

Tia was quiet a moment. "I'm torn between arguing that you're better than any society witch bitch and relief you understand this thing has an expiry date."

Leah did laugh now, loving her friend for helping ease the discomfort that lodged, hard and tight, in her chest. "We both get it. We originally said one night but then…"

"The dress got ripped out from under you?"

Leah sighed. "Oh, yeah."

"Gabriel Goodnight." Emma's expression was funny. "Ripping a dress in half."

"I'm telling you, tip of the iceberg."

Tia reluctantly toasted with her empty glass. "Always the quiet ones."

21

"You *have* to be Leah."

At the unfamiliar feminine voice, Leah twisted from where she was tugging rope with the energetic collie, Buster. The cool air fluttered loose curls around her face as she peered up against the sun. "Yeah. Can I help you?"

The figure moved to the right and Leah saw it was a girl, around Sloane's age, with the coltish frame of someone who hadn't yet grown into her limbs. She held the promise of beauty, with a swing of black hair that framed a heart-shaped face topped with hazel eyes and an infectious smile. She wore snug jeans and a white T-shirt that exposed her stomach beneath a cute lilac denim jacket. Something familiar tugged at Leah but she couldn't place what.

"I've come to help out," the girl announced, as though it were a done deal.

Despite the American accent, it was that authority that clicked it for her. Surprise shot through her veins. "You're Gabriel's sister."

"Yes!" Melly's smile widened. "I guess we kinda look alike, right?" She looked around. "Is he here?"

"Not yet." Discomforted, Leah arced her arm back and let the rope fly. A delighted Buster charged after it, joined by the other dogs she'd had out in the fresh air. She who was rarely lost for words found it suddenly hard to form a sentence. With no idea how much Gabriel had told her—and Leah really hoped he hadn't told his fourteen-year-old sister everything—she felt like she was trying to drive through fog. Her smile turned vaguely queasy as she faced Melly.

Who didn't appear to notice. "Perfect. That gives us time for a tour before he comes." Melly linked her hands in front of her, a silver charm bracelet dangling from her wrist. "He'll hate that I'm here."

Leah had a feeling.

"But I won't get you in trouble."

When Leah couldn't hold back her snort, Melly looked at her with as much delight as Buster. "You're not scared of my brother?"

Only when he withholds orgasms and I feel like I might die.

Right. Like she could say that to his little sister.

Deflecting, Leah pushed hair behind her ear. "Should I be?"

"Please, Gabriel's all bluster. Not that I won't get in trouble, but it'll be worth it. I've been dying to come here." Melly took everything in with a fascinated expression. It reminded Leah of herself whenever Emma or Tia spoke about the witch community. "He's talked about this place a lot." Her eyes went sly as only a teenager's could. "And you."

Leah's stomach jittered ridiculously.

"And Mrs. Q likes you. So, I thought, why should I stay home alone when I could come and check it out myself?"

Gabriel would blow a fuse. Two fuses. Hell, the power would be out in the whole state for days. If she was smart, she'd tell the girl to go home before her brother got there.

But she didn't do that. Mostly because Leah didn't see the harm in letting Melly hang out for a bit. Leah had often been the one left out of things, and she knew how bad it felt. Besides, if Melly's control over her magic slipped, Leah could always just steer her away from the others.

"You can help me with some of the chores if you want," she said, making the decision and whistling for the dogs.

After herding them back into their kennels, Leah put a mop in Melly's hand, grabbing a broom for herself. Even the prospect of cleaning didn't dampen the girl's enthusiasm. Over the next fifteen minutes, she chattered about her school, movies, even a hairstyle she was thinking of getting before moving on to how cool it must be to work with animals every day.

No wonder Gabriel put up with *her* so well, Leah thought with some amusement. He had his own chatterbox at home.

"Have you ever had animals?" Leah asked as she deposited swept-up dirt in the bin.

Melly, who was swinging the mop around with more enthusiasm than skill—definitely Gabriel's sister—shook her head. "I think Gabriel was overwhelmed enough looking after me; an animal would've been too much."

"A handful, huh?"

A grin brightened Melly's face. "Only when some of my, uh, experiments go awry."

Potions, Leah hazarded, with a strike of envy. She was obsessed with potions, had even talked Emma and Tia into letting her try to make a few, but they never worked. If she could only talk openly to Melly, she could've asked so many questions, but the last thing she wanted was to endanger the little Goodnight.

"I bet he handles that well."

"He's okay." Melly leaned on the mop handle with both hands. "He sighs, he groans, he curses the ceiling, but he's back the next day with a new, um, experiment to try."

"A good brother, then."

"The best."

"You must miss him while he's here."

She nodded. "The house feels too big. Uncle August says I could go over to his, but then Mrs. Q would be alone. She... she said you call Gabriel 'Gabe.'" Curiosity shone in the girl's eyes, with not a little speculation.

"It annoys him. I enjoy annoying your brother." Leah shrugged, focused on keeping it light. Surface. From the direction of Melly's questions, she had a feeling Gabriel had done just that.

Whether he'd tell his sister about the change in their relationship, well, that was his choice.

But she hoped.

Melly laughed again, swiping the mop across the soaked floor. "I know," she said in answer to Leah's comment. "He used to grumble how you were out to make his life hell."

Leah's eyebrows went up.

"It made me want to meet you even more. It's *so* obvious he doesn't want to answer questions about you. That he, you know, likes you. Like, *likes* you likes you."

Ah, to be fourteen. Unsure what to say, Leah fell back on a vague, "Huh."

"He's only dated a few women and they were all different, so I don't think he has, you know, a type." Thoughtfully, Melly swirled the mop in the bucket as Leah tried and failed not to be interested. "Well, looks-wise. They all scramble to agree with his every word. They don't stick around long. I think he wants a woman who'll push back. Who'll *annoy* him."

It could've been a billboard, for all its subtlety. Leah wondered if Gabriel knew his little sister was matchmaking. With a human, for that matter. "You don't say."

Melly slapped more water on the floor. Leah didn't have the heart to tell the girl she was doing it wrong if you could see your own reflection.

"He's stubborn," Melly continued, wrinkling her nose in thought. "He needs someone to push back or he'll get bored.

And too full of himself." Her sneakers squeaked in the water as she twirled the mop to the right. "He's, uh, not bad looking."

"No," Leah allowed, conjuring intense green eyes, sharp cheekbones, a soft mouth curving in the barest hint of a smile.

"He's funny. Sometimes."

"I've seen it."

"And he's strong. Like, if you needed to lean on someone, Gabriel would be there. He's always been there."

A lump appeared in Leah's throat.

Melly looked up at Leah, her parents' ghosts dancing between them. She frowned a little, the barest furrow. "Some people make fun of him for being too quiet or too blunt, but that's not the important stuff. He's…solid. Someone you can rely on."

The Warlock of Contempt. And yet.

Leah heaved a breath through her clogged throat. "Some people don't look beneath the obvious."

"No." Melly smiled, approving, the specter of grief disappearing. Dimples winked at her. "But you do."

Well, she'd stepped into that one.

Luckily for her, Sloane also stepped into it—it being the lake of water that ran over the kennel hallway.

"Gah." The teenager gawked at the water pooling around her sneakers. "Did we have a leak?"

Melly lifted a hand from the mop, gestured. "I'm mopping!"

"Uh…" Sloane slid her gaze from the grinning girl to Leah to the floor. Something shifted on her face. "You're Gabriel's sister."

"Yes! Is there a resemblance?"

"Something like that," Sloane murmured, gingerly stepping toward a dry patch of floor.

Leah choked back her laughter. "Melly, this is Sloane." She debated for a second, then went with her gut. "You might know her sister, Emma Bluewater?"

Melly's eyes rounded and then fired with excitement. "Oh, my Goddess! You're the hidden love child?"

Sloane's face went slack, and Leah winced.

Immediately, Melly's face twisted with contrition. "I'm sorry, sometimes words come out before I've thought them through. It's a bad habit."

"It's okay." Sloane rubbed her elbow, crossed her arms around her stomach. Her brown hair fell forward as she stared at the ground.

"I heard about Bastian's proposal." Clearly trying to make Sloane feel at ease, Melly switched gears and audibly sighed, all drama as she clutched the mop to her chest. "It sounded so romantic. I wish I'd been there."

"I saw it," Sloane ventured.

Melly darted forward to clutch her wrist. "You *have* to tell me all the details. Did he really have the ring that was promised when they did their—um…" She stopped, slid Leah a look.

She took pity on her. "How about I finish mopping and you two fetch us some drinks from the café across the street? Just tell Joanne to put it on my tab."

Sloane shot her a betrayed look as she was carted off by the chattering girl. Leah was unrepentant. She might not know magic, but she knew people, and she would bet on those two becoming fast friends before she had her coffee in hand. It would be good for both of them—and get Melly away from Leah before she figured out the truth about her and Gabriel.

Yeah, Leah would let Melly's big brother explain that one.

Gabriel stopped short as he caught the sound of his sister's belly laugh pealing out from the shelter's yard. His chest tightened as he hurried forward, telling himself he had to be wrong. Melly was in New Orleans, she was at the manor, she was…

…playing tug-rope with Chuck.

Stupefied, he fielded emotions like Leah's beloved baseballs as he watched Melly laughing with the Labrador. Pleasure at seeing his sister; anxiety, the kind that wrings out your insides; irritation, the kind that only a brother would know.

Chuck noticed Gabriel first, releasing the rope with an over-joyed woof and hurtling toward him. He went up on his hind legs but dropped before making contact. Progress.

His tail swished violently along the ground as he pushed his head into Gabriel's crotch.

Or not.

It was hard to maintain dignity when scooping a Labrador's head out of his groin, but he managed a narrow-eyed look to-ward Melly. "What are you doing here?"

"Gabriel!" His sister charged him with a whoop, just like Chuck. Trapped, he caught her but remained stiff in her em-brace.

"I told you not to come here," he murmured into her hair as his hands briefly gripped her before nudging her away.

"I'm a Goodnight," she said with a twinkle, drawing back. "We don't let anyone tell us no. Besides," she added before he could comment, "I wanted to meet Leah."

Every nerve inside him went on red alert, a hundred flags raised at the comment. "Why?"

"You know why."

Hot color ran up him as he fought not to shift like a guilty teenager. His sister couldn't know about what had happened between him and Leah, but she had an uncanny ability to read people. "I'm sure I don't."

She hiked up her eyebrows, delighted. "You're blushing."

"I am *not* blushing," he hissed at her.

She patted his cheek, pinched it, and then giggled as he swat-ted her away.

Melly turned to include the others in the conversation, walk-ing with Gabriel back to them. "I've been put to good use. I mopped," she told him, dropping down to her haunches and rubbing Chuck's chin. His back leg lifted and he scratched at the air in ecstasy. "And I cleared out some cats' cages. And then Sloane and I went to get coffee."

"What?" Alarm rippled through him. "You went out?"

"Uh-huh. We went to the coffee shop across the road. I had hot chocolate as Sloane said they were the best. Leah said we could put it on her 'tab' but I used your card."

He looked at her drolly. "Naturally."

She grinned. "And then we came out here to exercise the dogs. I like Chuck. Leah says he's your favorite, too."

Without asking permission, his gaze sought Leah across the small distance that separated them. She was windblown, capless, curls flying everywhere, in jeans and a snug sweater. Her small breasts rose and fell beneath the thin material. An erotic memory of teasing them with his teeth ran through his mind, so vivid that he felt heat of every kind flushing his cheeks.

As if Leah could hear his thoughts, she shivered. Or...

No coat, he realized.

"You need a coat," he told her.

"I'm fine."

He didn't frown but he wanted to. "You'll catch cold."

"I'm fine." Her stare drilled into him. He almost heard the words in his head: *I'm not fragile.*

If they'd been alone, he might have argued the point, but with his sister and Sloane keenly watching, he swallowed the retort. He wasn't sure what to tell Melly about their arrangement, but he knew he didn't want a big public display.

He refocused. "Chuck is a project," he told Melly. "I'm attempting to make him more dog than beast."

"He's doing well," Sloane ventured, in her shy way. "Chuck never sat before. He doesn't always listen, but he'll pay attention for a treat."

"In other words, your typical male."

Both girls hooted at Leah's dry comment.

Gabriel shook his head, gesturing to Melly to walk inside. "I need to talk to you."

"Here comes the lecture." Melly pushed to her feet, not looking at all worried about his wrath. "I'll probably be headed home after so—Sloane, you've got my number. We'll text. Right?"

Anyone else might not see the slight anxiety that her potential friend might not follow through. Consequences of being a Goodnight. It was hard to find genuine people.

Sloane nodded with a timid smile. She ducked her head. "It was fun, like, hanging out."

"You could come to me next. I can show you Bourbon Street."

"No, you cannot." Gabriel shuddered to think what Emmaline would say if his sister corrupted hers. He pointed ahead of him. "If you please, Amelia."

With a final roll of her hazel eyes, Melly headed into the building.

Even as he followed, he couldn't help but look back at Leah. A hint of a frown marred her forehead as she watched him go, her arms coming up to wrap around her stomach.

Was she annoyed that he was lecturing his sister? Surely she had to understand his concern. Melly was young, untried in society, witch or human, and was still not in full control of her magic. Letting her run loose in the human world was asking for trouble.

As soon as they were both inside, he cast a soundproof spell, sealing it with, "*Susurri*." At his strongest, he wouldn't have had to say the word, but he fell back on his schooling now.

The magical feedback ripped through him, and he clenched his teeth.

Melly touched his arm. "Gabriel?"

He nodded to let her know he was okay, breathed out through his nose as much for calm as to get his breath back.

Then he turned on her. "I cannot tell you how angry I am with you."

"Oh, Gabriel."

"No, you don't get to play the teenager card. I had reasons why you shouldn't come here. Reasons that begin and end with your safety."

"But I'm fine," she protested, patting all parts of her body like a strange game of head and shoulders. "See? All working parts still attached. I know you don't trust humans, but—"

"It isn't that," he cut her off, then, when her gaze called him out, he amended it to, "Not exactly. But you went out to the streets of Chicago."

"You make it sound like some kind of war zone. Dealing with teenage witches is more treacherous."

Because she had a point, he regrouped. "Do you know the crime rate in Chicago? Because I do."

"Okay, but I have magic to protect me."

"Which you can't use in front of humans." Sticky fear at the reminder of how their parents had died clutched in his belly, numbing him for an instant. To think of his sister being in the same situation…

Her mouth opened, closed. Something softened in her eyes. "It's not the same, Gabriel."

He rubbed a hand down his face, his chest, trying to ease the grip of anxiety.

"It's a safe street, a cute neighborhood café. Sloane was with me," she pointed out.

He didn't laugh but another man might have. "A fourteen-year-old half witch as a bodyguard. That changes everything. Please. Go play in the streets."

"Being around humans has affected you," Melly teased, still with that sympathetic glint. "I just meant, if it was dangerous, she would've said something. And I'm not *them*. I'd fight, even if it meant exposing witches." Sounding older than her years, she added softly, "I'd never choose to leave you."

Undone, he put his hand over hers, love a sharp blade in his throat.

"Besides," she continued, lighter now, an element of mischief warning him what was coming, "Leah wouldn't have sent us to the coffee shop if she thought we'd be in trouble. I like her, Gabriel."

He only heard one thing. "*Leah* sent you?"

"I think she wanted me and Sloane to bond."

It would be just like Leah to encourage a friendship. She never wanted to see anyone be alone. But the idea of his sister, his younger sister, wandering unprotected had his system on high alert. While she was right that she could defend herself and ultimately, if it came down to her life and exposing the secret, he would always have her choose herself, he wasn't so sure the High Family would agree. A cold sweat broke out at the idea of their summons.

"Promise me you'll be more careful," he demanded, trying to temper the fear. "You have to think before you act."

"Sometimes you can think too much." Her challenge was gentle but her eyes, when she lifted them to his, were hot. "I'm not a little girl anymore. You can't protect me forever."

"I can try."

That lifted the corners of her lips. "Gabriel, you have to let me make mistakes sometimes. Step outside the safety lines. I did, today, and look, nothing happened. Let me grow." She squeezed his forearm. "You're not my dad. You're my brother."

His words got stuck in his throat as he stared down at the girl he'd raised, suddenly a young woman.

She grinned, an impish curve. "You should be helping me make mistakes, not stopping me."

"I don't know about that," he said, his voice rusty. He looked up at the ceiling, then back. "When they died... You were so young. But it...affected me. I can't change overnight, Mells."

"I know. One step. That's all I'm asking."

He struggled with the instinct to say no, to wrap her up in bubble wrap. But he knew she was right, even if he hated it. Hadn't he accepted that living, working with humans wasn't always a bad thing? How could he admit that and then not trust Melly to navigate it herself? Under guidelines, of course. His points about the danger of losing control of magic were valid. But if another witch or someone he trusted was there to intervene...

He'd been allowed to make mistakes, though his parents had always despaired of his "acting out." He didn't want Melly to feel stifled, to be friendless. To have bitterness eat away at her soul. He didn't trust all humans, hell, he didn't trust all witches, but he could trust her. Even if it made him feel vaguely nauseous.

At some point, he thought, tracing her face, you had to take a leap.

He closed his eyes, gave in. "Fine. You can come back, but only when I'm around."

"I'll accept that. For now." Melly bounced up, kissed his cheek. "Thanks, big brother." She drew back, an impish dimple creasing hers. "About Leah...maybe you should start thinking about stepping outside some safety lines with her, too."

He shifted, uncomfortable.

Her eyes went round as crystal balls. "Shut. Up."

Resigned to nosy sisters, he nudged her toward a seat. This would take a while.

22

"Are you blind?" Leah cupped her hands around her mouth as she bellowed at the umpire. She'd shot out of her plastic seat at the call and now gestured wildly. "He was safe!"

Around her, other Cubs fans shouted in agreement. A large man eating a chili dog next to her lifted it in agreement. "You tell 'em, honey."

She made a disgusted sound and plopped back in her chair. "Ridiculous. Can you believe that?"

On the other side of her, Gabriel sat with perfect posture, dressed in designer jeans, a cashmere sweater the color of his eyes and a brown suede jacket. His hair was windblown and he wore sunglasses, which reflected her outrage as he turned to look at her.

In honor of making their remaining time count, they'd decided on equal opportunity: his and hers activities. Leah had nominated baseball as their first date.

From his expression, she didn't think he was feeling America's pastime.

"You're so angry," he commented, his accent out of place in

a stadium full of people who spat, scratched and swore, "about a baseball game."

"That could have cost us," she explained, voice hot. She curled her hands into fists, bashed them against her knee. "And this is our year."

"It's my understanding Cubs fans believe every year is their year, when statistics say—"

"Do I need to explain the rules again?"

"Please, Goddess, no."

She eyed him with some humor. "You're loving this, aren't you?"

"Every second is an experience in pleasure," he said, deadpan.

She shook her head. "Maybe you're not in the proper spirit because you're not dressed right."

"I'm wearing jeans."

"Aw, baby, you miss your suits?"

"Jeans are constricting."

"You're so weird."

"Unlike you, the model of normal."

She grinned, reached up and took off her hat. She undid the band to make it larger and then leaned over to place it on his head. Backward.

He sat perfectly still. "What are you doing?"

"Seeing you as a baseball fan." Gabriel, darkly, sleekly handsome, in jeans, sweater, jacket and a backwards cap. A shiver slid through her. "It's working for me."

His head cocked. "Really?"

"Mmm." She felt restless as she continued to look at him. "You sure wear the hell out of a hat, Gabe."

He considered, sliding his sunglasses off and hooking them on his sweater. He turned the cap around so the brim shaded his eyes. "How much do you like it?"

She saw where this was going and wagged a finger playfully. "Not enough to skip the rest of the game."

"What if I...helped the Cubs win?"

Shock halted her thoughts. She spluttered, insult raging. "The Cubs do not *need* your help to win."

His eyes went to the field, the scoreboard, then back to her. Hers narrowed.

To her further shock, he smiled. "You're very easy."

She sat back. "You're saying you *wouldn't* have cheated and broken the...you're right, I fell for that way too easily." Like Gabriel would ever. The guy probably dreamed in black-and-white.

To his credit, he was giving the game a go, scrutinizing it as he did with everything new. Probably trying to figure out how they could improve their game. *Without* magic, even though he had implied otherwise. Teasing. He'd teased her.

She held the delight in her secret heart and hugged herself. She chose to focus on that, on the good parts rather than the negative. And there was so much good here.

But only for a little while.

On the echoes of that thought, she studied him. "What'll you give me if we leave early?"

Everything about him came to attention. His head tilted to her, gaze intently green under the brim of the Cubs cap. God, he'd never looked more attractive than he did wearing her team's merch.

"Is that a possibility?"

A slow sly grin. "Put the offer on the table."

"I could put you on the table."

Someone shouted on the field and the crowd shouted in return, yet it all went fuzzy as her body roared to life.

"Feast on you like my own personal dessert." Lazily, his gaze drew down her body. "All three courses. It could take a while. If we leave now, we might finish before midnight."

The cotton of her bra rasped her nipples until she felt like squirming, did squirm. Her hand gripped the plastic chair.

"Thoughts?"

She dragged in a breath that did nothing to help. The baseball game faded to the background. "I want my turn."

His expression turned hunting quiet. "Is that a yes?"

She gave him a jerky nod.

He didn't waste time, gripping her hand to lead her out of their row. As a cheer went around the stadium, he pulled her up the steps and then out into the echoing hall, where he backed her against the wall. He braced a hand above her head, the other arm bracketing her. "I don't like baseball."

"I figured." God, he smelled good.

"But I like you."

Little pops of lust burst within her and she went up on tiptoe, gripping his sweater to yank him down for a hot, drowning kiss.

"I like you, too," she said against his mouth. "But Gabe? You're keeping the hat on."

She felt the smile against hers before he propelled her into motion and out of the stadium.

"This is inappropriate," Gabriel complained the next night from his seat on the couch. He'd refused to cuddle up with Leah in front of his sister, somewhat embarrassed at the idea, and now perched on the end as Leah, Melly and Sloane all lumped together. A blanket covered them and a giant bowl of buttered popcorn Leah had insisted on was clutched by Melly, who sat in the middle with a grin just as giant on her face. It warmed him, even as he shook his head, lips set.

Leah rolled her eyes. "*Pretty Woman* is a classic."

"It has—" He gestured to his sister. "Inappropriate content."

Who rolled *her* eyes. "Gabriel, I know about sex."

"Please," he said, cringing.

"I'm almost a woman. And Sloane says this movie is awesome."

Sloane peered past Melly, nodding. "It is. Julia Roberts kicks ass."

"I'm not sure that a fourteen-year-old—" He broke off as a handful of popcorn hit him in the face.

Leah grinned at his stupefaction, popping the next kernel in her mouth. "Loosen up, Gabe."

"Yeah, Gabe," his sister echoed.

"You're a bad influence," he informed Leah. "I cannot watch a dirty movie with my sister."

"But you've watched them alone?"

He scowled. "I don't like you."

Melly hooted a laugh. "You broke him. I don't believe it." She tipped her head onto Leah's shoulder. "You're awesome."

As annoyed and embarrassed as he was, Gabriel's heart spasmed at the sight of the two of them together. The strong reaction unnerved him, pushing him to stand, get some space from the tableau. "I'll get drinks."

"For the whole movie?" Leah's voice laughed as he strode away.

He needed to get a grip. He opened the fridge, pulled out cans of Diet Coke he'd stocked for Leah. The past couple of days had been fun, light. As they should be, as he would expect when dealing with Leah. He was enjoying it all. There was no need to get antsy about how well she fitted into this family.

"You're not really that much of a prude, right?"

Her voice made him want to smile, a growing reaction he curbed as he turned toward her. Today, she wore one of her sweaters that slipped off her shoulder and worn jeans. Cozy. Touchable.

He had an audience of teenage girls, he reminded himself, one of which was his sister. There would be no touching.

"I have *some* inhibitions."

A sinful gleam in her eyes made him wary. "Didn't seem like that yesterday at the art show in the back room."

His blood rushed hot through his system. Sister, he reminded himself. And Sloane.

Still, not trusting himself completely, he took a step back as she advanced and put up his hands.

Her lips twitched. "Are you warding me off?"

"Yes." Primly, he gestured. "You stay on that side."

She held up her own hands, tucking them in her back pockets. Her breasts rose, guiding the sweater down her shoulder to expose her lickable tattoo.

"You should really go and watch the movie," he said, voice betraying his desire. "Better they not catch us together."

The teasing light died.

He didn't like that. "There would be questions," he tried to explain. God knew Melly had peppered him with them the other day, to the point his ears still rang.

"Wouldn't want that." Sounding off in a way he couldn't explain, Leah picked up the cans of Diet Coke, balancing the three. "I'll give these to the girls. If you want to go do something, I'll stay here until the movie's done."

He watched as she walked around the breakfast bar and delivered the drinks, plopping back into her seat. She didn't curve into the cushions like before, just stared at the screen.

Her reaction ate at him. He'd said something wrong. He'd hurt her.

With a burning hole in his gut, he returned to the couch, biding his time until Melly had hugged him and left with Sloane to portal back to New Orleans.

When he turned, he discovered Leah had wandered onto his small balcony, leaning on the wrought iron as a breeze played through her hair.

He quickened his pace outside. "You shouldn't be so close to the edge," he warned.

Humans couldn't conjure anything to save themselves. One slip and she'd be hurt.

Fragile. She denied it, but it wouldn't take much, and she could be gone. It was enough to have him move to her side, prepared to grab her if she so much as teetered.

She sent him a smile over her shoulder, but with no real sparkle. "Always taking care."

"You do have a habit of needing rescue on balconies."

At the reference to their first meeting, her smile gained some warmth. He felt it in his soul.

"As I recall," she said, shifting to watch him, "I didn't need rescuing." She tilted her head. "When did you figure it out?"

"The night you almost kissed me."

It made her choke. "I think actually *you* almost kissed *me*." She chuckled, glancing at the view. "I wonder if we'd have got here without that first meeting."

"You shouldn't have been there." It had been so dangerous, it still made his heart stop.

She stilled, then nodded. "You're probably right."

And that was off, too. Leah didn't passively accept what she should or shouldn't do. She pushed, fought for what she wanted.

He watched her in the darkness, the glow of the inside lights painting that false expression. "I did something," he said abruptly. "What?"

She tipped her head back to the stars. "So far away," she murmured. "You ever think just how far away the stars are? How out of reach."

"Not especially." Impatient, he set his hand on hers where it curled around the railing. "Tell me."

One last look at the sky, and then she faced him, studying his face with the same contemplative expression. "Are you ashamed to be with me, Gabriel?"

Shock punched into his chest. "I beg your pardon?"

She didn't move. "Ashamed. I'm human, after all. And you're the Warlock of Contempt."

He pulled his hand back. For once, he didn't make any effort to guard his expression from her. "I didn't cultivate that. And I don't particularly care what others think of me. I thought you understood that."

"I know you say you don't care," she said, more to the railing than him.

"I don't."

She angled her head toward him. "Then why don't you want your sister to know about us?"

"What?" Confusion twisted as he frowned at her. "Melly already knows."

It wasn't hard to read the shock that jerked her back. He wasn't sure why she was so stunned. As awkward as it might be, he wasn't going to hide Leah from the one person who'd always been in his heart. Melly and he never had secrets.

Leah's eyebrows threaded. "Then why... Earlier, you said..."

He recalled the moment, relieved it was so simple to explain. "It's uncomfortable for me. Open affection." Honesty compelled him to add, "And it's hard having a younger sister ask questions you don't know the answers to."

Like where this was going. Except he knew the answer to that. He just didn't like saying it aloud.

"I guess talking to a fourteen-year-old about sex could be awkward."

He cringed.

It made her laugh. A small laugh, but it brightened the air like golden sparks. "Typical brother. You know she's probably going to start dating soon."

"Stop." He ran a finger around his neckline, tugging at it like it choked.

Her smile faded and she took a moment to look at him. Something soft, pleading, reflected in the blue. "It really has nothing to do with me?"

He'd assumed Leah was confident in her appeal, that she

knew he was wrapped around her little finger. But something wounded lurked beneath the pretty surface.

It called to his own aches, his own scars. And he wondered how deep the scars went, if her desire for constant company— be it animal or human—in fact stemmed from not wanting to be alone with whatever the voices whispered to her.

He knew what that was like.

He wasn't an eloquent warlock, at least he didn't think of himself that way. But he knew what he said next meant everything. "Anyone that makes you feel less than the incredible person you are isn't worthy of your time. You're a gift, Leah."

Clearly uncomfortable, Leah ducked her head. "Yeah, well... Sorry to ask, it's just with the whole...magic thing between us, it's hard not to feel like I'm not being kept out for a reason." When he went to speak, she hurriedly added, "I know it's for my protection. Bad consequences, etc. But it sucks sometimes, you know?" She gazed out at the view, twin flags of color on her cheeks as she spoke her truth. "Being on the outside, looking in."

The words lodged in his gut. He heard what she didn't say. The feelings of not being worthy, of being found wanting. Maybe that's even why she pushed so hard to know more about their world—because it hurt to be kept out. It tore him up, shredded something inside him, knowing she felt that way. Bright, bold Leah with more shadows than he'd ever guessed.

"God, shut me up now." She made a noise somewhere between a groan and a laugh, leaning out over the railing to look at the ground below. "I wonder if I could make that."

He tugged her back, unsure if she was joking. Words jumbled in his head, along with a fiery burn in his throat. But he knew he wanted to fix this, ease her pain.

With one hand on hers, he led her to the striped outdoor couch Mrs. Q had conjured for him. He gently pushed her down and stepped back against the railing. He needed some space for this. The breeze ruffled his hair, felt cool against his skin.

"My parents," he said, a hitch in his voice, "were the first Goodnights in hundreds of years to make a mark. They'd come from generations of pampered aristocrats who used their—" he hesitated, forced himself to say it "—magic for nothing but their own convenience. An attitude many of the Higher families share today."

She sat still, hands braced on the cushions. He focused on her fingernails—pink and yellow, happy colors—as he continued. "They wanted to be different, *make* a difference, and forged a completely unique company." His thumb smoothed his signet ring. "They wanted to help. Nobody dared to naysay them; when you have bloodlines like ours, you can get away with almost anything."

"Even being a jackass?"

"You'd have to talk to Kole about that," he said pleasantly.

She shot him a semi-warning look. "Go on. Your parents formed the company."

"Yes. As I said, they were determined to help. And they did—we do, in the company that carries their name." He tightened his fingers, took a breath. "But they met a stumbling block in me."

It felt like wrenching open a rusted door without magic: painful, a lot of effort. But he wanted, needed, to do this for her. "I was their firstborn. Their living legacy. They hoped to have a child to be proud of. I did not live up to their ideal."

"You?" Doubt underscored the word.

"Yes. I slacked off, pulled pranks. Generally, I behaved like the spoiled, proud warlocks they'd wanted nothing to do with. They despaired."

"Sounds like a typical teenager."

"Except I behaved that way up until they died." He lifted his chin, prepared to take her disgust. "They wanted more from me, but I couldn't be bothered to fulfill their wishes. I didn't want to go into the family business."

"What did you want to do?"

Her question made him stop. "I'm not sure."

"Nobody ever asked you?"

"They made it clear they expected that I follow their footsteps."

Her painted fingernails tapped. "When did they—can I ask when they…passed?"

A hard ball was stuck in his throat. It made breathing difficult. "I was eighteen. They'd been visiting with a human hospital in South America and a rebel band stormed through. They were shot."

Her face went white. So did her fingers around the cushion. "Gabriel. I'm… I don't know what to say."

"Melly was only two," he said softly, turning to watch the lights across the way. "She barely remembers them, but I know they'd be proud of her."

"They'd be proud of you, too."

"I promised myself they would be." He counted the lights. "I swore I'd live up to their expectation. Even to the point of coming here and mopping floors in an animal shelter."

He sensed her before her hand slid into his. Unsure, he looked down where their fingers interlinked before looking back at her. Her expression was fierce.

"You're not a disappointment," she told him.

"I caused them pain when I didn't live up to my potential."

She made a noise. "You were a kid. You're allowed to make mistakes, decide who you are. They should've let you, not focused more on a cause than their child." Her eyes suddenly rounded. "Shit. Sorry. I didn't mean to badmouth your parents. It's just… I didn't get to be a free teenager, either. My mom and all. Kids should have a childhood, you know? To be reckless or wild or whatever."

"Hence your corruption of Melly." But her words chimed against something cold and hard he'd harbored for years.

She squeezed his hand. "You're a great brother. A great son. A passable lover." The droll look he sent her made her laugh. "And for what it's worth, I think anyone with that much expectation piled on them would have rebelled more than you did. A few pranks?" She puffed out a breath. "Please. What matters is that you grew into the man you are. And a disappointment he isn't."

He lifted her hand to his mouth. Kissed her knuckles. "Thank you." He wasn't sure he fully believed her, but it meant something that she believed it. And she did; every word shone in her eyes. It prompted him to admit softly, "I've never felt good enough either."

That truth tangled them together like strings that would never be unknotted.

She watched him with those eyes, deep, drowning blue. "Thank you for letting me in."

"You're welcome."

Her small laugh settled inside him. He adjusted his grip and backed toward the entrance to the apartment. "It's still early. Stay with me tonight?"

"I'll need to go grab the dogs."

He sighed, more for form than anything else. "Only for you."

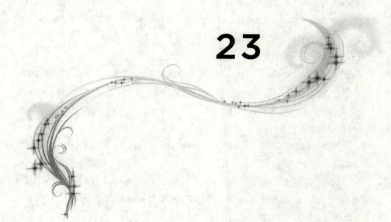

23

*L*eah idly swished a cloth over the clean bar, eyeing Gabriel, who sat in a booth with Bastian and Henry. It was karaoke night, Lord help them all, and a man clutching a beer bottle swayed along to his choice of Take That's "A Million Love Songs." None of the men even looked up from their conversation.

What were they talking about? Potions, spells, society gossip? Bastian and Gabriel weren't exactly similar, while Henry seemed to be a chameleon, able to slip into whatever skin suited his purposes best.

"What do you suppose that's about?" Leah posed the question to Emma as her friend built a Witch's Heart for a customer. The blackberry liqueur shimmered in the martini glass, topped by a dramatic smoking mist.

Emma handed the drink to the customer, accepting the money before running a harried hand through her hair. "What?" She followed Leah's pointed gaze, winced. "Henry's here again?"

"Pretty sure he's got Tia bugged. He seems to know exactly when she's not around." Leah smiled automatically at another customer and dropped the cloth to pour two large glasses of red wine. Transaction complete, she got back to eyeballing the men. "You haven't told her he's been in?"

"It hasn't come up."

"Same." Leah tapped her fingers. "Are we bad friends?"

"Probably."

"Should we kick him out?"

"Probably."

Leah grimaced. "You're sure she'd have a problem with him being here?"

"Tia's not exactly rational when it comes to Henry." Emma gnawed her bottom lip. "But he's Bastian's friend. Puts me in an awkward situation."

"Whereas it's fine for the human to kick the all-powerful warlock out?"

Emma just shrugged.

"Fine. I'll go over there. But you owe me."

"I'll pick up extra shifts volunteering this week."

"Done." Leah looked back at the booth. "Seriously, what do you think they're talking about?"

"What song they're going to sing together?"

Leah let out a snort of laughter as Take That man finally finished and the next ballad cued up for a drunken twosome. She'd heard the friends arguing about whether to brave the stage or not earlier. Now, three drinks in and buzz firmly on, they wrapped their arms around each other's waists and belted out an Adele number.

Emma winced, tried to hide it. "I never get why anyone would do that," she commented. "Even drunk."

Leah nudged her hip against the bar as an idea formed. She considered the men, then turned to her friend. "I bet I could get Gabriel up there."

Emma scoffed. "Not even you can get Gabriel Goodnight to do karaoke."

"All I'll have to do is ask. He's a marshmallow when he cares about someone."

"I don't believe it."

"Bet you a dollar."

"A dollar?"

"And whoever loses has to kick Henry out."

Emma's gaze was full of pity. "You're biting off more than you can chew."

"Have you ever known me to fail?"

Doubt flickered briefly before she nodded. "No, I'm calling it. There's no way. We have a bet."

They soberly shook hands.

Leah reached up, tugged the band out of her hair so her curls fell loose across her shoulders. She slipped the band over her wrist and shot a cocky grin at Emma. "Watch the master work."

"Uh-huh."

With Emma's skepticism powering her, Leah moved around the counter toward the booth. Purpose drove her steps. It might seem like a bit of silliness, but for Leah, it began and ended with revealing Gabriel's sweet side. While her friends had accepted she was sleeping with him, they didn't like him. And worse, Gabriel didn't expect any different.

After the story he'd told her a couple of nights ago, she understood why he kept himself apart; he was used to being judged or rejected. Better to reject everyone first, to act like you didn't care.

She refused to leave it like that. He deserved to be seen for all his facets. Especially when she was…gone.

Emma would be the first domino to topple in Leah's campaign.

When he noticed her approaching, he slid out of the booth to stand. Society manners, she supposed. She couldn't say she hated it.

"Hi, men," she greeted, halting at Gabriel's side. She wished she could lean into him, wrap an arm around his waist. Even though he'd assured her that he wasn't ashamed of their relationship, she knew it wouldn't be smart to openly claim him in front of Henry. Still, she wished.

Bastian sent her a two-fingered salute as Henry nodded in acknowledgment.

"Couldn't stay away?" she directed at the latter in an arch tone.

To his credit, he winced.

"I asked him to come," Gabriel surprised her by saying. The back of his hand brushed hers and her stomach dipped like a teenager with a crush. "You're working the late shift, so I thought we could...hang out while I wait."

She cocked her head, at more than his testing use of the human phrase. "Wait?"

"To walk you home. It's not safe."

Bastian plonked his elbows on the table, framing his face with his hands. "Awww."

Baffled, Leah wasn't sure how to respond. Before she could settle on an action, he decided for her, clasping her hand, lifting it to his mouth. He kissed her knuckles before adding, "You look tired."

Amusement at the blunt statement trembled into a sweet ache as he lowered their hands but kept them joined.

Are you ashamed to be with me, Gabriel?

He'd really heard her.

God, her heart might spasm too hard and kill her. She knew he wouldn't be doing this in front of people he didn't trust, but the gesture still slayed her.

"Well, well," Henry murmured. His eyes were sharp as he studied them, lifting his beer for a sip.

Okay. Awkward.

She angled her head to Gabriel, pretending not to be affected. "I, uh, need you to sign up for karaoke."

Henry choked on his beer, chest convulsing as Bastian hooted a laugh.

Gabriel didn't move. "No."

"Please?"

"No."

"For me?"

"How would getting up there and humiliating myself be for you?"

"Because you'd do anything for me?"

One perfect eyebrow slid up an inch.

"Wouldn't hurt you to pretend," she grumbled. Then, because it was *right there*, added, "I thought you liked playing pretend."

His eyes heated to a simmer.

"Go on, Gabriel." Henry's encouragement held a touch of hoarseness as he regained his breath. His grin was wide. "I'll help you pick the perfect song."

"AC/DC?" Bastian asked.

"That or Phil Collins."

Gabriel ignored them. He leaned down so his murmured words were only for her. "Why are you asking me to do this?"

Leah pursed her lips. So low her voice wouldn't travel, she admitted, "I want Emma to like you."

"Why?"

"Because she's my friend."

"So?"

"So, I want her to like you."

"Why?"

Her eyes narrowed. "Don't make me hit you, Goodnight." At his perplexed expression, she couldn't stop the wave of affectionate sympathy. He was so obtuse sometimes. "I want them to see who you are."

"A karaoke singer."

"No." The word came out on a laugh. She tugged on his

jacket, pulling him down even closer. "As a man who'd do anything for those he cares for." Awkwardness swamped her as the words left her mouth. *Shit.* She found her next breath difficult as he studied her, the green of his eyes vivid even in low lighting. "Um. That is… If you do care for me. A little."

This close, she saw every micro-movement in expression. "This is important to you?"

"Yes." She lifted her hand to cup his cheek, unable to stop herself. "I know you don't care how people see you, but I don't want anyone to think of you as the Warlock of Contempt. I want them to see you."

"And the best way is karaoke."

She huffed a small laugh, her thumb smoothing over the hint of stubble that had grown in throughout the day. "Maybe."

He was quiet for a long moment, the only noise the clink of glasses, the murmur of conversations, and the violent thump of her heart.

When he sighed, that heart leaped.

But five minutes later, as Gabriel reluctantly climbed on stage to the enthusiastic applause of Bastian and Henry, it was all she could do to hold her jittering nerves together. Oh, God. What if he was terrible? What if he was about to make a fool of himself?

"If they make fun of him, I'm going to sic my dogs on them." Leah glared at Bastian and Henry. "No! I'm going to call Tia and sic her on them."

"I can't believe you got him up there." Emma blinked fast, as if that might make Gabriel disappear. "I seriously underestimated you. Or him." Speculation crept into her face. "There's more to this than karaoke, isn't there?"

Leah barely heard her. *Please be okay, please be okay,* she chanted inside her head.

Then the first notes of the song he'd selected came through the speakers. Leah froze, processed, and broke into a grin so wide, it hurt her cheeks. "Unbelievable."

Even Emma laughed as Gabriel stepped up to the mic. He didn't sway or bounce his feet, just stood there tall and elegant as he waited for his cue. And when it came, he leant to the mic, hands linked behind his back, and politely said in a British monotone perfect for the song: "Tequila."

"All right," Emma murmured in Leah's ear as Gabriel didn't react to the cheers from the bar. "Maybe there's more to him than meets the eye."

Leah just grinned.

Gabriel didn't feel as at home as he'd expected as he claimed the seat in the conference room at Goodnight's Remedies. He'd left Leah asleep in his bed, nudging Delilah off his foot as she'd plopped on it when he'd stopped to brew coffee—he had the hang of it now—petting Rosie as she'd pranced over and then Louie as he toddled behind. He'd dressed in one of his suits, the act like donning armor.

A long-distance portal meant cold sweat was still drying down the small of his back, but at least his temples had stopped pounding as he faced his uncle and the rest of the board down the long rectangular table.

All heads turned to August as he began. "I know we're all busy, so I'll get right to it. The board has asked you to come here to express congratulations at how well you've been doing in Chicago."

Gabriel absorbed that without expression. When he'd been summoned unexpectedly, he'd assumed trouble, that the board suspected Leah knew the truth. He threaded his fingers together to hide his relief.

"We're all so impressed," James said, adjusting his body as he sat forward. "I'm not sure *I* could've gone this long with barely any magic."

"It's been an adjustment."

At Gabriel's dry comment, laughter rippled around the room.

The atmosphere was relaxed, pleased. Strangely, Gabriel felt stirrings of resentment at their approval.

"Will even says you've learned how to cook?" another witch asked from across the table.

"Cook is a bit of a stretch." He glanced at his uncle's assistant, who stood unobtrusively in the corner, a pad and pen taking minutes at his side. "I can use a toaster." He allowed a moment of self-satisfaction at that fact.

"And how are you finding mixing with humans?" Fiona, a witch who'd been on the board with his parents, watched him with interest. "In the past, you've always been vocal about wanting to keep your distance."

And the company was keen to increase their human employees, encourage more melding for expansion purposes. They were clearly looking for an indication that he could follow through on that.

He shifted, barely aware of the telling gesture. "It's been an experience," he said carefully. "A valuable one. Now I've lived there, my understanding of them is clearer. They are, after all, very similar to us. But," he added, without thinking, "also more."

From the head of the table, August raised his eyebrows. "More?"

Fuck. Gabriel rushed to cover the slip. "We're dependent on our magic," he explained. "Because they don't have magic, they're forced to be more resourceful. Creative. Determined. Stubborn." Leah's face came to mind. "Definitely stubborn. And brave. Kind." Realizing the board was staring, he cut himself off. His cheeks felt hot.

"Sounds like someone has been wooed by the humans," Peter, a warlock who'd been voted in ten years ago, said with a smile. It wasn't snide, but it still made Gabriel desperately want to hunch in his chair.

"He makes a point." August sat back, gazing at Gabriel over

steepled hands. "You forget: humans are not altogether altru-
istic, just as we aren't. They can be manipulative and grasping,
out for money or power." He paused. "Your...friend from the
shelter, for example. Leah."

Every nerve, every atom, in Gabriel's body stilled. "Excuse
me?"

"We want to help humans here; that is the whole raison
d'être of this company. But let's not get swept away. Leah used
your connections to organize a charity event to further her
own ends."

"No."

"I'm delighted you've learned from this experience," August
went on, rolling over Gabriel's denial. "But keep it in perspective. Don't romanticize them."

Gabriel couldn't believe his uncle was lecturing to him, especially in front of the board. Many of whom sported uncomfortable expressions as if they didn't want to witness this,
either. "I'm not."

"That isn't what I've observed or been told."

Gabriel's gaze winged to Will, who had the decency to
wince, before returning to his uncle.

He made an effort to keep his voice calm. "I believe the
terms of the will have been met. My experiences will further
my role when I take over from you as CEO in two weeks."

"And your human friend?"

Gabriel kept his eyes steady. "Will be left behind."

Another witch who'd only been voted in last year spoke up.
"Glad to hear it. You don't want to lose sight of what's important because of a manipulative human out for anything she
can get."

The window behind the witch shattered without warning,
throwing glass in every direction. The closest board members
yelped, gabbling a barrier incantation as shards rained down
on them. From where he'd leaped up, August gaped at Gabriel.

Mortification ran through him like a river. It lapped at his feet as he stood, smoothing a hand down his tie. Only those closest to him would see that it trembled.

"Apologies," he said through the groaning ache in his temples. He nodded at them all, registering their shock alongside his own. "I will see you in two weeks."

If they still voted him in after that display. Panic flapped in his chest and he barely made it out of the room before bracing a shaking hand against the wall. He bent his head, breathing deeply.

He needed to get a handle on himself. That outburst was unacceptable. Even if the insult had made his vision go red, even if the lecture from August had been beyond humiliating. He should have better control than to create such a scene.

Especially since it could lose him everything he'd ever worked for.

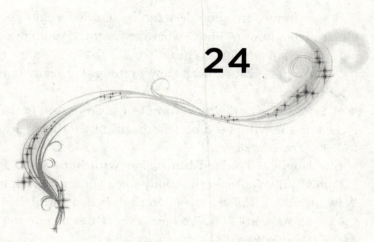

24

"It was so sweet." Leah smiled over her beer bottle at Gabriel. The candle she'd plucked from her living room flickered merrily between them on her kitchen table, her dogs curled at their feet. "Chuck sat at the yard door for at least ten minutes, hoping you'd show."

Gabriel nodded, gaze on his plate as he pushed spaghetti around. He'd been like that since he'd arrived. Not cold but moody, pensive.

"Nothing could tempt him," she went on. "I mean, nothing. I tried a ball, a toy, a chew."

"Hmm."

Leah tucked her tongue firmly in her cheek. "And then I sprayed whipped cream all over my body. Offered myself to Mitch, who proposed we make it a threesome."

"Sounds good."

Leah set her beer down. "Okay. What's wrong?"

She nudged him under the table with her foot, startling him into looking up. Candlelight moved over his troubled expression before he blanked it.

Her eyes narrowed. "Don't do that. I hate that."

A sigh moved his shoulders and he set his fork down. He didn't pretend not to know what she meant. "Apologies. I'm not great company this evening."

"You're not great company any evening. I'm really only in it for the sex."

A brief smile curled one corner of his mouth. He finally picked up the wine she'd bought specifically for him, lifted it to her. "You're welcome."

She laughed. Nudged him again with her socked foot. "C'mon, spill. You've been moody since you came back from New Orleans." *With the board.* Dread uncurled within her and she sat up straight. "They're not…they're not taking you out of the running for CEO?"

"No." But even as her shoulders dropped in relief, his brow furrowed. "No."

"But…?" she prompted.

"It's nothing."

Leah set her chin on her hand, elbows on the table. And stared.

He swirled his wine. "It was something my uncle said."

"Oh." She shoved away the instant distaste. "What?"

"It's petty."

She scratched Rosie's head absently as the sprocker leaned against her chair. "What did he say?"

"It's fine. I overreacted."

"I've always said that about you, you're *such* a drama queen."

He rolled his shoulders, clearly uncomfortable. "He said… some things about my time here. How he didn't want it to change me, not if I want to be a suitable CEO."

"Real nice." Leah soothed her dog, watching Gabriel as he concentrated on his plate. Something clicked. "Was it about me?"

He stayed silent.

Her stomach pitched in response. "He doesn't like me. He made that clear."

His gaze snapped up.

"The gala," she elaborated. Shrugged. "He made some comments."

The air thickened palpably. "What comments?" he demanded.

"Stupid stuff. Along the lines of how lucky I am that you and the Goodnight name came along to help and how I clearly saw that opportunity. Which is what he said today," she guessed, gauging his face. "In front of the board? Damn it. I'm sorry."

"Why should you apologize?"

"Because I've caused an issue. I know what this company means to you. I don't want to be an obstacle."

"You won't be."

She reached out, set a hand on his. Her fingernails were sherbet pink and contrasted with his more masculine hand. "I promise I won't ever be."

"I know." He turned his hand over so their fingers linked. "You were telling me about Chuck?"

"He missed you." Leah took a beat, unsure she should let the subject drop. "Gabriel…"

"He'll get used to it." Gabriel set down his wineglass to pick up his fork again. "Maybe I should stop visiting him. Make the transition easier."

"No, don't do that." They had, after all, only two weeks left with him.

Two weeks. How was it already only two weeks?

Gabriel took a bite of pasta, swallowed. "He'll only get more attached."

Too late for that, she thought. For both of them. "You're sure you wouldn't want to take him? He loves you."

"No."

"You could use a friend when you go back. And he could use a family."

"Leah, I said no."

The words were sharp and cut the strings holding her smile in place.

For a lingering moment, the only sounds were Delilah's soft snores.

"He loves you," she repeated, a hollow ache setting up camp. "It'll break his heart when you go."

"He'll find someone else to love."

"He's getting older. He may only have two years or so left."

"Exactly," he bit out, putting down his fork and rising. He carried his plate over to the sink, bracing his now-free hands on the counter. His back was rigid. "I am not setting Melly up to lose someone else. We've been through enough."

She stared at that unbending back. "You're serious?"

"We've lost enough," he repeated stubbornly, turning to her. His expression matched his voice. "Two years is nothing for a witch. A blip of time. She'll have him, love him, only to watch him die. Better not to have him at all." He shook his head irritably, leafing a hand through his hair. "You don't understand, you're not of my world."

She sat back, feeling like she'd taken a punch to the gut. Instead of feeling the hurt, she chose annoyance.

"Maybe I don't," she retorted. "I don't understand why you'd deprive a dog who loves you of a family for the final years of his life." Or himself of anyone willing to care for him, she admitted quietly to herself. Dog—or person.

A muscle ticked away in his jaw, and he linked his hands behind his back the way she'd noticed he did whenever he was uncomfortable.

Might as well go for broke. Get it all out.

"And maybe it's being human," she continued, pressing her hands onto her thighs as nerves tickled in her belly, "but I don't see why you're letting your uncle do this to you."

He frowned. "What?"

"Everything. The whole weird will." She blew out a breath. "Say that three times fast."

Her joke fell flat. "He didn't *force* me," Gabriel countered, each word bristling. "He wants me to prove myself, gain respect from the board and show how I can lead them into the future."

"And you didn't earn that already by working your way up through the company?" she shot back. She'd loved how that one example demonstrated his willingness to try, his curious mind. It deserved appreciation. And so, she pushed. "Tell me, Gabriel, what exactly do you like about the idea of being CEO? Why do you want it so much? Is it because you actually want it or because..." She stopped before she went too far.

He only lifted his chin. "This is what I was born for. It's what I'm good at."

She could quit but that just wasn't her. "Running things from a distance? Sitting behind a desk? That isn't you, Gabriel. You told me about going into each department and seeing what made it tick. How you like improving everything, thinking of new ways to do things at ground level. That's what you're good at."

"I could do that as CEO," he said stubbornly. "My uncle still dips a hand in every so often."

"But he focuses on the bigger picture, not the minutiae. The details are where you shine." She paused. "And from the sounds of things, your uncle might like being in charge. Maybe a little too much."

She swore she felt the abrupt chill in his gaze, sliding ice into her skin.

"What is that supposed to mean?"

Careful, she warned herself. "I'm just...look, if he wants you to succeed so much, why talk down to you today? Why make you do this at all?" She wet her lips. "Maybe he's setting you up to fail—because he doesn't want to give up being CEO."

"Stop it." Gabriel came forward so abruptly, it startled Rosie from her position next to Leah. His hands clenched, a storm in his eyes. That storm flared out, little green sparks flickering and flashing around him. "You don't know what you're saying. August has always wanted the best for me, for Melly. He's been there my entire life, *especially* when my parents died. He sat with me in silence for two weeks until I was ready to talk. He helped me sort out details when I could barely breathe. He's family."

Leah's heart softened. She lifted her hands in pacification. "Okay. I'm sorry. I didn't know."

Another man, another warlock might have pounced on the vulnerability. Pointed out again that the reason for that was because she was outside his world. Maybe even use what she'd told him that evening on the balcony to cut into her.

Gabriel merely stared at her, that muscle in his jaw beating away.

The divide between them yawned. She felt every inch of it viciously. His world, she thought with a pang. It would always be his world and she would always be on the outside.

Good thing she wasn't attached like Chuck.

"He's always accepted me," Gabriel said into the quiet. Her gaze flew up, found his. The green was fierce. "My entire life, he's always been there, supporting me."

Unlike his parents.

Leah swallowed down regret. Maybe she'd been wrong. Just because she didn't like his uncle didn't mean he was a bad guy. Taking a chance, she rose and went to Gabriel, tilting her head back to maintain eye contact. She slid her hand down his arm to his hand. His signet ring brushed her fingers as she linked them.

"I guess I owe him for that." She squeezed, letting it go. She'd said her piece and it was up to him what to do with it. "Wanna make up and make out?"

Grave, he studied her. Then he cracked, lips tilting to a smile.

And everything was alright in her world.

★ ★ ★

Peggy came back five hours later to find them arguing on the couch.

"It's irresponsible," Gabriel said, waving a hand at the television where Simon, Duke of Hastings, was striding around and looking damn fine doing so. He'd offered to watch something she wanted after dinner. He probably regretted it now. "Just because his father was harsh does not mean he should be so petty."

"He was hurt," Leah argued hotly. "Admittedly, it's not the best idea, especially now he has Daphne, but people can't be ruled by logic alone."

"Of course, they can."

"Well, *of course* you'd think so." Leah jabbed his chest from where she was curled up next to him. "But the rest of us aren't robots. We feel, we act."

"His father isn't even around anymore to see him take his ridiculous revenge." Gabriel shot her a superior look. "Tell me how it's harming anyone other than himself."

Peggy leaned on the back of the couch. "He's got you there."

"Don't you have somewhere else to be?" Leah directed at her and Peggy laughed, said good-night and drifted upstairs. When she'd gone, Leah turned back to Gabriel. "It's not," she said, returning to her argument. "But the point is emotion makes you a little wild. Human."

"Impractical," Gabriel corrected. "Life should be looked at with sensible eyes."

How he could be so obtuse was both irritating and laughable. Leah raked her hands down her face and peeked at him through them. "You're going to love Anthony's season."

"The rogue who's infatuated with the opera singer?"

Leah sighed, swinging her legs into Gabriel's lap. His hand went there instantly, cupping her thigh. "Trust me," Leah said with a small shake of her head, pretending to be annoyed when what she really felt was just…happy. "You'll love him."

They both turned back to the TV, while underneath, Ralph's unblinking eyes watched them as if they were far more entertaining than any show.

The night had been a kind of dream, the sort nobody wanted to wake up from.

The day swiftly devolved into a nightmare.

Leah stared at Sonny across his cluttered desk, dropping into the padded chair opposite. The plant she'd bought him with the inscription, *Dog dad, plant papa*, drooped in its corner. She knew how it felt.

She'd known. As soon as he'd said he wanted to talk to her, she'd known.

"You have an offer," she repeated dully. Her head throbbed.

Sonny nodded, hands restlessly organizing his papers into a pile. He avoided her gaze. "Someone from the charity gala. They came by for a visit, really took to the place."

"That's good, but…" She gripped her thighs so she wouldn't leap up. "You can't seriously be thinking of accepting."

His shoulders slumped and he bent to his chair, his weight making the old furniture squeak. "You know it's been tight. And I'm tired."

"But the gala raised all that money," she began.

"It's a good offer," he interrupted. Lines streaked around his eyes, making him look every one of his years. He fiddled with a pen, turning it over and over. "And they haven't ruled out me staying on in some capacity. If I want."

"But it's your place." *Mine.*

"I know." And the look he shot her told her he did. He rubbed tiredly at his forehead. "Part of me thinks Mabel would come down from heaven itself to scold me for even thinking of giving it up."

The mention of his wife almost made her smile. "She loved this place."

"So do I." He pressed his lips together. "But the love has to be balanced with the practical. And the truth is, running everything is becoming too much for me. What with the recent vandalism, the police. And the expense—"

"So, I'll help out more," Leah said with a tinge of desperation. Her hands curled into her jeans, picking at the rip over her knee. "I'll put in more hours."

"And what about your bar?"

"I'll manage. There's twenty-four hours in a day, right?" She'd always believed that, never truly felt right sitting around doing nothing. Okay, she didn't have much free time, but she could make it work.

"Leah, I don't want to hurt you." He grimaced, squeezed the pen. "I just…thought you should know. I'm considering."

Leah sat back, struggling to breathe past the fear or panic or whatever it was blocking her throat. She gazed at Sonny, the familiar face that had been there for her since she'd been fifteen. Except now she really looked.

The line that carved through his brow had become permanent this past year. Worry had made him pale, almost haggard. He was at retirement age. He should be enjoying life.

I can't lose this place, she wanted to cry like a child.

But she didn't. Instead, she fixed a smile to her face. It was like a poorly-made table—rough, wobbly—but it held.

"Don't worry about me." She stood, leaning to cover his hand where it lay on the desk. "Us. We'll be fine, no matter what you decide. Just do what's best for you."

She made it to Chuck's kennel before she broke. Tears slid down her cheeks as she sank to sit by the enclosure. She wrapped her arms around her knees and buried her head, warmed by the Labrador as he nosed as best he could against her.

"Leah?" Gabriel's voice was sharp. He was beside her the next moment. He dropped, ignoring Chuck when the dog started a series of happy barks. "What's wrong? Are you sick? Hurt?"

He had her standing the next minute, patting her down. An overly warm sensation bloomed beneath her skin.

Recognizing it, she batted at his hands. "Don't use magic," she said thickly, sniffling. "You'll hurt yourself."

He trapped her hands in his. "What's wrong?"

"Nothing. I'm fine."

He gave her a bland stare, then cut a look at Chuck. "Enough."

The Labrador relented after one more woof, sitting and sweeping his thick tail across the ground.

Gabriel's hands warmed hers. "Talk to me."

"It's nothing. Okay, it's not nothing," she expanded after an impatient huff from him. "It should be nothing. It's not health, it's not death." She sank her teeth into her lip, tried to stop another tear from falling. "It's Sonny."

Gabriel studied her. When he let go, it was to gently wipe away the next tear. "He's selling."

"He got an offer." Leah impatiently scrubbed at her eyes. "God. I hate crying. It's pointless." She breathed out, blinked to quell the next wave.

"Is he going to take it?"

"I don't know. Maybe. And the idea of this place not being his anymore, not being mine in the same way..." She fisted a hand at her heart. "And how selfish is that? He's getting old, *is* old. I never see him play with the dogs or cats anymore. He's stressed, overworked, underpaid, and I'm *sad* that he's found a solution?" She snorted. "I'm a terrible person. A terrible, selfish, stupid—"

Gabriel kissed her. Soft, sweet.

Her hands were pressed against his chest, his on her upper arms when he stopped. "You're not a terrible person."

"You're biased," she murmured.

"Goodnights are nothing if not truthful." He'd adopted that stuffy tone. She had no idea why it struck her as adorable. Maybe because he was trying to hide the fact that he cared. After all, this, them, was one level, one note and then the song would end. It made her feel like crying all the more.

"If I had the money," she said, "if I hadn't invested in my property, the bar…"

Wanting to block it out, she pressed her face into his chest. When he patted her head uncomfortably, she couldn't stop the faint smile. It didn't last long, couldn't when her emotions were fighting for supremacy. They churned and crashed and bruised her insides. To be held like this, to be in his arms where she felt safe, like she could manage anything as long as he was beside her. Her hidden heart screamed into the abyss, desperate to keep it. But she couldn't and she knew that. She had to stand alone.

"It will be fine." Gabriel's voice was uncompromising, as firm as his hand was gentle. "You will be fine. Turners are resilient."

The truth in his words and her own steadied her just enough. His chest muffled her response. "Damn straight."

"That's better." Still with his hand against her head, he continued, "Tonight."

She concentrated on breathing, on repairing her cracks. "What's tonight?"

"Wait and see."

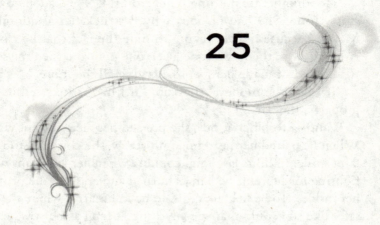

25

*L*eah's gaze wandered across Gabriel's breakfast bar. An array of ingredients, some she recognized, some she didn't, in glass jars, pots, paper packages, lay strewn across the counter. She fought not to let her disappointment show. "We're cooking?"

Across the room, Louie sniffed the new amethyst throw blanket she'd bought to bring some color to Gabriel's apartment before turning around three and a half times and plopping onto it. Rosie was glued to Gabriel's leg as he attempted to work the Alexa he bought.

Leah hid a smile. "You need some help?"

"No." He fiddled with it and then a blue light lit up the device. He sent her a smug look. "Alexa, play music."

"She'll need more direction than that."

"Alexa, play jazz music."

"You like jazz?"

"I live in New Orleans. You develop an appreciation."

"But it doesn't have rules or structure." Leah pressed a hand to her cheek in mock horror. "They just follow their hearts and instincts."

He ignored her, stroking a hand down Rosie, then Delilah as she bustled over like a mini dictator, pushing in. When he rose, the sultry sounds of sax mixed with the upbeat percussion.

He'd dressed down, as he often did now, in jeans and a soft shirt, with the sleeves rolled up to expose his forearms. A tickle in her belly warmed her as she leaned her hip against the breakfast bar, watching him walk toward her.

"What?" he asked, catching her drooling stare.

"You're cute."

The look he shot her questioned her sanity. "How do you like your surprise?"

"I mean," Leah said, glancing down, once again reaching for enthusiasm. "It's great. I like cooking."

"We're not cooking." He scoffed at the idea. "Although I *can* toast with the best of them now."

"Then what…?"

He waved a hand over a bare section of the counter. Air shimmered, forming to a dark green leather-bound book. In gold lettering, the title read: Potions for Beginners.

Leah shot out a hand, dug into his arm. "Potions?"

He nodded. "I'm going to teach you one."

"A *potion*?" Excitement throttled her heartbeat up to a near-dazzling speed. She threw herself at him, wrapping both arms around his waist and squeezing python-hard.

He'd barely returned the gesture when she moved back. "Hang on, I thought you wanted to keep everything…you know. On the DL."

Blank.

"The down-low," she elaborated. "Hush-hush. Quiet."

"A little late for that." Irony ran through the words as he turned to the book. "I'm not suggesting you shout about it, but I thought you'd enjoy learning an easy one."

"They never work." She fought the urge to pout. "I've tried before with Emma and Tia."

"Even when they added their magic to it?"

She frowned. "Added their…?" Her teeth clicked together as realization struck. Babied again, not trusted.

"I'm assuming they didn't." His hand slid onto her hip, supportive. "You'll have no problem with this, not with me lending a spark of power. And…I want to give you a piece of my world."

Ridiculously she felt like bawling. "This magic—it's not going to hurt you, right? Because if it is, I don't want to do it." She cast a longing glance at the book, then away.

"I'll be fine," he assured her, convincing enough to make her reservations drop.

"Gabriel. This is…" She trailed off, blown away by the gesture. Swept up by emotion, she went up on tiptoe and snagged his shirt to bring him down for a short kiss. "Thank you."

God, how was she going to let him go?

Because she had to. But for now, he was here and there was a potion.

Another woman might have played it cool. Leah danced in place and clapped her hands like an infant. "This. Is. Awesome. Where do we start? Is it safe? What is the potion for?"

Apparently it was for levitation. A dash of this powder, a dollop of purple gel, a few herbs and other assorted ingredients all went into a cast-iron pot he had out on the stove. He cracked a smile when she asked about cauldrons.

She listened to him as carefully as any student, insisting she measure and add and stir on her own.

Finally, he rubbed his thumb and forefinger together and produced an iridescent green spark that floated in the air until he batted it to the pot below. "It has to simmer now. When it turns midnight blue, it's ready."

Leah peered in at the bubbling purple liquid. "Looks kind of like a Witch's Heart. Cocktail," she explained with a laugh at his expression. Turning her attention back to the pot, she jigged. "This is so fun. How long will it take?"

"Potion-making is an art as well as a science." Gabriel glanced at the clock on the oven. "An hour or two."

"That long?" She watched the bubbles pop. "I can't believe Emma and Tia never explained they had to add magic."

"Most likely they were trying to keep you safe."

"I know. Still, they could trust me."

"They told you about us," he pointed out, leaning back against the counter. "That carries a huge risk."

"I know," she repeated, angling her head back to look him in the face. "I don't mean to sound ungrateful or anything."

He considered her in his aloof Gabriel way. "Have they told you the consequences if you're ever discovered?"

"Not really. I know I'd get brought before the High Family— like, your version of a royal family?" At his nod, she continued, "But other than that, details are a little hazy. Memory wipe, most likely—which, can I just say, not cool."

"Witches aren't known for ethics."

"Apparently."

"Did they discuss what would happen to them?"

The question made her still. She stared at him. "What do you mean happen to *them*?"

"If they were unmasked as the ones who told you without seeking permission, they could also face severe penalties."

Chilled at the sound of those two words, she wrapped her arms around her waist. "Like what?"

"In truth, it's been that long since the rules have been broken that it's mostly rumor."

He was avoiding the question. Not a good sign. "They didn't tell me." She thought of how often she'd pushed to know more, not even considering that she might be putting her friends in danger, and dropped her arms. "Shit. I'm such an idiot. And so are they for not telling me. I know, probably trying to protect me. Still, they should've said something."

"When you want to protect someone, sometimes that trumps what you 'should' do." Experience rang through the wry words.

Leah shook her head, still jittery. "It's stuff like this that makes me feel so out of touch. I'm an adult; I deserved to know all the facts, right?"

He stayed silent, but the fact that he'd drawn her attention to it was its own point.

She tapped her fingers against her hips. "You think I should focus on the fact that they told me in the first place, don't you?"

"Why did they?"

The memory brought a rueful smile. "Emma got drunk."

Shock splashed over his face.

She had to laugh. "It's why she's so OTT about me slipping up, because she feels responsible—and it's also why she can out-drink anyone now, because she swore it wasn't going to happen again. It was like a year after we met, a few months after she'd introduced me to Tia, and I was hosting a girl's night. Nothing fancy. And Emma pounded too much gin. Next thing I knew, she was claiming to be able to make magical cosmos and cooing to my plants."

"And Tia?"

Leah tilted her head thoughtfully. "She could've intervened. But all she did was sit there with a smile on her face. Apparently, she had a 'premonition' that I could be trusted. It's why she let me in so quickly, why we all gelled as a unit enough to open the bar when I suggested it."

"Tia has premonitions?"

Leah knew precious little about it except that it wasn't Tia's primary power, but that she sometimes got strong feelings, emotions, about people, places. She nodded. "Sometimes, at least. Anyway, it shocked the hell out of me when I saw a glass float to Emma—and that was it. I was obsessed."

His eyes followed the lines of her face, absorbing it. "Why?"

It made her blink. "Why? Because…it's magic. It's telekinesis and conjuring and spells. Fun."

"Fun," he said, as though tasting the word.

"Or it should be. But I guess…it's not for you?"

"Being a witch is about society, bloodlines, reputation. Not fun."

"You've never enjoyed having magic?"

He blinked. "I've never thought about it." His serious expression didn't change as he asked, "Would *you* want magic?"

"Uh…*yeah*."

"Even if it came tangled with my world?" he pushed.

She almost said yes out of habit, having longed for that for so many years. But something caught the word before it left. Hers had always been a child's answer, one without thinking through the consequences. Now…

"I don't know," she said after a minute, the truth quiet. It made his eyes darken. "Part of me says yes," she admitted, looking at the potion that simmered. "Your world…glitters. But the idea of watching my back for a knife at all times, being careful what I say, who I say it to, constantly fearing rejection or being cast out…" She spread her hands. And as she'd already thought, she'd deliberately turned away from a similar world once.

His response hung on a timeless second before he nodded, short, sharp. As if he had no feeling one way or the other. "Understandable. It's a game, but we don't play. It's not fun."

"No."

The mood had darkened, twisting his offer of a piece of his world to her rejecting it. She hated that.

She brought the topic back to her friends with some effort. "I don't regret that they told me. Or…anything else." *You*, she thought, fingers curling into her palms. Not brave enough to say it aloud.

"It's the greatest show of trust they could ever give." Gabriel inclined his head. "We, none of us, trust easily."

She read between the lines and swore she heard her own heart crack in two. But that was to think about later. For now, she wanted to give something back to Gabriel. For the warlock who never played for fun. "You're right."

"I'm sorry?"

"You're right."

"One more time?"

She poked him, smiling. "I said, you're right, Goodnight. They trusted me enough to let me in the door." She tilted her head back, basked in his gaze. "And so did you."

The music had shifted to something bluesy, an outpouring of soul that shivered through her blood. Just as he did.

Her smile turned sly. "The question is, how *much* do you trust me?"

The snap of lust in his blood was tempered by wariness. Leah's face spelled nothing but trouble.

"Why?" Gabriel asked, standing perfectly still.

She toyed with one of his buttons, quirking a brow. "Why don't we play pretend?"

His mind flashed back to the first time she'd said those words, the night that had followed. "Pretend?"

"Mmm." Her eyes were so blue, they could lure a man in, under. "How about I'm the all-powerful witch and you're the powerless human?"

"You have never been powerless."

Her hand paused for a second before it slipped his button free. "Very smooth."

"Truth," he countered, watching her undo his buttons and spread open his shirt. "I don't think you know what you do to me, Leah." What she created inside him, more than just desire. More than just affection, concern. If she didn't, perhaps her rejection wouldn't have cut so deeply. But he shied away from that. Because this was temporary anyway. No point in examining feelings that had nowhere to go.

For a moment, her gaze connected with his and an acknowledgment ran between them. The sharp ache, the sweet torment of now. Only now.

Then she smiled, as only Leah could. "Wait until you see what I'm *about* to do to you."

"Should I be concerned?"

"Depends on if you're willing to play."

He allowed her to slide the shirt off, pulse thrumming as her fingers skimmed bare skin. "What does the powerless human have to do?"

"It's simple." She pressed her mouth against his chest. Her tongue flicked out, made his breath catch. "You have to let me have my way with you. My way. My rules."

He was always the one giving the pleasure before taking his own. It was easier to stay removed.

But this was Leah.

The hint of anxiety after he nodded was soothed by her bright smile. She tangled their fingers together as she led him toward his bedroom.

"No," she said, command vibrating in her tone, and he turned his head to see Rosie skitter to a halt, her body drooping in denial. Delilah huffed and yipped, cantering forward despite the order.

Gabriel conjured three bones, one directly in the dachshund's path. The way the little dog's eyes bugged out was worth the ache that vibrated through him, clanging in his temples.

Leah's laugh floated around him as she walked them into his bedroom. Then his back was against the closed door and her mouth was fixed greedily on his.

His hands clamped on her hips and she broke free.

"First rule," she said breathlessly. "Hands off."

Like she'd spoken in Cantonese and he'd forgotten a translation spell, he blinked at her owlishly.

"I'm all-powerful, remember?" She backed away, perched on his bed. She sat there, dressed in black jeans and a navy sweater covered in dog hair, curls wild. She might as well have been in sheer lingerie.

As he stood, helpless against her, she leaned back on one elbow. "Strip."

"Sorry?"

"Strip." Laughter sparkled in her eyes. "And make it good."

"I've never told you to strip."

"When it's your game, you make the rules." Her sweater slipped down, exposing her tattoo and a lacy black bra strap. "Strip, warlock boy."

He threw her a haughty look, but his hands went to his belt. "I'm not dancing."

"What if I gave you something to work with?" She sat up, cupped her hands around her mouth and made what he presumed she thought were beatboxing noises.

He couldn't prevent the smile as he pulled the belt free. "This is an excellent seduction."

She stopped, beamed. "Thanks. But it's not a seduction, remember? I have you at my mercy."

Yes, she did.

When he shucked his jeans and stood there in only black boxer briefs, Leah's smile faded, and she swept her tongue over her bottom lip. Heat rolled over him as he started toward her.

Her hand flew up like a traffic cop. "Uh-uh. My game."

"I just want to touch you."

"My rules," she insisted, stubbornly, then scooted off the bed. "Where do you keep your ties?"

Surprise had him gesturing at the closet before he thought better. She laughed at his circular tie rack, though what there was to laugh about, he had no clue. She selected two, a pinstripe and a solid black.

"On the bed."

Eyeing the ties, he did as ordered, moving to the head when she gestured.

"Arms out."

"Why?"

"Trust me."

Warily, he spread his arms. When she began to wrap the pinstripe around the slats of the headboard and then around his wrist, the question slipped out. "What are you doing?"

"Tying you to the bed."

"I see. And the reason for this is?"

She knotted the tie, tugged. Nodded before clambering over him to mirror the action with his other wrist and the black tie. "To immerse you in your role." She pointed. "Powerless human."

"But I don't technically need my hands." Although telekinesis wasn't his specialty, he stroked a fine line down her neck and saw her shiver. Clamped down on the vicious ache that gripped his neck.

Blue eyes cut to his. "No. It causes you pain. I don't ever want to cause you pain."

Something hard lodged in his chest. Because he knew, despite her best efforts, she would.

"Besides," she added with a nod of satisfaction at her other knot. "Hands off was the rule, in *every* sense. And you're a rule follower, aren't you?"

"I'm beginning to feel I shouldn't have agreed to this." He tested the restraints. They weren't incredibly tight but were tighter than he'd expected.

She knelt next to him. "We can stop."

He studied the ties, then her face. "I trust you."

Everything about her softened. She shifted to swing a leg

over his waist. The rough fabric of her jeans abraded his belly as she planted her hands on his chest. "You ready to lose control?"

"Do you think you can make me?"

Challenge gleamed in her face. "Take it like a human, Gabe." And so saying, she kissed him.

It was a study in sin, a deep caress of tongue, the perfect pressure of lips, the nip of teeth. He sank into it, into her, desperate for more, for what he could get. He wanted to absorb this memory, hide it away to always remember.

She broke away when his chest was heaving, her own breathing unsteady. She dragged her mouth down his throat and beyond. She left no part of his chest untouched, her lips and tongue and teeth tracing every square inch until his breath was short and sharp and he throbbed everywhere. When she settled over him, he ground his teeth, pleasure a sharp arc.

"Please," he ground out. "I want you naked."

"Compromise." Her voice was raw, as affected as him. She pulled off her sweater, tossing it behind her. She was left in a black lacy bra, black jeans and sky-blue nails that she scored lightly down his belly, heading for his underwear.

He couldn't help the bump of his hips, even as he said through his teeth, "Leah, you don't…"

She hushed him, sliding her hands into his underwear, pushing them down his thighs, his shins, off. She moved back up, smoothing hands that were soft but intent up his legs, making him shudder. When she gripped him, his spine arched and a muffled groan flew from his mouth.

She didn't let him have a respite, one hand firm at the base. Every inch of him was alive as he watched her mouth near his cock.

"Leah," he said again in a near-moan. "You don't have to—"

Her tongue darted out, licked the drop of pre-come off. His hips arched and his eyes slammed shut. Every breath was an effort as she teased him, her tongue working him like she knew

every secret fantasy, every hidden desire. Any thought of resisting so he could stay in control fled. All his thoughts were
of her, her and her hot, talented mouth.

When she took him in, he heard something smash into the
wall, but neither stopped. The bed shook under them as his
magic leaked out, sending a fine shiver of pain into the pleasure as she worked him, her hand below what her mouth could
manage.

Pleasure was a fever inside him and he braced, his hands
straining at the bonds to grip her, hold her, work her in return. Black spots danced with the green sparks and he shouted
as she firmed her hold, as she sucked so hard her cheeks hol-
lowed. And then he was there, his whole body shaking as he
shot into the stratosphere, touched the stars before slamming
back into his boneless body.

Sweat glistened over him as she sat back. Her nipples strained
against her thin bra and her skin was sheened, body trembling.
Aroused even as she slid a hand over her own stomach. He
couldn't not watch as her head fell back.

"Gabe," she moaned.

"Release me." It was half command, half plea.

"Yes."

Before she could move, he'd snapped a word that undid any
bindings. The crack of pain barely registered.

He captured her mouth in a searing kiss, tasting both of
them as he ran his hands over her breasts. She pushed into his
hands, undulating. Desperate. He'd bet she was dripping and
groaned at the image.

He nudged her to stand next to the bed, unsnapped her
jeans himself. The zipper tugged down to reveal white lacy
underwear, and why the sight of mismatched underwear excited him, he didn't really care. All he knew was he needed to
get inside them.

She moaned as his fingers trailed over her, pushing inside

the panties to cup her. He'd bet right; she was soaked. Pleasure caught him in its teeth, in its demand that he make her crave him like he did her.

"Take them off."

Their pretense was done and she complied, kicking them off and getting rid of her bra. Whether he reached for her or she dove onto him wasn't clear, but he rolled so she was underneath, sucking in a breath at the feel of her body against his.

He slid his hand back down, lazily playing with her as he grazed his teeth over her nipple. Dark satisfaction rolled over him as she called his name, as he used his tongue to bring the nipple to an even stiffer peak. Then he moved to the other, still languid with her even as she moaned, writhed, pleaded for him to go faster, press harder against that small bundle of nerves.

Only when her breaths were sobbing did he give in and slip a finger, then two, inside, hooking them so they grazed the right spot. He used his thumb to circle her clit as he moved his fingers in a rhythm designed to drive her wild, teasing, squeezing lightly. When he added a third finger, stretching her, her hands fisted the sheets and she arched her upper body off the bed.

"Goddess," he dragged out, unable to help quickening the rhythm, lost to her. "I love watching you like this." For his eyes only. Primal, he shoved her over with a few quick gestures. Her cries echoed in the room as her body stiffened, quivered. Beautiful.

He didn't give her time to recover, leaving only for the time it took him to grab a condom, roll it on. Then he was on her, thrusting home while she was still quaking. He felt the fine edge of her orgasm dance through him. And lost his mind.

He didn't think to control the pace, didn't stop to consider whether he could. His hips drew back, slammed in. Pleasure fired up his spine, white-hot and blinding him to anything but her.

He caught her lips in a rough kiss as he set an almost savage rhythm. Her legs wrapped around his hips, meeting him, challenging him as their mouths clashed. This was war, a battle for something neither knew. Her fingernails dug into his skin, his teeth nipped her. The air was saturated with the sounds of their bodies meeting, her short cries, his harsh breathing.

Pain mingled with the pleasure once again, heightening it, as magic leaked from him. He forced his eyes open and met glazed, pleasure-drunk blue.

When she threw her head back on a silent scream, rippling around him, he heard himself snarl, his hips increasing, hitting hard and fast and making her clutch at him in ecstasy. He couldn't catch his breath, didn't want to, as he watched her through narrowed eyes until he finally broke. Pleasure ripped them both apart, leaving them a shattered mess.

And as he gasped for air, sweat slicking both of them, as her nails released his skin and she sank into the mattress, the bed dropped the foot it had been levitating. The wood trembled, cracked, fell in, the mattress slamming to the floor.

Leah's startled yelp faded as Gabriel lifted his head and stared at the wreckage.

Before he even knew what to say, Leah's shoulders began to shake and she hooted with laughter.

Embarrassment at his loss of control faded at the sight of her, sated, sexy and so damned happy. And as an echo of the same ran through him, he gave in and laughed with her.

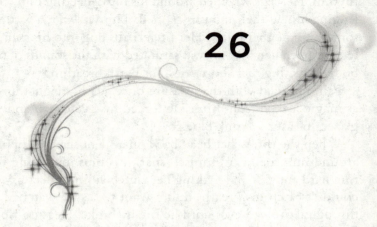

26

Their final two weeks together passed in a blur. Before Leah knew it, D-Day was upon them, with only one more night left.

One more night. Every time she thought it, nausea ran up her throat. She tried not to dwell—after all, what would be the point? They'd both known this was the arrangement. Short-term, no strings. Except now they'd got to this point, Leah wanted to take some strings, wrap them around Gabriel, around herself and knot them together.

She didn't let it show as she maneuvered the breakfast tray up the stairs, mumbling a curse as Delilah shot past her. Rosie was hot on her heels and the orange juice sloshed in the glass, almost over the French toast Leah had sweated over until it was crisp and perfect. She righted it quickly, passing a chastising glance over her dogs as she reached the top, where they waited outside her bedroom door.

Balancing the tray on her hip, she managed to get the door open, then watched in muted resignation as Rosie charged in and made a flying leap for the bed.

Gabriel, peacefully sprawled across the mattress until this

point, shot up with a pained *oomph* as the sprocker landed on his gut.

"Rise and shine," Leah called out merrily as Gabriel cast her a glower she knew he didn't mean. Not when he was already scratching Rosie behind the ear, making her back leg thump in earnest. Delilah yipped from the floor, demanding to be picked up.

"Not when there's food," Leah told him before he could reach down. She proffered the breakfast tray. "For you."

"You made me breakfast?" He accepted the tray, flipping out the legs.

"In bed. And bonus, you get me, too." She pushed Rosie off before the dog could sniff too earnestly at the French toast and pointed at both troublemakers. "Where's Peggy? Go find Peggy."

They gamboled off. Louie appeared two minutes later, obviously deciding the bed was better than the couch. Leah scooped him up and sat with him on her lap, sitting cross-legged and diagonal to Gabriel, who had yet to touch his breakfast.

"You like French toast, right?"

Gabriel smiled his smile, the barely-there curve which always looked brand-new. "Yes. Thank you."

"I figured the last full day before you go home deserved something special."

His green eyes slid to the side as he picked up his fork. "Not the last morning?"

"I thought you'd want to make me breakfast," she teased. "Some burnt toast? Rubbery eggs?"

He arched his eyebrows and cut a piece of French toast. "Who will keep my ego in check when you're not around?"

That fist around her heart squeezed mercilessly. She shrugged a careless shoulder, cuddling Louie closer for comfort. "I'm sure you'll find some society witch to do it. From what I hear, they ain't no marshmallows."

"No." He stared down at the plate.

She indulged in a long stare, drinking him in. "Did you say you're meeting with the board tomorrow afternoon?"

He nodded. "They'll review the past three months, but I'm not concerned how the vote will go."

Except she knew a part of him was. She set Louie down on the comforter and the King Charles sleepily curled up on the spread. She reached out, touched Gabriel's knee. "They won't be able to vote you in fast enough. They'll be like, 'Congrats, you're the big fish we all want. Tell us, oh mighty one, what shall we do to serve?'"

He huffed what might have been a laugh.

"Seriously, how do you feel?" She drew a design on his leg beneath the blankets. "Nervous? Excited?" *Devastated?*

"I'm not sure." He set the plate aside, still uneaten. Put a hand over hers to lift it so he could fiddle with her fingers. "Relieved? I've been waiting for this for so long, it feels surreal to know by tomorrow afternoon I'll have everything I've ever wanted."

Words bubbled up, desperate to be voiced.

She swallowed them down. He'd just said he was relieved it was almost over. She reached into herself and produced a bright smile she didn't feel. "So, what do you want to do on your last day?"

"Actually, I promised I'd meet Bastian and Henry at the bar."

"Henry is still going to Toil and Trouble, even after Emma forbade him?"

"When did she forbid him?"

Leah narrowed her eyes. "She didn't?" *Traitor.*

He shook his head. Hesitated. "I apologize. I didn't know if you'd be busy at the shelter."

On his last day? As if she'd be anywhere else. "I'm here for your whim."

"I like the sound of that."

Leah leaned forward, looped her arms around his neck. *Keep it light*, she ordered herself. Playful. "How about you meet me at the shelter after and you can say bye to Chuck then, too?"

She didn't know whether to find it funny or insulting that he actually looked grieved at the idea. Oh, sure, saying goodbye to her was easy, but a Labrador? Whole different story.

If she didn't find it so sweet how much he loved that dog, she'd resent it. Okay. Maybe she did, a little. It'd be nice to know she wasn't the only one twisting over this.

"We could do that," he agreed, sliding his hands up her arms.

"We could have dinner."

"That, too."

"You could say you'll miss me." The words came out without any plan. Mortification sank into her bones. "Um…"

His hands stopped their sensual slide. "What?"

Oh, well. She'd done it now.

"Even if it's not true," she hedged, toying with the wisps of hair at his nape. "You could say you'll miss me."

"Will you miss me?"

Careful, she cautioned. "Maybe."

"Your enthusiasm stuns me. Please, let me take a moment to recover."

She pinched his neck. "Okay, fine. Yes." Her voice turned soft. Sincere. Too much so. "Yes, I'll miss you, Gabe."

Before she could regret it, he leaned in, pressed his forehead to hers. "I'll miss you, too," he said, deep, grave. The simple words winged into her heart.

It gave her the courage to unlock her own. "What if we didn't end things?"

He stilled. Three seconds counted down before he spoke. "What do you mean?"

Her pulse picked up as she drew back. "I just… I know some humans are accepted into your world. What if I was one of them?"

He said nothing, his face betraying *nothing*. It felt like a chill across her skin.

Everything in her wanted to curl into a ball, to hide, to retreat. But this was too important to risk not opening herself up. He was as guarded as she could be. One of them had to take the first step.

Even so, she withdrew her hands, fisting them on her lap. "There's something here," she said. "Something real. You said you'd miss me—what if you didn't have to?"

When his silence continued, she felt words scrape her throat with the need to fill it. Her nails pinched her skin as she curled her hands tight. "There are humans in your company and at some point another witch must have wanted a human. It must be possible to—appeal?" She wasn't sure of the word, wasn't sure of anything except that Gabriel didn't look like a man given the key to his heart's desire. She pushed. "I could swear not to tell anyone, if we could just go to the High Family—"

"No."

That one syllable snapped her back. Her chest shuddered as she stared at him. "No?" she echoed.

He moved then, fast, before she'd realized he would. He wore only boxer briefs but he may as well have been wearing one of his suits. His expression was set as he stood next to the bed.

"We will not be going to the High Family," he intoned, voice razor-sharp in its directness. "The idea is ridiculous."

She chose to stay seated, wasn't sure if her legs would hold her. "The idea of being with me is ridiculous?"

His jaw set and he turned to gather up his clothes. As he pulled them on, he kept his movements brusque and efficient, much like his words. "The High Family do not welcome everyone in simply because one witch—*likes* a human. Business requirements can be examined, and in limited cases special circumstances can be allowed, but a sacrifice is needed to show that the party is serious. That is not what we have here."

"Oh?" Her voice sounded off to her own ears. "What do we have here, Gabriel?"

He refused to meet her eyes as he shrugged on his sweater.

Brittle, she wrapped her arms around her waist to keep herself together. "I'll say it then, shall I? A good fuck."

He whirled on her, the excessive movement so unlike Gabriel that it surprised her. "Don't reduce it to that."

"Why not? You are. Leah Turner, good enough to screw, not good enough to sacrifice something for."

Something flashed in his eyes but he didn't come any closer. "You're being dramatic."

Her vision bled to red. "Because I have actual feelings instead of being a good little robot doing as he's told?"

"Careful."

She ignored that. "Everything you've ever wanted, huh?" She parroted his earlier words with a heaping of scorn. "Why? You don't even *want* the job, Gabriel, not really. You're only doing it because——" She stopped.

Green glinted dangerously. "Because?"

Fury and hurt still battled in her blood, but she chose her next words with care. "They can't come back and approve of you, Gabe." She flinched when something—the bedside table drawers—banged. "You can't, you shouldn't, live for them. You should do what makes you happy."

"And I suppose that's you?" He didn't sneer but she felt it anyway. "A woman so desperate to be included when she's not even sure why she wants to be?"

She pressed her lips together tight enough to hurt.

"Grow up," he snapped. "This isn't magical cocktails and portalling abroad. It's real and dangerous. And you pushing your way in because you hold a child's fantasy that magic is amazing is not going to end well."

"That's not why," she protested, stomach cramping from the

look in his eyes. Not her Gabe. "I told you; I don't know if I'd *want* to live in that kind of world again."

"Then why even suggest putting yourself in the High Family's line of fire?" he shot back.

"Because *I love you*."

Her words, ripped from the depths of her, might as well have been a slap as he took a step back. A surge of emotions lit his eyes, and she swore something like terror flared bright before everything got sucked out. His mask rolled down. "No."

She had to take a breath. "Yes," she said, quieter. "Believe it or don't, but I love you. I would sacrifice living a normal life for you." She pleaded with her eyes as she looked across the divide at him. Hope gave her one last push. "Wouldn't you do the same for me?"

She read it in his face before he'd made his decision.

And the rejection sliced her heart in two before he even crossed to the door and walked away.

"What the hell?" Tia's voice rang out across the bar, slicing neatly through the murmur of casual conversations.

Across from where Gabriel sat, Henry's entire body stiffened.

Bastian whistled silently and cast his eyes down, rolling his beer bottle in his hands. "Uh-oh."

Gabriel barely noticed. He hadn't really been present this entire time, his whole body locked up with the effort not to betray the emotion rattling around inside of him.

I love you.

He'd known Henry would only hound him if he hadn't shown, so he'd dutifully reported to the bar and sat in silence as the other two traded friendly insults. If he could have left without arousing suspicion, he would have.

She didn't love him. It was impossible. A terrible thought. Terrifying. And so tempting his body trembled.

Desperate for relief, he looked up to see Tia barreling down on them, dressed in a violent red sweater and jeans ripped at the knee. Violent was the right word, he thought, as murder glinted hotly in her eyes. With another witch, he might have expected a physical manifestation of the temper, but not Tia Hightower. She stopped in front of their table, hands on hips.

"What do you think you're doing?" she shot at Henry.

He sent her a steely look. Just like that, the easygoing man transformed into a stiff, combative warlock. "Hello, Tia."

"You're drinking. At my bar."

"Seems like it. Why?" He arched one deliberate eyebrow. "Does it bother you?"

Gabriel swore he felt heat coming off her as she snapped, "*You* bother me."

"I understand. Old ties can be so hard to cut for some people." Gabriel knew when his friend was being deliberately baiting.

"I cut ties with you the second you didn't stand with me."

Henry's face quivered, the effort of restraining an expression.

Seeing it, Tia laughed harshly. "Of course, how could I forget? Can't possibly show too much emotion in front of anyone. Easier to walk away."

"I didn't walk away," he bit out.

"Yes. You. Did."

Bastian's sharp whistle cut through their debate and he made a time-out gesture. "Guys, chill before hex bags get thrown."

Tia smirked, tossed her hair back. "I wouldn't waste the ingredients on such a small man. And I mean that in every sense."

Bastian touched his forehead and then his lips in a symbol of prayer.

Given his own mood, Gabriel decided to interrupt. "Tia, this is not the appropriate setting." He locked down the instant of sudden fear when those blazing eyes turned on him. "I, ah, understand you and Henry have history but we're all adults."

"Yet to see evidence of that," Henry muttered.

"How droll." Tia crossed her arms, focused on Bastian. "Just because you have the bad taste to have this man as a friend doesn't mean I should suffer his presence in my bar."

"We're having a last drink with Goodnight."

Her gaze swung his way again. "You're leaving? What about Leah?"

His throat hurt. Everything did. It wasn't true. What she'd said.

She couldn't love him.

He couldn't let that thought surface, locked down on it like a drowning man desperate for air. "I'm not sure what you mean?"

"I see *his* stupidity is rubbing off on you."

Henry's jaw clenched.

"I mean, is she all right with this?" she emphasized. "I won't let you hurt her, Goodnight."

Too late.

The memory of those perfect blue eyes shattered by his rejection chilled him to his marrow. He'd done that. And why? *Why?*

When she'd spoken of going to the High Family, he'd been both elated and terrified out of his wits. To have her exposed like that. He couldn't stand it. Better to make her angry, as long as it kept her safe.

Except it wasn't anger in her eyes, at the end.

A mournful cry reverberated in his soul at the memory.

Tia looked at him sharply, as if she'd heard it. "You've already done something."

He took a shallow breath, gripping the table to maintain an even expression. "I reminded her that what we have is temporary. She...didn't take it well."

Tia's stare drilled into him. It might have been just them two as he fought the urge to explain. He owed Tia nothing. Even if Leah would need her when he went. When he left her.

He admitted defeat and closed his eyes.

"Good," he heard Tia say, causing him to flinch. "Leah deserves someone who'd fight for her, sacrifice anything, and let's face it, you're not that guy."

I would sacrifice for you. Wouldn't you do the same for me?

The statement was shocking; even more so was the answer that had whispered from his heart.

So, he'd left her before any damage could be done. It was safer that they stick to the rules they'd laid out. Safer for her.

For him.

Struck, he swallowed as those words dug inside him. Safer for him. Because…

Because it was safer to keep her at a distance. Because losing Leah would crush his heart.

Because…he loved her.

Nearby the chairs around an empty table flew out without warning, causing customers to squeak in surprise. Murmurs of confusion quickly followed.

Gabriel ignored it, their sounds, the hum of Tia's voice berating him for using magic.

All of it receded as he focused on the glowing truth.

He *loved* Leah.

His chest seized as their conversation tore through his mind. He'd fallen back on old habits. Attacked because he'd needed her to stay at a distance, panicked he'd lose someone else he loved if they got too close. But it was too late. She'd already slipped behind his barriers, become so integral that he couldn't imagine a day without her in it. And in return…he'd hurt her.

That pit in his stomach widened. An urge shoved through his body, to go to her, to fix it. But…

It wasn't simply a matter of loving each other; his world could be cutthroat. Even if the High Family accepted her, other witches wouldn't. Leah hated to be excluded, rejected, and she would be, time and time again.

She'd be welcomed in only to be left outside again.

As he sat there, the words of the others falling like misty rain upon his senses, Gabriel played over his every memory of Leah, from the balcony where she had coyly flirted with him, to the bar where she had openly challenged him, to another balcony, where she'd exposed her hidden pain for him. To the bedroom, to their fight, where once again she'd proven to be the stronger one.

And he knew what he had to do.

"We'll be okay, right?" Leah stroked a hand down Chuck's head as the Labrador sprawled across her lap, panting happily. She'd meant to only drop by his kennel on her way to updating the shelter's website and social media, but hadn't been there thirty seconds before the tears had started. She'd cried into his fur as he'd sat as her anchor, hating that she did so but unable to stop the flood. Her mom had always said crying was therapeutic, but the hole inside Leah still gaped, no better for the tears.

Her mom.

God, she hated this stupid secret even more now because even if Leah picked up the phone and called her, poured out her troubles, she couldn't *really* speak to her. Not about the real reason Gabriel was pushing her away.

She wasn't an idiot. Hurt might have buried her better sense for a minute, but she *knew* Gabriel. She knew what he did when he was protecting someone he cared about—he kept them away from any threat. He did it to Melly. He was doing it to her now.

Old insecurities tried to wedge in but she refused to let them. Gabriel wasn't cruel for no reason. That *had* been terror she'd seen on his face before he'd rebuffed her. Because he cared more than he wanted to. How many times had he said that he didn't want her hurt?

It was irritatingly, exasperatingly presumptuous of him to lock her out of any decision and she was so furious with him for it. Love was about trust, in her, in *them*. That they could do anything together.

But maybe he didn't love her enough to try.

And that was what kept her away from Toil and Trouble when she'd thought about going after him. She'd gone to him too many times. She'd put herself out there for him, in a way she'd never done for anyone. If he wanted her, he would have to come on his knees.

She focused on Chuck, pushing aside the whispering fear that Gabriel would crawl for nobody. "He's going to realize he needs you, too," she told him. "Idiot warlock." She pressed a noisy kiss to Chuck's head to hide the wobble in her voice. He grunted and squirmed until he lay on his back.

"What do you—" she began, startled when the lights went out.

They had a skylight so it wasn't completely pitch-black, but even so, all she could see were shapes and shadows.

"Perfect." A fuse must have blown. Or a power surge. Something expensive that would tie Sonny's decision to sell into a bow. The cherry on this fantastic day.

She maneuvered to her feet, hitching her phone out of her back pocket to turn the flashlight on. When she reached Chuck's door and felt him close behind her, she gently pushed him back with her free hand.

"Sorry, baby. You have to stay here."

Shutting the door behind her, she peered into the gloom and headed for where the fuse box was. She'd let Georgia, another volunteer, leave early, so she was the only one on-site before the next shift started.

Well, she was an independent woman, wasn't she? She could probably figure out what the problem was. She pushed open the door that led out of the dogs' section, the thin stream of her phone's flashlight a beam in front.

The next thing she knew she was sent sprawling, a hard blow

to her cheek crashing her into the wall. Her head knocked into the concrete painfully, face throbbing where she'd been hit.

Dazed, she glanced up, saw the outline of a figure, his hands moving in a pattern she recognized. *Magic.*

Fear chilled her skin and she scrambled to move, to get away. A weapon, she needed a weapon. She staggered up, a wild thumping in her ears all she could hear.

At least until a hand gripped the back of her head, forcing her still. "You're just the right leverage," a man murmured, voice too low to make out who. "*Incantartum.*"

Instant lethargy hit her bloodstream. She wanted to fight— sleep was the enemy—but she was only human. Fragile after all.

Gabe, her mind called out. God, she wanted Gabriel.

Then she was lost to unconsciousness.

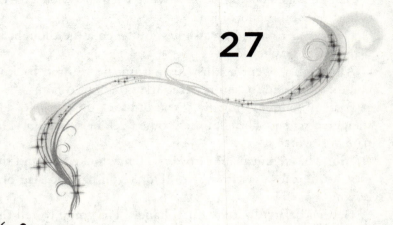

27

"Say it again."

Gabriel gritted his teeth. Henry was drawing too much pleasure out of this. "I fucked up," he enunciated.

Henry shook his head like there was water in his ears. "Sorry, just once more."

"I'll go get Tia."

"Asshole."

Gabriel flicked him a look. They stood waiting for a cab—or Gabriel did. Both of them had been kicked out of Toil and Trouble, and his former friend now seemed content to needle him. He should've kept his mouth shut.

The noise on the street was overwhelming, cars rumbling past, the people swarming and chattering like magpies. Yet, there was quiet inside him now. A stillness he'd never felt before.

Shame Henry wasn't letting him appreciate it.

"Explain to me again how you fucked up."

Bastian piped up from the other side. "Yeah, I'd like to know that, too."

Gabriel scowled. "I don't even know why you're here."

Bastian affected a hurt look. "We're friends. When a friend is hurting, you support them."

He was surrounded by assholes. But even as he thought it, Gabriel's lips twitched.

Although it went against his nature, he figured backup couldn't hurt and so, summarized the situation. Again.

Bastian nodded shrewdly. "You did fuck up. *Oomph.*" He staggered when Gabriel pushed some telekinesis at him. The pain was worth it.

"So, what's your plan? Grovel?" Henry looked around the city, at the cabs crawling past. "Don't you have to flag one down?"

Gabriel belatedly stuck out a hand. "I'm going to tell the truth." He was supposed to be good at that.

"And the truth is…?"

He refused to say those important three words to anyone but Leah for the first time. "I took the decision away from her," he said, nerves skittering down his spine. He flexed his hands. "She deserves to know everything and then…" Then he'd see.

His protective instincts went haywire, jockeying for control, but he breathed through it. By holding on too tight, he'd lose her. He had to try. Had to take this risk.

A few seconds went by. So did two cabs.

"Well." Bastian clapped his hands together. "Bro trip, then?"

"Bro trip?" Gabriel echoed, and found his arm seized by Bastian, who towed him away from the road toward an alleyway. When they stopped, he blinked at the piles of garbage. "Excellent destination."

Having followed them, Henry snickered as Bastian threw up a shield. "We'll portal."

"We?"

"Backup, man."

Henry nodded sagely.

The last thing Gabriel wanted was these two there when he

spoke with Leah, a front-row audience to whatever happened… but portalling would be faster than human travel.

He gave in. "Fine."

"Where to?"

"The shelter."

Henry had barely flicked his fingers before a shimmering portal whirled into existence. Gabriel didn't waste time, hearing footsteps behind him as he strode in and out the other side.

What he saw had his stomach diving into his throat. Bastian and Henry both cursed as they exited and closed the portal, but Gabriel was already streaking toward the shelter, where smoke billowed out the broken windows in thick clouds.

"Henry!" he yelled. Henry's specialty was fire magic. He could contain the blaze.

"I'm on it."

As Bastian raised another shield, to keep the fire from spreading to the other buildings and also to keep humans from seeing too much, Henry braced both hands and began to work on the inferno. His hands shimmered white as he spat out a curse, strained. "Something's wrong. It's not natural. Gabriel! You can't go in until we've managed it. *Gabriel.*"

He barely heard his friend as he crashed through the door. A wave of heat knocked him back and he threw up a magical barrier against the dancing flames, gritting his teeth against the jolt of pain. Even with the block, the heat was incredible and sweat slicked his skin as he barreled through the fire. Was Leah in here? Horrible scenarios ran though Gabriel's head.

The animals, he thought in the next breath. *Chuck.* But as he turned down the first hallway, his eyes fell upon empty kennels and cages, their doors open.

Bastian and his telekinesis. He must have released them. Temporary relief made his head pound, not helped by the thickening smoke or the continued drain of magic. The heat intensified until it felt like his clothes could melt from him. Still, he forged ahead, needing to check each pen, unable to let it rest until he'd seen for himself that no animals were trapped in the blaze.

He nearly missed her. Later, it might make his heart stop to think of how close he'd been to passing by the kennel. The only reason he paused was because it was the only closed door. And there she was, curled up on the floor, pale, unconscious, blond curls splayed around her like a death shroud.

He might have screamed; his mouth moved but all he could hear was his heart throbbing wildly against his rib cage. He threw himself at the kennel door, yanking on it to get her out, to get her away. It wouldn't budge. He applied pressure, feeling the burn in his biceps, triceps, shoulders. He threw all his magic at it, draining himself to the point where his teeth locked together. Nothing.

More sweat dripped and from somewhere in the building, something crashed. He vaguely heard Henry's shouts amidst the roar of the fire. Remembered his friend's words.

It's unnatural.

Swallowing the dark fear, he placed a hand on the kennel door. Magic leaped at his palm like iron shavings to a magnet, forcing a bad taste into his mouth. Someone had sealed the door with a high-level spell. Who? Why?

His mind was a jumble of thoughts, not all of them making sense as he beat the door again, over and over and over, until his skin scraped away and blood bloomed. All outer walls had crumbled, every society manner that made up Gabriel Goodnight burned to ash. That was all he tasted as he finally braced his fists and let his head fall on the door. He stared at Leah with desperation.

Bastian and Henry could get her without issue, but neither were here, and the flames were licking closer. The air was thick with smoke and she was breathing it all in. She might already have suffocated.

The idea had something wild ripping at his insides, shredding him into something less than man. *No.* This wasn't supposed to happen. He couldn't let this happen.

An unnatural calm blanketed the panic. He couldn't let this happen. Wouldn't.

There was only one choice.

Part of him grieved, would grieve more when they were out and he had to face the consequences. But now he focused inside, sank his consciousness down until he reached the binding that held back his power. And, without hesitation, sliced through it.

His body arched, lifting into the air as magic flooded his body. It was ecstasy and torture as his cells rebonded with the power that had always been a part of him. His mouth opened on a silent scream as his body spasmed for endless seconds, until finally he crumpled to the floor.

Gabriel lay there for a blank moment, breathing hard until the lingering pain melted away. Then he lifted his head and pushed to his knees, his feet. Strength coursed through him and he barely broke stride as he focused on Leah's cell, crushed his fist. The spell sealing the kennel door shattered.

He threw a barrier of protection around her instantly, lunging forward to gather her into his arms. Her head lolled as he stood; her chest didn't move. Sick terror gripped him as he created a portal to outside.

Bastian shouted as Gabriel carried Leah through the portal, cradling her in his arms.

"Help," he shouted back, falling to his knees. He stared at her face, tracing every inch as panic swarmed his cells. "She's not breathing," he told Bastian as the other warlock dropped down next to them.

Bastian tore off his jacket. "Lay her on the ground. You know CPR?"

Gabriel shook his head.

"I need you to blow in her mouth when I say." Bastian positioned Leah, moving her chin, her arms, her legs, before laying his hands on her chest. Then he pressed down hard, once, twice, three times, again and again. "When I say, tilt her chin back, pinch her nose and seal your mouth over hers. Breathe into her. *Now.* Stop. Again. Stop. Good." He resumed his compressions, stopping after thirty. "Again."

Gabriel wanted to beat his fists on the ground, scream. Magic could do a lot of things, but it couldn't bring someone back to life.

Not that she was dead. He held that thought like he held her hand, like he could keep her here by force, the depth of his will strong enough to beat back the Goddess and anyone who'd dare take her from him. He had to tell her what she must *know*: that she was in every beat of the heart that now labored for both of them.

"Breathe," he demanded, vaguely aware of Henry still battling to keep the blaze from consuming the building. Unaware of him, thanks to Bastian's shield, groups of people gathered, gawking, distressed as sirens rent the air.

Gabriel barely noticed. His entire focus was on the woman lying so still, too still, when everything she was was energy. "Breathe, Leah." He clutched her as Bastian counted off the compressions. His face was ashen, the expression there close to grief. He slowed, chin tilting to Gabriel.

Something broke inside him, just crumbled, slid away.

"No," he managed, a broken syllable for a broken man. "*No.*" He squeezed her hand tight.

And her eyes flew open.

Instantly she turned, gagging, coughing a raw, painful sound. Gabriel's chest tensed until it hurt as he dragged in a breath.

"Leah." His voice was stricken. "Leah." It was all he could say. But not all he could do. He conjured a vial of Goodnight's Remedies' tonic to soothe a burn patient's innards. As she tried to sit up, he supported her head, then her body as he angled himself to sit behind her.

"Drink this," he urged, wrapping her hands around the pretty blue bottle as his own trembled. "It'll help."

He allowed himself to stroke the hair off her face, focusing on the faintest scent of coconut beneath the acrid smoke. He felt her heart beat, felt his settle into a slower, less jerky rhythm.

Except it didn't feel whole anymore, not completely. The other half was cradled in his arms.

He skimmed his lips over her forehead as she drank the potion with only a wrinkling of her nose. His eyes met Bastian's. "Thank you." He would be forever in his debt.

The warlock inclined his head and patted Leah's knee. "Glad you're back with us, Leah." His words were casual but the raw note in them revealed how close it had been. Saying nothing about that, he hiked a thumb. "I'm going to go help Henry."

"I'll come. Rest here for a minute," Gabriel said to Leah and eased away.

"What's...?" She turned her gaze onto the building and panic leaped to her eyes. "The animals." She struggled to rise.

"They're not in there." He soothed her back to sitting. "Rest. I'll be back."

He found it hard to keep his gaze off her, how she breathed, *that* she breathed, as he walked backward for a few steps. Then he turned and helped Bastian and Henry beat the mystical fire into submission.

Leah's mind was still foggy hours later as she curled up in her bed. Next to her, Rosie sprawled, snoozing, while Delilah and Louie lay together at the footboard. Sylvie had abandoned her for Peggy, who'd fluttered around Leah until she'd finally been ordered away. Yet she hadn't been the worst offender.

Emma had gripped her hard in a hug that wouldn't end, while Tia had paced the bedroom floor, ranting about how when she found out who'd done this, she'd hex their insides to be their outsides and force them to eat every slimy inch. Just…ew.

Leah hadn't seen Gabriel once her friends had descended.

She couldn't blame him. He must be…was there even a word for what he must be feeling?

He'd voided his contract, or word, or whatever was the right term. On the final day, when he'd made it three months, he'd been forced to throw away all of his dreams, his chance at redeeming himself—in his head, anyway—because of her.

She knew it wasn't her fault that she'd been knocked out and locked up. But she'd promised him she'd never be an obstacle.

Well, congratulations, Leah, she told herself as she stared at the figures moving around on the TV. *You weren't an obstacle, you were a dead end.*

The expression made her wince. *Dead end.*

She shied away from the words as they echoed in her mind. As gut-wrenching as Gabriel's situation was, it was still easier to focus on than the fact that she'd apparently stopped breathing.

It could've been so much worse. And she still had no idea who would want to set the shelter on fire. Mitch was right, it was like they were being targeted for some reason.

At least the animals would be okay, having been saved by being rounded into the yard. Unfortunately, although Bastian had done his best, smoke damage had still caught some of them before they'd got the fire out.

Sonny had immediately linked with their on-call vet to come assist, Joanne and other neighbors also offering help once the all clear was given. Luckily, thanks to the warlocks filtering the magic out of the blaze, firefighters had finished putting out the fire shortly after Leah had woken up. She'd been bundled off to the hospital for a checkup, but she'd been told Gabriel had also contacted his sister in search of something to help the animals. None of their usual elixirs would work for non-humans, but Melly, as he'd told Leah once, loved to experiment, so she'd been tasked with tweaking some of their existing medicines. According to Emma, the early results were promising.

Gabriel had also solved the problem of where to house the animals longer term and volunteered his manor, at least temporarily, until the shelter could be assessed and repaired. Leah couldn't even imagine how his housekeeper would cope, but she knew Melly would be in heaven. And luckily, with Gabriel and all her other witch friends to help, the shelter wouldn't be a write-off. Everything would be okay. For her.

But Gabriel was going to lose everything.

"Leah."

His voice had her gaze flying to the open door. He stood in the doorway, dressed in one of his three-piece suits. Immaculately armored once again. His hair was freshly washed, face freshly shaved. He looked perfect and unattainable, not like the man who'd held her so tenderly when he'd taken her away from the shelter.

They still hadn't talked and their last words before the fire throbbed between them. She'd hoped he'd come but now he was here, her stomach knotted at his watchful gaze. He'd only worried she was fragile before; now he knew it.

She scooted up to sit, making the mattress dip. Rosie moaned in her sleep.

Unsure what to do with her hands, she tucked hair behind her ear. "Hi." Her voice was scratchy, uncomfortable.

"How are you feeling?"

"Fine. Alive."

He nodded and stayed in the doorway.

Her heart dropped farther, to her toes. She curled them under the covers. "Did I say thank you?"

"Yes. But there's no need."

"Sure. When I save someone's life, I always think it's no big deal."

Delilah stirred. On seeing Gabriel was there, she lifted her little body and wiggled it, yipping.

He hesitated then crossed the threshold to scratch her behind her ear. He focused on the dog. "I have to go to New Orleans."

Leah chewed the inside of her cheek, lifting her knees up so she could wrap her arms around them. "To tell them."

"They'll already know. The binding… Breaking it forcefully will have caused a ripple effect back through their magic, since they created it." He smoothed a hand down Louie's back as the lazy spaniel lifted a paw. "I have to explain."

"Maybe they'll understand."

"Maybe." But his tone wasn't encouraging. It wasn't anything really.

Any hope she might have harbored about the two of them melted away in that moment of silence.

Tears burned at the backs of her eyes, for him, for her. For what they may have been. She held them back. "Do you want me to…would it help if I came? Explained?"

"No. It's best I face the consequences alone." Another marked hesitation lapsed into silence. Then he shifted to look at her. His eyes were vibrantly green. "We need to talk."

Hope, a thing more dangerous than a blade or gun, unfurled in her chest.

His gaze caressed her, a frown marking his brow. "You're tired."

"I'm fine."

That same gaze called her a liar.

"Mostly," she allowed. "You wanted to talk."

"Later. You should rest first and I have to deal with…this." He paused for the longest second. "But I am sorry, Leah. For what I said."

That hope shivered. "I'm sorry, too." For springing it on him. The words about his parents.

He withdrew his hand from the dogs. "Do you need anything? Peggy or Emmaline or Tia?"

She shook her head. "The board might understand," she added, hating the gulf between them but knowing now wasn't the time. "You were helping a human, right?"

"Maybe." To her surprise, after a marked hesitation, he came around the bed. He bent, pressing his lips to her forehead. She inhaled, wanting to grip his tie, hold him to her, using it for leverage. But she let him go as he stepped back.

And it came to her.

"Gabriel?"

He stopped, angled a look back in question.

"I remember…the man who knocked me out. He said something. About me being the perfect leverage." She searched his face. "Do you think that means anything?"

His lips pressed together, something dangerous flaring to life in his expression. "It means someone knows what you mean to me. Someone close."

She didn't dare react to his statement. "Close? Like…?"

"Someone who would benefit from my failure."

"You didn't—" Understanding dawned. She gripped the duvet. "Your uncle."

He didn't let her continue, though what she'd have said, she wasn't sure. "I have to go."

"And do what?" Worried, she tried to catch his hand, but he'd moved away. "Confront him?"

"If I have to."

His brittle voice made her wince. "It might not be what it looks like."

For a split second she saw the utter pain in his eyes before he blanked them. "I'll give him the chance to tell his truth. Even if it's not one I want to hear."

"I'm sorry." It was useless but all she could think of.

He was already in motion. "I'll come back."

He was gone the next second. And then it was just her, the dogs and the quiet.

"I'll be waiting," she said to the empty room.

Gabriel met Henry and Bastian in front of the shelter. The windows were blown out, plastic tape making Xs across them. It flapped in the wind, drawing attention to the destruction caused. If it wasn't for the fact that all the employees were human, Gabriel would've worked a spell or seven, but they might be suspicious of a building that withstood a fire without a scratch. Better to ensure the innards were sturdy, if smoke-damaged.

Not that it had changed Sonny's mind, as the owner had told Gabriel that morning. It was the final straw for the old human. He was selling.

"She's going to hate me," Sonny had said, staring at his blackened shelter with swimming eyes. He didn't acknowledge the tears so neither had Gabriel. "But I just don't have the heart anymore."

Gabriel wiped that from his mind as he greeted the warlocks with a nod. "Thanks for coming."

"Shit." Henry winced at the deep-fried structure. "Though with the strength of that fire, I'm surprised it's still standing."

He'd told Gabriel that the magical fire had been set to withstand the interference of magic, and considering it had taken Henry with assistance from Bastian and Gabriel to put out the blaze, Gabriel believed him.

It added to his dark mood. "It was set to lure me out."

Bastian cocked an eyebrow. "What makes you think that?"

When he told them what Leah had said, they both grimaced.

"Shit," Henry said again, rubbing the back of his neck. "You know, only a high-level warlock can cast that kind of magic."

"I do."

"And you have a suspect?"

Gabriel wanted to beat his already torn-up fists against the brick, lift all the stones in the area and crush them with tele-kinesis. He held it in as he said, "My uncle."

"August?" Henry goggled. "Are you serious?"

"There's nobody else who stands to gain anything from my failure. Now he stays CEO."

"He likes the job?" Bastian voiced.

"He does. He says he's happy to hand it back, but power, that kind of power, can do strange things to a person." Gabriel's hands tightened into fists, signet ring cutting into flesh. "He doesn't like Leah, made a point of berating me in front of the board for letting myself be weak."

"Putting you down to make you look even weaker." Henry rubbed his hands over his face. "But Gabriel, August's been there since..."

"Since my parents died." Gabriel firmed his jaw before it could tremble. "I know. I don't want to believe it. Which is why I'm asking for your help."

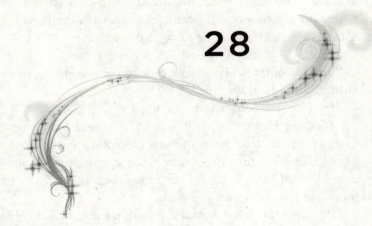

28

*I*t was like facing down a firing squad.

Gabriel stood by the windows, hands locked behind his back. His uncle and the board members sat at the long rectangular table, judge and jury. He couldn't read their faces but he could imagine how disappointed they were. Just like his parents always had been. He'd failed once again.

Leah's voice crept into his head. *You don't even* want *the job, Gabriel, not really.*

At the far end of the room, Henry and Bastian lounged against the walls, expressions neutral. His uncle had at first questioned their presence but conceded when Gabriel explained they were here for his defense. Will echoed their posture on the other end of the room, closest to August, pen and paper at the ready.

Gabriel studied his uncle now, framed by the light from the afternoon sun. August had always absorbed light, mirrored it back to encourage everyone around him. Was all that a lie? Was everything?

The idea was like shaving a grater over his heart.

Finally August linked his hands together on the table. "Ultimately," he said, deep, regretful, "we are where we are. It falls to you, nephew. Tell us why you voided the clause. Speak your truth."

Gabriel ignored the tremble in his hands, tightening their grip on each other. "Actually, Uncle," he said with no trace of emotion. "I was hoping you would speak *your* truth."

August cocked his head. "I'm sorry?"

"The shelter I've been working at for the past three months has been plagued by incidents. Multiple counts of vandalism. Phony reports to the police. Irritants designed to trigger a reaction." Gabriel swept his gaze across the table, ensuring he made eye contact with each member. This was a guess at most, but the idea had formed when he'd looked at all the pieces. "Meant to provoke me into getting frustrated enough to use magic or even leave entirely."

"Why would any witch do that?" James spoke up, sitting back in his chair.

Because the question wasn't combative, Gabriel answered. "The same reason someone knocked out the human I've formed an attachment to and locked her in a burning building behind a high-level spell."

Murmurs of surprise, dismay, rippled.

"Is she okay?" someone ventured.

"Only because I cut through the binding."

More murmurs. August's chair squeaked as he leaned forward. "Was there no other recourse?"

"Henry and Bastian were outside. By the time I got to them, it might have been too late. It almost was." He would never get the image of Leah, lifeless in his arms, scrubbed from his mind. "I believe the person who had the most to gain from my failure to complete this clause was responsible for this final act."

"And who is that?"

Gabriel let the truth drop like a witch's grenade hex. "You."

Gasps ran around the room, one witch half rising, shaking their head.

August pushed up, slow, incredulous. "You honestly believe I'd harm a human?"

"You don't like her."

"I don't harm everyone I dislike."

"You also have the most to gain." Gabriel forced himself to keep eye contact. "You love being CEO."

August's hands slammed onto the table in a rare show of temper. "You believe I'd jeopardize my nephew for a job?" he demanded. "You've been like a son to me, Gabriel."

Gabriel felt sickness rise in his throat at the word *son*. Manipulation. It had to be manipulation.

"Facts are facts," he said steadily.

"And what are these facts?" August spat, anger alive and hot. "That the human is angling for whatever she can get? That I tried to tell you how she's making you weak? That I have done nothing but support and care for you and your sister since the day I got the mirror message telling me Alec was dead?" His voice broke. He took a moment, grief touching his face, hollowing it. "I've only ever wanted the best for you."

Gabriel struggled with the emotion clogging his throat. He wanted, with everything inside him, to believe his uncle.

"There's an easy way to prove it," Henry spoke up. He nudged Bastian and both came forward. They may have been dressed casually, but nobody would deny the Higher warlocks passage. They stopped next to Gabriel's uncle, who stared at them like he smelled something bad.

Henry's smile was thin. "Take a test."

August's confusion flipped to consternation. "You expect me to let Bastian Truenote into my mind?"

No. But it was the only way that all of them would know the truth.

"Do it, then."

Gabriel's breath left his body at his uncle's words. His hands unlinked, drifting forward. "Sorry?"

August glared at Bastian. "Do it. I won't have my nephew think I betrayed him. Not that he should."

Doubt trickled like a leak from a pipe, eroding Gabriel's beliefs.

A bluff, he told himself, eyeing August. So, despite the conflict screaming inside him, he gave Bastian the go-ahead. "Do it."

Bastian turned toward August. "Lower your barriers."

"You can't just crash through them?" August's voice was icy.

Not that it touched Bastian. "Sure, I can, but it's polite to ask." With a twist of his lips, he touched his fingertips to August's temples.

"Maybe you shouldn't——" a witch from the other side of the table began.

"Quiet," Henry cut her off.

August stood statue-still as the other warlock's brow furrowed. Gabriel knew he'd be sifting through the layers, searching in the rooms that made up August's mind.

He'd asked a mind master once what it was like to search inside a person's head. She'd described it as like looking through a house, with each person completely unique, cluttered or tidy, big or small, many doors or one open space. It took precision to leave everything untouched, no damage. It was why only mind masters were called upon when spells, hexes or curses rendered a witch locked inside their own mind, or when the High Family wanted someone interrogated. Bastian could make a fortune if he wanted but he'd left society too young to go down that road.

When Bastian's fingers left August's temples, the whole room held their breath like an audience in a bad detective show, like the ones Leah had made him watch.

Surprise marked Bastian's face as he stepped back. "It wasn't him."

Gabriel gripped the back of a chair to keep his knees from buckling. "What?"

"It wasn't him. But I did find something interesting." Bastian's voice was deceptively casual. "Someone reporting how influenced you were by a greedy, grasping human. And how the best thing might be to call you out in front of the board, shaming you to be strong. Whispering about how, sadly, maybe you weren't ready to be CEO." Bastian's eyes flashed as he sought the person in question. "Someone who likes his position as ear to that power very much. Right, Will?"

Shock resonated through Gabriel as his head swung to his uncle's assistant.

Will's expression mirrored the emotion. "I—you think *I*...?" he spluttered, putting up his hands, pen and paper falling to the floor. The pen hit, rolled to where August stood staring.

"You kept talking about the human." August's brows drew together. "How she was corrupting Gabriel. How he was turning back into the child he'd been."

Gabriel squeezed the back of the chair and said nothing to that.

Will looked wildly between them all. "But...why would I? It's not like I have influence."

"As August's assistant, you get a certain amount of power," Henry countered, one platinum brow arching. "August trusts you absolutely, gives you assignments no normal assistants get."

"You recommend someone for promotion? Done." Bastian snapped his fingers. "You suggest firing someone for lackluster work? Bam. You push for a new trial; he'll consider it strongly. You want to be the power behind the throne."

"I didn't—I couldn't..." Will shook his head, seemingly helpless.

August turned fully to his assistant. "Then prove it." He gestured to Bastian.

"No." Will balled his fists. "Just because *you* agreed doesn't mean I have to. It's a violation."

"Do you have something to hide?" James asked from his seat.

"*No.*"

"Take the test."

"Yes, take the test."

"Take the test."

It ran around the room until August held up a hand, gaze locked on the warlock in question. "Will, your contract says you must submit to a mind scan if deemed necessary by the board." He kept his hand lifted. "All those in favor?"

Will snapped. One minute he was the sweet guy forever running around after Gabriel's uncle. The next, an ugly sneer curled his lips. "Fine." He shrugged, folding his arms. "I rigged the game a little. So what?"

Gabriel's blood rose, thick, frothing. "So. *What?*"

His power shot out and Will slammed into the wall, clawing at the phantom hand holding his throat. There were some exclamations of surprise, more that it was Gabriel doing it than out of objection. Nobody moved to stop him.

Henry let the other warlock struggle for thirty seconds before walking to Gabriel's side. "Ease off."

Gabriel's jaw clenched so tight, he thought he heard his teeth crack. "He hurt her."

"She's okay. And he'll get what's coming to him." Coolly, he looked at Will. "The High Family love sentencing dirt like you." His hand rested on Gabriel's shoulder. A reminder. A support. "He's not worth it, Gabriel."

A humming moment passed.

Gabriel closed his hand and dropped it, allowing Will to slide down the wall. He plopped to the carpet, chest heaving, gulping in air.

He struggled to sit up. "She's a human," he rasped. "Like they'll care."

Henry smirked, shoulder to shoulder with Gabriel. "I bet they will, considering the damage you could've caused this company."

"Speaking of." James looked around the room, received nods. "I think we can all agree you acted without bias and with pure intent to help a human, Gabriel. It's exactly what we want in a CEO for Goodnight's Remedies. You may have voided the clause by breaking the binding, but you did so in a way that would have made your parents proud."

Gabriel's throat went thick as other board members chimed in with their agreement.

"Are you kidding me?" Will snapped his open mouth shut, staggering to his feet. "He was weak, emotional. For a *human*."

"That's what this company is all about." James sent him a speaking look, one that had an overlay of warning sparks. "Humans are just as worthy of help as witches. Something you'll have time to ponder after the High Family is done with you."

Bastian chuckled, rubbing his hands in glee. "Maybe they'll strip you of your magic and sentence you to be human. The High Family love an ironic twist."

Will lost what color he had. Then he uttered five words that yanked Gabriel's feet from under him.

"Leah Turner knows about witches."

Gabriel froze. Through the haze of panic, he swung his gaze to his uncle, to the board, saw the horror dawn on Bastian and Henry's faces.

"He's lying," Bastian instantly said, scoffing, stepping forward as if to shut Will up personally. "How would she? Why would she?"

"She's a third owner in a witch bar. She's been sleeping with Gabriel Goodnight." Pleased with the upper hand, Will tucked his thumbs in his pockets. "I've been observing for a while. I've seen it all. And I'll have no problem telling everyone—including the High Family."

Henry shifted as if to shield Gabriel. "Nobody will believe a warlock who's looking to escape punishment."

August stayed silent.

"Lord Pearlmatter is correct." James steepled his hands, the beginnings of a frown tugging on his bushy eyebrows. "Nobody will believe him—provided you cut all ties."

Gabriel's mouth dried up.

No. The word echoed in his head.

"Keep the company," James went on, oblivious. "Your legacy. And end the relationship with the human, distancing yourself from her."

Gabriel made himself speak. "Or?"

"Or," August finally spoke up, face carefully blank. "Or you could go to the High Family and ask for clemency."

"Bullshit," Will sneered from his corner. "You know she's only interested in you because you're a warlock."

One of the board members waved their hand and tape appeared over Will's mouth.

August acted as though there hadn't been an interruption, gaze boring into Gabriel, through him. His voice gave nothing away. "Throw yourselves on their mercy, ask for forgiveness and permission to bring Leah fully into this world. And potentially lose everything. It's your choice."

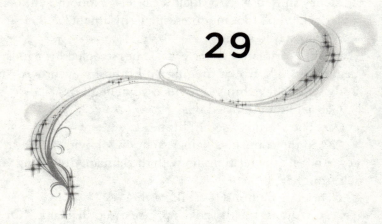

29

*G*abriel was on the manor's downstairs terrace, where he always went to think, when Melly flew out the French doors.

"Please tell me you're not considering this."

Chuck lifted his head from where he'd been lying in a pool of sunlight, wagged his tail in greeting as Gabriel turned to face her. "What?"

"Uncle August told me." She stopped in front of him, hands on hips. Her charm bracelet glinted in the afternoon light. "Will. The ultimatum they handed you. It's BS. Tell me you're not even considering it."

He took a breath, released it. "I'll make sure the company is safe for you, no matter what."

She blew a raspberry, making Chuck woof in response. "Screw that. I meant, tell me you're not even *considering* the answer. Tell me you're only out here thinking up ways to persuade the High Family to let Leah in."

It made him smile, faintly. Of course she'd be on Leah's side.

He gave her a searching look. "Are you mad I didn't tell you she knew?"

"No. Because I already guessed." She laughed a little as she joined him at the railing, diverting to give Chuck a quick fuss. "C'mon, Gabriel. She never questioned why or how I'd show up from New Orleans so quickly, or any of the small magic I accidentally used. Besides." She leaned back, eyes on the landscaped gardens. "Leah can't lie for shit."

It startled him into a laugh.

She grinned up at him. "That's a nice sound. I've heard it more since she's been around." She slid her hand over the railing so she brushed his fingers. "You love her, don't you?"

He exhaled. Saying nothing, he faced the gardens, too. When he spoke, his voice was low, but strong as spelled steel. "Yes."

Melly's whoop made him start. "I'm so happy for you," she crowed. "And me. Leah's cool."

"For a human?"

"For anyone. Better than the legacy lovers that always primp when you walk into a room."

He ignored that, focusing on the more important point. "You've never had an issue with humans," he said. "The opposite, in fact. Why?"

"Why did you?"

He hesitated.

"Gabriel." Melly angled her body toward his, eyes suddenly serious in her young face. "I'm fourteen, almost fifteen. I can handle it."

She really was growing up on him. "Because of how Mother and Father died," he admitted. "And not just…the rebels." His shoulders rode a discomforted wave as he stumbled for words. "I felt like they'd chosen them. The humans."

"Over us?" Her voice was soft.

He moved his head in a small nod.

Sunlight dappled over features that spoke of both of their parents as his sister drew her bottom lip between her teeth, darting him a glance. "Can I tell you a secret?"

"Yes."

"I don't remember them." She didn't look at him now, focused on the gardens. "I feel guilty that I don't, and a little sad. But I don't have that connection with them. Everything you've told me, everything I've read or heard, it makes me proud to be their daughter. They dedicated their lives to helping others. But…" Her mouth pinched. "I just don't feel it."

He had no idea what to say. "I didn't know."

"I didn't want to tell you in case you, I don't know, thought less of me."

He covered her hand. "I would never think less of you."

"Not even when I blew the roof off with that potion?"

"Maybe then."

They both smiled.

Something churned inside him, an ocean he'd worked to keep inside. But as he looked at his sister, at the young adult she was becoming, Gabriel realized it was time to let it out. "Can I tell *you* a secret?"

"Always."

She meant that. He held the brilliance of that to him as he removed his hand from hers, gripped the railing. "I'm so damn mad at them."

"Mother and Father?"

"They were never around. They chose to leave you, to help other people instead of spending even a fraction of time with you."

"With us."

He shook that away. "And even worse—" His voice caught as the truth he'd tried to bury stuck in his throat. He felt Melly's hand slide onto his, drew strength from it. "Even worse," he continued, gruff, "was that they chose not to risk exposure and live for us." The words left him after a lifetime in the dark, leaving him raw and open. Somehow free.

A flock of birds passed overhead, their calls the only sound for several heartbeats. "You grew up alone, Gabriel," were his sister's first words, surprising him. "I had you, Uncle August." Her hand tightened on his. "You grew up alone, and with their disapproval when you tried to get their attention. Please," she said as he glanced at her, "you don't think Mrs. Q tells stories?"

He winced.

"I think it's okay to feel angry, hurt, that they chose everyone but you. In a way, they still chose reputation over family, even if they went against normal society to do it. And I love you for showing up for *me*, for trying to be the parent they never could. Even living with humans so you could demonstrate responsibility to our name." Her tone turned teasing. "Though that worked out for you, huh."

He smiled faintly as the wind caressed the tips of his hair. "Will says Leah only likes me because I'm a warlock."

"That's stupid. And you're not stupid, right?"

"You can't deny there'd be an allure." He paused, shook his head. "No. I think she might actually like me for being…me."

"Arrogant jackass with a marshmallow interior." Melly nudged his shoulder with her own. "So, you love her. You're obviously going to the High Family, right?"

"You aren't disappointed with me for potentially throwing away our legacy?"

"What legacy? The company?" She gestured between them. "*We're* our legacy, Gabriel. You and me, Uncle August, Mrs. Q. Chuck," she added with a laugh. "As long as you live up to that, I won't be disappointed."

"I love you, Melly."

"I love you, too." She grinned, bright and brilliant. "Now, c'mon. What's next?"

It had been five hours and nothing. Nada. Not a carrier pigeon or flying broom. No talking mirrors, either, and Leah had made sure to keep a compact nearby just in case.

Gabriel had said he'd come back but now he was with his own kind, maybe he'd decided to skip the awkward breakup conversation altogether. That or he'd been right about his uncle and had lost the company and it was too painful for him to face.

She didn't *do* patient. Sitting on her ass was driving her nuts, even if her body still felt weak. She'd made it downstairs, at least, lying on the couch and stroking Delilah, who lay on Leah's belly, her other hand on Rosie's head where the sprocker curled on the floor. Louie nestled between her legs and Sylvie stretched on the back of the couch. Even Ralph had shown his support by venturing forward to nudge Leah's hand before streaking back to his hiding place.

"Get used to it, gang," she murmured. "This is it now."

Just her and her animals. Sounded perfect.

With a sigh, she turned off the TV and stared at the ceiling. What was this? She wasn't the type to sit around. She went out and got what she wanted, knocking down every wall she came across. In some ways, her fear of rejection had become her drive to succeed—and wasn't that a kicker to realize? She might've put up her own walls but everything she'd gone after, she'd got.

The question was, what did she want now?

Gabriel. Every screwed-up, annoying, loving inch of him. She was even willing to brave the twisted society that came with. The trouble was two hearts were involved here. He had to bend toward her as well. And she doubted her warlock, forged in discipline, would ever bend that much.

"Leah."

She choked on the chocolate-covered pretzel she'd just crunched down on, her chest seizing as she coughed. The dogs leaped off her, scrambling to greet the owner of that wonderfully sinful voice. By the time she'd got her breath back and had risen from the couch, he'd petted them all, even little Louie, who'd deigned to leave his comfortable position.

Gabriel's face was achingly familiar as she took in every inch, trying and failing to read his expression. He wore a suit still, perfectly pristine and gorgeous.

And she wore a tattered hoodie, and sweatpants with the word *juicy* on the ass.

"Hi," she said for lack of anything better. She shifted her weight, swallowing down the nerves that wanted to flutter. "I didn't know if you'd come back."

"I said I would."

"And Goodnights always keep their promises." It was said with some affection, a tinge of longing.

If he caught it, he didn't let on. "I wanted to talk to you. About Chuck."

Leah's mind halted. "You…came back to talk to me about Chuck?"

"Yes. I want to adopt him."

She could almost hear the high-pitched whine of her ego deflating. Or was that her soul crying? Could be either. "Okay."

"Melly already adores him. No matter how long he has left, he's going to get as much love as he can stand."

He was staring at her in a way that made her feel like she should be getting some kind of message. She wasn't.

"Okay… Will that be cash or credit?" she asked, seriously confused and not a little pissed.

His throat moved as he swallowed. "I'm trying to say…you were right."

"I usually am."

He ignored her. "Blocking out something I love in case it leaves me isn't possible. Not when loving is worth the risk of pain."

A glimmer of something danced across her mind. It clutched in her belly, painful, raw. *Hope.* "You love Chuck?"

"I do."

Her throat constricted but she forced the words out. "Only Chuck?"

He moved then, coming forward to clasp her arms. One tug and she was against him, her hands pressing into his hips as she fought for balance. A joke. She'd never found her balance again after that first night on the balcony.

Those intensely green eyes scanned her face as he confessed, "I never had a chance, Leah. I was a breath away from falling for you since the moment you first punched Laurence."

She hiccupped a small laugh.

"I didn't want to admit it. As if that would make it hurt less. So, I pushed you away like a fool. Like a dick," he corrected, making her laugh again, stronger this time. "I was the weak one. Blaming it on your being a human, the obstacles we'd face, the chance I could lose you. I lost you anyway and it fucking gutted me. It made me realize I would sooner have one moment of life with you than years alone." His hands tightened on her arms a fraction, as did all the muscles in his body. "I don't know... I honestly don't know how someone as bright and warm as you could love someone like me, but I'm willing to spend a lifetime learning how to make you smile." He paused, and the edge of uncertainty just about killed her as he traced her face with his gaze. "Leah," he said, voice unsteady. "I love you."

Emotion burst inside her like fireworks, joy bubbling into laughter that wanted to spill out. "I love you, too," she choked out. "I love you, Gabe. You're everything I want. *Everything.* You're generous and loving and just enough of a dick so you're not perfect." His rare dimple danced. "You make me happy. You make me feel chosen. Just like I will always choose you." She watched the relief, the elation rise before she hauled him down to her, crushing her mouth to his.

When he broke the kiss, he pressed his forehead to hers. "I'm sorry it took me so long."

"It was worth the wait." She breathed him in for several seconds before forcing herself to say it. To burst the bubble. "But are you sure? What about—?"

He shifted to kiss her, silencing the words. "The second part of my plan."

"There's a plan? What am I saying? Of course, there's a plan." Leah grinned up at him when he gave her an arch look. It helped mask the flicker of sudden fear. "So? Tell me."

He squeezed once before he explained what had happened in the board meeting, his uncle's PA's betrayal and worse, the bomb he'd dropped.

The aftershock rippled through Leah as she dropped to the couch on weak legs. "They know." She didn't know what to feel. Except, "You could've denied it. It would've been the safer, sensible thing."

"Please. I'm a rebel."

It made her smile as she knew he knew it would. She reached up and drew him down to sit next to her, so close his knee pressed hers. She kept her grip on his hand. "The company…"

He stroked his thumb down her palm. "Melly and I talked. About a lot. Including how my parents might have loved us, but they loved each other and their cause more. Their name. Their legacy. And that sucks," he said, using a word she'd never thought he'd say. "But being in that fire with you made me realize how far a person will go for someone they love. It doesn't excuse my parents for abandoning us. But it means they were flawed. They weren't perfect, and they shouldn't have expected me to be. I have to start living my life for me. If that means I'm out of the company, so be it."

"No, Gabe." She shook her head, gripping his hand in denial. "It means everything."

"You mean more," he said simply. But even under the truth of that, his inner turmoil trembled through, enough that Leah inched closer, pressing her thigh against his.

"We won't let it come to that," she vowed.

He gave her a grateful look but didn't comment.

For now, she moved on. "So, August gave you the choice." She searched his face, nerves a lead ball in her stomach. "Does that mean you're going to the High Family?"

"No." He let go of her hand only to cup her face, his own grave. "We are. If you'll be by my side."

Knowing how scared he must be for her to face his worst fears made her fall a little more in love with him. If the High Family ruled against her, it would destroy him. All her life she'd feared rejection but this time, she welcomed the chance to face it. She wouldn't be taken from this man so easily.

She leaned into his touch and put her heart into her answer. "Always."

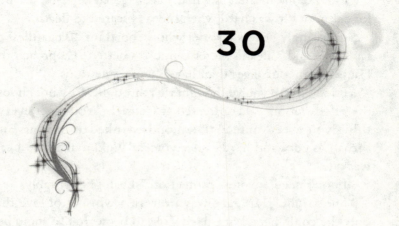

30

*H*er friends didn't take their decision as well.

Tia sat perched on one of Toil and Trouble's stools as Emma stood behind the bar, arms folded, where they'd been when Leah and Gabriel had walked in five minutes ago. Where they'd stayed as they were told everything, including the plan to meet the High Family on their turf.

Emma's face was a mask of fear. Tia was already shaking her head. "No."

"Yes." Leah sounded calmer than she felt. As if he knew, Gabriel took her hand in his. A united front. "This isn't asking for permission. We're here because…" She stumbled.

"Because you're worried you won't come back," Tia bit out. Emma made a sound.

Gabriel's hand tightened around hers, but his face was smooth, unrippled glass. "That will not be happening."

"I thought you said you were leaving." Tia's tone was vicious in its accusation. "This is your fault."

"Don't put this on Gabriel. He didn't tell me about magic."

"No, I did." Emma's voice was raw. "It's my fault."

"Em, I didn't mean it like that." Leah closed her eyes, reached for calm, but it was hard when she was scared to death.

Surprisingly, it was Gabriel who stepped in. "Regardless of fault," he said, "Leah's secret is out. It's better to approach the High Family ourselves than have them come to us."

"I don't think you've thought this through. Why not choose the other option?" Tia directed at Gabriel. "You'd get everything you ever wanted." Diamonds winked at her ears and throat, as cool and hard as her voice. "We'd make sure Leah was safe."

"I don't need anyone's protection," Leah said irritably.

"She's right." His gaze was a caress, a whisper of love that only she could hear. "She has a right to be heard. To stand before them and speak for herself."

Tia put a fisted hand to her belly and looked away, her face agitated. Violent.

Emma's voice, in contrast, was soft. "You love her."

"Yes."

Leah nodded as Emma angled her head toward her in question. "Yes."

A sound from Tia, low, pained. Like she knew that was the beginning and end of it.

With an understanding born of friendship, Emma reached out and took Tia's hand, uniting them. The latter let out a shaky breath. They both reached to Leah at the same time.

She held their hands and fought not to give in to tears. "Come on," she teased. "Have some faith in me. If I can talk Gabriel Goodnight into karaoke, I can talk anyone into anything."

Tia squeezed her hand hard. "I want to say don't go," she murmured, voice strained. Her eyes were dark. "I want to lock you up in the cellar. But..." Her shoulders slumped and she kicked out a foot. "The damn warlock's right."

Out of the corner of her eye, Leah saw Gabriel open his mouth and then think better of it.

"It's not that I don't think you can handle yourself," she insisted. "But you have such a spark, Leah. You don't even know. I didn't want our ways to snuff it out. Nobody gets through society unscathed." Something old and painful moved through her gaze. "But you're an adult and you deserve to make your own choices. Even if they're wrong." The last was said with a snarky undertone and a pointed tip of her head toward Gabriel.

Leah laughed wetly. "Thanks, T."

Emma sighed. "Well, now I can't think of anything that sounds as good as that." She shrugged. "Go get 'em?"

Leah laughed again, loving these two so much. She held on one moment longer before letting go of their hands.

Gabriel curved a hand around her waist and turned them to go. Stopped. "I'm going to say I told her." He looked back over his shoulder at Emma, then Tia.

They hadn't discussed this, but Leah wasn't surprised he'd take the fall. He knew how much these two meant to her. And being a protector would always be a part of him.

Emma's lips parted in surprise. "Gabriel…"

"We can't let you take all the blame." Tia ran a hand through her hair in one agitated movement. "Aren't you meant to be an asshole?"

"Aren't you meant to be a bad-tempered shrew?"

Her lips curved. "Yes. And I am. But I have layers."

"Then you understand."

She considered him. "I think I do."

Leah took them in, their bar, but didn't go so far as to say goodbye. She refused to believe this was it. Not when she had so much to fight for. "We'll let you know. How it goes."

"Sure," Tia murmured. "Good luck."

With one last nod, they turned and headed out.

★ ★ ★

Back in the bar, Emma glanced at Tia. "We're not seriously sitting back here, are we?"

"What do you think?" Tia clambered up on the stool, balancing the stool with a flick of telekinesis. She clapped her hands. "Folks, if I can have your attention? The bar's going to be closing early today for a family emergency…"

Gabriel's heart was pounding but he didn't let it show as he offered his calling crystal to the butler. Dressed in a form-fitting navy suit, Bianca accepted it with a nod toward one of the high-backed chairs that sat in the grand foyer. Not by a flicker of an eyelash did she show surprise at Leah's appearance. "You may wait there, Lord Goodnight."

He didn't take the chair, didn't think he could contain the nervous energy that thrummed within him if he did. Instead, he stood perfectly still, calling on a lifetime of training to appear nonchalant. He could feel the fine tremors running through Leah's body as she stood next to him, dressed in a simple tea dress that matched her eyes. He'd ensured they both presented a respectful appearance, knowing the High Family set store by such little gestures. He'd dressed in his best suit, a navy three-piece Prada, and even pinned the symbol of his family crest to his tie, as was traditional at High functions. Every little bit helped. He wouldn't consider the alternative, not now he'd put his trust in *them*. In her.

Instead of pacing, as he longed to do, he let his gaze roam the elegant foyer, from the Italian marble terrazzo floor to the two gleaming staircases at either end, curving delicately upward. He lingered near the round walnut table, where an abundance of flowers and a statue of the Goddess waited, and where he could see the many closed doors that lined the hall. They could be called into any of them.

"So, who will we be meeting?" Leah's voice was barely a

whisper, showing how ill at ease she was. He hated it, hated that they'd had to come here, but more, he hated that her confidence had faltered with every step into the mansion. Appearances mattered, in more ways than one. If they saw her as weak now, that would be it.

He grazed his knuckles along hers, making sure she looked at him. "You got this," he said, deliberately using the human phrasing to make a glimmer of humor dance in her eyes. Goddess, he adored that.

When she nodded, inhaling, he focused on her question. "Each member of the High Family takes responsibility for different sectors of witch society." He was aware that he could be making things worse by telling her these intimate details, but at this point, he doubted it. That she knew was enough. "Some focus on relations with other High families around the world, others take an interest in developments in potions and spell-casting. Others manage the security forces that could be called on in an act of terrorism or war."

"So, will we be seeing the ones that oversee security?"

He shook his head. "It's always a panel of at least four when hearing and deciding on pleas of this magnitude." A panel of judges and executioners, if need be. The thought was like ice spreading through his soul. *Never.*

"Four." Her breath was soundless as she exhaled. "I can deal with four."

He almost smiled. There she was.

The butler appeared out of nowhere, her skill clearly teleportation, a rare gift.

"They will see you in the Rose Room." She gestured for them to follow and clipped off down the hall.

He'd been to the Rose Room before. It was one of their grandest salons. Their choice of it now indicated respect for him. Perhaps they didn't know why he'd requested an audience and the butler hadn't revealed he'd brought a human—

perhaps they did know, and were toying with him. The latter sounded more likely. They put a hard line on revealing magic to humans without permission.

It was the siblings they'd see, he realized, entering the salon ahead of Leah to gauge the threat. His gaze fell on the golden twins first, a man and woman with light brown skin and gleaming blond hair. Their faces were relaxed and almost identical, both retaining certain quirks that gave them their own edge. Two sets of amber eyes surveyed him neutrally before sliding to Leah. Their job was overseeing the security forces and both were prone to protection over all. Not a bad thing, as they weren't aggressive idiots, but if they deemed his actions a threat, he couldn't count on their vote.

"Luisa, Julian." He nodded at both so Leah would know who was who.

"Gabriel," both replied in dusky tones that rang in harmony. "And *guest*…"

He didn't linger, moving to the third sibling, a man with dark brown skin who stood at six foot five with a shock of white hair and dark brows over darker eyes. He was large in every way that counted and yet, he was their most persuasive talker and was often sent on diplomatic missions when a High Family member needed to be present.

"Arlo."

Arlo inclined his head. "Gabriel." He made no mention of Leah, which could be good or bad.

Finally, he looked at the fourth sibling, a startling amalgamation of the others with curling white hair and amber eyes. Isabella was the sibling most embroiled in local politics, a compassionate nature firmed with the hard edge witchkind demanded. Most Higher childhoods could be competitive between siblings, especially as magic weakened with each sibling born. Not so in the High Family, one of the reasons they *were* the High Family. Each member was as powerful as the next. Childhood must have been…interesting.

She was his best chance at clemency, so he bent his upper body to her and bowed. "Isabella."

"It's good to see you, Gabriel. And you've brought such diverting company." She waved a delicate hand. "Sit. Would you like sweet tea?"

"Thank you, no." As none of them moved to sit on the provided velvet couches in the rose silk wallpapered room, he continued to stand. "I came for a purpose. We have," he corrected. He looked at Leah, then back with his jaw set. "We want to set the record straight."

"It's thoughtful of you to come to us," Julian said, arching his golden brow. "It's rare witches have the nerve to yield so willingly for their punishment."

Leah's heart stopped for three excruciating seconds at the blond male's lazy pronouncement. Just being in front of these four had sweat pooling at the base of her spine, little hairs lifting of their own accord. Their power was like static, on the edge of painful, and it butted against her skin. She'd understood intellectually the witches would be potent, but facing them all, every instinct whispered in warning not to make a target of herself.

"You already know." Gabriel's voice remained even.

The one he'd called Isabella cast him a pitying look as she opted to sit on one of the couches. She wore a pretty summer dress the color of raspberries, with a high collar and capped sleeves. The skirt swirled before settling around her legs. "This is witch society. The only thing that travels faster than gossip is Bianca," she added, presumably referring to the butler who'd escorted them in. That was what Gabriel had greeted her with.

As Isabella's gaze fell on her, Leah wondered if she should speak.

"You are a pretty toy," the witch murmured.

Leah frowned before she could control herself. It made something like delight flicker in Isabella's eyes.

Gabriel interrupted the byplay, voice steely. "Will you permit us to state our case?"

"You've broken the law." The blonde female twin moved to sit next to Isabella, dressed in a long white skirt and an off-the-shoulder crimson top that bared her stomach. "Why should we hear you out?"

"Because I'm a Goodnight. And because I'm asking."

The handsome warlock called Arlo looked at each of the others, then nodded. "Please."

"Wait." Isabella held up a hand. She tapped a finger against lips curled in a playful smile. "I say we let the human speak."

Leah felt Gabriel's instinctive *no* form as he locked in place next to her. But he didn't let it out. Instead, he pressed his lips together, holding to his promise to trust her.

Part of her wished he hadn't, as all four witches cocked their heads at her expectantly. All waiting for her to fail.

"Well," she said, her voice cracking. It was that crack, and the hint of derision in the blonde twin's—Luisa's?—face, that snapped her spine straight. She wouldn't let her fears control her, not now. Not ever again.

She set her shoulders. "My name is Leah Turner. I run a bar in Chicago and work in an animal shelter. And I'm in love with Gabriel Goodnight."

It wasn't easy, and she fumbled several times as they sat in stony silence, but Leah told them everything. Or at least, the version of everything that she and Gabriel had agreed on. The clause that had brought Gabriel to her, his time in the human world, the sabotage. And how they'd fallen in love. She hated exposing them like this. But she didn't stop until she'd said everything she thought they needed to hear.

"She says *you* told her about us?" Luisa cocked her head,

vaguely doubtful, talking to Gabriel as if Leah wasn't there. "Doesn't she own the bar with Emmaline Bluewater and Tia Hightower?"

Yes, she does, Leah retorted in her head, going to cross her arms before second-guessing the action.

Apology was in the quick flick of Gabriel's eyes as he answered for her. "Yes. But they kept her in the dark."

Isabella frowned as she sipped the sweet tea she'd conjured, but she didn't say anything.

"It was me." Gabriel fisted his hands at his sides and then immediately unclenched them. "I dragged her into this. I alone should face the consequences, should you deem consequences necessary."

Leah's head whipped toward him with a scowl. "No."

"But I ask that you bend the law this once. I love her." He said it again, firmer, louder, as the family—siblings?—stared. "I love her. If a punishment must be had, I will take it, but I ask for clemency."

Isabella put down her sweet tea on a gold circular end table that carried a vase of lilies. Death flowers. Leah tried not to focus on that.

"I think it's interesting," she said in her melodic voice, one that carried a note of amusement. "I don't think I've ever heard Gabriel plead for anything—or ask for anything, for that matter."

"Indeed." Luisa watched him as one did something new and fascinating. "He must really love this human. But the law is the law. It is there to protect us."

Julian nodded, hard-faced. "I agree."

"You two are not romantics." Isabella sighed, then tapped her manicured nails on her lap. "So, your argument is that you were swept away by passion? How very...un-society-like of you." Her tone didn't make it clear whether she approved or not.

She switched her focus to Leah. "And you? You're happy for Gabriel to take punishment?"

Leah's nails bit into her palms but she met that gaze head-on. "No. We're partners. I'll take whatever he does."

"I see." Intrigue shimmered in Isabella's face. "What if the punishment was to give each other up? You could keep your memories, but would not be permitted to be with each other. What would you say to that, Gabriel?"

Gabriel's eyes glittered bright green. "Fuck. That."

Leah had never truly got what it meant to hear a pin drop until right then.

"How delicious." Isabella smiled, proving to Leah she was only toying with them. "One more question, Ms. Turner. Why do you think you *deserve* to be welcomed into our world?"

Leah absorbed the question, the little stings across her exposed skin. Memories rushed up, of being shut out, of being kept in the dark. One more test and she could be in the ultimate club.

Well, to use Gabriel's phrasing: Fuck. That.

"I don't care if you think I deserve it or not," she said, standing tall beside the man she loved. "I don't really care if you like me or want to have me around. I might not be able to do magic, but I have value. I don't have to prove myself to anyone," she said, realizing it was true as Gabriel's hand tangled with hers. She looked up and saw him smiling at her, in full view of others. With maybe a hint of healthy fear. She looked back at the witches who thought to judge her. "I love Gabriel and he loves me. That should be enough."

Arlo grunted. A punctuation mark to her speech, but she wasn't sure which one.

Isabella considered her, and if Leah wasn't imagining things, she swore she saw some respect there. Then the witch clapped and the look was gone.

"So," Isabella said, as if Leah hadn't completely disrespected them, and in hindsight, it hadn't been the best time for her epiphany, "it comes to a vote. Do we wipe the human's memory? I say nay."

"I say—"

Luisa's vote was cut off as the sounds of an argument broke out beyond the room. They all swiveled to the door, which burst open to emit a snarling Tia, followed closely by Emma, who looked one "boo" away from melting into the floor. Leah's mouth fell open at the sight.

"I said we need to talk to them," Tia was insisting to Bianca, who had a grip on her wrist. "You teleport me again and we're going to throw down."

"That will not be necessary." Isabella didn't rise, but nodded at Bianca. The butler let go and with one steamed look at Tia, who returned it in kind, drifted away.

Tia brushed off her jeans. "I apologize for the lack of etiquette."

The male blond—Julian's—eyes glinted in quiet amusement. "Do you?"

"We had to see you, Your Excellencies." Tia bent in a formal bow, as did Emma. "We have an objection to make."

Leah's stomach took a dive as Gabriel spun back to the family. "No, they don't."

"Yes, we do." Emma's voice squeaked and her face went bright red as everyone turned their attention to her, but she didn't cringe away. "We're not letting you do this, Gabriel."

"Do what?" Arlo wanted to know.

"Leah already knew about witches before Gabriel said anything." Tia's voice trembled on the last word before she coughed, clearing it from her throat. "We told her. We're here to plead for her."

"Not for yourselves?" Luisa asked from the sofa.

Emma shook her head. "Leah is an exceptional person," she said on a swallow. "She deserves to be welcomed, not wiped."

"She's known for years," Tia pointed out, hands in fists, posture stiff. Only her eyes showed her nerves. "Never said anything. Even when Gabriel came to work for us, she didn't tell him she knew."

Leah and Gabriel shared a look, both silently agreeing not to point out that he'd guessed anyway.

"Doesn't her knowing that long prove she can be trusted? And she helped Gabriel out when he needed to work in the human world, to fulfill the terms of his father's will. She didn't have to. All we're asking for is a chance." Tia tipped up her chin, a proud legacy witch. "She's our sister in every way that matters."

"That's interesting, but—" Luisa began and was once again interrupted as two men barreled through the doorway.

"Bastian? Bluewater?" Gabriel's shock echoed through Leah at the sight. "How did you know about this?"

Kole eyed him with distrust. "Emma told him, Bastian told me."

"Where's Henry?" Tia spoke up.

"His father—"

"Typical," she muttered.

Bastian went to Emma, brow knit. "You shouldn't have come without me."

"I didn't want to get you in trouble."

"I'd face anything for you. You're not alone."

She cupped his cheek. "I know."

Kole, meanwhile, was glaring at Leah. "You're in *so* much trouble. What was the first rule?"

"Well." Isabella ventured a smile, lifting her glass again. "It's becoming quite the party, isn't it?"

Kole faced her, bowed. "Your Excellencies. Please consider pardoning my sister and Tia."

"Not me?" Gabriel muttered. Leah hushed him.

"Their actions were wrong, but I hope you can find it in your kind and just selves, especially in light of what all our families have done for you, to grant clemency." Kole held Arlo's eyes, adding emphasis to the words. "And if there are consequences for Emma, I ask to bear them in her stead."

"No, you idiot." Emma rounded on him. "I'm ready to face whatever needs to be faced. Just so long as Leah can keep her memories and be welcomed here."

"You're the idiot." He poked her.

"Agreed. Hush." Bastian tugged her back.

Kole continued. "But I concur, Your Excellencies. Let us take the consequences, not Leah. She has proven herself to be a valued, trusted human whose presence here could add to our society, not take away. She truly is…exceptional."

Leah felt on the edge of bawling at all of them showing up for her. But deep inside, she'd never doubted them. They were, all of them, hers, and she was theirs.

"We appreciate all of your arguments," Luisa said. "And— now what?" she said with exasperation as the door opened again.

And Leah's heart stopped as Gabriel's uncle stepped through.

Gabriel stared at his uncle, hardly daring to breathe.

They hadn't spoken, not since Gabriel had accused August of betraying him. He'd tried to apologize, but August had simply walked off, bristling, face set in implacable lines. Gabriel couldn't blame him. He'd thrown years of love and attention and family back in his face. *He* had betrayed *him*.

And now he was here. He didn't like Leah—was he here to speak against her?

Gabriel's chest constricted, making it hard for him to draw a full breath. "Uncle," he managed. His hold on Leah tightened.

August's gaze was sharp as it briefly landed on his nephew, then moved to where he linked with Leah. Something flickered on his face before he faced the family with a bow. "Your Excellencies."

"Are you also here to speak for Leah Turner?" Arlo asked. Humor rose for an instant. "Are there any more of you?"

"That I don't know. I'm here to lend my authority and weight to my nephew." August didn't show emotion, only the pulse throbbing in his throat an indication of how he felt. "This human—Leah," he corrected himself, pausing to seek her out, "has opened him up in ways I haven't seen since before my brother passed. He understands what it means to show weakness, and that showing weakness can sometimes be strength. He's a better man for her."

Gabriel's throat was tight, crowded with emotion.

Eyes so like Gabriel's father's held onto his, bright, searing. Then August turned to the High Family. "Please don't take her from him."

Luisa waited a beat, pointedly looking at the door. When no more interruptions came, she allowed a thin smile. "I'm moved. And it says a lot that she has the weight of such powerful families on her side."

The Bluewaters weren't powerful, but otherwise, Gabriel realized she was right. Leah had made friends with the right people.

"It's unprecedented." Luisa shared a look with her siblings. "But as you know, humans have been allowed into society on a trial basis before. She would have to be monitored until the probation passes. Are you considering bonding with her?" she directed to Gabriel.

Bonding with a human was rarely done. Once done, a bonding could not be undone, similar to witch marriages. The human would take a sliver of their bonded one's magic into them and it would enhance their body, allowing them to live longer. A true mate.

Sensing Leah's confusion, he turned to look at her. And saw his future.

"Well, you have time to consider that." Julian waved that off, the golden twin huffing in small amusement. "Give the man a break, Luisa. He's known her three months."

She rolled her eyes.

Gabriel didn't let his guard down. The High Family liked to toy with prey, coaxing them to believe all was okay before hitting them between the eyes.

Arlo spoke up. "We may be willing to allow this human into society on a trial basis."

Gabriel still didn't celebrate. Neither did Leah or any of the others ranged around the room.

"But you broke the law," Arlo finished. The siblings' faces turned implacable, Luisa and Isabella rising to present a united front. The four of them stared back at Gabriel and Leah, who faced them together.

Isabella spread her hands. "There must be a price paid."

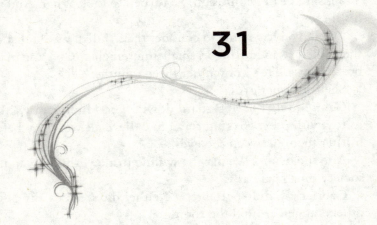

31

"Leah, can I have a word?"

Leah pulled away from Tia's hard hug and made a face. "Uh-oh," she said lightly, turning to Kole. "I'm in for a spanking." She used the light words as a defense against the rolling nausea in her belly as they grouped together like sitting ducks.

But he didn't come back with a quip. Face set, he jerked his head to a corner of the waiting room they'd been marched into to await the High Family's verdict. If her life hadn't been at stake, she'd have found the large room lovely with its paneled walls, faded Persian rugs and wide, wonderful windows that let in the twilight. As it was, it was all she could do to keep from staining the rugs. Gabriel had been drawn away to speak with Bastian and Emma, which was probably why Kole was making his move.

Casting Tia a look, she followed Kole to the windows. He gazed out at the view of the bayou, one so close she figured magic had to be at play. His profile was as handsome as ever, but there was something remote about him at that moment.

It unsettled her. "Kole?"

"You love him."

It wasn't a question, not in that careful voice, and it wasn't where she thought he'd start his lecture. But she nodded.

"It wasn't something I was looking for but he kind of snuck up on me." She laughed a little at the understatement. "He got through all my walls. He...sees me."

Kole shifted. "Leah." He took one of her hands in his. The seriousness of his expression caused her stomach to flip.

"What is it?"

"Can I ask you something?"

"Always."

He hesitated. "Did you ever...?" He struggled for words. "With me, did you...?" He stopped, staring at their joined hands.

"Did I...?"

Kole's face filled with something she couldn't name, strong, powerful enough to make his eyes glow.

"Hey." She squeezed his hand. "You can ask me anything. You're big brother Kole." She smiled, hoping to coax whatever was riding him out. "We're family. Always." She felt her stomach pitch. "No matter what their price is."

The glow faded. "Right." He took a breath, squeezed her hand back. "It's nothing."

"You sure?"

"Yeah." He smiled, then, back to normal as he patted her hand. "Don't worry. I'm sure they'll let you in."

She snorted, full of confidence she didn't feel as time ticked on. "They should be worried about keeping me out if they try and push me away from Gabriel."

"I pity them."

"Pity us, Lord Bluewater?" It was Luisa who cut in, whose voice made Leah flinch in surprise. Luisa smiled thinly, as if she enjoyed the reaction.

Gabriel hurried over, only one hint of fear leaping out before his society mask hid it all. He slid next to Leah. Or slightly in front of her.

Protector. She might have rolled her eyes if she wasn't so grateful for it.

At Luisa's silence, a fist clenched in Leah's gut, a tightness that didn't allow for air.

One second.

Two.

Three.

"His price has been met." Luisa didn't allow for celebration before adding, "Now it must be yours."

Out of the corner of Leah's eye, she saw thunder roll over Gabriel's brow. "That wasn't the deal," he demanded.

"Sacrifice," the High witch stated without much emotion, "must come from all parties."

Leah's heart deafened her to anything else as she watched the witch that reminded her of a snake. Able to strike without warning and just a little unnerving. "What's the price?"

"You alone are permitted entry to this world." Luisa's eyes glowed. "No family, no friends, nobody must know. And if you breathe one word, the magic I bind you with now will punish you accordingly."

Leah swallowed. "My mom—"

"Nobody."

Her stomach felt tight as she looked to Gabriel. The emotional bruise blossomed, quick, without warning, as she thought of the gulf that would separate her and the only parent who had ever really cared about her.

Except...

Did she want her mom in this world? Did it matter so much that she couldn't be told?

Leah was looking at the only person she really needed her mom to know. As long as her mom knew Gabe, the man, she didn't need to know Gabriel, the warlock.

She nodded.

Luisa inclined her head. "Congratulations."

Once, she might have clicked her heels for joy at being let into this world. Now, she latched onto Gabriel's arm, the only thing that really mattered. "Thank you."

"Isabella wants you to come for tea." Luisa smiled slowly at Leah's obvious surprise. And alarm. "Soon."

As she strode off without waiting for an answer, Kole slid a look at Leah. "Trouble."

"Charm," Leah corrected, but even she felt shaky at the idea. "Maybe it's their version of *we will be watching*."

"Oh, they'll be watching," Tia said from behind her, then gripped Leah tight. Emma followed suit. "Thank the Goddess."

Leah relished their embrace, even as she sought Gabriel, who stood next to Kole. Two men couldn't be more different on the surface, she thought, but underneath, both had that protective core, an honor that made them fight for what they loved. It was strange but somehow Kole seemed the more isolated one now, loneliness a black ribbon that twined around him. She hoped he found someone soon. And she hoped the female made him work for it.

The idea for a celebration rose but Gabriel rejected it, curling his hand around Leah's. "I need to borrow her for a second."

"I pity you if it's just a second." Tia's smirk wiped away any hint of the vulnerability she'd just displayed. "Well, we'll see you crazy kids at the bar."

All of them walked through the portal Bastian created, laughing, talking, joking. Only Kole paused. His head angled back. "I don't like you, Goodnight," he said flatly. "Honestly, I think you're a dick."

Gabriel lifted his chin, boredom playing over his face. Leah tightened her hand on his.

"But you risked it all. Leah deserves someone who'd fight the world for her." He ran a hand over his hair, dullness dimming his usual light. "Not someone who's content with what little he thinks he can get."

Mystified, Leah turned to him, but he was already stepping through the portal.

Gabriel didn't give her time to question. He tugged. "Come."

"Where are we going?" She stopped him with a hand, curling her fingers around his arm. "And what did Luisa mean about the price having been met?"

He hesitated.

"Gabriel."

At his uncle's voice, every muscle on Gabriel's body locked. Regret moved across his face as he visibly steeled himself before swiveling to August. Leah stepped close, ready to throw down if needed.

The two men, so alike, stared at each other.

Gabriel broke first. "Thank you, Uncle." The tone was husky with gratitude. "That you'd show up even after... I can't even—" He trailed off.

August merely held out a hand. Gabriel slowly put his own into it, cautious as an animal looking for a trap. That changed when August pulled him in, wrapping his arms around his nephew in a tight embrace. Leah watched a tremor shudder through Gabriel's body, felt the same pass through her heart.

When they pulled apart, August nodded at her. "We'll talk."

It was obvious to Leah that Gabriel was too choked up to speak so she took up the reins. If August was making an effort, she supposed she could, too. "Maybe you could come to dinner."

"I'd like that. You know how to reach me." With one last look at Gabriel, he walked away.

"Intense few hours," Leah observed in the silence that followed.

Gabriel grunted.

She grinned. "Quick. Before anyone else comes. Take me away."

A faint smile before his hand tangled in hers. With a gesture, he opened a shimmering portal behind them, leading her through it.

She marveled as she had the first time, how it was just like stepping through a door, the only indication of travel a small *pop* in her ears. God, she'd never walk again if she could do this. Which, considering the many dogs she had to walk each day, was why it was probably a good thing she couldn't.

They exited onto an unfamiliar balcony. Vines wove through iron railings, flowers creeping up the old brick. The air was warm, sultry, scented.

And there was a black Labrador flopped on the stone floor.

As he caught sight of her, Chuck woofed in delight, throwing himself from his sprawl against her legs and almost knocking her back through the portal. She steadied herself, bending down to give him a hug. He licked her face and she grinned. "Hey, big guy. Where are we, huh?"

"My home."

Chuck barreled into his master, overjoyed to see them both. He danced around until Gabriel conjured a tennis ball and heaved it to the gardens that dropped away from the balcony. Claws scraped stone as Chuck threw himself down the stairs after it. Leah winced.

Then turned to Gabriel, arms crossed. "So?" she ordered. "What price did you pay?"

He ignored her crossed arms and touched her cheek lightly as if to reassure himself she was there. "I'm sorry about your mum."

"Gabriel, I only need her to know *you*. Screw the rest." She prodded him. "What price?"

He relented. "The company. I'm out."

"*What?*"

"I'm forbidden from taking my place as CEO—or any position—at Goodnight's Remedies." He said it matter-of-factly, as if it wasn't tearing him apart. And it had to be.

"No," she breathed. She slipped her arms free, pressed her hands into his chest. "Gabriel. I'm so… We can fix this. I can do something, I'm sure."

"Leah."

"No. That company is everything to you. It's all you ever worked for, ever wanted."

"Leah."

"I swore I wouldn't be an obstacle and—"

He kissed her.

Their lips clung until he broke it off. He stayed close. "Leah. I'm fine."

"You're only saying that."

"I'm telling the truth. Look at me." He forced her to do it, hands on her elbows. His gaze was open to her as it moved over her face. "You were right when you said I didn't really want to be CEO."

"But you wanted to be involved." She felt like crying. "You were forced to give it up because of me."

"No. I chose to." He stroked his thumbs over the soft skin of her upper arms. "You heard them. A sacrifice must be made. What is true sacrifice if what you're giving up doesn't draw a little blood?"

"But that's worse. I—"

"Leah." This time his voice held an edge of laughter, so foreign to Gabriel's voice that it made her stop. His dimple made an appearance. "You're my future. Goodnight's Remedies holds too many memories, too many regrets for me to ever be truly happy there, in any capacity. It was time to say goodbye."

She absorbed that, heard the truth for what it was. "But what will you do?" She knew he wasn't the kind to sit around the manor.

"Melly and I are going to open our own company."

She laughed, then saw he was serious. "You're going into business with your fourteen-year-old sister? Doing what?"

"We're going to branch out from what Goodnight's Remedies does. We're going to focus on helping animals."

"You're—" As the idea took hold, a smile curved her lips and she threw her head back on a laugh. "I *love* that. The next generation of the Goodnights' legacy. It's perfect for you."

He agreed with a dip of his chin. "The first place I ever truly felt accepted was at the shelter," he said, contemplative. "Animals never expect you to be anything other than you are. I want to give back, help them as they've helped me…which is why I bought the shelter from Sonny's buyer."

"You…you what?" Her legs felt weak so she leaned against him before she ruined the moment by cracking her head on the stone floor. Boy, when he committed, he *committed*. She shouldn't have expected any different. And she couldn't love him any more. "Thank you."

"You're welcome." He caught her hand, brushed a kiss over it. "But I did it for both of us. That is a special place. It needs to be run by people who appreciate that."

Chuck nosed in between their legs, pressing his big head into her belly. She stroked his ears and smiled up at Gabriel. Everything was perfect. The only thing that would make it more so would be—

A cocktail stick appeared on the railing.

Leah frowned at it quizzically. "You felt the need for a tiny weapon?" When she looked up, she tensed at the expression on Gabriel's face. "What?"

"I didn't conjure that."

"Then who…?"

"What were you just thinking about?"

"A Cauldron Cosmo." Unease slicked her insides at his expression. "Gabriel, that's not a cosmo."

"But it's an element. The smallest, easiest one." Pale, he picked up the cocktail stick between finger and thumb. "Let me see if I can get an energy signature." When his eyes flashed open, locked on her face, she shook her head at the answer she saw there.

"I don't have magic. I'm human. How could that possibly have been me?"

He scrubbed his face with his free hand. "Honestly, I have no…" He trailed off. Understanding, consternation, resignation all played over his features. He dropped his hand. "You died."

"Okay, but—"

"I willed you to live. I breathed into you and willed you to live." His throat worked. "We must have bonded out of sheer desperation."

"Bonded?"

"If a witch decides their life mate will be a human, the High Family bonds them in a ceremony. It can't be undone. I don't actually know anyone that has done it. It allows the human to take a small segment of magic to link them to their partner, extend their life, their health. It means we're linked."

Uncertainty had her teeth sinking into her bottom lip. "Are you okay with that?"

Something lightened in his expression and he cupped her cheeks. "Yes. I told you you're my future; I meant it." He paused. "But nobody is meant to bond without the High Family's permission."

Well, shit. Those two words rang in Leah's head as she worried her lip. "Do we tell them?"

He exhaled. "No. You're not about to become all-powerful, and we can hide one secret."

"Well, what about—"

"Enough." He lowered his head, catching her in a soft kiss. "Enough. Whatever comes, we'll handle it. But for now, all I want to do is celebrate. We made it."

They'd made it.

Music suddenly played, the soft sounds of jazz filtering in with the fading light.

"You're going soft," she teased as he began to sway her. "What will people say about the Goodnights when they see Gabriel being a fool for love?"

He curled an arm around her waist, swirling her in an intricate turn. As she whirled, her simple shift disappeared, replaced by her flowing pink evening dress, either mended by magic or completely new. He smiled at her surprised pleasure, drew her close. "They'll say I'm one hell of a lucky warlock."

"Damn right." And she kissed him on a balcony at sunset while a Labrador panted happily at their feet. Followed closely by a fourteen-year-old's loud, excited, *"Hell, yeah!"*

★ ★ ★ ★ ★

ACKNOWLEDGMENTS

I want to thank, first of all, all of the WONDERFUL booksta-grammers and bloggers that made this book possible by end-lessly and helpfully promoting *The Witch is Back* and asking for a book two. A special thanks to TheReyloReader, Temma Thomas, TwiceUponaBook, LinnaReads, Mile.High.TBR, Surakajanebooks, booked.by.allie, EdwardandDamon, Books-withBoz, BecsBookNook, and TheStephWord for all of your love and support—everyone go check out their accounts; they're amazing! Apologies for anyone I've missed.

The thanks continue to the librarians and bookshops who ordered *The Witch is Back* and shared their love for it, again making *De-Witched* possible. We wouldn't be where we are without them and I'm so grateful!

Of course, I have to thank my brilliant fellow spaniel lover of an editor, Stephanie Doig. You have this amazing ability of seeing exactly what a story needs to evolve and make it the best it can be and I'm so thankful for your time and insights.

Cole Lanahan—you rock as an agent and you have a million dogs. That alone proves how cool you are.

To my friends and family who put up with me hermiting

when under deadline and don't get bored (at least outwardly) when I discuss my book over and over.

To Molly, aka Moll, aka Moo, aka Bubba, aka Pidge. You're the reason I get up in the morning. Seriously. We need to discuss lie-ins. But also the reason I smile every day and get off my butt and out into nature, for being the greatest sounding board, the worst wing woman, and truly the weirdest animal I've ever known. You're never alone when you're with a dog, for better or worse, and even when I can feel your stare boiling the back of my head at walk time, I wouldn't be without you.

And for every reader that takes a chance on a book by an unknown author—thank you so much!